THE OLD MAN LOOKED LONG AND EARNESTLY
AT THE PICTURE.

—*The Ralstons.*

THE COMPLETE WORKS OF
F. MARION CRAWFORD

In Thirty-two Volumes ✒ *Authorized Edition*

THE RALSTONS

BY

F. MARION CRAWFORD

WITH FRONTISPIECE

P. F. COLLIER & SON

NEW YORK

THE COMPLETE WORKS OF F. MARION CRAWFORD

—23—

THE RALSTONS

THE RALSTONS.

CHAPTER I.

ALEXANDER LAUDERDALE JUNIOR was very much exercised in spirit concerning the welfare of his two daughters, of whom the elder was Charlotte and the younger was Katharine. Charlotte had been married, nearly two years before the opening of this tale, to Benjamin Slayback, the well-known member of Congress from Nevada, and lived in Washington. Katharine was still at home, living with her father and mother and grandfather, in the old house in Clinton Place, in the city of New York.

Mr. Lauderdale, the son of the still living philanthropist, and the nephew of the latter's younger brother, the great millionaire, Robert Lauderdale, sat in his carefully swept, garnished and polished office on a Saturday morning early in April. In outward appearance, as well as in inward sympathy, he was in perfect harmony with his surroundings. He resembled a magnificent piece of

1

mechanism exhibited in a splendid show-case — a spare man, extremely well proportioned, with a severe cast of face, hard grey eyes, and a look all over him which recalled a well-kept locomotive. He sat facing the bright light which fell through the clear plate glass. One of his hands, cool, smooth, lean, lay perfectly still, spread out upon the broad sheet of a type-written letter on the table; the other, equally motionless, hung idly over his knee. They were grasping hands, with long, curved nails, naturally highly polished. It was not probable that the great Trust Company, in which Alexander Junior held such an important position, should ever lose the fraction of a fractional interest through any oversight of his.

So far as his own fortune was concerned, he often said that he was poor. He lived in an old house which had been his grandfather's and father's in turn, but which, although his father was alive and continued to live in it, had become his own property some years previous to the beginning of this story. For Alexander Lauderdale Senior was a philanthropist; and although his brother, the rich Robert, gave liberally toward the support of the institutions in which he was interested, Alexander had little by little turned everything he possessed into money, applying it chiefly to the education of idiots. The consequence was that he depended, almost unconsciously, upon his only son for the actual necessities of life. The old house was situated on the north side of Clinton Place, which had never been a fashionable street, though it lay in what had once been a most fashionable neighbourhood. No one need be surprised if the near relatives of such a very rich man as Robert Lauderdale lived very quietly, so far as expenditure was concerned. He was a very generous man, and would have done much more for his nephew and the latter's family if he had believed that they wished or expected it. But in his sensible view, they had all they needed, — a good house, a sufficient amount of luxury, and a very prominent position in society. He knew, moreover, that, however much he might give, the money would either find its way into the vast charities in which his brother was interested, or would disappear, as other sums and bits of property had disappeared before now, to some place — presumably one of safety — of which his nephew never spoke. For he suspected that Alexander Junior was not nearly so poor as he represented himself to be, and he was not exactly pleased with the fact that he himself was the only person before whom Alexander Junior bowed down and offered incense.

For this younger Lauderdale was a very rigid man in almost all respects: in his religion, which took the Presbyterian form, and took it in earnest;

in his uprightness, which was cruelly sincere; and
in his outward manner, which was in the highest
degree conventionally correct.

It was this extreme correctness which lay at the
root of his present troubles, since, in his opinion,
both his daughters had departed from it in opposite directions and in an almost equal degree. He
did not recognize himself in either of them, and, as
he believed his own character to be an excellent
model for his family, his vanity was wounded by
nature's perverseness. Furthermore, he distinctly
disliked that sort of social prominence which is
the portion of those who are not like the majority,
or who do not think with the majority and say so.
Both Mrs. Slayback and Miss Lauderdale attracted
attention in that way.

Mrs. Slayback was handsome and vain, and believed herself to be proud in the better sense of the
word. She had married her husband for two reasons: because she found the paternal home intolerable, and because, besides being rich, Benjamin
Slayback was thought to be a man who had a brilliant future before him in the world of politics.
Charlotte had believed that she could rule him,
and herself become a power. In this she had
been disappointed at the outset, having been deceived by a certain almost childlike simplicity
of exterior, which was in reality one of Slayback's
strongest weapons. He admired her very much;

he looked up to her with admiration for her superior social acquirements, and he treated her with a sort of barbaric liberality to which she had not been accustomed. But within himself he followed his own political devices without consulting her, and with a smiling reticence which convinced her most unpleasantly that she was not intellectually a match for him. This was all the more painful as she considered him to be her social inferior, a point of view which was popular with some of her intimate friends in New York, but much less so in Washington, and not at all in Nevada.

The immediate consequence of this state of affairs was that Charlotte and her husband did not agree. Both were disappointed, though in an unequal measure. Slayback claimed that any woman should be contented who had what he gave his wife. Charlotte thought that she showed great forbearance in not leaving a man whom she could not rule. It was not worth while, she said to herself, to have accepted a man who had, at her first acquaintance with him, worn a green tie; whose speech at home was remarkable rather for its 'burr' than for its grammar, and who did queer things with his knife and fork — unless his undeniable intelligence and force were to be at her service in such a way as to make her feel that she was at least as powerful a person as he. She had condemned the green tie, and he had submitted, and she had successfully conveyed hints against cutting fish and potatoes with a steel knife; but in the matter of grammar she had been less successful. When Benjamin was on his legs on the floor of the House, as he often was, he could speak very well indeed, which made it all the more unpleasant when he relapsed into the use of dialect, not to say slang, at his own table. He was a jovial man over his dinner, too, and she particularly detested jovial men, especially when they spoke English not altogether correctly. She had vaguely hoped that Benjamin would be spoken of as Mrs. Slayback's husband, but it had turned out that, in spite of her beauty and brilliant conversation, she was spoken of as Benjamin Slayback's wife. By way of outshining him, she had conceived the plan of outshining everybody else in matters of fashion and fashionable eccentricity. She had spoken to more than one member of the family of obtaining a divorce on the ground of incompatibility of temper, which, she said, could be managed in Nevada, since New York was so absurdly strict about divorces. It was evidently within the bounds of the possible that she might have spoken in this sense to friends who were not related to her, as her father knew. Altogether, he was aware that she was talked of and he suspected that she was laughed at. She had been seen to smoke cigarettes, it was reported that she had driven four-in-hand, and Alexander would have been less surprised than shocked if he had heard that she played poker with her intimates and bet on horse-races.

It was hard that such a man should have such a daughter, he thought, and that all this should be the result of so much careful and highly correct training and education. It was harder still that his younger child should be as completely out of sympathy with him as her elder sister, especially as Katharine outwardly resembled him, at least a little, whereas Charlotte had inherited her fair complexion from her mother.

Of the two, Katharine was the more difficult to deal with, and he was glad that her peculiarities were mental rather than outwardly manifested in her behaviour, as her sister's were. But of their kind, they were strong and caused him great anxiety. There was a mystery about her thoughts, too, which he could not fathom, and which influenced her conduct, as though she had some secret motive for some of her actions and for many of her opinions, which might, perhaps, have explained both, but which she was not willing to divulge. Katharine held views upon religion which were of the most disquieting character, and Katharine flatly refused to speak of being married. These were Alexander Junior's principal grievances against her.

So far as the second of these was concerned, he

might have found plenty of excuse for her, had he
sought it, in his own character. Whatever his
faults might be, he had been a very faithful man.
He had married Emma Camperdown, the famous
beauty from Kentucky, when they had both been
very young, and he had loved her all his life, in
spite of the fact that she was a Roman Catholic
and he a very puritanically inclined Presbyterian
of the older school.   Love that will bear the strain
of religious differences, when religious conviction
exists on both sides, must be of a very robust
nature, and Alexander's had borne it for a quarter
of a century.   It was true that his wife, who had
been born a Catholic, was not aggressively devout;
but in his view of the matter, her errors were
mortal ones, and the thought of her probable fate
in a future existence had really saddened the hard
man's life.   But it had not diminished nor shaken
his love.   About that, there was nothing romantic,
nor Quixotic, nor emotional.   It had none of the
fine, outward qualities which often belong abun-
dantly to transient passions.   There was in it a
good deal of the sense of property, which was very
clearly defined with him, and he lacked in most
ways the delicacies and tendernesses which are the
rarest and most beautiful ornaments of the strong.
But such as it was, its endurance and good faith
were unquestionable.   Indeed, endurance and uprightness were Alexander's principal virtues.   Both

were genuine, and both were so remarkable as to raise him high in the respect of his fellow-men. If he had secrets, he had a right to keep them, for they concerned nobody but himself, and he was naturally reticent.

Katharine had some similar qualities. She had loved her distant cousin, John Ralston, a long time, and she was as faithful and enduring as her father. Ralston loved her quite as dearly and truly, but Alexander Junior would not have him for a son-in-law, and had told him so in an exceedingly plain and forcible manner. His objection was that Ralston seemed unable to do anything for himself, and had, moreover, acquired a reputation for being fast and dissipated. He was not rich, either. His father, Admiral Ralston, had been dead several years, and John lived with his mother on twelve thousand a year. The young man had made two attempts at steady work and was now making his third, the previous ones having resulted in his leaving the lawyer's office in which he had placed himself, at the end of three months, and the great banking establishment of Beman Brothers, in Broad Street, after a trial of only six weeks. He had now gone back to Beman's, having been readmitted as an especial favour to Mr. Robert Lauderdale, with no salary and with an unlimited period of proba-tion before him. He was a popular young fellow enough, but he was not what is called a promising youth, though his ways had improved considerably during the last few months. Mr. Beman said that he came regularly to the bank and seemed disposed to work, but that his ignorance of business was something phenomenal. Nevertheless, to please old Robert the Rich, John Ralston was tolerated, so long as he behaved himself properly.

And Katharine loved him, in spite of her father's disapproval and her mother's good advice. For during the preceding winter Mrs. Lauderdale, who had once favoured the match, had gone over to the enemy, and showed a very great and almost unbecoming anxiety to see Katharine married. Hamilton Bright, another distant relative and the junior partner of Beman Brothers, would have married her at any moment, and he was a very desirable man. The fact that he was a relative was in his favour, too, for both he and Katharine would probably in the end inherit a share of the enormous Lauderdale fortune, and it would be as well that the money should not go out of the family. Robert Lauderdale had never married, and was now well over seventy years of age, though his strength had not as yet come to labour and sorrow.

Katharine did not talk of John Ralston. Especially of late, she avoided saying anything about him. But she would look at no one else, though she had no lack of suitors besides Hamilton Bright, and in spite of her reticence it was easy to see that her feelings towards Ralston had not undergone any change. Once, during the preceding winter, Alexander had been visited by a ray of hope. Ralston had been reported by the newspapers as having got into a bad scrape, winding up with an encounter with a pugilist, and ending in his being brought home by policemen in the middle of the night. It had actually been said that he had been the worse for too much champagne, and during a few hours Mr. Lauderdale had hoped that Katharine would be disgusted and would give him up. But it turned out to have been all a mistake. No less a personage than the celebrated Doctor Routh had at once written to the papers, stating that he had attended John Ralston when he had been brought home, that he had met with an accident, and that the current statements about his condition were utterly false and libellous. And there the matter had ended. Alexander might congratulate himself upon having got the alliance of his wife against John, but their united efforts to move their daughter had proved as fruitless as his own had been when unassisted.

There was nothing for it but to wait patiently, and to hope that she might forget her cousin in the course of time. Meanwhile, another anxiety presented itself, almost as serious, in her father's opinion. She had been brought up as a Presbyterian, like her sister, in accordance with his wishes,

and in this respect Mrs. Lauderdale had been conscientious, though her antagonism to her husband's
church was deep-seated and abiding. But of late
Katharine had begun to express very dangerous
and subversive opinions in regard to things in general and in respect of religion in particular. Her
mind seemed to have reached its growth and to
have entered upon its development. Katharine
was going astray after strange new doctrines, Alexander thought, and he did not like the savour of ·
mysticism in the fragments of her conversation
which he occasionally overheard. Though he could
not with equanimity bear to hear any one deny the
existence of the soul, he disliked almost more to
hear it spoken of as though humanity could have
anything to do with it directly, beyond believing in
its presence and future destiny. Whether this was
due to the form of the traditions in which he had
been brought up, or was the result of his own
exceedingly vague beliefs in regard to the soul's
nature, it is of no use to enquire. The fact was
the same in its consequences. He was very much
disturbed about Katharine's views, as he called
them, and at the same time he was conscious for
the first time in his life that no confidence existed
between her and him, and that their spheres of
thought on all subjects were separated by a blank
and impenetrable wall.

Then, too, Katharine had of late shown a strong

predilection for the society of Paul Griggs, a
man of letters and of considerable reputation, who
was said to have strange views upon many subjects, who had lived in many countries, and who
had about him something half mysterious, which
offended the commonplace respectability of Alex·
ander Lauderdale's character. Not that Alexander
thought himself commonplace, and as for his respectability, it was of the solid kind which the
world calls social position, and which such people
themselves secretly look upon as the proud inheritance of an ancient and honourable family. Everything that Paul Griggs said jarred unpleasantly
on Alexander Lauderdale's single but sensitive
string, which was his conservatism.

Griggs disclaimed ever having had anything to
do with modern Buddhism, for instance. But he
had somehow got the reputation of being what people call a Buddhist when they know nothing of
Buddha. As a matter of fact, he happened to be
a Roman Catholic. But Mr. Lauderdale had heard
him use expressions which had fixed the popular
impression in his mind. The conversation of such
a man could not be good for an impressionable
girl like Katharine, he thought. He took it for
granted that Katharine was impressionable because
she was a girl and young. Mr. Griggs said very par·
adoxical things sometimes, and Katharine quoted
them afterwards. Mr. Lauderdale hated paradox

as he hated everything which was in direct opposition to generally received opinion. It was most
disagreeable to him to hear that there was no such
thing as a future, as distinguished from past or
present, when so much of his private meditation
had for its object the definition of the future state
for himself and others. He did not like Mr.
Griggs' way of referring to the popular idea of the
Supreme Being as a ' magnified, non-natural man '
— and when Griggs quoted Dante's opinion in the
matter, Alexander Lauderdale set down Dante Ali-
ghieri as an insignificant agnostic, which was unjust, and branded Mr. Griggs as another, which
was an exaggeration. Now, whatever the truth
might be, he considered that Katharine was in
great danger, and that although Providence was
necessarily just, it might have shown more kindness and discretion in selecting the olive branches
it had vouchsafed to him.

It need hardly be said that of the two extremes
to which his daughters seemed inclined to go, he
preferred the one chosen by Katharine. That, at
least, gave no open offence. Morally, it was worse
to dissect the traditional soul as it had been handed
down in its accepted form through many generations of religious men, than to smoke a cigarette
after a dinner party. But in practice, the effect of
the cigarette upon the opinion of society was out
of all proportion greater, and Charlotte was there-

fore worse than Katharine, as a daughter, though she might not be so bad when looked upon as a subject for potential salvation.

All this disturbed Alexander Lauderdale very much, for he saw no immediate prospect of any improvement in the condition of things. For once in his life his daughters were almost his chief preoccupation. If he had been subject to absence of mind, something might, perhaps, have got out of order in the minute details of the Trust Company's working. In that respect, however, he was superior to circumstances. But when he was momentarily idle, his mind reverted to its accustomed channels, and the problem regarding the future of his daughters got into the way and upset his financial calculations, and made him really unhappy. For his financial calculations were apparently of a nature which made them pleasant to contemplate, although he declared himself to be so very poor.

On that particular Saturday morning he was interrupted in his solitude by the sudden appearance of his wife. It was not often that she had entered his office during the ten years since he had been installed in it, and he was so much surprised by her coming that he positively started, and half rose out of his chair.

Mrs. Lauderdale was a beautiful woman still, and would be beautiful if she lived to extreme old age. But she was already past the period up to

which a woman may hope to preserve the freshness
of a late youth. The certainty that her beauty
was waning had come over her very suddenly on a
winter's evening not long ago, when she had noticed
that the man who was talking to her looked per-
sistently at Katharine instead of at herself; and
just then, catching sight of her face in a mirror,
and being tired at the time, she had realized that
she was no longer supreme. It had been a bitter
moment, and had left a wound never to be healed.
The perfect, classic features, the beautiful blue
eyes, the fair waving hair, were all present still.
Her tall figure was upright and active, and she
had no tendency to grow stout or heavy. She had
many reasons for congratulating herself, but the
magic halo was gone, and she knew it. Some
women never find it out until they are really old,
and they suffer less.

At the present moment, as she entered her husband's office, it would have been hard to believe
that Mrs. Lauderdale could be more than five and
thirty years of age. The dark coat she wore
showed her figure well, and her thin veil separated
and hid away the imperfections of what had once
been perfect. She was a little agitated, too, and
the colour was in her cheeks — a trifle too much
of it, perhaps, but softened to the delicacy of a
peach blossom by the dark gauze.

She paused a moment as she closed the door

behind her, glancing first at her husband, and then looking about the unfamiliar room, to satisfy herself that they were alone.

"This is an unexpected pleasure, Emma," said Alexander Junior, rising definitely and coming to meet her.

"Yes," answered Mrs. Lauderdale. "I don't often come, do I? I know you don't like to be disturbed. But as this is Saturday, and I knew you would be coming up town early, I thought you wouldn't mind. It's rather important."

"I trust nothing bad has happened," observed Alexander, drawing up a chair for her.

"Bad? Well—I don't know. Yes—of course it is! It's serious, at all events. Uncle Robert's dying. I thought you ought to know—"

"Dying? Uncle Robert?"

Alexander Lauderdale's metallic voice rang through the room, and his smooth, lean hands grasped the arms of his chair.

An instant later he looked a little nervously at the door, as though hoping that no one had heard his words, nor the tone in which he had spoken them. A dark flush rose in his face and the veins at his temple swelled suddenly, while his grip on the chair seemed to tighten, and he turned his eyes on his wife.

"Dying!" he repeated in a low voice. "What has happened to him? When did you hear of this?"

Mrs. Lauderdale had not expected him to show so much feeling. She, herself, was far from calm, however, and did not notice his extreme agitation as though it were anything unnatural.

"Doctor Routh came to tell me," she answered. "He's been there all the morning — and as there was time before luncheon, I thought I'd come — "

"But what's the matter with the old gentleman? This is very surprising news — very sad news, Emma."

A rather spasmodic, electric smile had momentarily appeared on Alexander Lauderdale's face, disappearing again instantly, as he uttered the last words.

"I'm very much overcome by this news," he added, after a short hesitation.

He did not appear to be so deeply grieved as he said that he was, but the words were appropriate, and Mrs. Lauderdale recognized the fact at once.

"It will make a great difference," she said.

"Yes, I should say so. I should say so," repeated Alexander Junior, not with emphasis, but slowly and thoughtfully. "However," he continued, suddenly, "we mustn't count — I mean — yes — we — we mustn't altogether place our confidence in man — though Doctor Routh certainly stands at the head of his profession. It's our duty to see that other physicians are called in consultation. We must do our utmost to help. Indeed — it might have been wiser if you had gone there at once and had sent a messenger for me, instead of coming here. But — yes — you haven't told me what the matter is, my dear. Is it — anything in the nature of apoplexy — or the heart — you know? At his age, people rarely — but, of course, while there's life, there's hope. We mustn't forget that."

He seemed unable to wait for his wife's answer to his questions.

"Why, no, my dear," she replied. "You know he's not been very well for some days. He's worse — that's all. It was nothing but a cold at first, but it's turned into pneumonia."

"Pneumonia? Dear me! At his age, people rarely live through it — however, he's very strong, of course. Difference!" he exclaimed, softly. "Yes — a great difference. It — it will make a great gap in the family, Emma. We're all so fond of him, and I'm deeply attached to him, for my part. As for my poor father, he will be quite overcome. I hope he has not been told yet."

"No — I thought I'd wait and see you first."

"Quite right, my dear — quite right — very wise. In the meantime, I think we should be going. Yes — it's just as well that you didn't take off your hat."

He rose as he spoke, and touched one of the row of electric buttons on his desk. A man in the livery of the Company appeared at the door, just as Alexander was taking up his overcoat.

"I'm going up town a little earlier than usual, Donald," he said. "Inform Mr. Arbuckle. If anything unusual should occur, send to Mr. Harrison Beman."

"Yes, sir."

"That's all, Donald."

The man faced about and left the office, having stood still for several seconds, staring at Alexander. Donald had been twenty years in the Company's service, and did not remember that Mr. Lauderdale had ever left the office before hours in all the ten years since he had been chief, nor in the preceding ten during which he had occupied more or less subordinate positions.

Mrs. Lauderdale daintily pulled down her veil and pulled up her gloves, shook out her frock a little and looked at the points of her shoes, then straightened her tall figure and stood ready. Alexander had slipped on his coat, and was smoothing his hat with a silk handkerchief which he always carried about him for that purpose. He had discovered that it made the hat last longer. Both he and his wife had unconsciously assumed that indescribable air which people put on when they are about to go to church.

"We'll take the Third Avenue Elevated," said Mr. Lauderdale. "It's shorter for us."

Robert Lauderdale's house was close to the Park. The pair went out together into Broad Street, and the people stared at them as they threaded their way through the crowd. They were a handsome and striking couple, well contrasted, the dark man, just turning grey, and the fair woman, still as fair as ever. It might even be said that there was something imposing in their appearance. They had that look of unaffectedly conscious superiority which those who most dislike it most strenuously endeavour to imitate. Moreover, when a lady, of even passably good looks, appears down town between eleven and twelve o'clock in the morning, she is certain to be stared at. Very soon, however, the Lauderdales had left the busiest part of the multitude behind them. They walked quickly, with a preoccupied manner, exchanging a few words from time to time. Lauderdale was gradually recovering from his first surprise.

"Did Routh say that there was no hope?" he asked, as they paused at a crossing.

"No," answered Mrs. Lauderdale. "He didn't say that. He said that uncle Robert's condition caused him grave anxiety. Those were his very words. You know how he speaks when a thing is serious. He said he thought that we all ought to know it."

"Of course — of course. Very proper. We should be the first, I'm sure."

It would not be fair, perhaps, to say that Alexander's voice expressed disappointment. But he spoke very coldly and his lips closed mechanically, like a trap, after his words. They went on a little further. Then Mrs. Lauderdale spoke, with some hesitation.

"Alexander — I suppose you don't know exactly — do you?" She turned and looked at his face as she walked.

"About what?" he asked, glancing at her and then looking on before him again.

"Well — you know — about the will — "

"My dear, what a very foolish question!" answered Alexander, with some emphasis. "We have often talked about it. How in the world should I know any better than any one else? Uncle Robert is a secretive man. He never told me anything."

"Because there are the Ralstons, you know," pursued Mrs. Lauderdale. "After all, they're just as near as you are, in the way of relationship."

"My father is the elder — older than uncle Robert," said Alexander. "Katharine Ralston's father was the youngest of the three."

"Does that make a difference?" asked Mrs. Lauderdale.

"It ought to!" Alexander answered, energetically.

CHAPTER II.

"I'm not dying, I tell you! Don't bother me, Routh!"

Robert Lauderdale turned impatiently on his side as he spoke, and pointed to a chair with one of his big, old hands. Doctor Routh, an immensely tall, elderly man, with a long grey beard and violet blue eyes, laughed a little under his breath, and sat down.

"I'm not at all sure that you are going to die," he said, pleasantly.

"That's a comfort, at all events," answered the sick man, in a husky voice, but quite distinctly. "What the deuce made you say I was going to die, if I wasn't?"

"Some people are stronger than others," answered the doctor.

"I used to be, when I was a boy."

"It won't do you any good to talk. If you can't keep quiet, I shall have to go away."

"All right. I say — mayn't I smoke?"

"No. Positively not."

Doctor Routh smiled again; for he considered it a hopeful sign that the old man should have a distinct taste for anything, considering how ill he had been. A long silence followed, during which the two looked at one another occasionally. Lauderdale was twenty years older than the doctor, who was the friend, as well as the physician, of all the Lauderdale tribe — with one or two exceptions.

The room was larger and higher than most bed-rooms in New York, but it was simply furnished, and there was very little which could be properly considered as ornamental. Everything which was of wood was of white pear, and the curtains were of plain white velvet, without trimmings. Such metal work as was visible was of steel. There was a large white Persian carpet in the middle of the room, and two or three skins of Persian sheep served for rugs. Robert Lauderdale loved light and whiteness, a strange fancy for so old a man; but the room was in harmony with his personality, and, to some extent, with his appearance. The colour was all gone from his face, his blue eyes were sunken and his cheeks were hollow, but his hair, once red, looked sandy by contrast with the snow-white stuffs, and his beard had beautiful, pale, smoke-coloured shadows in it, like clouded meerschaum. It was not surprising that Routh should have believed him, and believed him still, to be in very great danger. Nevertheless, there was strength in him yet, and if he recovered he might last a few years longer. He breathed rather painfully, and moved uneasily from time to time, as though trying to find a position in which he could draw breath with less effort. Routh sat motionless by his bedside in the white stillness.

"What's the name of that fellow who's written a book?" asked the sick man, suddenly.

"What book?" enquired the doctor.

"Novel — about the social question — don't you know? There's an old chap in it who has money — something like me."

"Oh! I know. Griggs — that's the man's name."

"What is Griggs, anyway?" asked Robert Lauderdale, in the hoarse growl which served him for a voice at present.

"Griggs? He's what they call a man of letters, or a literary man, or a novelist, or a genius, or a humbug. I've always known him a little, though he's younger than I am. The only good thing I know about him is that he works hard. Now don't talk. It isn't good for you."

"Well — you talk, then. I'll listen," grumbled old Lauderdale.

Thereupon both relapsed into silence, Doctor Routh being one of those people who cannot make conversation to order. Indeed, he was a taciturn man at most times. Lauderdale watched him, coughed a little and turned uneasily, but made a sign to him that he wanted no help.

"Why don't you talk?" he enquired, at last.

"About Griggs ?   I haven't read but one or two of his books.   I don't know what to say about him."

"Do you think he's a dangerous friend for a young girl, Routh ? "

"Griggs ? "   Routh laughed in his grey beard. "Hardly ! He's as ugly as a camel, to begin with — and he's getting on.   Griggs — why, Griggs must be fifty, at least.   Did you never see him ? He's been about all the spring — came back from the Caucasus in January or February.   What put it into your head that he would be a dangerous acquaintance for a young woman ? "

"I don't mean his looks — I mean his ideas."

"Stuff ! " ejaculated Doctor Routh.   "He's only got the modern mania for psychology.   What harm can that do ? "

"Is that all ?   Alexander's an ass."

Robert Lauderdale turned his head away as though he had settled the question which had tormented him.   Again there was a silence in the room.   The doctor looked at his patient with a rather inscrutable expression, then took out his watch, replaced it, and consulted his pocket-book. At last he rose and walked toward the window noiselessly on the thick, white carpet.

"I shall have to be going," he said.   "I've got a consultation.   Cheever's downstairs."

Doctor Cheever was Doctor Routh's assistant, who did not leave the house during Mr. Lauderdale's illness.

"And you can send away the undertaker, if he's waiting," growled the sick man, with an attempt at a laugh. "I say — can I see people, if they call? I suppose my nephews and nieces will be here before long."

"It's no use to tell you what to do. You'll do just what you please, anyway. Professionally, I tell you to keep quiet, not to talk, and to sleep if you can. You're not like other people," added Routh, thoughtfully.

"Why not?"

"Most men in your position are badly scared when it comes to going out. The efforts they make to save themselves sometimes kill them. You seem rather indifferent about it. Yet you have a good deal to leave behind you."

"H'm — I've had it all — and a long time. But I want to see Katharine Lauderdale, if she comes."

"I'll send for her if it's anything important," said Doctor Routh, promptly.

The sick man looked quickly at him. It seemed as though his readiness to send for Katharine implied some doubts as to his patient's safety.

"I don't believe I'm going to die," he said, slowly. "What are my chances, Routh? It's your duty to tell me, if you know."

"I don't know. If I did, I'd tell you. You're a very sick man — and they'll all want to see you, of course. I — well, I don't mean to say anything disagreeable about them. On the contrary — it is natural that they should take an interest — ”

“ Devilish natural,” answered old Lauderdale, with the noise that represented a laugh. “ But I want to see Katharine.”

“ Very well. Then see her. But don’t talk too much. That’s one reason why I’m going now. You can’t keep quiet for five minutes while I’m in the room. Good-bye. I’ll be back in the afternoon, sometime. If you feel any worse, send for me. Cheever will come and look at you now and then — he won’t talk, and he’ll call me up at my telephone station, if I’m wanted.”

“ Well — if you think it’s touch and go, send for Katharine — I mean Katharine Lauderdale, not Katharine Ralston. If you think I’m all right, then leave her alone. She’s not the kind to come of her own accord.”

“ All right.”

Doctor Routh held his old friend’s hand for a moment, and then went away. He exchanged a few words with the nurse, who sat reading in the next room, and then slowly descended the stairs. He was considering and weighing the chances of life and death, and trying to make up his mind as to whether he should send for Robert Lauderdale’s grand-niece or not. It was rather a difficult question to solve, for he knew that if Katharine appeared, the sick man would take her coming for a sign that his condition was desperate, and the impression might do him harm. On the other hand, though he was so strong and believed so firmly that he was to live, there was more than a possibility that he might die that night. With old people, the heart sometimes fails very suddenly. And Routh could not tell but that his patient's wish to see the girl might proceed from some intention on his part which should produce a permanent effect upon her welfare. It would be very hard on her not to send for her, if her appearance in the sick-room were to be of any advantage to her in future.

It was natural enough that he should ultimately decide the matter in Katharine's favour, for he liked her and Mrs. Ralston best of all the family, next to old Robert himself. Before he left the house he went into the library, which was on the ground floor, to speak with his assistant, Doctor Cheever, whom he had not yet seen, and who had spent the night in the house. The latter gave him an account of the patient's condition during the last twelve hours, which recalled at once the discouragement Doctor Routh had at first felt that morning. Once out of the old man's presence, the personal impression of his strength was less vivid, and the danger seemed to be proportionately magnified, even in the mind of such an experienced physician. Doctor Routh had also more than once experienced

the painful consequences of having omitted, out of
sheer hopefulness, to warn people of a dying relation's peril, and he at once decided to go to the
Lauderdales himself and tell them what he thought
of the case.

He drove down to Clinton Place, and, as luck
would have it, he met Katharine just coming out
of the house alone. He explained the matter in
half a dozen words, put her into his own carriage
and sent her to Robert Lauderdale at once, telling
the coachman to come back for him. Then he went
in and saw Mrs. Lauderdale, and told her all that
was occurring. She at once asked him so many
questions and required such clear answers, that he
forgot to say anything about his meeting with
Katharine on the doorstep. As has been seen, he
was no sooner gone than Mrs. Lauderdale went
down town to speak to her husband. Before
Doctor Routh had left Clinton Place, Katharine
was sitting at old Robert Lauderdale's bedside.

Many people said that Katharine had never been
so beautiful as she was that year. It is possible
that as her mother's loveliness began to fade, her
own suffered less from the comparison, for her
mother had been supreme in her way. But Katharine was a great contrast to her. Katharine had
her father's regular features, and his natural,
healthy pallor, and her eyes were grey like his.
But there the resemblance ceased. Where her

father's face was hard as a medal engraved in
steel, hers was soft and delicate as moulded moon-
light. Instead of his even, steel-trap mouth, she
had lips of that indescribable hue which is only
found with dark complexions — not rosy red, nor
exactly salmon-pink, and yet with something of the
colouring of both, and a tone of its own besides.
Her black hair made no ringlets on her forehead,
and she did not torture it against its nature. It
separated in broad, natural waves, and she wore it
as it chose to grow. She had broad, black eyebrows. They make even a meek face look strong,
and in strong faces they give a stronger power of
expression, and under certain conditions can lend
both tenderness and pathos to the eyes they over-
shadow.

In figure, Katharine was tall and strong, well-
grown, neither slight nor heavy. In this, too, she
was like her father, who had been an athlete in his
day, and still, at fifty years, was a splendid speci-
men of manhood, though he was growing thinner
and smaller than he had been. His daughter
moved like him, deliberately, with that grace which
is the result of good proportion and easily applied
strength, direct and unconscious of effort. Katharine may, perhaps, have been aware of her advantages in this respect. At all events, she dressed
so simply that the colour and material of what she
wore never attracted a stranger's eye so soon as

her figure and presence. Then he might discover
that her frock was of plain grey homespun, exceedingly well made, indeed, but quite without
superfluity in the way of ornament.

Long-limbed, easy and graceful as a thoroughbred, she entered the white room and stooped
down to kiss the old man's pale forehead. His
sunken blue eyes looked up at her as his hand
sought hers, and she was shocked at the change in
his appearance. She sat down, still holding his
hand, and leaned back, looking at him.

" You've been very ill, uncle Robert," she said,
softly. " I'm so glad you're better."

" Did Routh tell you I was better ? " asked the
old man, and his gruff, hoarse voice startled Katharine a little.

" Not exactly getting well — but well enough to
see people," she answered. " That's a good deal,
you know."

" I should want to see you, even if I were dying,"
said Robert Lauderdale, pressing her hand with
his great fingers.

" Thank you, uncle dear ! A lover couldn't say
it more prettily." She smiled and returned the
pressure.

" Jack Ralston could — for your ears, my dear."

" Ah — Jack — perhaps ! "

A very gentle shadow seemed to descend upon
Katharine's face, veiling her heart's thoughts and

hiding her real expression, though she did not turn her eyes away from the old man. A short silence followed.

"I hear that Jack is doing very well," he said, at last. "Jack's a good fellow at heart, Katharine. I think he's forgiven me for what happened last winter. I was angry, you know — and he looked very wild."

"He's forgotten all about it, I'm sure. He never speaks of it now. I think he only mentioned it once after it happened, when he explained everything to me. Don't imagine that he bears you any malice. Besides — after all you've done — "

"I've done nothing for him, because he won't let me," growled Robert Lauderdale, and a discontented look came into his face. "But I'm glad he's doing well — I'm very glad."

"It's slow, of course," said Katharine, thoughtfully. "It will be long before he can hope to be a partner."

"Not so long as you think, child. I've been very ill, and I am very ill. I may be dead to-morrow."

"Don't talk like that! So may I, or anybody — by an accident in the street."

"No, no! I'm in earnest. Not that I care much, I think. It's time to be going, and I've had my share — and the share of many others, I'm afraid. Never mind. Never mind — we won't talk of it any more. You're so young. It makes you sad."

Again the two exchanged a little pressure of hands, and there was silence.

"It will be different when the money is divided," said old Lauderdale, at last. "You'll have to acknowledge your marriage then."

Katharine started slightly. She had her back to the windows, but the whiteness of everything in the room threw reflected light into her face, and the blush that very rarely came spread all over it in an instant.

Only four living persons knew that she had been secretly married to John Ralston during the winter; namely, John and herself, the clergyman who had married them, and Robert Lauderdale. At that time she had with great difficulty persuaded John to go through the ceremony, hoping thereby to force her uncle into finding her husband some congenial occupation in the West. Half an hour after taking the decisive step, she had come to Robert Lauderdale with her story, and he had demonstrated to her that John's only path to success lay through the office of a banker or a lawyer, and John had then returned to Beman Brothers, after refusing to accept a large sum of money, with which old Lauderdale had proposed to make him independent. He had not been willing to give his uncle the smallest chance of thinking that he had married Katharine as a begging speculator, nor had the old gentleman succeeded in

making him change his mind since then. Nor had
he referred to the marriage when speaking with
Katharine, except on one or two occasions, when it
had seemed absolutely necessary to do so. And
now that he had spoken of it, he saw the burning
blush and did not understand it. Women had
entered little into his long life. He fancied that
he had hurt her, and was very sorry. The great
hand closed slowly, as though with an effort, upon
the white young fingers.

"I didn't mean to pain you, my dear; forgive
me," he said, simply.

Katharine looked at him with a little surprise,
and the blush instantly disappeared. Then she
laughed softly and bent forward with a quick
movement.

"You didn't, uncle dear! You didn't pain me in
the least. It's only — sometimes I don't quite
realize that I'm Jack's wife. When I do — like
that, just now — it makes me happy. That's all."

Robert Lauderdale looked at her, tried to understand, failed, and nodded his big head kindly but
vacantly.

"Well — I'm glad," he said. "But you see, my
dear child, when John's a rich man, you can acknowledge your marriage, and have a house of your
own. You really must, and of course you will.
John can't refuse to take his share. We never
quarrelled, that I know of, but that once, last win-

ter, and you say he has forgotten that. Has he?
Are you quite sure?"

Katharine nodded quickly and a whispered
'yes' just parted her fresh lips. In her eyes there
was a gentle, almost entreating look, as though
she besought him to believe her.

"Well," he said, and he spoke very slowly —
"well — I'm glad. He can't refuse to take his
share when I'm dead and gone — his fair share and
no more." He paused for some seconds. "Katharine," he said, very earnestly, at last, "there's a
great deal of money to be divided amongst you all.
Many of them want it. They'll all have some —
perhaps more than they expect. There's a great
deal of money, child."

"Yes, I know there is," answered Katharine,
quietly.

"When I'm gone they'll say that the old man
was richer than they thought he was. I can hear
them — I've heard it so often about other men!
'Just guess how much old Bob Lauderdale left,'
they'll say. 'Nearly eighty-two millions! Who'd
have thought it!' That's what the men will be
saying to each other. Eighty millions is a vast
amount of money, child. You can't guess how
much it is."

"Eighty millions." Katharine repeated the
stupendous words softly, as though trying to realize their meaning.

"No — you can't understand." The old man's eyes closed wearily. A few moments later they opened again, and he smiled at her.

"How did you ever manage to make so much?" she asked, smiling, too, and with a look of wonder.

"I don't know," answered the great millionaire, as simply as a child. "I worked hard at first, and I saved small things for a purpose. My father was rich — in those days. He left us each a hundred and fifty thousand dollars. Your uncle Alexander gave it to the poor — as much of it as the poor did not take without asking his leave. Ralph spent some of it, and left the rest to Katharine Ralston when he was killed in the war. I saved mine. It seemed good to have money. And then it came — it came — somehow. I was lucky — fortunate investments in land. I ran after it till I was forty-five; then it began to run after me, and it's outrun me, every time. But I wasn't a miser, Katharine. I don't want you to think that I was mean and miserly when I was young. You don't, do you, my dear?"

"No, indeed!" Katharine gave the answer readily enough. "But, uncle Robert, aren't you talking too much? Doctor Routh said you were not to — that it might hurt you. And your voice is so hoarse! I am sure it can't be good for you."

The old man patted her hand laboriously, for he was very weak.

"I want my talk out," he said. "It doesn't matter much whether it hurts me. A year or two, more or less, when I've had it all, everything, and so long. I'm tired, my child, though when I am well I look so strong. It isn't only strength that's needed to live with. It takes more."

"But there are other things — there is so much in your life — so many people. There are all of us. Don't you care to live for our sakes — just a little, uncle ?"

"If they were all like you — more like you — well, I might. I'm very fond of you, Katharine. You know it, don't you ? Yes. That's why I sent for you. I don't believe I'm going to die — I told Routh so half an hour ago. But I might — I may. I didn't want to go over without having had my talk out with you. That's it. I want to have my talk out with you. I should be sorry to slip away without seeing you. There are things — things that come into my head when I'm alone — and I've been alone a great deal in my life. Oh, I could have married, if I had liked. Queens would have married me — queer, little, divorced queens from out-of-the-way little kingdoms, you know. But I didn't want to be married for my money, and there were no Katharine Lauderdales when I was young."

Again, with an unsteady, laboured movement, the old hand caressed the young one as it lay on

the soft, white, knitted Shetland shawl which covered the bed, and again Katharine smiled affectionately and laughed gently at the flattery. Then
all was quiet. She leaned back in her chair, thinking — the aged head rested on the white pillow,
thinking.

"Katharine," — the eyes opened again, — "what
does it all mean, child ?"

"What?" asked the young girl, meeting him
again out of her reverie.

"Life."

"Ah — if I knew that —"

"You're at the beginning of it — I'm at the end
— almost, or quite, it doesn't matter. What's the
meaning of all those things I've done, and which
you're going to do ? They must mean something.
I ought to have got at the meaning in so many
years."

Katharine was silent. Of late, she, too, had
heard the great question asked, which rattles in
the throat of the dying century, and is to-day
in the ears of all, whether they desire to hear it
or not. And no man has answered it yet. A year
earlier Katharine would have said but one word
in reply. She could not say it now.

In the still, white room she sat by the old man's
side and bowed her head silently.

"It's puzzled me a great deal," he said, at last,
in his familiar speech. "So long as I cared for

things,—money, principally, I suppose,—it didn't puzzle me at all. It all seemed quite natural. But when I got worn out inside — used up with the wear and tear of having too much — well, then I couldn't care for things any more, and I began to think. And it's all a puzzle, Katharine. It's all a puzzle. We find it all in bits when we come, taken to pieces by the people who have just gone. We spend all our lives in trying to put the thing together on some theory of our own, and in the end we give it up, and go to sleep — 'perchance to dream' — that's Hamlet, isn't it? But I never dreamt much. If it's anything, it isn't a dream. Well, then, what is it?"

Katharine looked up at him with a little, half-childish glance of wonder.

"Why, uncle Robert," she said, "I always thought you were a religious man — like papa, you know."

"No." The old man smiled faintly. "I'm not like your father. I fancy I'm more like you—in some ways. Aren't you religious, as you call it, my dear?"

"I'm religious, as I call it—but not as 'they' call it." She laughed a little, perhaps at herself. "I seem to see something, and I believe in it, without quite seeing it. Oh, I can't explain! I've tried so often, but it's quite hopeless."

"Try again," said old Lauderdale. "It can't

do any harm, and it may do me good. I'm so lonely."

Katharine was perhaps too young to understand that loneliness, but the look in the sunken blue eyes touched her. She rose and bent over him, and kissed the pale, wrinkled forehead twice.

"It's our fault — the fault of all us," she said, sinking into her seat again.

"No; it's not," he answered. "I didn't want you all, and I couldn't have the ones I wanted. It doesn't matter now. I want to hear you talk. Try and tell me what you think it all means, from your end of life. I've forgotten — it's so long ago."

He sighed, then coughed, raising himself a little, and then sank back upon his pillow and closed his eyes, as though to listen.

"People say so many things," Katharine began. "Perhaps that's the trouble. One hears so much that disturbs one's belief, and one hears nothing that settles it in any new way. That's what happens to every one. In trying to find reasons for things, people ruin the things themselves with the tools they use. You can't find out the reason of a flower — certainly not by sticking the point of a steel knife into it and cutting the heart out. You can see how it's made — that's science. But the reason of its being a flower has nothing to do with science. If it had, science would find it out, because science can do anything possible in its own line. But it's always the steel knife — always, always. You can't tell why things exist, by taking them to pieces, can you ? "

"No—no—that's it." The old man turned his head slowly from side to side. Then it trembled a little and lay still again. "And the short cut is to say there is no reason for things—that they're all accidents, by selection."

"Yes ; that's the short cut, as you say," answered Katharine. "The trouble is that when we've taken it, if we don't want to go back, we ought to want to go on to the end. Nobody will do that. They meet you with a moral right and wrong, after denying that there's a ground for morality. I know—I've talked with a great many people this winter. It's very funny, if you listen to them from any one point of view, no matter which. Then they all seem to be mad. But if one listens inside, — with one's self, I mean, — it's different. It hurts, then. It would break my heart to believe that I had no soul, as some people do. Better believe that one has one's own to begin with, and the fragments of a dozen others clinging to it besides, than to have none at all."

"What's that ? " asked the old man, opening his eyes with a look of interest. "What's that about fragments of other people's souls ? "

"Oh — it's what some people say. I got it from

Mr. Griggs. Of course it's nonsense — at least — I don't know. It's the one idea that appeals to one — that we go on living over and over again. And he says that in that theory there's an original self, sometimes dormant, sometimes dominant, but which goes on forever — or indefinitely, at least; and then that fragments of the other personalities, of the people we have lived with in a former state, better or worse than the original self, fasten themselves on our own self, and influence its doings, and may put it to sleep, and may eat it up altogether — and that's why we don't always seem to ourselves to be the same person. But I can't begin to remember it all. You should get Mr. Griggs to talk about it. He's very interesting."

"It's a curious theory," said old Lauderdale, evidently disappointed. "It's an ingenious explanation, but it isn't a reason. Explanations aren't reasons — I mean, they're not causes."

"No," answered Katharine, "of course they're not. The belief is the cause, I suppose."

The sick man glanced at her keenly and then closed his eyes once more. Katharine rose quietly and went to the windows to draw down the shades a little.

"Don't!" cried Lauderdale, sharply, in his hoarse voice. "I like the light. It's all the light I have."

Katharine came back and sat down beside him again.

"I wasn't going to sleep," he said, presently. "I was thinking of what you had said, that belief was the cause. Well — if I believe in God, I must ask, 'Domine quo vadis?' — mustn't I? You know enough Latin to understand that. What do you answer?"

"Tendit ad astra."

It was one of those quick replies which any girl who knew a few Latin phrases might easily make. But it struck the ears of the man whose strength was far spent. He raised his hands a little, and brought them together with a strangely devout gesture.

"To the stars," he said in a whisper, and his eyes looked upwards.

Katharine rested her chin upon her hand, leaning forwards and watching him. An expression passed over his face which she had never seen, though she had read of the mysterious brightness which sometimes illuminates the features of dying persons. She thought it must be that, and she was suddenly afraid, yet fascinated. But she was mistaken. It was only a gleam of hope. Words can mean so much more than the things they name.

And a dream-like interpretation of the two Latin phrases suggested itself to her. It was as though, looking at the venerable and just man who was departing, she had asked of him, 'Sir, whither goest thou?' And as though a voice had answered her,

'Starwards' — and as though her own eyes might be those stars — the stars of youth and life — from which he had come long ago and to which he was even now returning, to take new childish strength and to live again through the years. Then he spoke, and the dream vanished.

"I believe in Something," he said. "Call it God, child, and let me pray to It, and die in peace."

CHAPTER III.

KATHARINE said nothing, not knowing what to say. During what seemed to her a long time, old Lauderdale lay quite still. Then he seemed to rouse himself, and as he turned his head he coughed painfully.

"I want you to know how I've left the money," he said abruptly, when he had recovered his breath.

"Do you think I ought to know?" asked Katharine, in some surprise.

"Yes — I don't know whether you ought — no. But I want you to know. I've confidence in your judgment, my dear."

"Oh, uncle Robert! As though your own were not a thousand times better!"

"In matters of business it may be. But this is quite another thing. You see, there are a good many who ought to have a share, and a good many who expect some of it, whether they have any claim or not. I want to know if you think I've acted fairly by everybody. Will you tell me, quite honestly? Nobody else would — except Katharine Ralston, perhaps."

"But I don't want to be made the judge of your actions, dear uncle Robert!" protested Katharine.

"Well — make a sacrifice, then, and do something you don't like," answered the old man, gruffly.

It would have pleased Doctor Routh to see how soon his temper rose at the merest sign of opposition.

"Well — tell me, then," said Katharine, reluctantly.

"It's a simple will," began the old man, and then he paused, as though reflecting upon it. "Well — you see," he continued, presently, "I argued in this way. I said to myself that the money ought either to go back to its original source — I've thought a great deal about that, too, and I've made sketches of wills leaving everything to the poor, in a big trust — I suppose every rich man has made rough sketches of queer wills at one time or another." He paused a moment and seemed to be thinking. "Yes," he resumed, presently, "either it should go back to the people, or else it ought to go amongst the Lauderdales, as directly as possible. Now there's my brother, first — your grandfather. He's older than I am, but he's careless and foolish about money. He'd give it all away — better leave something to his asylums and things, and give him an income but no capital. He doesn't want anything for himself — he's a good man, and I wish I were like him. Then there's your father, next, and Katharine Ralston — my nephew and niece. They don't want a lot of money, either, do they?"

Katharine's eyes expressed a little astonishment in spite of herself, and the old man saw it. He hesitated a while, coughed, cleared his throat, and then seemed to make up his mind.

"It's been my opinion for a long time," he said, slowly, "that your father has a good deal of his own."

"Papa!" exclaimed Katharine. "Why — he always says he's so poor! You don't know how economical he is, and makes us be. I'm sure he can't be rich."

"Rich — h'm — that's a relative expression nowadays. He's not rich, compared with me — but he has enough, he has quite enough."

"Oh — enough — yes," answered the young girl. "The house is comfortable, and we have plenty to eat." She laughed a little. "But as for clothes, you know — well, if my mother didn't sell her miniatures, I don't know exactly what she and I should do — nor what Charlotte would have done, before she was married."

Robert Lauderdale looked at her intently for several seconds.

"Do you mean to say," he asked, at length, "that when your dear mother sells her little paintings, it's to get money for her and you to dress on ? "

" Yes — of course. What did you think ? "

" I thought it was for her small charities," he answered, bending his rough brows with an expression of mingled pain and anger. " It seemed to me a good thing that she should have that interest. If I'd known that your father kept you all so close—"

" But I really think he's poor, uncle Robert."

" Poor! Nonsense! He's got a million, anyway. I know it. Don't look at me like that — as though you didn't believe me. I tell you, I know it. I don't know how much more he has, but he's got that."

He moved restlessly on his side, with more energy than he had yet shown, for he was growing angry.

" There's some money in the drawer of that little table," he said, pointing with his hand, which trembled a little. " It's open — just get what there is and bring it here, will you ? "

Katharine rose.

" I don't want any money, if you mean to give it to me," she said, as she crossed the room.

She brought him a roll of bills.

" Count it," he said.

She counted carefully, turning back the crisp green notes over her delicate fingers. It was new money.

"There are three hundred and fifty dollars," she said. "At least, I think I've counted right."

"Near enough. Make a note of it, my dear. There are pencil and paper on the table. There —just write down the figure. Now put the money into your pocket, and go and spend it on some trifle."

"I'd rather not," answered Katharine, hesitating.

She had never had so much money in her hand in her whole life, though she was the grand-niece of Robert the Rich.

"Do as I tell you!" cried the old man, almost fiercely, and in a much stronger voice than he had been able to find hitherto.

Katharine obeyed, seeing that he was really losing his temper.

"You may as well spend it on toys as leave it to the servants," he said. "They'd have stolen it as soon as I was dead. Not that I mean to die, though. Not till I've settled one or two things like this. I feel stronger."

"I'm so glad!" exclaimed Katharine.

"So am I," growled the sick man. "You've saved my life."

"I?"

"Yes, child. Go and tell Routh that I said so. Upon my word!" he grumbled, half audibly. "Selling her poor little miniatures to buy clothes for herself and her children — my nieces — that's

just a little too much, you know — can't see how
I could die decently — well — without telling him
what I think about it. Katharine," he said, more
loudly, addressing her, "it amounts to this. I've
left a few charities, and I've left the Miners a
little something to make them comfortable, and
I've given a million to the Brights — Hamilton and
Hester and their mother — and I've left the rest
to you three young ones — you and Charlotte and
Jack Ralston. That ought to make about twenty-
five millions for each of you. I want to know if
you think I've done right?"

Katharine's hands dropped by her side. For the
first time in her life she was literally struck dumb.

"That doesn't mean," continued the old man,
watching her keenly, as the light came back to his
eyes, "that doesn't mean that I give you all that
money, just as I gave you that roll of bills just
now. It's all tied up in trusts, just as far as the law
would allow me to do it. You couldn't take it and
throw it into the street, nor speculate, nor buy a
railway, nor do anything of the kind. You and
Charlotte will have to pay half your income to
your father and mother while they live, and you'll
have to leave it to your children — at least, Charlotte must, and I hope you will, my dear. And
Jack must give half of his income to his mother.
You see, as there are three parents, that will make
it exactly equal. And all three of you have to

pay something to make up an income for your
grandfather. So it will still be equally shared. I
like you best, my dear, but I couldn't show any
favouritism in my will. The end of it will be that
you will each have something less than half the
income of twenty-five millions to spend. That's
better than selling miniatures to buy clothes, any·
way. Isn't it, now?"

He laughed hoarsely and then coughed.

"Go home, child," he said, presently. "I've
talked too much. Stop, though. What I've told
you is not to be repeated on any account. I wanted
to know what you thought of the right and wrong
of the thing — but I've taken your breath away.
Go home and think about it. Come and see me
day after to-morrow — there, I shouldn't have said
that an hour ago — give me a little of that beef
tea, please, my dear. I'm hungry — and I'd rather
have it from your hand than from Mrs. Deems's.
Thank you."

He drank eagerly, and she took the cup from
him and set it down again.

"She's a good creature, the nurse," he said. "A
very good creature — a sort of holy scarecrow. I
shan't need her much longer."

"You really do seem better," said Katharine,
wondering how she could ever have believed that
he was dying.

"I'm going to get well this time. I told Routh

this morning that I wasn't going to die. You've saved my life. There's nothing like rage for the action of the heart, I believe. I shall be out next week."

He began to cough again.

" Go home — go home," he managed to say, between the short spasms. " I'm talking too much."

Katharine bent down and kissed his forehead quickly, looked at him affectionately and left the room, for she saw that what he said was true. She closed the door softly and found her way to the stairs. She was in haste to get out into the air and to be alone, for she wished, if possible, to realize the stupendous possibilities of life which the last few minutes had brought into her range of mental vision. It was not a light thing to have been told that she was one day to be among the richest of her very rich acquaintances, after having been brought up in such a penurious fashion.

In the hall she came suddenly upon her father and mother, who were parleying with the butler.

" Here's Miss Katharine, sir," said the servant, and he immediately fell back, glad to avoid further discussion with such a very obstinate person as Alexander Junior.

" Why, Katharine!" exclaimed Mrs. Lauderdale, in surprise. " Do you mean to say you're here?"

" Yes — didn't you know? Doctor Routh sent

me up in his carriage. He met me on the steps
just as he was going in to see you. Didn't he tell
you?"

"No — how very extraordinary!"

Mrs. Lauderdale's face assumed a grave expression not untinged with displeasure.

"This is very strange," said her husband. "And
Leek has just been telling us that uncle Robert
could see no one."

"I beg pardon, sir," said the butler, coming forward respectfully. "There were orders that when
Miss Katharine came, Mr. Lauderdale was not to
be disturbed."

"Yes," answered Alexander Junior, coldly. "I
understand. Come, Emma — come, Katharine —
we shall be late for luncheon."

"It isn't half-past twelve yet," observed Katharine, glancing at the great old clock, which at that
moment gave 'warning' of the coming chime for
the half-hour.

"It's of no consequence what time it is," said
her father, more coldly than ever. "Come!"

They went out together, and the door closed
behind them. Alexander Lauderdale stood still
upon the pavement and faced his daughter, with a
peculiarly hard look in his eyes.

"What does this all mean, Katharine?" he
enquired, severely. "Your mother and I desire
some explanation."

" There's nothing to explain," answered the young girl. " Uncle Robert wanted to see me, and Doctor Routh told me so, and was kind enough to send me up in his carriage. I was coming away when I met you. There's nothing to explain."

Alexander Junior very nearly lost his temper. He could not recollect having done so since he had refused to accept John Ralston as his son-in-law, nearly eighteen months ago. But his steely grey eyes began to gleam now, and his clear, pale skin grew paler. It was evident that his mind was working rapidly in a direction which Katharine could not understand.

"I wish to know what he said to you," he replied.

" Why do you want to know?" asked Katharine, unwisely, for she herself was agitated.

" I have a right to know," answered her father, peremptorily.

It was unlike him to go to such lengths of insistence at once, and even Mrs. Lauderdale was surprised, and glanced at him somewhat timidly.

" Shall we walk on?" she suggested. " I'm cold — there's a chilly wind from the corner."

They began to move, Alexander Junior walking between them, with Katharine on his left. She did not reply to his last speech at once, and his anger rose.

"When I speak to you, Katharine, I expect to be answered," he said.

"Yes," replied Katharine, coolly. "I was thinking of what I should say."

She had been taken unawares, and found it hard to decide how to act. She thought he was angry because he suspected her of trying to influence the old millionaire to do something which might facilitate her marriage with John Ralston, little guessing that in the eyes of the church and the law she was married already. So far as revealing anything about the dispositions of her great-uncle's will might be concerned, she had not the slightest intention of saying anything about it, nor of even hinting that he had spoken of it. She was capable of quite as much obstinacy as her father, and she was far more intelligent; but she disliked a quarrel of any sort, and yet, placed as she was, she could not see how to avoid one, if he continued to insist. Mrs. Lauderdale saw that trouble was imminent, and tried to come to the rescue.

"How did he seem to be, dear?" she enquired, speaking across her husband. "Doctor Routh was not very encouraging."

"He is better—really better, I'm sure," answered Katharine, seizing the opportunity of turning the conversation. "When I first went in, he looked dreadfully ill. His eyes are quite sunken and his cheeks are positively hollow. But gradually, as we talked, he revived, and when I left him he really seemed quite cheerful."

She paused, not seeing how she could go on talking about the old gentleman's appearance much longer. She hoped her mother would ask another question, but her father interposed again, with senseless and almost brutal persistence.

"I'm glad to hear that he is better," he said. "But I'm still waiting for an answer to my question. What was the nature of the conversation between you, Katharine? I insist upon knowing."

"Really, papa," answered the young girl, looking up to him with eyes almost as hard as his own, "I don't see why you should be so determined to know."

"It's of no consequence why I wish to know. It should be sufficient for you to understand my wishes. I expect you to obey me at once and to give a clear account of what took place. Do you understand me?"

"Perfectly — oh, yes!"

It was evident from Katharine's tone that she did not intend to satisfy him. Her mother thought that she might have excused herself instead of refusing so abruptly. She might have even given a harmless sketch of an imaginary conversation. But that was not her way, as she would have said.

Alexander's anger increased with every moment, in a way by no means normal with him. He said nothing for a few moments, but walked stiffly on, biting his clean-shaven upper lip with his bright teeth. He felt himself helpless, which made the position worse.

"So uncle Robert is really better," said Mrs. Lauderdale, pacifically inclined.

"I think so," answered Katharine, mechanically.

"I'm very glad. Aren't you glad, Alexander, my dear?" she asked, turning to her husband.

"Of course. What a foolish question!"

Mrs. Lauderdale felt that under the circumstances it had certainly been a very foolish question, and she relapsed into silence. She was, on the whole, a very good woman, and was sincere in saying that she was glad of the old man's recovery. This was not inconsistent with her recent haste to inform her husband of the supposed danger. It had seemed quite natural to her to think of going instantly to old Robert Lauderdale's bedside, if there were any possibility of his dying. She knew, also, far better than Katharine had known, what an immense sum was to be divided at his death, and considering the life she had led under her husband's economic rule, she might be pardoned if, even being strongly attached to the old gentleman, she was a little agitated at the thought of the changes imminent in her own existence. There is a point at which humanity must be forgiven for being human. In the memorable struggle for the great

Lauderdale fortune, which divided the tribe against itself, it must not be forgotten that Mrs. Lauderdale was sincerely fond of the man who had accumulated the wealth, though she afterwards took a distinct side in the affairs, and showed herself as eager as many others to obtain as much as possible for her husband and her children.

Meanwhile, in spite of her, the opening skirmish continued sharply. After walking nearly the length of a block in silence, Alexander Junior once more turned his head in the direction of his daughter.

"Am I to understand, Katharine, that you definitely refuse to speak?" he enquired, sternly.

"If you mean that I should tell you in detail all that uncle Robert and I said to each other this morning, — yes. I refuse."

"Do you know that you are disobedient and undutiful?"

"It isn't necessary to discuss that. I'm not a child any longer."

"Very well. We shall see."

And they continued to walk in silence. Alexander was fond of walking and of all sorts of exercise, when it did not interfere with the rigid punctuality of his business habits. He had been a very strong man in his youth.

This was the beginning of hostilities, and the events hitherto described took place in the month of April.

Robert Lauderdale's instinct had not deceived him, in prompting him to say that he was not going to die when he seemed most ill. He rallied quickly, and within a fortnight of the day on which he had sent for Katharine, he was able to be driven in the Park, in the noon sunshine. He was changed, and had grown suddenly much thinner, but most of his friends thought that at his age this was no bad sign.

Ever since that crisis there had been a coldness between Katharine and her father. She felt that he was watching her perpetually, looking, perhaps, for an opportunity of making her feel his displeasure, and assuredly trying to find out what she knew. The subject was not mentioned, and Alexander Junior seemed to have accepted his defeat more calmly than might have been expected; but Katharine knew his character well enough to be sure that the humiliation rankled, and that the obstinate determination to find out the secret was as constantly present as ever.

Katharine's life became more and more difficult and complicated, and she seemed to become more powerless every day, when she tried to see some way of simplifying it. She found herself, indeed, in a very extraordinary position, and one which requires a little elucidation for all those who are not acquainted with her previous history.

In the first place, she had been secretly married

to her second cousin John Ralston, nearly five months before the beginning of this story. John Ralston had faults which could not be concealed. It had been said with some truth that he drank and occasionally played high; that he was a failure, as far as any worldly success was concerned, was evident enough, although he was now making what seemed to be a determined effort at regular work. He was certainly not a particularly good young man. His father, the admiral, who had been dead some years, had been a brave sailor and distinguished in the service, but there were many stories of his wild doings, so that those who trace all character to heredity may find an excuse for John's evil tendencies in his father's temperament. Be this as it may, he had undoubtedly been exceedingly 'lively,' as his distant cousin and best friend, Hamilton Bright, expressed it.

But he had his good points. He was honourable to a fault. He loved Katharine with a single-hearted devotion very rare in so young a man,—for he was only five and twenty years of age,—and for her sake had been making a desperate attempt to master his worse instincts. He could be said to have succeeded in that, at least, since he had made his good resolutions. Whether he could keep them for the rest of his life was another matter.

Katharine's father, however, put no faith in him, and never would. Moreover, John was a poor

man, a consideration which had great weight. No
one could suspect that his great uncle intended to
leave him a large share of the fortune, and it was
very generally believed that they had quarrelled
and that John Ralston was to be cut off with
nothing. This opinion was partly due to the fact
that John kept away from Robert Lauderdale's
house more than the rest of the family, because
he dreaded the idea of being counted among the
hangers on of the tribe. But Alexander Lauderdale could not forbid him the house, because he
was a relation, but altogether refused to hear of
a marriage with Katharine. He hoped to make for
her a match as good as her sister's, if not better.
The scene with John had been almost violent, but
the young lovers had contrived to see each other
with the freedom afforded by society to near
relatives.

Almost a year had passed in this way, and there
had seemed to be no prospect of a solution, when
Katharine had taken the law into her own hands,
being at that time nineteen years old. She had
persuaded John that if he would marry her secretly,
she could at once prevail on old Robert Lauderdale
to find him some occupation in the West. After
much hesitation John Ralston had consented, on
condition that uncle Robert should be told immediately. The pair were secretly married by a clergyman whom John persuaded to perform the ceremony,

and an hour later Katharine had told the old gentleman her secret. He at once offered to make her and
John independent — for the honour of the family;
but John had stipulated that he was to receive
nothing of the nature of money. That would have
been like begging with a loaded pistol. What he
wanted was a position in which he might do some
sort of work, and receive an equivalent sufficient to
support himself and his wife. Robert Lauderdale
at once proved to his grand-niece that such a scheme
was wholly impracticable. John could do nothing
which could earn him a dollar a day. Katharine
had to own at last that he was right. He said that
if John would work steadily in an office in New
York, even for a year, it would be easy to push him
rapidly into success.

The compromise was accepted as the only way
out of the difficulty. The secret marriage remained
a secret, and a mere accomplished formality. John
continued to live with his mother as though he were
a bachelor; Katharine stayed under her father's
roof as Miss Lauderdale. John returned to Beman
Brothers, and was now working there, as has been
said more than once. Katharine had to bear all
the difficulties of a totally false position in society.
These had been the results of the secret marriage,
so far as actual consequences in fact were concerned. Morally speaking, there could be no question but that John Ralston, at least, had profited

enormously by the sense of honourable responsibility Katharine had forced upon him.   He had made
one of those supreme efforts of which natures
nervous by temperament, melancholy, and sometimes susceptible of exaltation, are often capable.
The almost divine dignity which his mother had
taught him to attribute to the code of honour stood
him in good stead.   He saw by the light which
guides heroes, things not heroic in themselves to
be done, but brave at least, and they were easy to
him, because, for Katharine's sake, he would have
done much more.

So far as Katharine was concerned, the effect
upon her was different.   It might even be questioned whether it were a good effect.   She was
helpless to do anything which could improve her
position, and the result was a feeling of hostility
against her surroundings.   The whole fabric of
society seemed to her to rest upon a doubtful
foundation, since two young people so eminently
fitted for each other could be forced by it into
such a situation.

They were of equal standing in every way; she
had even lately learned that their prospects of
fortune, which were little short of colossal, were
precisely the same.   They loved each other.   They
were married by church and law.   Yet between
John's code of honour, on the one hand, and
Alexander Lauderdale's determined opposition, on

the other, they dared not so much as own that they were husband and wife, lest some enormous social scandal should ensue. They had but one alternative — to leave New York together, which meant starvation, or else to accept Robert Lauderdale's help in the form of money, which John was too proud to do. And though John would have been quite ready to starve alone, he had no intention of subjecting Katharine to any such ordeal. He blamed himself most bitterly for having accepted the secret marriage at all, but since the thing was done, he meant to do his share and bear his burden manfully and honourably. It was all he could do to atone for his weakness in having yielded, and for the trouble he had caused Katharine.

But she had no such active part as he. He must work, for he had chosen that salvation for his self-respect, and it was her portion to wait until he could win his independence on his own merits, since he would not be indebted for it to any one. The waiting is often harder to bear than the working. Katharine grew impatient of the conventions in the midst of which she lived, and found fault with the system of all modern society.

She was strangely repelled, too, by the attentions of the young men she met daily, and danced with, and sat beside at dinner. They had amused her until the last winter. She was not one of those girls who either feign indifference to amusement, or really feel it, and so long as she had been free to enjoy herself without any secondary thoughts about the meaning of enjoyment, she had found the world a pleasant place. Now, however, she was for the first time made conscious that several of the young fellows who surrounded her at parties really wished to marry her. The genuine and pure-hearted convictions concerning the inviolable sanctity of marriage, which are peculiarly strong in American young girls, asserted themselves with Katharine at every moment. Being the lawfully wedded wife of John Ralston, it seemed an outrage that young Van De Water, for instance, should seek occasion to assure her of his devotion. Yet, since he, like the rest, knew nothing of the truth, she could not blame him if he had chanced to fall in love with her. She could only refuse to listen to him and discourage his advances, feeling all the while a most unreasonable and yet womanly desire to hand him over to her husband's tender mercies, together with a firm faith that John was not only able, but would also be quite disposed, to slay the offender forthwith.

This seems to prove that woman is naturally good, and that harm can only reach her by slow stages. And it is a curious reflection that generally in the world good, when it comes, comes quickly and evil slowly. Great purifying religions have arisen and washed whole nations clean, almost in one man's lifetime, whereas it has always required generations of luxury and vice to undermine the solidity of any strong people. A first sin is rarely more than an episode, too often exaggerated by those who would direct the conscience, and who leave the offenders to the terrible danger of discovering such exaggerations later, and then of setting down all wrong-doing as insignificant because the first was made to appear greater than it was.

Katharine hated the falseness of her position, and the perpetual irritation to which she was exposed unsettled the balance of her girlish convictions as they had emerged from the process of education, ready-made, honest, and somewhat conventional. The disturbance awakened abnormal activity in her mind, and she fell into the habit of questioning and discussing almost every accepted article of creeds social and spiritual.

Hence her liking for the society of Paul Griggs, whose experience was a fact, but whose convictions were a mystery not easily fathomed. Alexander Lauderdale especially detested the man for his easy way of accepting anybody's religious beliefs, as though the form of religion were of no importance whatever, while perpetually thrusting forward the humanity of mankind as the principal point of interest in life. But when he was alone with Katharine, or with some kindred spirit, Griggs sometimes talked of other things.

The day on which Katharine, returning from
Robert Lauderdale's house, refused to answer her
father's questions was an important one in her
history and in the lives of many closely connected
with her; and this has seemed the best place for
offering an explanation of such preceding events
as bear directly upon all that followed. Here,
therefore, ends the prologue to the story which is
to tell of the lives of John Ralston and his wife,
commonly known as Miss Lauderdale, during the
great battle for the Lauderdale fortune. It has
been a long prologue, and, as is usually the case
in such tiresome preliminary pieces, the majority
of the actors in the real play have not yet
appeared, and the few who have come before the
curtain crave as yet indulgence rather than ap-
plause. They have shown their faces and have
explained the general nature of what is to be
represented, and they retire as gracefully as they
can, under rather difficult circumstances, to re-
appear in such actions and situations as should
explain themselves.

CHAPTER IV.

In itself, Robert Lauderdale's will was a very fair one. It provided, as has been seen, that each of the living members of the family in the direct line should have an equal income, while insuring the important condition that the money should remain in the hands of the Lauderdales and Ralstons as long as possible, since the income paid to the four elder members, Alexander Lauderdale Senior, Alexander Junior, the latter's wife and Mrs. Ralston, John's mother, should revert at the deaths of each to the three younger heirs, John Ralston, Katharine, and Charlotte Slayback, and afterwards to the children of each.

This result seemed just and, on the whole, to be desired. Robert Lauderdale had devoted much thought to the subject, and had seen no other way of acting fairly and at the same time of providing as far as possible against the subdivision and disappearance of the great fortune he had amassed. The will was to constitute three separate trusts, one for each of the direct legatees and their children, at whose death the trusts would expire, and the property be further divided amongst the succeeding generations in each line.

The old millionaire was a very enlightened man, and had honestly endeavoured during his lifetime to understand the conditions and obligations to which the possessors of very large fortunes should submit. Looking at the matter from this point of view, he had come to regard the accumulation and dissipation of wealth as a succession of natural phenomena, somewhat analogous to those of evaporation and rain, beneficial when gradual, destructive when sudden. As water is drawn up in the form of vapour, in invisible atoms, gradually to accumulate in the form of clouds, which, moving under natural conditions, are borne towards those regions where moisture is most needed, to descend gently and be lost in showers that give earth life, until the sky above is clear again, and all the fields below are green with growing things — so, thought Robert Lauderdale, should wealth follow a reasonable and beneficial course of constant distribution and redistribution, to promote which was a moral obligation upon those through whose hands it passed. He was not sure that it was in any way his duty to leave vast sums for charities, nor to hasten the subdivision of the property in any violent way; for he knew well enough that sudden divisions generally mean the forcible depression of values, in which case wealth, of which the

income being spent regularly should find its way
to the points where it is most needed, must, on
the contrary, become dormant until values are restored, if indeed they ever are restored altogether.

If he had been the father of one or more children, there is no knowing how he might have
acted. If there had been in the whole family one
man whom he sincerely trusted to act wisely, he
might have left him the bulk of the fortune,
giving each of the others a sum which would have
been large compared with what they had of their
own, but wholly insignificant by the side of the
main property. But no such selection was possible. His brother was a very old man, wholly un-
fitted for the purpose. His brother's son was a
miser, and a dull one at that, in Robert's estimation. John Ralston was not to be thought of for
a moment. Hamilton Bright would have answered
the conditions, but he was far removed in relationship, being a descendant of Robert Lauderdale's
uncle through a female line. Nevertheless, Robert
Lauderdale hesitated.

It was perhaps natural that Alexander Junior
should believe that he was the proper person for
his uncle to select as the principal heir. He was
the only son of the eldest of the family. He was
a man of stainless reputation, occupying a position
of high importance and trust. No one could have
denied that he was scrupulous in business matters

to a degree rare even amongst the most honourable
men of his own city. He was comparatively young,
being only fifty years old, and he might live a
quarter of a century to administer and hold together the Lauderdale estate, for his health was
magnificent and his strength of iron.

He had thought it all over daily for so many
years, that he could see no possible reason why he
should not be the principal heir. In arguing the
case, he told himself that his uncle was not capricious, that he would certainly not leave his fortune
to Hamilton Bright, who was the only other sensible man of business in the whole connection, and
that it was generally in the nature of very rich
men to wish to know that their wealth was to be
kept together after they were dead. No one could
possibly do that better than Alexander Lauderdale
Junior.

Nevertheless, he felt conscious that his uncle
disliked him personally, and in moments of depression, when he had taken too little exercise and his
liver was torpid, the certainty of this caused him
much uneasiness. There was no apparent reason
for it, and it suggested to his self-satisfied nature
the idea that some caprice entered, after all, into
the nature of his uncle. On such occasions he
rarely failed to instruct Mrs. Lauderdale to ask
uncle Robert to dinner, and to be particularly careful that the fish should be perfect. Uncle Robert

was fond of fish and a quiet family party. Katharine was his favourite, but he liked Mrs. Lauderdale, and his brother, the old philanthropist, was
congenial to him, though the two took very different views of humanity and the public good.
Alexander Senior's dream was to get possession of
all Robert's millions and distribute them within a
week amongst a number of asylums and charitable
institutions which he patronized. He should then
feel that he had done a good work and that his
benevolent instincts had been satisfied. He sometimes sat in his study in a cloud of smoke — for
he smoked execrable tobacco perpetually — and
tried to persuade himself that ' brother Bob '
might perhaps after all leave him the whole fortune. There would be great joy among the idiots
on that day, thought old Alexander, as the two-
cent ' Virginia cheroot ' dropped from his hand, and
he fell asleep in his well-worn armchair. And
then came dreams of unbounded charity, of unlimited improvement and education of the poor
and deficient. The greatest men of the age should
be employed to devote their lives to the happiness
of the poor little blind boys, and of the little
girls born deaf, and of the vacantly staring blear-
eyed youths whom nature had made carelessly, and
whom God had sent into the world, perhaps, as a
means of grace to those more richly endowed.
For old Alexander was charitable to every one —

even to the Supreme Being, whose motives he ven-
tured to judge. He was incapable of an unkind
thought, and in the heaven of his old fancy he
would have founded an asylum for reformed devils
and would not have hesitated to beg a subscription
of Satan himself, being quite ready to believe that
the Prince of Hell might have his good moments.
He would have prayed cheerfully for 'the puir
deil.' There is no limit to the charity of such
over-kind hearts. Nothing seems to them so bad
but that, by gentleness and persuasion, it may at
last be made good.

He knew, of course, for Robert had told him,
that he was not to have the millions even during
the few remaining years of his life, and he bore
his brother no malice for the decision. Robert
promised him that he should have plenty of money
for his poor people, but did not hesitate to say that
if he had the whole property he would pauperize
half the city of New York in six months.

"You'd give every newsboy and messenger boy
in the city a roast turkey for dinner every day,"
laughed Robert.

"If I thought it might improve the condition
of poor boys, I certainly should," answered the
philanthropist, gravely. "I'm fond of roast turkey
myself — with cranberry sauce and chestnuts
inside. Why shouldn't the poor little fellows
have it, too, if every one had enough money?"

"If there were enough money to go round, creation would be turned into a kitchen for a week, and into a hospital for six months afterwards," observed Robert Lauderdale. "Fortunately, money's scarcer than greediness."

And on the whole, there was much wisdom in this plain view, which to Robert himself presented a clear picture of the condition of mankind in general in regard to money and its distribution.

It would not have been natural if even the least money-loving members of the family had not often speculated, each in his or her own way, about the chances of receiving something very considerable when old Robert died. He had been generous to them all, according to his lights, but he had not considered that any of them were objects of charity. The true conditions of his brother's household life had been carefully concealed from him, until Katharine had, almost accidentally, given him an insight into her father's family methods, so to say. Nevertheless, he had long known that Alexander Junior must have much more money than he was commonly thought to possess, and his mode of living, as compared with his fortune, proved conclusively that he hoarded what he had. He must have known that a large share of the estate must ultimately come to him, and he could assuredly have had no doubts as to its solidity, since it consisted entirely in land and houses. What was he hoarding his income for? That was the question which naturally suggested itself to Robert, and the only answer he could find, and the one which accorded perfectly with his own knowledge of his nephew's character, was that Alexander was a miser. As the certainty solidified in the rich man's mind, he became more and more determined that Alexander Junior should know nothing of the dispositions of the will.

And he had rigidly kept his own counsel until that day when he had confided in Katharine. When he was well again, or, at all events, so far recovered as to feel sure that he might live some time longer, he regretted what he had done. Weakened by illness, he had acted on impulse in making a young girl the repository of his secret intentions. Moreover, he had not intended to part with the right to change them whenever he should see fit, and the problem of the distribution of wealth continued to absorb his attention. He had great faith in Katharine, but, after all, she was not a man, as he told himself repeatedly. She might be expected to confide in John Ralston, who might, on some unfortunate day, drink a glass of wine too much and reveal the facts of the case. He would have been even more disturbed than he was, had he known that Alexander Junior suspected his daughter of knowing the truth.

Robert Lauderdale had certainly not made her

life easier for her by what he had done. During
several days her father from time to time repeated
his questions.

"I hope that you are in an altered frame of
mind, Katharine," he said. "This perpetual obstinacy on the part of my child is very painful to me."

"I might say something of the same kind," Katharine answered. "It's painful — as you choose to
call it — to me, to be questioned again and again
about a thing I won't speak of. Why will you do
it? You seem to think that I hold my tongue
out of sheer eccentricity, just to annoy you. Is
that what you think? If so, you're very much
mistaken."

"It's the only possible explanation of your undutiful conduct. I repeat that I'm very much
pained by your behaviour."

"Look here, papa!" cried Katharine, turning
upon him suddenly. "Don't drag in the question
of duty. It's one's duty to keep a secret when
one's heard it — whether one wanted to hear it or
not. There's no reason in the world why I should
repeat to you what uncle Robert told me — any
more than why I should go and tell Charlotte, or
Hester Crowdie, or anybody else."

"Katharine!" exclaimed Alexander Junior,
sternly, "you are very impertinent."

"Because I tell you what I think my duty is?
I'm sorry you should think so. And besides, since

you seem so very anxious that I should betray a secret, I'm afraid that it wouldn't be very safe with you."

Alexander Junior did not wince under the cut. He was firmly persuaded that he was in the right.

"If you were not a grown-up woman, I should send you to your room," he said, coldly.

"Yes, I realize the advantage of being grown up," answered Katharine, with contempt.

"But I shall not tolerate this conduct any longer," continued Alexander Junior. "I will not be defied by my own daughter."

"Charlotte defied you for twenty years," replied Katharine, "and she's not half as strong as I am. And I never defied you, and I don't now. That's not the way I should put it. I'm not so dramatic, and as long as I won't, — why, I won't, that's all, — and there's no need of calling it defiance, nor by any other big name."

Alexander was a cold man, and it was not likely that he should lose his temper again as he had when he had walked home with her from Robert Lauderdale's. He began to recognize that in the matter of imposing his will forcibly, he had met his match. He had generally succeeded in dominating those with whom he came into close relations in life, but his hard and freezing exterior had contributed more to the effect than his intellectual gifts. Finding that his personality failed to produce the usual result, he temporized, for he was not good at sharp answers.

"There's no denying the fact," he said, "that uncle Robert has told you about his will. Can you deny that?"

The latter question is a terrible weapon, and is the favourite one of dull persons when dealing with truthful ones, because it is so easily used and so effective. Katharine was familiar with it, and knew that her father had few others, and none so strong. She met it in the approved fashion, which is as good as any, though none are satisfactory.

"That's an absurd question," she answered. "You've made up your mind beforehand, and nothing I could say would make you change it. If I denied that uncle Robert had told me anything about his will, you wouldn't believe me."

"Certainly not!" replied Alexander, falling into the trap like a school-boy.

"Then it's clear that nothing I can say can make you change your mind — in other words, that you're prejudiced," said Katharine, in cool triumph. "And as that's undeniable, from your own words, I don't see that it's of the slightest use to ask me questions."

Her father bit his clean-shaven upper lip and frowned severely.

"I don't know where you get such sophistries from!" he answered, in impotent arrogance. "Unless it's that Mr. Griggs who teaches you," he added, taking a new line of aggression.

"Why do you say 'that' Mr. Griggs, as though he were an adventurer or a fool?" enquired Katharine, arching her black brows.

"Because I suspect him of being both," answered Alexander Junior, jumping at the suggestion with an affectation of keenness.

Katharine laughed.

"That's too absurd, papa! You'd have said just the same thing if I'd said 'murderer' and 'thief.' You know as well as I do that Mr. Griggs is a distinguished man, — I didn't say that he was a great genius, — who has got where he is by hard work and good work. He's no more of an adventurer than you are."

"I've heard strange stories of his youth, which I shall certainly not repeat to you," answered Alexander, snapping his lips in the fine consciousness of his own really unimpeachable virtue.

One proverb, at least, is true, amidst many high-sounding, conventional lies. Virtue is emphatically its own reward. The scorn of those who possess it for those who do not, proves the fact beyond all doubt.

"I'm not going to discuss Mr. Griggs, and I don't want to hear about his youth," answered Katharine. "You've taken an unreasonable dislike for him, and there's no necessity for your meeting any oftener than you please."

"Fortunately, no — there's no necessity. I should be sorry to associate with such men, and I regret very much that you should choose your friends amongst them. Since you've announced your intention of defying me and disregarding all my wishes, we'll say no more about that for the present. Perhaps I shall find means to bring you to reason which will surprise you. In the meantime, I consider that you are acting very unwisely in refusing to communicate what you know about the will."

"Possibly — but I'm willing to abide by my mistake," answered Katharine, calmly.

"It is of course certain," continued her father, "that a very large sum of money will come to us when my uncle Robert dies — some day. Let us hope that it may be long before that happens."

"By all means, let's hope so," observed Katharine.

"Don't interrupt me, Katharine. You can at least show me the common courtesy of listening to what I say, whatever position you may choose to take up against me. As I was saying, a great deal of money will come to some of us. We do not know exactly how much it will be, though I've no doubt that you're acquainted with all the details. But I admit that you can't possibly appreciate how important it is for us all to know how this great fortune is to be disposed of, and who has

been selected as the administrator. The happiness
of many persons, the safety of the fortune itself,
depend upon these things being known in time."

"I don't see what they can have to do with the
safety of the fortune. Houses don't run away.
I've often heard you say that uncle Robert has
everything in houses. I suppose one person will
get one house and another will get another."

"I'm not here to explain the principle of business to you," said Alexander. "Those are things
you can't understand. The death of a man of such
immense wealth necessarily affects public affairs
and the market, even if his fortune is largely in
real estate. It is a security to the world at large
to feel that a proper person has succeeded in the
management of the estate."

"I suppose that uncle Robert understands that,
too," observed Katharine.

"In a way, of course — yes, in a certain way he
must, I've no doubt. But these great men never
seem to realize what will happen when they die."

"You speak of uncle Robert's death as though
you expected to hear of it this evening. He's
almost quite well."

Again Alexander Junior bit his lip. He had,
perhaps, never before been so conscious that when
his personality failed to produce the effect he desired, his intelligence had no chance of accomplish-
ing anything unaided.

"This is intolerable!" he exclaimed, with profound disgust. "Since you can be neither decently civil nor in any way reasonable, I shall leave you to think over your conduct."

This is a threat which rarely inspires terror in the offender. Katharine did not wish to go too far, and received the announcement in silence, sincerely hoping that he would really go away and leave her to herself. Such scenes occurred almost every day, and she was weary of them, — not more so, perhaps, than Alexander was of perpetual defeat. She could not understand why he was so persistent, for it seemed to her that she showed him plainly enough how determined she was to keep silence. His reproof did not affect her in the least, for she knew she was right. She wondered, indeed, from time to time, that a man so undoubtedly upright as he was should so press her to betray a confidence, when he had all his life preached to her about the value of reticence and discretion, and she rightly attributed his conduct to his excessive anxiety for the money, overriding even his rigid principles. She had often admired him, merely for that very rigidity, which appealed to her as being masculine and strong. She despised him the more when she had discovered that the only motive able to bend the stiff back of his scrupulous theory and practice was the love of money, pure and simple. She did not believe that he would have so derogated to save her life. The very arrogance of his manner showed how far he knew himself to be from his own ideal. He was trying to carry it through as a matter of right.

Katharine longed to confide in John Ralston. He was not so free as he had been in his idle days, a few months earlier. Having accepted a position, he was determined to do his best, and he stayed down town every day as long as there was the least possibility of finding anything which he could do in the bank.

Not long after the last-recorded interview with Katharine, Alexander Junior, being down town, had some reason to speak of a matter of business with the senior partner in Beman Brothers', and entered the bank early in the afternoon. It was a vast establishment on the ground floor, a few steps above the level of the street. Being a place where there was much going and coming and active work, the office had not the air of icily polished perfection which characterized the inner fane of the Trust Company. The counters and seats were dark, and rubbed smooth with use, like the floor; the doors were worn with constant handling, but moved easily and noiselessly on their hinges. The brass gratings and rails were bright with long years of daily leathering. Everything was large, strong, and workmanlike, as a big engine, which is well kept but gets very little rest. There was the low,

breathing, softly shuffling sound in the air, which
is heard where many are busy and no one speaks a
superfluous word.

Alexander Lauderdale passed through the great
outer office and caught sight of John Ralston,
bending over some writing at a small desk by himself. Ralston was at that time between five and six
and twenty years of age, a wiry, lean young man,
with a dark face. There was more restlessness
than strength in the expression, perhaps, but there
was no lack of energy, a quality which, when it
does not find vent in a congenial activity, is apt to
produce a look of discontent. Possibly, too, there
might be a dash of Indian blood in the Ralston
family. There was certainly none in the Lauderdales. John's bright brown eyes were turned upon
his work, as Alexander passed near him, but
glanced up quickly a moment later and saw him.
A look of contempt darkened the young man's features like a shadow, and was instantly gone again.
The two men had not exchanged half a dozen words
in eighteen months. The brown eyes went back to
the page, and the sinewy, nervous hand went on
writing, and the straight, smooth hair on the top of
Ralston's head, as he bent over the desk, became
again the most prominent object, for its extreme
blackness, in that part of the office.

Alexander Junior was ushered into the elder Mr.
Beman's private room, by a grave young man in a

jacket with gilt buttons. The name of Lauderdale
was a passport in any place of business in the city.

"By the way," he said, after exchanging a few
words about the matter which had brought him
there, "you've taken back that young cousin of
ours, Jack Ralston. How's the fellow getting
on ?"

"Ralston? Oh, yes — Mr. Lauderdale wanted
him to try again — yes — well, he's doing pretty
well, I'm told. But they tell me he can't do anything, though he wants to. Praiseworthy, though,
very praiseworthy, to try and work, when he's sure
to have plenty of money one of these days. I like
the boy myself," added Mr. Beman, with slightly
increasing interest. "He's got some good in him,
somewhere, I'll be bound."

"Does he keep pretty steady ?" enquired Alexander Junior. "You knew he drank, I suppose ?"

"Drinks !" exclaimed Mr. Beman, rather incredulously. "Nonsense — don't believe it."

Mr. Beman hated society, and spent many of
his leisure hours in a club chiefly frequented by
old gentlemen.

"Oh, no ! It's quite true, I assure you. I thought
you knew, or I wouldn't have mentioned it — being
a relation. I hope he won't make a fool of himself, now that he's with you. Good morning."

"Good morning, my dear Lauderdale," answered
the banker, cordially shaking hands.

Alexander left the bank and returned to his own office, questioning himself by the way concerning the right and wrong side of what he had just done, in undermining whatever confidence Mr. Beman might have in John Ralston. By dint of moral exertion, he succeeded in inducing his Scotch business instinct to admit that it was fair to warn an old friend if the habits of a young man he had lately taken into employment were not exactly what they should be. He resolutely closed his eyes to the fact that he had waited several days, until something had required that he should see the banker, in order to ask the careless question, and that, during all that time, Katharine's obstinacy had rankled in his brooding temper like an unreturned blow. He did not wish to think, either, that he had perpetrated a small act of indirect vengeance. He was very intent upon being conscientious — it would not do even to remember that any under-thoughts had floated through his brain beneath the current which he desired to see.

It was easy enough to forget it all, by merely allowing his mind to turn again to the question of his uncle's millions. That subject had a fascination which never palled. If he is to be excused at all for this and many other things which he subsequently did, his excuse must be stated now, or never.

Let this one fact be remembered, for the sake of

his humanity. He had spent the best years of his
life in the inner office of a great Trust Company.
That alone explains many things. Having originally been in moderate circumstances, he had been
brought into daily contact for a long period with
the process of hoarding money. He had seen
how sums, originally insignificant, doubled and
trebled themselves, and grew to fair dimensions by
the simplest of all means, — by being kept locked
up. He had not been by nature grasping, nor
covetous of the goods of others in any inordinate
degree, but he had that inborn craving for the actual
money itself, for seeing it and touching it, and
knowing where it is, which makes one small boy
ask his father for a penny 'to put by the side of
the other,' while his brother spends his mite on a
sugar-plum, eats it, and runs off to play. Day by
day, month by month, year by year, he had seen
that putting of one penny by the side of the other
going on under his eyes and personal supervision.
It had been his duty to see that the pennies stayed
where they were put. It is not strange that, with
his temperament, he should have done for himself
what he did for others. And with the doing of it
came the habit of secrecy, which belongs to the
miser's passion, the instinctive denial of the possession, the mechanical and constantly recurring
avowal of an imaginary poverty. All that came
as surely as the dream of countless gold, to be

counted forever and ever, with the absolute certainty of never reaching the end, and as the nightmare of the empty safe, more real and terrible than the live horror of the waking man who comes home and finds that the wife he loves has left him.

He knew that hideous scene by heart. It visited him sometimes with no apparent cause. He knew how in the night — he always dreamed that it happened at night — he went to his own box in the Safe Deposit Vault, his own familiar box, as in reality he went regularly twice in every week. He felt the thrill of secret, heart-warming anticipation as he came near to it. His heart began to beat as it always did then, and only then, giving him a queer, breathless sensation which he loved, and that peculiar thirsty dryness in the throat. He turned the key, he pressed the spring, and out it came against his greedy, trembling hand — empty. At that point he awoke, clutching at the thin, tough chain by which the real key hung about his neck. His worst fear for years had been to dream that dream — his highest pleasure had been to go, after dreaming it, and find it false, the drawer full, all safe, the good United States Bonds filed away in dockets of a hundred thousand dollars each, untouched and unfingered.

He knew the fascination, the dumb horror, the soul-uplifting delight of a great passion, of one which is said to be the last and greatest, if not the worst, that plays the devil's music on the wrung heartstrings of men. That is his only excuse for what he did. Dares humanity allege its humanity in extenuation of its humanity ?

CHAPTER V.

BEFORE John Ralston had gone back to Beman Brothers', it had been easy enough for him and Katharine to meet in the course of the day, but the difficulties had increased unavoidably of late. Of course they saw each other in society, and as members of the same tribe they were often asked to the same parties, though that was by no means a matter of certainty. It was necessary to have a fixed understanding which should enable them to be sure of meeting and communicating with one another, and of knowing from day to day whether the next meeting were positively certain or not. John's hour for going down town was fixed, but the time of his returning was not. That depended on the amount of work there chanced to be for him at the bank, — sometimes more, sometimes less.

The habits of the Lauderdale household in Clinton Place were also very exact. Alexander Junior took charge, as it were, of the day, as soon as it appeared, and doled it out in portions. Breakfast was at half past eight, and he expected his wife and daughter to make their appearance in time to

see him at least finish the solid steak or brace of
chops with which he fortified himself for work.
His father always came down late, in order to be
able to smoke as soon as he had finished eating,
without annoying any one, for the old man seemed
to subsist largely upon tobacco smoke and fresh
milk — which is a strange mixture, but not un-
healthy for those who are accustomed to it. That
he smoked 'Old Virginia Cheroots' at two cents
each, was his misfortune and not his fault. Practically he lived upon his son, for he had long ago
given away everything he possessed, and even the
old house had passed into Alexander's hands — for
a very moderate equivalent, which the philanthropist had already spent in advance upon the intro-
duction of a new heating apparatus in his favourite
asylum. Alexander Junior supplied him with the
necessaries of life, and by almost imperceptible
degrees of change had at last substituted the cheroots for the fine Havanas to which his father had
been addicted in his comparative prosperity. From
time to time the old man made a mild remark
about the deterioration of cigars. The observations
of his friends, after smoking one of his, were less
mild. Alexander Senior attributed the change to
the McKinley Bill. Alexander Junior did not
smoke. He left the house every morning at a
quarter past nine, before the fumigation had begun.

Katharine had always been free to go out for a

walk alone in the early hours since she had been considered to be grown up, and she took advantage of the privilege now in order to meet John Ralston. He was expected to be at the bank at half past nine, and, as it was near the Rector Street Station, he could calculate his time with precision if he found himself near a station of the elevated road.

He and Katharine had a simple system of signals. John came down to Clinton Place by the Sixth Avenue elevated, and got out at the corner. Thence he walked past the Lauderdales' house to Fifth Avenue, and crossed Washington Square to South Fifth Avenue, by which he reached the Bleecker Street Station of the elevated railway. The usual place of meeting was on the south side of the Square. If Katharine were coming that morning there was something red in her window, a bit of ribbon, a red fan, or anything she chanced to pick up of the required colour. John could see it at a glance. He, on his part, let fall a few seeds or grains on the well-swept lower step of the house as he passed, to show that he had gone by. The convention was that the signal should consist of any kind of seed or grain. If, when she went out, there was nothing on the step, which very rarely happened, Katharine went back into the house and waited, easily finding an excuse if any one remarked her return, by alleging a mismatched pair of gloves, or a forgotten parasol or umbrella.

The **system** worked perfectly. Two or three
grains of wheat, or rice, or rye, a couple of pepper-
corns, a little millet, varied daily, according to the
supply John had in his pockets, and dropped near
one end of the step, were all that was required, for
it was rarely that more than a few minutes elapsed
between their being deposited there and the moment
when Katharine saw them. Generally, the sparrows
had got them before any one else came out. The
only person who ever noticed the frequent presence
of seeds of some kind on the doorstep was the old
philanthropist, who made illogical reflections upon
the habits of the birds that brought them there, as
he naturally supposed.

With regard to the place of meeting, the two
changed it from time to time, or from day to day,
as they thought best. Their minutes were counted,
as John could not afford to be late at Beman
Brothers', and sometimes they only exchanged a
few words, agreeing to meet in the evening, or,
since the spring had come, after John's business
hours. Hitherto, they believed that none of their
acquaintances had seen them, and they believed
that none ever would. There seemed to be no reason why people they knew should be wandering in
the purlieus and slums about South Fifth Avenue
and Green Street, for instance, at nine o'clock in
the morning. A few women in society patronized
the little foreign shop in the Avenue, near the

Square, where artificial flowers were made, but if they ever went there themselves, it was much later in the day.

They met on the morning after Alexander Junior had spoken to Mr. Beman about John. The latter was standing before the church on the south side of Washington Square, puffing at the last end of a cigarette, when he saw Katharine's figure, clad, as usual, in grey homespun, emerging from one of the walks which ended opposite to him. The colour came a little to her face as she caught sight of him.

She walked quickly, and began to speak before she reached him.

"Oh Jack! I do so want to see you!" She held out her hand as he lifted his hat.

Their hands remained clasped a second longer, perhaps, than if they had been mere acquaintances, and their eyes were still meeting when their hands had parted.

"Yes — so do I," answered Ralston, with small regard for grammar. "You look tired, dear. What is it?"

"It's this life — I don't know how much longer I can stand it," answered Katharine, and they began to walk on.

"Has anything happened? Has your father been teasing you again?" John asked, quickly.

"Oh, yes! He leaves me no peace. It's a succession of pitched battles whenever we meet. He's

made up his mind to know what uncle Robert said
to me, and I've made up mine that he shan't.
What can I do? Why, Jack, I wouldn't even tell
you!"

"I don't want to know," answered Ralston.
"Uncle Robert isn't going to die for twenty years,
and I hope he may live thirty. Of course, when
he dies, if we're alive, we shall have heaps of
money all round, and your father and grandfather
will probably get the biggest shares. But there'll
be plenty for us all. Your father seems to me to
have lost his head about it."

"He really has. It's the same thing every day.
He tells me that I'm all kinds of things — undutiful, and impertinent, and intolerable — altogether a perfect fiend, according to him. Then he
threatens me —"

"Threatens you?" repeated John, with a quick
frown and a change of tone. "He'd better not!"

"Well — he says that he'll find means to make
me speak, and that sort of thing. I don't see
myself what means he has at his command, I'm
sure. I suppose when he's angry he doesn't know
what he's saying. So I try to smile — but I don't
like it."

"I should think not! But as you say, he can't
really do anything except talk. He's permanently
angry, though. He came into the bank yesterday
and passed near me. I saw his face."

John added no comment, but his tone expressed well enough what he felt.

"I know," answered Katharine. "He always has that expression now, — one only used to see it now and then, — as though he meant to have something, if he had to kill somebody to get it. It's the strangest thing! He, who has always preached to me about keeping the secret of other people's confidence! It's perfectly incomprehensible! It's as though his whole nature had suddenly changed."

"He's wild to know how much he's to have," observed John, thoughtfully. "It attacked him when they expected uncle Robert to die. And now that he knows that you know, he means to wring it out of you. I hate him. I should like to wring his neck."

"Jack!"

"Oh, well — of course he's your father, and I'm very sorry for expressing myself — all the same — " he finished his sentence inwardly. "At all events, he's got to treat you properly, or I shall interfere. This can't go on, you know."

"You, Jack dear? What could you do?"

"What could I do? Take you away from him. of course. I'm your husband. Don't forget that, Katharine."

"No, dear — I'm not likely to. But still — I don't see — nothing's changed, you know. The difficulties are just the same as they ever were."

"Yes. But the reasons are different. I can't
allow you to suffer. You know that after all that
trouble last winter my mother insisted on making
over half the property to me. Of course things go
on just as they did, and we share everything. But
I've got it all the same — six thousand a year, if
I choose to call it my own. The reason why we
don't tell everybody that we're married is, first,
because it would make such an incredible row in
the family, and secondly, because, as my mother
and I have so little between us, she would have to
reduce ever so many things if we set up at house-
keeping with her, until I can make something. As
long as you're happy at home, that's all very well.
We're young enough to wait six months or a year,
though we don't like it, and I'm going in for earn-
ing the respect of the Beman Brethren — they're
really awfully nice to me, I must say. Anything
more ignorant than I am you can't imagine!"

"Never mind, Jack — you're learning, at all
events," said Katharine, in an encouraging tone.
"And I know, dear — I know how you care for me,
and how brave you are to wait for the sake of
what's nice to your mother — "

"Oh, don't talk of courage! It's what I ought
to have done long ago, if I hadn't been a born
loafer and idiot. But if things are going to be
different since your beloved father has got this
idea into his head, if he's going to torment you

perpetually, and make your life a burden, and call
you bad names out of the prayer-book — that sort
of thing, you know — why, then, we must just do it,
that's all — just face the row, and the economies,
and all, and you must come to my mother's."

"But, Jack — just think of what would happen — "

"Well — just think what's happening now. It's
much worse, I'm sure, and if it's going to last, I
shall just do it. My mother always says that she
wishes we could be married. Well — we are married. There's nothing to be done but to tell her
so. Besides, for her part, she'd be delighted.
You don't know her! She's just like a man in
some things. She'd put up with anything — boiled
beef and cabbage, and a horse-car fare on Sundays
by way of an outing. Only, of course, if it can
possibly be helped, I don't want her to have to
pinch and screw about her gloves, and her cabs,
and the little things she likes and has had all her
life. That's why I'm working. If I could only
get a salary of two thousand a year, we could manage. I've figured it all out — it's just that two
thousand that would make the difference — it's
ridiculous, isn't it ? "

"It's worse," said Katharine. "It's abominable."

"Yes — it's everything you like — or don't like,
rather. But if you're going to suffer, we must do

as I say. I'll tell you how we'll manage it. You'll just go up to our house some morning about ten o'clock, and go out of town with my mother for a few days. I'll get a holiday from Beman's, and I'll go and see your mother and tell her, and then I'll go down town and face your father. His office is a nice, quiet place, I believe. He's nothing much to do but to be trusted, and he sits all day long by himself in the company's showcase, and people trust him. That's his profession. He represents the moral side of business. Once I've told him, I'll disappear for a while, — going to you, of course, — and we three will come back together and tell the world that we've been quietly married — which is quite true. Lots of people do that nowadays to get out of the expense and fuss of a dress parade wedding. How does that strike you ?"

"Oh, it's clever enough, and brave of you — as you always are — to be ready to face the parents alone. We shall have to do something of the kind in the end, you know, because we can't be married over again. Uncle Robert suggested the same sort of plan last winter; only he wanted us to go to his place up the river, and he was going to ask the whole family. The dear old man forgot that his servants would remember for the rest of their lives that there had been no marriage service. It wasn't practical."

"By the bye, where's our marriage certificate ?"

asked John, suddenly. "You took it, you know. You never told me what became of it."

"Oh, uncle Robert said he'd keep it with his papers. I suppose it's as safe there as anywhere. Still — if he were to die — "

"It's all right, if he's kept it. It will be in a safe place, properly endorsed. As he's the only person who knows the secret, he'd much better keep it, and he's not at all likely to die now that he's recovered. I'd been meaning to ask you for ever so long. But to go back — if things get any worse, or go on as badly as they're going now, do you see any possible objection to doing what I propose ? "

"Well, the principal objection is that it will hamper your mother, Jack. I'd rather suffer a great deal more than I'm likely to, than thrust myself upon her. I know — you'll tell me that she's very fond of me and wants to see us married, and I know she's in earnest about it and means every word she says. But I've lived in a rigidly economical household, as they call it. I know what it means, and it would be very difficult for any one who's never been used to it. Don't think about it, dear. Please don't. You know I come to you with all my little woes — but you mustn't take them too seriously. You'll prevent me from speaking freely if you do, dear."

"It's my business to take your happiness seri-

ously. I'm not prepared to stand the idea of having your life made miserable on my account."

"But it isn't about you, Jack. It's altogether
about the question of uncle Robert's will."

"Never mind. I won't have you made unhappy
by anybody, do you understand? I've got the right
of loving you, and the right of being your husband,
and if that isn't enough I'll take the right. I'm in
earnest, Katharine."

He stood still on the pavement; she stopped,
also, and faced him.

"Yes, dear; I know and I thank you," she said,
gently. "But it really isn't as bad as I made out.
I'm irritated, and I want to be with you all the
time, and then the least little thing seems so much
bigger than it is. Please, please don't do anything
rash, Jack, or without telling me just what you're
going to do! You know you are rash, dear — I'm
always a little afraid of what you may do when
you're angry."

"I certainly shan't be rash where you're concerned," answered Ralston. "You're too much to
me — we are to each other — and we mustn't risk
anything. But don't imagine, either, that if anything goes wrong I shan't know it, even if you
won't tell me. I can guess what you think of
from your face, you know — I've often done it."

"That's true — I'm sure I couldn't conceal anything from you for long," answered Katharine,
womanly wise.

She was concealing something from him at that very moment, something which she had meant to tell him, and would have told him, had he not spoken so decidedly of what he meant to do if her life were made unhappy. But she knew that he was quite capable of doing anything which he said he would do, no matter how rash. When she had at first spoken, she had not altogether realized how he would take up the question of her present unhappiness as a matter for immediate and decisive action. She loved him all the better for it, but she began to understand how careful she must be in future.

John paused a moment after his last speech, and looked into her grey eyes. Perhaps some little doubt assailed him as to whether, if she tried, she could not, perhaps, keep from him something he wished to know — the doubt from which men who love are very rarely quite free.

"But promise me, Katharine," he said, presently, "promise me that if you are really suffering you will tell me, instead of just leaving me to guess."

"Ah — you see!" She laughed softly and happily. "You're not so sure as you thought! Oh, yes — I'll tell you if anything dreadful happens."

"You'd better!" Ralston laughed, too, out of sheer delight at being with her, and his laugh pleased her, for it came rarely. "And about your father — I'll tell you what I think. His excitement will cool down as he sees that uncle Robert's getting better, and he'll leave you alone. You see, he'll be afraid that you'll go to uncle Robert and say that you're being tormented to give up his secret. And then uncle Robert will descend upon Clinton Place and make a raid and raise Cain — and there'll be something to pay all round and no pitch particularly hot. Do you see?"

Katharine laughed again, but she understood that what he said was reasonable enough.

"Now I must be going," said Ralston. "I'm so angry about it all that I'm on the verge of being funny, which isn't in my line. Can you come to-morrow? Is there any chance of seeing you to-night?"

"I don't know. There's a little thing at the Vanbrughs' — are you going?"

"Not asked, worse luck!"

"Then I won't go. How stupid of them not to ask you. I suppose you haven't been near them for months. Have you? Confess!"

"How can I do the card-leaving business now that I'm down town all day? It isn't fair on a man. Besides, the Vanbrughs needn't be so particular. She's nice, though — much nicer since she's given up Sunday-schooling. The last time we talked she knew all about the universe and the Bab faith and the life everlasting — and she was telling everybody. She hates me because I laughed. By Jove!

I must be going, though. To-morrow, then? As
usual. I say, Katharine — if you get a chance to
give your father the sharp answer that wrath particularly dislikes, I hope you will — and tell me
about it. Good-bye, sweetheart — only sixteen
minutes to get to the bank!"

"You did it in fourteen and a half last week,
Jack," answered Katharine, holding his hand.

"Yes — but I just caught the train — I wouldn't
do it at all, if I could help it, you know."

"Of course not — I mustn't be selfish. Run,
dear — and good-bye!"

In a moment he was gone. She watched his
wiry, elastic movements as he ran at the top of his
speed towards the station of the elevated, to the
vicinity of which they had directed their walk
while they had been talking. As he disappeared,
flying up the covered iron stairs, two steps at
a time, she turned and walked briskly homeward.
The neighbourhood is a safe and quiet one, though
it is largely inhabited by foreigners, but she did not
care to slacken her pace till she got back to Washington Square. Then she moved more slowly.

The spring was in the air and the sun was bright.
She sauntered leisurely through the walks, wondering what the coming summer was to bring forth for
her, and all the months after people began to go
away. And she thought all the time of Ralston.
It seemed such an absurd and senseless thing that

they two, who were to be one day among the richest, and would be masters of all that the world can
give to people not endowed with what is not in the
world's gift or market — that they two, being lawfully and christianly married, should be forced to
meet by stealth for a few moments, to be separated
again almost immediately by the necessity which
drove John every day to his desk as a junior clerk
in Mr. Beman's employment. A week — a year —
ten years, if uncle Robert lived so long — and then,
if John went into the bank, the clerks, who were all
his seniors, would lift their pens from the paper in
the middle of a word to watch the representative of
so much wealth go by.   And old Mr. Beman would
rise from his seat and offer Twenty-Five Millions
a chair, as though he were a man of years and
weight.   Not but that the Bemans and John's
fellow-clerks, some of whom were acquaintances
in his own world and beginning their life as he
was, were all well aware that he had a good chance
of getting something handsome in the end. But
mere potential wealth is too common in the neighbourhood of Wall Street to be noticed or much
respected.   It is not the man who may have it,
but the man who has it, who commands respect.
Even the only son, the man who is sure to get
it if he lives, is treated with a certain indifference.
But when time has brought down his heavy hand
upon the millionaire, and crushed him into the

earth-darkness and his memory into a bit of stone
with his name on it, when the last well-greased
screw has been run into the polished coffin, when
the black horses have waved their black plumes
and the last carriage that followed the funeral is
being washed down in the coach-house yard—then
the man who is next stops, and lets future run
ahead of him and himself becomes present fact,
strong, gorgeous, worshipful. For at his mighty
nod the wilderness may become real estate, or the
secret places of Nassau Street and Exchange Place
may be hideous with the groaning of the bulls he
has beared out of the ring—and the solid security
may to-morrow be wild-cat if he wills it, and the
wild-cat emerge in the dawn with a gilt edge and
an honest countenance, to be a joyful investment
for the widow's mite.

Meanwhile, Jack was nobody down town. His
cousin Hamilton Bright, who was a junior partner
in Beman Brothers', was a vastly more important
person than he. For he had behind him what
Ralston had before him, and a fair amount of
capital in the present, besides. It was all very
ridiculous, Katharine thought, and depended on
the false state of society in which she was obliged
to live.

She thought bitterly of her father. He was a
prominent figure in that false state—a man of
fine principles and opportunist practice — she

had caught the latter expression from Walter
Crowdie, Bright's brother-in-law, the well-known
painter, who had painted a portrait of her during
the winter, and who, as the husband of a distant
cousin, was counted in the Lauderdale tribe.

Her father, she thought, preached, prayed —
and then acted far worse than average people who
prayed little and sat still to be preached at on Sundays, in order that Providence might have a sort of
weekly photograph of their souls, so to say, and
because others did the same and it was expected of
them. She and her father had never agreed very
well, and had come into open conflict about John
Ralston; but hitherto she had respected him for
his uncompromising, unashamed piety. There had
seemed to her to be something masculine and bold
about it, and such as it was, she had believed in it.
It had been far from being an idol, but it had been
a very creditable statue, so to say, and now, on a
sudden, the head had been knocked off it, and she
saw, or thought she saw, that it was hollow and
a sham. She was too young yet to admit the presence of good in the same place with evil, and the
evil itself had been thrown directly in her path as
a stumbling-block for herself, and in the hope that
she might fall over it.

And as though it were not enough to torment
her perpetually with questions, there was that
other thing which she had just concealed from

John, because he had been so angry about the first.
Her father and mother were apparently determined
that she should be married before the summer was
out, and were thrusting a match upon her in a way
of which she would not have believed them capable. Ever since her mother had discovered that
she was losing her beauty and that Katharine received three-fourths of all the admiration which had
once been hers, the relations of the two had been
changed. Mrs. Lauderdale was constantly between
two conflicting emotions, which almost amounted
to passions, — her real affection for Katharine, and
her detestable envy of the girl's freshness and
youth. She was a good woman, and she despised
herself more than any one else could possibly have
despised her, for wishing that she might not be
daily compared with her, handicapped, as she was,
with nearly twenty years more to carry. To marry
her daughter was to remove her from home, and
perhaps from New York — and with her, to do
away with the foundation of envy, the cause of
the offence, the visible temptation to the sin
which was destroying the elder woman's happiness and undermining her peace of mind. Mrs.
Lauderdale, whose sins had hitherto been few and
pardonable, felt that if Katharine were once away,
she should become again a good woman, and find
courage to bear the terrible loss of her once supreme beauty.

For she was keenly alive to the wickedness of what she felt, though she could not quite understand it. No man could boast that he had ever had a meaning look or an over-sympathetic pressure of the hand from Mrs. Lauderdale, during the five and twenty years of her married life, though she had loved society intensely, and enjoyed its amusements with a real innocence of which not every woman in her position would have been capable. But no man who had laid eyes upon her could boast — and it would have been a poor boast — that he had turned away at the first glance, without looking again and wondering at her loveliness, and saying to himself that Mrs. Lauderdale was one of the most beautiful women he had ever seen.

It hurt her bodily to miss those eyes turned upon her from all sides, as she began to miss them now. It hurt her still more — and in spite of secret prayers and solemn resolutions and litanies of self-contempt, she turned pale with quiet, deadly anger against the world — when, as she entered a crowded room with Katharine, she felt, as well as saw, that those same eyes sought the pale, severe face of the dark-haired young girl, and overlooked her own fading perfection. The stately rose was drooping, just as the sweet white summer myrtle burst the bud.

Let her not be judged too harshly, if she longed

to be separated from Katharine just at that time.
There was no ill-will, nothing like hatred, no touch
of cruelty in the simple desire to be spared that
daily contrast. It was rather that wish which
many have felt, despairing of grace and strength
to resist temptation, to have the cause of it
removed, that they may find peace. A worse
woman would not so long have been satisfied with
beauty alone, and with compelling by her mere
presence the admiration of a crowd in which no
one face was dearer than the rest, nor than it
should be.

She longed with all her heart to see Katharine
married, as her husband did from very different
reasons. Nor were his arguments bad or unkind
from his point of view. He feared lest she should
marry Ralston in spite of him, and he honestly
believed Ralston to be a worthless young fellow,
who could make no woman happy. As for his
daughter, he was attached to her, fond of her,
perhaps, in his cold way; though loving with him
seemed to be a negative affair and not able to go
much further than a cessation of fault-finding, except for his wife, who had overcome him and kept
him by her beauty alone. It was not until Katharine aroused the deep-seated passion of his unsatisfied avarice that he ceased to be kind to her, as he
understood kindness.

CHAPTER VI.

KATHARINE was in her room that afternoon towards five o'clock, when a servant knocked at her door, disturbing her as she was composing a letter to her best friend, Hester Crowdie. She looked up with an expression of annoyance as the door opened and the maid entered.

"Oh — what's the matter?" she asked, impatiently striking the point of her pen upon the edge of the glass inkstand.

"Mr. Wingfield's downstairs, Miss Katharine," answered the girl.

"Oh — is he? Well — "

Katharine tapped her pen thoughtfully upon the glass again, and a quick contraction of the brow betrayed her displeasure.

"Shall I tell the gentleman that you'll be down, Miss Katharine?" enquired the other.

"No, Annie. Tell him I'm out. That is — I'm not out, am I?"

"No, Miss Katharine."

Katharine let her pen fall, rose and went to the window in hesitation. The bit of red ribbon which had served as a signal to John was pinned

112

to the small curtain stretched over the lower sash. She looked at it thoughtfully, and forgot Mr. Wingfield for a moment.

"Shall I show the gentleman into the library, Miss Katharine?" asked Annie, in an insinuating tone.

"Oh, well! Yes," said Katharine, turning suddenly. "Tell Mr. Wingfield that I'll be down in a few minutes, if he doesn't mind waiting. I suppose I've got to," she added, audibly, before Annie was well out of the room.

She glanced at herself in the looking-glass, but without interest. Then she slipped her unfinished letter into the drawer of the little writing-table by the window, at which she had been sitting, and turned towards the door. But before she left the room she paused, hesitated, and then went back to the table, locking the drawer and withdrawing the key, which she slipped behind the frame of an engraving. She had become unreasonably distrustful of late.

Instead of going down to the library, she knocked at the door of her mother's morning room. It chanced that Mrs. Lauderdale was at home that afternoon, which was unusual in fine weather. Mrs. Lauderdale was sitting by the window at the table she used for her miniature painting. She had talent, and had been well taught in her girlhood, and her work was dis-

tinctly good. Amateurs more often succeed with
miniature than in any other branches of art. It
is harder to detect faults when the scale of the
whole is very minute.

Mrs. Lauderdale was bending over a piece of
work she had lately begun. All the little things
she used were lying about her on the wooden
table, the tiny brushes, the saucers for colours,
the needle-pointed pencils. She looked up as
Katharine entered, and the latter saw all the
lines in the still beautiful face accentuated by
the earnest attention given to the work. The
eyelids were contracted and tired, the lips drawn
in, one eyebrow was raised a little higher than the
other, so that there were fine, arched wrinkles in
the forehead immediately over it. The faces of
American women of a certain age, when the complexion is fair, favour the formation of a multitude of very delicate crossing and recrossing lines,
not often seen in the features of other nationalities.

"What is it, child?" asked Mrs. Lauderdale,
quietly, with her soft southern intonation.

"Mr. Wingfield's there again," answered Katharine, with unmistakable disgust.

"Well, my dear, go down and see him," said
Mrs. Lauderdale, blandly. "Did you send word
that you'd receive?"

"Yes. I'm going to tell him not to come any
more."

Katharine went behind the table, so that she faced her mother and looked directly into her eyes. For several seconds neither spoke.

"I hope you won't do anything so rude," said Mrs. Lauderdale at last, without avoiding the gaze that met hers. "We all like Mr. Wingfield very much."

"I daresay. I'm not finding fault with him, nor his looks, nor his manners, nor anything."

"Well, then — I don't see — "

"Oh, yes, you do, mother, — forgive my contradicting you, — you know very well that he wants to marry me, and that you want me to marry him. But I don't mean to. So I shall tell him, as nicely as I can, to give up the idea, and to make his visits to you, and not to me."

"But, Katharine, dear — nobody wishes to force you to marry him. We don't live in the Middle Ages, you know."

"There's a resemblance," answered Katharine, bitterly.

"Katharine! How can you say anything so unjust!"

"Because it's true, mother. I'm not blind, you know, and I'm not perfectly insensible. I see, and I can feel. You don't seem to think it's possible to hurt me — and I don't think you mean to hurt me, as papa does."

"You're quite out of your mind, my child!

Your father loves you dearly. He wouldn't hurt
you for the world. Don't talk such nonsense,
Katharine. Go and see Mr. Wingfield, and be
decently civil for half an hour — he won't stay
even as long as that. Besides, you can't tell
him not to come any more. He hasn't asked you
to marry him. You may think he means to, but
you can hardly take it for granted like that."

"No, but he means to ask me to-day," answered
Katharine. "And I haven't encouraged him in
the least."

"Then how do you know ?"

"Oh — one can always tell."

"It's not exactly true to say that you've not
encouraged him," said Mrs. Lauderdale, thoughtfully. "He's been here very often of late, and
you've danced the cotillion with him twice, at
least. Then there was his coaching party — only
the other day — and you sat beside him. He's
always sending you flowers, and books, and things,
too. It isn't fair to say that he's had no encouragement. You'll get the reputation of being a
flirt if you go on in this way."

"I'd rather be called a flirt than marry Archibald Wingfield," replied Katharine.

"At all events you might have some consideration for him, if you've none for yourself. Don't
be foolish, Katharine dear. Take my advice. Of
course, if you could take a fancy to him, quite

naturally, we should all be very glad. I like him — I can't help it. He's so handsome, and has such good manners, and speaks French like a Parisian. I know — you may laugh — but in these days, when people are abroad half the time — and then, after all, my dear, you certainly can't be really sure that he means to ask you to-day. Very likely he won't, just because you think he's going to."

"Of course, mother, you know that's absurd! As though it wasn't evident — besides, those flowers this morning. Didn't you see them?"

"What about them? He often sends you flowers."

"Why, the box was all full of primroses, and just two roses — extraordinary ones — lying in the middle and tied together with a bit of grass. Imagine doing such a thing! And I know he tied them himself, on account of the knot. He's a yachting man, and doesn't tie knots like the men at the flower shops."

"Oh, well, my dear — if you are going to judge a man by the way he ties knots —"

Mrs. Lauderdale laughed as she broke off in her incomplete sentence. Then her face grew grave all at once.

"Take my advice, my child — marry him," she said, bending over her table once more and taking up a little brush, as though she wished to end the interview.

"Certainly not!" answered Katharine, in a tone which discouraged further persuasion.

Mrs. Lauderdale sighed.

"Well—I don't know what you young girls expect," she said, in a tone of depression. "Mr. Wingfield's young, good-looking, well-educated, rich, and he adores you. Perhaps you don't love him precisely, but you can't help liking him. You act as though you were always expecting a fine, irresistible, mediæval passion to come and carry you off. It won't, you know. That sort of thing doesn't happen any more. When you want to get married at last, you'll be too old. You have your choice of almost any of them. For a girl who has no money and isn't likely to have much for a long time, I don't know any one who's more surrounded than you are. Of course I want you to marry. I don't believe in waiting till you're twenty-five or thirty."

"I don't intend to."

"Well, you will, my dear, unless you make up your mind soon. It's all — "

"Mother," interrupted Katharine, "you know very well that I've made my choice, and that I mean to stand by it."

"Oh—Jack Ralston, you mean?" Mrs. Lauderdale affected a rather contemptuous indifference. "That was a foolish affair. Girls always fall in love with their cousins. You'll forget all about

him, and I'm sure he's forgotten all about you.
He hardly ever comes to the house now. Besides,
you never could have married poor Jack, with his
dissipated habits, and no money. Uncle Robert
doesn't mean to leave him anything. He'd gamble
it all away."

"You called me unjust a moment ago," said
Katharine, in an altered voice, and growing pale.

"Of course — you take his part. It's no use to
discuss it —"

"It's not discussion to abuse a man who's bravely
doing his best. Jack doesn't need any one to take
his part. Do you know that he's altogether given
up his old life at the club — and all that? He's
at Beman Brothers' all day long, and when you
don't see him in society, he's quietly at home with
cousin Katharine."

"Yes — I heard he was doing a little better.
But he'll never get rid of the reputation he's given
himself. My dear, you don't seem to remember
that poor Mr. Wingfield is waiting for you all this
time downstairs."

"It will be the last time, at all events," answered
Katharine, in a low voice. "I'll never see him
alone again."

She turned from her mother towards the door.
Mrs. Lauderdale followed her with her eyes for a
moment, then rose swiftly and overtook her before
she could let herself out.

"Katharine — I won't let you send Mr. Wingfield away like that!" said Mrs. Lauderdale, in a quick, decided tone.

"Won't let me?" repeated Katharine, slowly.

"No — certainly not. It's quite out of the question — you really mustn't do it!" Mrs. Lauderdale was becoming agitated.

"Do you mean that it's out of the question for me to refuse to marry Mr. Wingfield?" Katharine had her back against the door and her right hand upon the knob of the lock.

"Oh — well — no. Of course you have the right to refuse him, if he asks you in so many words —"

"Of course I have! What are you thinking of?" There was a look of something between indignation and amusement in her face.

"Yes — but there are so many ways, child. Katharine," she continued, almost appealingly, "you can't just say 'no' and tell him to stop coming —you'll change your mind — you don't know what a nice young fellow he is —"

Katharine's hand dropped from the door-handle, and she folded her arms as she faced her mother.

"What is all this?" she asked, deliberately and with emphasis. "You seem to me to be very excited. I should almost fancy that you had something else in your mind, though I can't understand what it is."

"No — no; certainly not. It's only for your

sake and his," answered Mrs. Lauderdale, hurriedly. "I've known it happen so often that a girl refuses a man just because she's in a temper about something, and then — afterwards, you know — she regrets it, when it's too late, and the man has married some one else out of spite."

"How strangely you talk!" exclaimed Katharine, gazing at her mother in genuine surprise.

"My dear, I only don't want you to do anything rash and unkind. You spoke as though you meant to be as hard and cold as a mill-stone — as though he'd done something outrageous in wanting to marry you."

"Not at all. I said that I should refuse him and beg him to stop coming to see me. There's nothing particularly like a mill-stone in that. It's the honest truth in the first place — for I won't marry him, and you can't force me to — "

"But nobody thinks of forcing you — "

"I don't know. Perhaps not," answered the young girl, doubtfully. "But it's of no use, for I won't. And as for telling him not to come — why, it's rather natural, I think. It just makes the refusal a little more definite. I don't like that way girls have of refusing a man once a month, and letting him come to see them for a whole season, and then marrying him after all. There's something mean about it — and I don't think much of the man who lets himself be treated in that way,

either. If Mr. Wingfield is really all you say he
is, he may not be just that kind, and he'll understand and take his refusal like a gentleman, and
not torment me any more. But it's just as well,
to make sure."

"Promise me that you'll be kind to him, Katharine —"

"Kind? Oh, yes — I'll be kind enough. I'll
be perfectly civil —"

"Well — what shall you say to him? That you
like him, and hope to be good friends, but that you
don't feel —"

"Dear mother!" exclaimed Katharine, with perfect simplicity, "I've refused men before. I know
how to do it."

"Yes — of course — but Mr. Wingfield —"

"You've got Mr. Wingfield on the brain,
mother!" She laughed a little scornfully. "One
would think that you were his mother, and were
begging me to be kind and nice and marry your
son. I don't understand you to-day. Meanwhile,
he's waiting."

"One moment, child!" exclaimed Mrs. Lauderdale, laying her hand on Katharine's as it went out
towards the knob of the door. "You don't know
— there are particular — well, there are so many
reasons why you shouldn't be rough with him.
Can't you just say that you're touched by his proposal and will think it over?"

'   "Certainly not!" cried Katharine, indignantly.
"Why should I keep the poor man hanging on when
I don't mean to marry him — when I won't — I've
said it often enough, I'm sure. Why should I?"

"It would be so much easier for him, if you
would — to please me, darling child," continued
Mrs. Lauderdale, in an almost imploring way, "just
to please me! I don't often ask you to do anything
for me, do I, dear? And you're not like Charlotte
— we've always been such good friends, love. And
now I ask you this one thing for myself. It isn't
much, I'm sure — just to say that you'll think it
over. Won't you? I know you will — there's a
dear girl!"

Mrs. Lauderdale bent her head affectionately
and kissed Katharine on the cheek. The young
girl tried to draw back, but finding herself against
the door, could only turn her face away as much as
possible. She did not understand her mother's
manner, and she did not like it.

"But it's only a moment ago that you were
talking about my acting like a flirt!" she objected,
vehemently. "If it isn't flirting to give a man
hope when there is none, what is?"

"No, dear; that's not flirting; it's only pru-
dence. You may like him better by and by, and I
should be so glad! Flirting is drawing a man on
as you've done with him, and then throwing him
over cruelly and all at once."

"I've not drawn him on, mother! You shan't say that I ever encouraged him."

"I don't know. You've accepted his flowers and his books —"

"What was I to do? Send them back?"

"You might have told him not to send so many, and so often; you needn't have read the books. He'd have seen that you didn't care."

"Oh, this is ridiculous, you know!"

"No, it's not, my darling! And as for the flowers, of course you couldn't exactly send them back, but you weren't obliged to wear them."

"Nobody wears flowers now, so it wasn't probable that I should feel obliged to. Really, mother, you're losing your head!"

Mrs. Lauderdale shifted her position a little, moving towards the side of the door on which the lock was placed, and laying her hand affectionately on Katharine's, as though still to detain her.

"Yes," she said, "I'd forgotten that we don't wear flowers any longer. But that isn't the question, dear. I only ask you not to send him away suddenly, with a 'no' that can't possibly be taken back. I'm dreadfully afraid that you'll hurt the poor fellow, and I can't help feeling that he has reason — that you've given him reason to expect that you'll at least consider the question. Dear child, I only ask you this once. Won't you do it to please me? We're all so fond of Wingfield —"

"But why? why? If I don't mean to have him, how can I? I really can't understand. Is there any family reason for being so particular about Mr. Wingfield's feelings? We've never been so very intimate with his people."

"Reasons," repeated Mrs. Lauderdale, absently. "Reasons? Well, yes — but it isn't that —" She stopped short.

"Mother!" Katharine looked keenly into her face. "You've been talking to him yourself! I can see it in your eyes!"

"Oh, no!" answered Mrs. Lauderdale. "Oh, no — what makes you think that?"

But she looked away, and Katharine saw the blush of confusion rising under the transparent skin in her mother's cheek.

"Yes — you've given Mr. Wingfield to understand that I'm in love with him," said Katharine, in a low voice.

"Katharine, how can you!" Mrs. Lauderdale was making a desperate effort to recover herself, but she was a truthful woman, and found it hard to lie. "You've no right to say such things!"

"Yes — I see," answered Katharine, not heeding her. "It's all quite clear to me now. You and papa have drawn him on and encouraged him, and now you're afraid that I shall put you in an awkward position by sending him away. I see it all. That's the reason why you're so excited about it."

"Katharine, dear, don't accuse me of such things! All I said was —" She stopped short.

"Then you did say something? Of course. I knew that was the truth of it!"

"I said nothing," answered Mrs. Lauderdale, going back to a total denial. "Except, perhaps, we have given him to understand that we should be glad if you would marry him."

"We? Has papa been talking to him, too?" asked Katharine, indignantly.

"Don't be so angry, child. It's quite natural. You don't know how glad your father would be. It's just the sort of match he's always dreamed of for you. And then I think it was very honourable in young Wingfield, when he found that he was in love with you, to speak to your father first."

"Scrupulously! He might be French! He might have tried to find out first whether I cared for him at all. But I've no doubt you told him that he had only to ask and I should take him to my heart with pride and pleasure! Oh, mother, mother! You never used to act like this!"

"But, my dear child —"

"Oh no, — don't call me your dear child like that — it doesn't mean anything now. You're completely changed — no, don't keep me! That poor fellow's waiting all this time. You can't have anything more to say to me, for I know it all. A word more — which you may have said to him, or a word less — what does it matter? You've turned on me, and now you're doing your best to marry me, just to get rid of me. As for papa, he leaves me no peace about poor uncle Robert's will. And he calls himself an honest man, when he's trying to force a confidence that doesn't belong to him, out of — yes — out of sheer love of money. Oh, it's not to be believed! Let me go, mother! I won't keep that man wait- ing any longer. It isn't decent. There'll be one lie less, at all events!"

"Katharine, dear! Stay a minute! Don't go when you're angry — like this!"

But Katharine's firm hand was opening the door in spite of her mother's gentle, almost timid, resistance.

"No — I'm not angry now," answered the young girl. "It's something different — I won't hurt him — never fear!"

In a moment she had left the room, and her mother heard the quick footfall on the stairs, as she stood listening by the open door. Mrs. Lau- derdale had got herself into terrible trouble, and she knew it. Katharine had, in part, guessed rightly, for if Mrs. Lauderdale had not told young Wingfield in so many words that her daughter loved him, she had yet allowed him to think so, and had been guilty of a sin of omission in not

undeceiving him. There is a way of listening
which means assent, as there is a way of assenting
in words which mean a flat refusal. Alexander
Lauderdale had gone farther. He had distinctly
told Wingfield, in his wife's presence, that he had
no reason to believe that his daughter might not, —
he saved his scrupulous conscience by the 'might,'
— might not ultimately accept a proposal which
was so agreeable to his own wishes. Mrs. Lauderdale had been shocked, for, as it was spoken, the
phrase sounded very untrue, though when precipi-
tated upon paper and taken to pieces, it is found
to be cautious enough. 'Might,' not 'would' —
and 'ultimately,' not by any means at the first
attempt. Yet the impression had been conveyed
to Wingfield's mind that Katharine was predis-
posed in his favour, in spite of the reports which
had so long been circulated about her engagement
to Ralston. Mrs. Lauderdale had, for a moment,
almost believed that her husband had told an un-
truth. But on talking the matter over with him,
his dignity of manner, his clear recollection of
his own words, and the moderate stress which he
laid upon the 'might' and the 'ultimately,' not
only reassured her, but persuaded her to say
almost the same thing the next time she saw
Wingfield. The young fellow always sought her
out at a party, and confided to her all he felt
for Katharine, and Mrs. Lauderdale sympathized

with him, as she had once sympathized with Jack
Ralston, unconscious that she was doing anything wrong. He was handsome, frank, and win-
ning, and she longed to see Katharine married.
The reasons were plenty. Many cold and good
women enjoy being made the confidantes of young
lovers. The atmosphere of the passion is agreeable to them, though they may know little of the
passion itself. Mrs. Lauderdale had not fully
realized the meaning of what she had been doing
until Katharine made it plain to her that afternoon. And then, although her conscience told
her that she was in the wrong, and though she
had spoken to the girl entreatingly and gently,
she became angry with her as soon as she was
left to herself. The tortuousness of a good
woman's mind when she has hurt her own conscience surpasses by many degrees that of an ordinary criminal's straightforwardly bad ingenuity.

Meanwhile, Katharine descended to the library,
paused a moment in the entry, and then opened
the door. Archibald Wingfield's black eyes met
her as she entered the room. He was standing
before the empty fireplace, with his hands behind
him, warming them perhaps at an imaginary fire,
for they were cold. He was very much in love
with her, and Katharine's girlish instinct was
right, for he had come with the determined purpose of asking her to be his wife. She had kept

him waiting fully twenty minutes, and during that
time he had interpreted the delay in at least as
many different ways. As she came in, the colour
rose in his brown cheeks and his heart beat fast.

Archibald Wingfield was said to be the hand-
somest young man in New York society, which is
saying a good deal, notwithstanding those captious
persons who write and speak sarcastically about
the round-shouldered, in-kneed, flabby-cheeked,
youth of the present day. Of late years, during
the growth of what is now the young generation
in society, there has been a very sudden improvement in the race and type of boys and girls. Any
one can see that who does not wilfully close his
eyes.

Wingfield stood fully six feet four inches without his shoes, was broad-shouldered, deep-chested,
and thin-waisted as a young Achilles. His feet
were narrow, strong, and straight, his legs those
of a runner rather than a walker, his hands broad
and brown, with great, determined-looking thumbs,
marked sinews, and the high, blue veins of a thor-
ough-bred animal. The splendid form was topped
by a small, energetic head, with slightly aquiline
features, the clean-shaven lips that made a bold,
curved, bow-like mouth, flat, healthy, brown cheeks,
a well-rounded chin, deepened in the middle with
the depression which is nature's hall-mark on superior physical beauty — a moderately full fore-

head, very small ears, jet black, short, smooth hair, and wide, honest black eyes with rough black eyebrows. Under the brown colour there was rich blood, that mantled like scarlet velvet in summer's dusk.

He spoke in a low, self-possessed, unaffected voice, with an English accent, common enough to-day among young men who have been much abroad during their education. Wingfield had been at Christ Church, had got his degree in the ordinary course, and was hesitating as to his future career between the law, for which he was now reading, and a country life of gentleman farming and horse-breeding in western New York, which attracted him. His people were all rich, all good-looking, and all happy. His ideals were chiefly in his own family. When he had returned from England, he had been something of a hero among the young, owing to his having pulled five in the Oxford boat when the latter had won the University race in the previous spring, a very unusual distinction for a foreign-born athlete in England. With his great height, he was still proud of having trained to twelve stone eleven for the race.

In the matter of outward advantages John Ralston's spare figure and lean, Indian face could not compare favourably with such a man as Archibald Wingfield. Nor had Wingfield's reputation borne the strain and the shocks which John's had barely survived. The man seemed born to success, happiness and popularity, as many of his family had been successful, popular and happy before him. He himself believed that all he needed in order to be happier than any of them was to get Katharine Lauderdale's consent to be his wife. And he loved her so much, and was so nervous in the anticipation of what was to come, that his hands had turned cold, his healthy heart was bouncing like a football in his big chest, the blood rushed to his brown cheeks, and he almost dropped his silk hat as she entered the room.

"How do you do, Miss Lauderdale?"

He came forward with a gigantic stride, and then suddenly made a short little step, as he found himself already close to her.

"How do you do?" she asked, quietly repeating the inane question we have adopted as a form of greeting and recognition.

She looked up—far up, it seemed to her—into his brilliant black eyes, and understood how much in earnest he was, before he said anything more. Vaguely, as in a dream, she remembered how, several months earlier, in that very room and almost at that very hour, John Ralston had come to her and she had persuaded him to make her his wife.

"Thank you so much for the flowers," she said, sitting down in her favourite little arm-chair on one side of the empty fireplace.

He murmured in a pleased but incoherent fashion as he pushed a chair into a convenient position and sat down—not too near her—setting his hat upon the floor beside him. He rested his two elbows on his knees, and his chin on his folded hands, and looked at her with unblushing, boyish admiration.

"But please don't send me any more flowers, Mr. Wingfield," said Katharine, going straight to the point by an effort of will.

A puzzled look came into his face instantly. His hands dropped upon his knees, and he sat upright in his chair.

"Why not?" he asked, simply. "I mean," he added, fancying he had put the question roughly, "is it rude to ask why not? It gives me so much pleasure—if you like them a little, you know."

It hurt Katharine to see the simplicity of the man, and it made her face burn to think that he had been played upon.

"Because I'd rather not," she answered, very gently.

"I—I don't think I quite understand," said Wingfield, with some hesitation. "I know—you often say that I mustn't send them so much—but then, you know, one always says that, doesn't one? It doesn't seem to mean anything except a sort of second 'thank you'—"

"I mean more than that," said Katharine, smiling faintly, in spite of herself.

"But so do I!" exclaimed the young man. "I mean so much more than that — I always have, from the very beginning — "

"Please don't!" cried Katharine, anxiously, for she saw that he meant to speak at once — but it was too late.

"From the very beginning, since almost the first time I ever saw you — oh, my — my dear Miss Lauderdale — won't you let me say it at last?"

"No — no — please — "

"If you only knew how hard I've tried — not to say it before," he blurted out, as the blood rose warm in his brown cheeks.

CHAPTER VII.

KATHARINE turned her eyes from him and looked thoughtfully at the hearth-rug. A little silence followed Wingfield's last speech, as he sat gazing at her and hoping for a word of encouragement. But none came, and by slow degrees the eager expression faded from his face and left it anxious and pained.

"Miss Lauderdale — " he began, in an altered tone, and then stopped suddenly. "Miss — Katharine — " he began again, more softly, and still hesitated.

She looked up, and though her eyes were turned towards him, he fancied they did not see him. She was pale, and her lips were a little drawn together, and there was an incongruity between her attempt to smile and the weary tension of the brows. Everything in her face told that she pitied him with all her heart.

"I'm very sorry," she said, with real sympathy. "It's been a mistake from the beginning — a great mistake."

"Please don't say that!" he answered, impulsively — for he was impulsive, in spite of his solid, well-balanced strength. "Please don't answer me yet — "

"But I must!" she protested, and the look of pity became more set.

"No, no! Please don't! Wait a little — and — and let me tell you — "

"It can do no good," she answered, with a sudden rough effort. "You've been misled — I didn't know — "

"What?" he asked, softly. "That — that I cared so much — and meant always — all along — from the very first — it's always been so, ever since I saw you that first night at the Bretts', after I came back from Europe — only it's more so, every time, till I can't keep it back any more, and I've got to speak, and tell you — "

"Mr. Wingfield — " began Katharine, thinking, womanlike, to chill him by the formal enunciation of his name with a protest in the tone, kindly though it was.

"Yes — you think so now," he answered, irrelevantly. ".But I don't ask you to answer, I only ask you to listen to me — and, indeed, I don't want you to think that it's any one's fault, nor that there's any fault at all, because I know it will all come right, and you'll care for me a little, even if you don't now. I've spoken too soon, perhaps, and perhaps I've been rough or rude — or something — and I don't know how to tell you as I should —

because I've never told anybody such things — don't you believe me, Miss Katharine? But you wouldn't think any the better of me if I knew how to make beautiful speeches and phrases, and that sort of thing, would you?"

"Oh, no — no — and you've not been anything but nice — only — "

"I can't help it — you're my whole life, and I must tell you so now. Of course, lots of men worship you, and I daresay they know how to say it ever so much better — and that they're very much nicer men than I am. But — but there isn't one of them, I don't care who he is, who cares — who loves you as I do, or would do what I'd do for your sake, if I could, or if I had a chance. And even if you don't care for me at all yet, I'll love you so that you will — some day — and it's not the sort of love that's just flowers and attention and that, you know, like everybody's. It's got hold of me — hard, and it won't let go — ever! It's changed my whole life. I'm not at all as I used to be. You're in everything I do, and see, and think, and hear, as life is — and without you there wouldn't be any life in anything. Don't think I don't feel things because I'm so big, and I don't look sensitive, and all that — or because I can't put it into words that touch you. It's true, for all that, and all I ask is that you should believe me. Won't you believe me a little, Katharine?"

The great limbs of the young Achilles quivered,
and his strong hands strained upon one another,
and there was the clear ring of whole-hearted truth
in the deep voice, in spite of the incoherence and
poverty of the words.

"I believe you," answered Katharine, looking at
the rug again. "It isn't that. But I won't let
you think for one instant that there's the least
possibility of my ever caring for you, or marrying
you. It's absolutely impossible."

"Nothing's impossible!" he answered, impetuously. "Nothing except that you should never
care at all when I'd give my life for your little
finger, and my soul for your life — with all my
heart, and be glad to give either — "

"It hurts me very much to hear you talk like
this — because you've been misled and deceived —
my father and mother — "

"How can they know what you think and feel?"
asked Wingfield. "I only spoke to them because
it seemed right and fair, being so much in earnest,
and I couldn't tell but what there might be some
one else — I had no right to pry into your secrets
and watch you and try and find out — it wouldn't
have seemed nice. So I asked your father, and
then Mrs. Lauderdale — but I didn't suppose they
knew absolutely — of course they couldn't answer
for you — in that way. And I say it again — don't
make up your mind — don't send me off — wait —

only wait! You don't know how love grows out of what seems to be nothing till it's bigger and stronger than the biggest and strongest of us — you can't feel it growing any more than you could feel that you were growing yourself when you were small; and you can't remember when it began, any more than you can remember what you thought of when you were a year old. That doesn't make it less real afterwards — love's such a little thing at the beginning, and by and by it takes in everything, so that the whole world is nothing beside it. And if you'll only not make up your mind — "

"It's made up for me, long ago — in a way you don't dream of. It's absolutely, and wholly, and altogether impossible, and it always will be, no matter what happens. Oh, I can't say more than that, Mr. Wingfield — and it wouldn't be true if I said less!"

"But it can't be really true!" he protested, bending forward in his low chair. "Of course you think so — but how can you possibly tell? I don't mean to say that you're changeable, or capricious, or anything of that kind — but people do change, you know. Why — I hate to say it — but you couldn't say more than that if you were married and I didn't know it!"

Katharine started, though she was strong and her nerves were good. He had made the reflection very naturally, in answer to the very positive words she had spoken. But to her it seemed as though he must know, or at least guess, the truth. She lost her balance for a moment, as she gazed earnestly into his honest black eyes.

"Mr. Wingfield — do you know what you're saying?" she asked, in a low voice.

He was afraid he had said something monstrous, and his face fell.

"I didn't mean to offend you," he stammered, awkwardly. "I'm awfully sorry if I said anything I shouldn't — "

Katharine forgot his contrition, and forgot to reassure him in the anxiety caused her by the mere suspicion that he might know the truth. She sat staring at him in silence for several seconds, wondering what he knew. It was more than he could bear. He bent still nearer to her, from the edge of his chair, and his hands moved a little towards her, beseechingly, in as near an approach to an eloquent gesture as such a man could have used.

"Please don't be angry with me!" he said.

"Oh, no!" she answered, in an odd voice, with a little start. "I was only thinking — "

He did not understand, and he moved backward into his chair suddenly, crossed one knee over the other with an impatient jerk, and looked away from her.

"What a brute I am!" he exclaimed, in a barely audible tone.

Katharine paid no attention to this self-condemnation. Her eyes rested thoughtfully on his face, and she seemed to be reflecting. She was examining her own conscience, trying to find out how far her actions could have brought about the state of things she saw. A woman who loves one man with all her heart has small pity for any other, though she may know that she ought to feel pity and to show it. But she does not therefore lose her sense of justice.

"Will you tell me one thing, Mr. Wingfield? Will you answer me one question?" she asked, at last.

He turned to her quickly again, with a look of surprise. She was out of tune with him, so to say, and her words and tone jarred strongly upon his own mood.

"Certainly," he answered, much more coldly than he had spoken yet. "I'll try and answer any question you ask me."

"Do you really and truly feel that I've encouraged you, as though I meant anything?" she asked, slowly.

It would not have been easy to put a question harder to answer honestly. Wingfield did not like it. A man hates to be put in the position of either telling a falsehood or giving offence, with no alternative but an unmannerly refusal to speak at all. Wingfield felt that, in the first place, he had been badly used in spite of his protestations to the effect that no one was to blame. It had been unpardonable of Mr. and Mrs. Lauderdale to be so mistaken in their own daughter — he put it charitably — as to expose him to such an uncompromising and final refusal as he had received. He went no further in that direction. He did not think of himself as a very desirable son-in-law, and a very good match in fortune, because, like most people, he supposed that when the Lauderdale estate was divided, Katharine would ultimately have her share of it, a fact to which he was indifferent. He did not, therefore, accuse the Lauderdales of having intentionally led him on. But they had acted irresponsibly. And now he fancied that Katharine was very angry with him for what he had said a few moments earlier, and he thought she was unjust, since he had really said nothing very terrible. So he resented her last question as soon as she had asked it, and he hesitated before replying. Katharine waited patiently a few moments.

"Do you really think I've been flirting?" she asked at last, seeing that he did not answer.

"No!" he cried, at once. "Oh, no — not that! Never. If you ask me whether you've ever looked at me, or spoken to me as though you really cared — no, you never have. Not once. But then — there are other things."

"What other things? What have I done?"

Feeling that he had admitted the main point in her favour, she grew a little hard.

"Well — you've let me come a great deal to see you, and you've let me send you — oh, well! No — I'm not going to say that sort of thing. I got the impression, somehow — that's all."

"You got the impression, from what I did, that I liked you — that I encouraged you?" she asked, anxiously.

"Yes. I got that impression. Besides, you've often shown plainly enough that you liked to dance with me — "

"That's true — I do. You dance very well. And I do like you — as I like several other people. It isn't wrong to like in that way, is it? It isn't flirting? It isn't as though I said things I didn't mean, is it?"

"No," answered Wingfield, in an injured tone. "It's not. Still — "

"Still, you think there's been something in my behaviour to make you think I might care? I'm very sorry — I'm very, very sorry," she repeated, her voice changing suddenly with an expression of profound regret. "Will you believe me when I tell you that it's been altogether unconscious? You can't think — if you care for me — that I'd be so heartless and cruel. You won't, will you?"

"No — I don't want to think it. I misunderstood — that's all. Put it all on me."

He was very young, and he was cruelly hurt. He spoke coldly, lest his words should choke him.

"No," answered Katharine, speaking almost to herself, "there are other people to blame, whose fault it is."

"Perhaps."

A silence followed. It was warm in the room. One of the windows was a little raised, and the bells of the horse-cars jingled cheerfully in the spring air. At last Katharine spoke again.

"I suppose it doesn't mean much to you when I say I'm sorry," she said. "If you knew, it would mean much more. I'm very much in earnest, and I shall never forget this afternoon, for I know I've hurt you. I think you're a little angry just now. It's natural. You have a right to be. Since you think that I've made you understand things I didn't mean, I wonder you're not much more angry — that you don't say much harder things to me. It wouldn't really be just, because I'm very unhappy, whether I'm to blame or not. But you're generous. I shall always be grateful to you. You won't bear me any more ill-will than you can help, will you?"

"Ill-will? I? No! I'm too fond of you — and besides, I've not done hoping yet. I shall always hope, as long as I live."

"No — you mustn't hope anything," answered Katharine, determined not to allow him the shadow of any consolation. "It wouldn't be just to me. It would be like thinking that I were capricious. I'm not going to talk to you about friendship, and all that, as people do in books. I want you to try and forget me altogether — for I believe you — you really care for me. So there's no other way — when one really cares. Don't come here any more for the present — don't try to meet me at parties — don't ask me to dance with you. The world's very big, and you needn't see me unless you wish to. By and by it will be different. Perhaps you could go abroad for a little while again. I don't know what your plans are, but it would be better if you could. The season will be over — it's almost over now, and then you'll go one way and I shall go another, and there's no reason why we should meet. We mustn't. It wouldn't be fair to me, and it wouldn't be fair to you, either. You see — it's not as though you were disagreeable. If we meet at all, I couldn't help being very much the same as ever, and you know what I've made you think of that. You'll promise, won't you?"

"Not to try and see you sometimes? No, I won't promise that. I shall always hope — "

"But there is no hope. There's not the slightest possibility of any hope. If you knew about me, you'd understand it."

"Miss Lauderdale — will you think it very rude if I ask one question? I've — I've put my whole life into this — and you're sending me away without a word. So perhaps — I think you might — "

"What is it?" asked Katharine, kindly.

"Are you engaged to Jack Ralston? I've heard people say that you were, so often. Would you tell me?"

Katharine was silent for a moment. She did not know exactly how far it would be true to say that she was engaged to John, seeing that she was married to him. Her marriage, she thought, might be looked upon as a formal betrothal, and there would have been little harm in taking that view of it, under such circumstances. But she had inherited from her father something of his formal respect for the mere letter of truth, and she did not like to say anything which did not conform to it.

"We're not exactly engaged," she answered, after a short pause. "But we care for each other very much."

Wingfield's brow cleared a little. He had one of those dispositions which hope in spite of apparent certainty against them.

"Then I'll go away for awhile," he said, with sudden resolution and considerable generosity, from his point of view. "If you don't marry him, I'll come back, that's all. I'm glad you told me. Thank you."

It requires considerable self-control to act as Archibald Wingfield did on that occasion. His

voice did not tremble, and he did not turn pale,
because it was not in his nature to experience that
sort of physical weakness when he was making an
effort. But what he did was not easy. Even
Katharine could see that. He sat still a few
moments after he had spoken, glanced at her once,
as though to make sure that there was to be no
appeal, and then rose suddenly from his seat, and
stood towering above her.

"Good-bye," he said, holding out his hand, and
stooping to bring it within her reach. Now that
the effort had been made, his voice trembled a
little.

"Good-bye," answered Katharine, taking his
hand, and lifting her head almost without raising
her eyes.

There was something almost like timidity in
her tone. She felt how he had been wronged by
her father and mother, and in her trouble she was
willing to believe that she was really a little to
blame herself. She realized, too, that he was acting very bravely and honestly, and that he was
really suffering. It was not a grand, dramatic
agony, and eloquence was the least of his gifts,
but he was strong, young, and in earnest, and had
been made to undergo pain for her sake. She
was ashamed of having been the cause of it.

No other words suggested themselves to her,
but he waited one moment, as though expecting

that she would speak again.   Then he silently
dropped her hand, and bowing his head a little,
went quietly to the door without looking back.
She did not follow him with her eyes, but she listened for the sound of the latch, and it did not
come quite so soon as she expected.   He had
turned to look at her once more, his hand on the
door.

"God bless you — Katharine," he said, in a low
voice.

She looked round at him quickly, and the faint,
sorrowful smile came back to her face.   Her lips
moved, but no words came.   He gazed at her one
moment, and then took his young grief out into
the spring air and the evening sunshine.

When Katharine was alone, she sighed and
gazed at the hearth-rug, bending forward in a
thoughtful attitude, her chin supported in her
hand.

"How hard it is!" she exclaimed to herself.

It seemed to her that the difficulties of her life
grew with every passing day.   She had, indeed,
cut the knot of one of them within the last half
hour, and so far as Archibald Wingfield was concerned, the hard thing had been done, and he knew
the worst.   But she, on her part, had much to
bear yet.   She had seen to-day, for the first time,
how her father and mother longed to have her married.   Even now, she found it difficult to suspect

either of them of intentional cruelty, or of attempting to use anything more than persuasion in pushing her into the match. With her faculty for
seeing both sides of a question at once, she was
just. It was natural, perhaps, that they should
wish her to marry such a man. She had never
seen any one like him — such a magnificent speci-
men of youthful manhood. Even her father could
not compare with him. And he had much besides
his looks to recommend him, much besides his
fortune and his position and his popularity. He
was brave and honest, and able to love truly, as it
seemed.

He would recover, of course, she said to herself.
He was sought after, flattered, and pursued for
many reasons. He could find plenty of young girls
only too delighted to marry him, and he would certainly marry one of them before long. His life
was not blighted, and she had not broken his heart,
if hearts ever break at all. She remembered what
she had once borne, in the belief that John Ralston
.was disgraced for life on that memorable occasion
when all New York had learned that he had been
brought home, apparently drunk, after a midnight
encounter with a pugilist, who had found occasion
to quarrel with him in a horse-car. The belief had
lasted a whole night and a whole day, and she did
not think that young Wingfield could be suffering
anything like that. Moreover, her love for Ralston

made her ruthless and almost hard about every other man. Nevertheless, she was sincerely sorry for the man who had just left her — the more so, perhaps, because she had little or nothing with which to reproach herself.

Katharine was not left to her own reflections very long. By a process akin to telepathy, Mrs. Lauderdale was soon aware that Archibald Wingfield had left the house. In the half hour during which his visit had lasted, she had not touched her miniature, though she had looked at it, and turned it to and from the light many times. She was very nervous, and she wished that when he went away he might forthwith take himself off to China, at the very least. She did not wish to meet him that evening, nor the next, to be called to account by him for having exceeded her powers in the impression she had conveyed of Katharine's readiness to marry him. Yet she remembered that she had acted very much in the same way when Charlotte had married Benjamin Slayback. It was true that Slayback was a much older man, and well able to take care of himself, and that Charlotte had not at the time been showing any especial preference for any of her adorers. She had, in fact, just then dismissed one for the grievous offence of having turned out an unutterable bore after three weeks of almost unbroken conversation, during which she had exhausted his not fertile intellect,

as furnace heat dries a sponge. Charlotte's heart
had been comparatively free, therefore, and she
had been indulging in dreams of power and personal influence. But Mrs. Lauderdale and her
husband had on that occasion used to Mr. Slayback
almost the identical words which she had lately
repeated to Wingfield; Slayback had come, had
proposed, — in what manner Charlotte had never
revealed, — and had been immediately accepted.
Surely, there was nothing wrong in assuming that
Katharine might possibly behave in the same
way, seeing how very much more desirable a suitor
Wingfield was than Slayback. Thus argued Mrs.
Lauderdale, as she tried to trip up her conscience
and step over it. But she was too good by nature
to be successful in such a fraud upon goodness, and
in the midst of her involuntary self-reproaches,
her heart was beating with anxiety to know the
result of the interview.

It meant a great deal to her, for she was sure
that if Katharine could be removed from the
household, peace must descend upon her own soul
once more, and she longed for peace. Somehow,
she felt that if she could only enjoy that suprem-
acy of her wonderful beauty for one month more —
for one last month, before she grew old — she
could meet Katharine again, and forgive her all
her youth and freshness, and forgive herself for
having envied them. As her life was now, she

could not, try how she would. The pain was upon
her hourly, and she could not but resent it, and
almost hate the cause of it.

Though she constantly looked at her miniature,
and moved the brushes and little saucers on the
table, her hearing was preternaturally sharpened,
as it was in reality the barely audible sound of the
distant front door which told her that Wingfield
was gone. Instinctively she looked towards the
door of her own room, hesitated, then rose suddenly, and went out with a quick, nervous step,
and a determined look in her face. Without stopping to consider what she should say, she descended
to the library.

Katharine looked up with an expression of annoyance as her mother entered.

"He's gone, then?" said Mrs. Lauderdale,
interrogatively.

"Yes. He's just gone," answered Katharine,
in a voice that did not promise confidence.

"What did you tell him, dear?"

Mrs. Lauderdale sat down beside her daughter.
The smile she put on was as unnatural as the
endearing tone, and Katharine observed it. She
suffered in the artificiality which had developed
in her mother of late, so unlike the dignified personality which she had been used to love.

"Really, mother, I can't repeat the conversation.
I couldn't if I wished to. What difference does it

make what I said, since he's gone? I told you what I should say. Well — I've said it."

"You've sent him away for good — just like that?"

"I've told him the plain truth, and he's gone. He won't come back — unless he wants to see you," she added, rather bitterly. "I don't think he will, though. You've not exactly helped him to be happy."

"Katharine!" There was an injured protest in the tone.

"I don't see why you should be surprised," answered the young girl. "Of course he might take it into his head to be angry with you for what you've done. It wasn't very nice. I'm not sure that, in his place, I should ever wish to see you again."

"My child, what an exaggeration! You talk as though I had deliberately sought him out and asked him to the house — almost asked him to marry you."

"It comes to that," observed Katharine, coldly.

"Really, Katharine, you're — beyond words!" Mrs. Lauderdale drew back a little, in displeasure, and looked at her severely.

"I could forgive you," continued the young girl, "if you hadn't known that I love Jack and never shall marry any one else. You know it and you've always known it. That makes it much

worse. You've made that poor man suffer without
the slightest reason. You could just as well have
told him that you knew I cared for some one else,
and you could have been as nice to him as you
pleased. You've hurt him, and you've driven me
to hurt him, by no fault of mine, just to undo the
mischief you've done. Of course, it's papa who's
really done it all, but you needn't have let him
twist you round his little finger like a wisp of
straw."

"Oh, Katharine! Anything more unjust!"

"I'm not unjust, mother. But I'm too old to
think everything you do is perfect, merely because
it's you. When I see a man like Archie Wingfield
sitting there and straining his hands to keep himself quiet, and choking with the sound of his own
words, I know he's suffering — and when I know
that he's suffering uselessly, and that it's all your
fault and papa's, I judge you — that's all. I'm a
grown woman. I have a right to judge."

The door opened and Alexander Junior appeared
upon the threshold, just returned from his office.

"I heard your voice, so I came in," he said, with
an electric smile which was meant to be conciliatory. "Oh!" he exclaimed, in altered tones, as he
saw the faces of the two women, "has anything
happened?"

For a moment there was silence. Mrs. Lauderdale looked at the empty fireplace, avoiding the

eyes of both her husband and her daughter. But
Katharine leaned back in her seat and faced her
father. Her voice was almost as cold and steely
as his could be when she answered him at last.

"Mr. Wingfield has just asked me to marry
him," she said. "And I have refused him —
unconditionally."

"You've done an exceedingly foolish thing,
then," answered Alexander Junior. "And you'll
be very sorry for it before long."

He came nearer and stood by the fireplace, laying
one authoritative hand upon the mantelpiece, and
shaking the forefinger of the other in a warning
manner.

"I'm the best judge of that," answered Katharine, undaunted and unimpressed by his parental
tone.

"You're not," answered Mr. Lauderdale.
"You've acquired a habit of contradicting me
lately. It seems to be a part of your plan for
being as utterly undutiful and disobedient as you
can. I warn you that I won't submit to it any
longer."

"It's of no use to threaten me, papa," answered
Katharine, controlling herself as well as she could.
"And it doesn't do any good to call me undutiful
and disobedient so often. It doesn't make it true."

"Katharine!" cried her mother, in a tone of
distress which was not artificial.

"I know what I'm saying, mother —"

"Then you should be sincerely ashamed of your-self, Katharine," said Alexander Junior. "As sincerely as I'm ashamed that a daughter of mine should use such language."

Katharine rose slowly from her chair and stood up before him, while her mother remained seated.

"Neither of you have any right to say that you're ashamed of anything I've done," she said. "As for my language, it's mild enough — for what you've done. I've been ashamed of you both to-day — here, in this room, half an hour ago. You've told an honest man who's foolishly in love with me that I cared for him, and would have him if he would ask me, when you know that I will never marry any one but Jack Ralston. It seems to me that I've had good reason to be ashamed of you. It was hard to look him in the face, and tell him that my father and mother had misled and deceived him — to make him own that he had it all from you, and that I'd not given him the shadow of a reason for thinking that I cared for him — that he had it all from you. Oh, it was so plain! Not that you can deny it — and you tell me that you're ashamed of me! If I didn't love Jack, do you know what I'd have done? I'd have married Archie Wingfield to save you your respect for yourself, and a little of his for you!"

"I refuse to listen any longer to such insane

nonsense," said Alexander Junior, whose slow wrath was rising by degrees.

"You shall listen to me," answered Katharine. "I'm fighting with you for my life and happiness, and you've got to face me like an honest man — though you are my father!"

CHAPTER VIII.

"Katharine! This is too much!" cried Alexander Junior, his anger rising in his eyes.

The man's heavy hand fell emphatically upon the mantelpiece, making the old-fashioned gilt clock and the Chinese vases tremble and rattle. Mrs. Lauderdale was not a nervous woman, but she rose from her seat and stood beside her husband, not exactly as though she meant to take his side, and yet not exactly as a peace-maker. She felt herself accused as much as he did by the pale, strong girl who stood before them, one hand hanging by her side, the other pulling nervously at the little silver pin at her collar as though she felt that it was choking her. Of the three, at that moment, Mrs. Lauderdale was by far the most self-possessed.

"It's true," answered Katharine. "Every word of it's true!"

As she spoke she caught her breath, and was obliged to stop, white with anger.

"Katharine — my child! Don't!" cried Mrs. Lauderdale, fearing she was going to faint.

"I think you'd better go, my dear," said Alexander to his wife. "She's beside herself. I'll bring her to her senses."

The passionate blood rose in the girl's face and the words came again.

"No, mother — stay here!" she said. "You have no right to go away. Yes — I say that for months you've been doing your best, both of you, to destroy my happiness — and you'll destroy my life with it, if I stay with you longer. You've tried to separate me from the man I love, and you've been trying every day and every hour to make me marry another man — pushing him on, encouraging him, telling him that I would accept him — for all I know, telling him that I loved him. I've not forgotten the things you've done — I've not forgotten the day when you, mother, you who had stood by us so long, suddenly turned without reason and told Jack to go away. Here, in this very room, last winter — and you, papa — I've only to make you remember how you took that letter when it was brought, and kept it all day, and repeated all the lies that people told about Jack — and mother read me the things in the papers — and you made me believe that he had written to me when he was drunk. It was all a lie, a miserable, infamous lie! And you liked it, and repeated it, and turned it over and embroidered it and beautified it — to make it hurt me more. It did hurt me — it almost killed me — but for Jack's sake, I wish to God it had!"

"Katharine, this is blasphemy!" exclaimed her father, his cold eyes glittering with rage — but he was not fluent, he could find no words to dam the stream of hers.

"Blasphemy!" she cried, indignantly. "Is it blasphemy to pray — unless your God is my Devil?"

Beside himself with passion, her father made a step forward, and with a quick movement covered her mouth with one hand and grasped her arm with the other. But he miscalculated her quickness as against his strength. With a turn of the hand and wrist she was free and sprang backwards a step.

"It's like you to lay your hands on a woman, after trying to sell her!" she cried, her lips turning a dull grey, her eyes colder and brighter than his own.

Being roused, they were terribly well matched. Mrs. Lauderdale threw herself between them. To do her justice, she faced her husband, with one hand stretched out to warn him back.

"No, no, mother! don't come between us. I'm not afraid — I only got my mouth free to tell him that he's a coward to lay his hands on me. But that was his only answer, because the things I say are true — every one of them, and more, too. That's your one idea — both of you — to marry me off and get me out of the house, because you can't

look me in the face after the things you've done
— after coming between me and Jack, as you've
tried to do, and would have done, if we'd loved
each other less — after trying to force me upon the
first man who took a fancy to my face — after tormenting me to betray uncle Robert's confidence —
and it's all been for money, and for nothing else.
Money, money, money!"

"My child, you're mad!" cried Mrs. Lauderdale.
"What has money to do with it? What are you
talking about? Do you know that you're making
the most insane accusations?"

"Let her talk," said Alexander, in a low, sullen
voice. "She doesn't know what she's saying."

Ashamed of his outbreak, perhaps, or in sheer
helplessness against Katharine's desperate speech,
he had fallen back again and stood leaning against
the mantelpiece, his arms folded over his broad
chest, his hands twitching at his sleeve, his pale
mouth set like a steel trap, a dull, dangerous light
in his eyes.

"You're mistaken," continued Katharine. "It's
all for money. Money's at the root of every action
of your life. You didn't want me to marry Jack
because he's poor, and because uncle Robert might
not leave him anything. Money! You thought at
first you could make me take Hamilton Bright,
because he's cared for me so long — and because
he's beginning to be rich and is a partner in

Bemans' — money, again! Archie Wingfield —
how many millions will he have? Money — of
course. Uncle Robert's will — what shall you get
by it? Money — and you'd tear the figures out of
my head with red hot pincers if you could — just
to know how much you'll have when the poor
man's dead. Ever since we were children, Charlotte and I, you've preached economy and saving
and poverty — you've let my mother — your wife
—and you're the nephew of the great Robert
Lauderdale — you've let her work her hands and
her eyes till they ached to make a little money
herself — not for herself only, but for us. No —
don't smile contemptuously like that. She's done
it all my life, and she's doing it still. Your children could scarcely have been decently dressed, if
she hadn't earned a few hundred dollars for them.
There's hardly a thing I have on that she's not
paid for out of her earnings. We couldn't have
gone to our first ball, Charlotte or I, but for her.
And still, day after day, you say you're poor. Do
you think I don't see all the little meannesses?
Do you think I can't smell the vile cigars you
make grandpapa smoke, to save those few cents?
Is there a house among all our friends, poor as
some of them are, where there isn't a fire in the
library, at least in the evening, even when there's
nobody asked to dinner? Economy, saving, meanness of all sorts — even the poor housemaid who

broke her arm on the kitchen stairs! You sent to the hospital the day before she was to leave, half-cured and helpless, and made her sign the declaration that she made no further claim upon you. She came here when you were down town. Mother gave her five dollars — out of her earnings — but I heard her story. Oh, they're endless, your ways of saving that filthy, miserable money of yours!"

"Are you really mad, Katharine?" asked her father, in a dull, monotonous voice.

"Child! You know we're comparatively poor," said Mrs. Lauderdale. "Come — dear child — "

She laid her hand on the girl's arm as though she would lead her away and end the violent scene, but Katharine stood firm.

"Poor!" she cried, indignantly. "Comparatively poor! Yes — compared with uncle Robert or Mr. Beman, perhaps. But papa is not poor, though he has told you so for years, though he lets you work for money — you! Though he borrows five dollars of you — I've seen it again and again — and never returns it — borrows the poor little sums you earn by hard work! Oh, it's not to be believed! Borrows without ever meaning to give it back — like an honest man — oh, he wouldn't dare to do that with his dearest friend. But you! You can't help yourself — "

"My dear, he keeps an account — "

"I know, I know! He pretends that he keeps

the money for you and allows you interest! I've
heard him say so. Interest on five dollars. And
have you ever had it? Sordid — mean — there's
no word! And he keeps telling you that he's poor,
and that we must pinch and scrape or we shall go
beyond our income — when he has over a million
of dollars put away — "

"Be silent!" cried Alexander Junior, with sudden vehemence, his cheeks as grey as ashes.

"I won't be silent! I'll say every word I have
to say. Look me in the face. Deny, if you dare,
before God, that what I say is true — that you
have that money put away somewhere. Is it true,
or not, as you hope to be saved?"

Mrs. Lauderdale came between them again, laying her hands on Katharine's arm and trying to
make her leave the room.

"Take care, take care!" she cried, anxiously,
and hardly knowing what she said. "Alexander
— Katharine! Don't — oh, please don't quarrel
like this — my child, my child! You're beside
yourself!"

"I'm not — it's true as life and death!" answered the girl, resisting the pressure. "Ask him
if it's not! Make him swear that it's not true —
make him say, before heaven, that he has less than
a million, while he's selling his daughters and
forcing his wife to work. Wait — don't speak —
listen to what he says! If he can't say it, his

whole life has been a lie, and he knows it — wait — hush!"

Katharine held her mother fast by the hands, and seemed to hold her own breath, her angry eyes fixed on her father's face. Mrs. Lauderdale turned her head instinctively, and looked at him. He met their glances for a few seconds, and his dry, pale lips parted as though he were about to speak, but no sound came. In the waning light his eyes had a glassy look. It only lasted a moment, and then his mouth was twisted with an expression meant for a smile.

"Take her away — she's mad," he said, and his voice seemed to be suddenly weak.

Katharine laughed aloud, bitterly and cruelly, in her triumph.

"If I were mad, as you say I am," she said, a moment later, "that would not make it impossible for you to tell the truth. Yes, mother — I'm going now. I've said it all — and you know it's true."

She dropped her mother's hands, turned contemptuously away, and left the room. Neither her father nor her mother moved as she went, though they followed her with their eyes until the door closed behind her with a soft click.

Alexander Lauderdale was torn by the strongest emotions of which he was capable — anger and avarice. But avarice was the stronger. So long as

Katharine had accused him of unkindness, of dishonesty in his treatment of Wingfield, of meanness in his household, his wrath, though powerless, had kept the upper hand. But at the sudden and unexpected accusation of possessing a fortune in secret, he had been cowed. It was characteristic of him that even in that moment he would not swear falsely, and he saw the folly of denying the statement if he could not support his denial with something like an oath. When passions have reached such a crisis, they are not satisfied with less than they demand. On the whole, it had been wiser to say nothing. He could admit afterwards that he had saved something — he would assure his wife that Katharine's statement had been exaggerated — little by little, calm would be restored. And there would not necessarily be any increase of expenditure. At that crucial moment two thoughts had been uppermost in his mind. The miser's dismay at the discovery of his wealth, and the miser's visions of ruinous expense in the immediate future. In a flash, he had seen himself forced to spend fifty or sixty thousand a year, instead of ten or twelve, and all possible forms of reckless extravagance had appeared to him in a horror of kaleidoscopic confusion. It was torture to think of it — to realize that his secret was out.

The strong man stood, half-stunned, leaning against the mantelpiece, pulling nervously at the bit of embroidered velvet which covered it, his face drawn in an expression of suffering and fear. He dreaded the question which he knew that his wife would ask him, but he had not even the power to speak at that moment, in order to ward it off.

Mrs. Lauderdale hesitated a moment, wondering whether it might not be better to follow Katharine to her room and try to calm her and make her more reasonable. Never, in all the girl's life, had her mother seen her so passionately angry nor heard her use the tone of defying strength which had rung in her voice as she accused her father. Mrs. Lauderdale herself was frightened, and almost feared for Katharine's reason. But there had, nevertheless, been so much assurance of truth in what she had said, that her mother was half convinced. Before she left the room to follow her daughter, she turned to her husband, and the inevitable question came. It could not be otherwise. The girl's accusation had vividly brought before Mrs. Lauderdale the labour she had expended in all the past years, and of which the result had been to give her children what it was their father's duty to give them if he had anything to give. Many a time, too, she herself had chafed under the necessity of lending him small sums for an emergency, accepting a promise of payment which was never fulfilled, and forced to be satisfied with the assurance that he kept an account of

what he owed her. He seemed never to have
money about him. · He always said that he was
afraid of losing it — he, the most careful of men!
The cumulative force of those many small meannesses extending over a quarter of a century of
married life was tremendous when they were
brought up in a body and made to face the positive
statement that he was in reality a rich man. A
good wife she had been to Alexander Junior in
every sense of the word, but of that early trusting
love which hides more sins than the multitude of
them which charity can cover, there was not left
even the warmth where the spark had glowed.
There was no 'a priori' judgment of one heart
against all possible offence and sordid meanness
in the other. Katharine's blow had been heavy
and direct, and had gone straight to its mark.
Her mother loved her — in spite of her terrible
envy of her. It would need the man's solemn oath
to outweigh the girl's plain statement. The inevitable question came, as Alexander knew that it
must. He moved nervously as she began to speak.

"Alexander, dear," she said, speaking gently
from force of habit, "it would be very easy for you
to deny this."

He had thought of what he should say.

"My dear, I think that after spending half a
lifetime together, during which you've had occasion to find out that I'm truthful, it's scarcely

necessary to pay any attention to an angry child's ravings."

But Mrs. Lauderdale was not satisfied with this poor excuse. Katharine had roused her own resentment, and she remembered many things now, which Katharine herself did not know — little things — the dry sticks that will make a smouldering fire blaze.

"It's precisely because you're so truthful that it seems strange when you refuse to answer a simple question, Alexander," observed Mrs. Lauderdale, quietly enough.

She did not wish to take up Katharine's quarrel, nor to give the present conversation the air of an argument. She therefore did not stay beside him, as though they were discussing any point, but moved about the room, pretending to arrange small objects and books and generally to set the room in order, which was a work of supererogation, to keep herself in countenance while she renewed the attack.

"You admit that I'm truthful," said Alexander, coldly. "I'm glad you do. That settles the question at once. If I've been a rich man all these years, then I've not been telling the truth, nor acting it, either. It's all too absurd for discussion. I confess that at first I was angry. The girl spoke to me in the most outrageous manner. I don't remember that any one has ever said anything of the kind to me in my life. It's wrong to be angry, and I repent of it, but I think I may be pardoned — considering what she said. It's been a disgraceful scene. I'm sincerely thankful that none of the servants were present."

"Oh — it was natural that you should lose your temper, of course!"

"Human, at all events," said Alexander, with dignity; "I don't think I've ever made any pretence of possessing superior virtues. A man may justifiably lose his temper sometimes. 'Be angry and sin not.' I did not intend to be violent."

"No — of course not! Still —"

"Yes. I took her by the arm and deliberately laid my hand upon her mouth. That was not violence. Few men of sincere convictions would have done less, considering the blasphemous words she was uttering. It's the duty of parents to hinder their children from committing such sins, when they can. In the case of a man, I should have used my strength to enforce silence. As it was, I merely covered her mouth with my hand. I recollect that you came between us, as though you thought I meant to be violent. Nothing could have been further from my thoughts, I assure you."

"I trust so," said Mrs. Lauderdale, taking a package of envelopes out of the little stationery rack on the writing-table, turning it round and putting it back again.

"With regard to Archibald Wingfield," continued Alexander, getting further and further from
the question of the money, "you know as well as
I do, that we have treated him precisely as we
treated Slayback, when he wished to marry Charlotte. As for me, I told him that I saw no reason
why Katharine might not — 'might not ultimately,'
mind you — accept an offer which was so agreeable
to me personally. I fail to see anything which
can be criticised in that answer. I should by no
means like to say positively, even now, that Katharine 'might not ultimately' accept him. That
would amount to denying the existence of an
evident possibility, which is absurd. She may, so
far as that goes. I don't say she will. I say,
she may. Young women frequently change their
minds, and sometimes for the better. Let us hope
for the best. Of course I don't know every word
of what you said to him, though you did your best
on each occasion to tell me all about it. I
gathered that you gave him very much the same
sort of negative encouragement that I did. Practically, we told him to try his luck."

Mrs. Lauderdale had rarely heard her husband
speak so long consecutively. He was not fluent,
as a rule, and in the recent quarrel with Katharine
he had been almost speechless. But now he was
talking for his life, as it were. If he lost the
position of domination which he had held so long

with his wife, his existence must be shaken to its foundation. He barely gave her a chance to introduce a word.

"I'm not so positively sure, myself," she said. "Of course I didn't mean to convey any wrong impression to young Wingfield, but — "

"But you may perhaps have pardonably exceeded your powers," interrupted Alexander, anxious that she should not commit herself. "Very pardonable, my dear, very pardonable. Such things happen constantly, even in business. Of course the party who goes beyond his instructions bears the responsibility in case anything goes wrong. Just so in the present case. If there is any responsibility, which may be doubted, it's yours and not mine, for I'm positively certain of the words I spoke — of the very words. I said 'might not ultimately accept' — I recollect very distinctly, and you know how accurate my memory is."

"Yes — I know," answered Mrs. Lauderdale, in a tone which might have been thought to give the words a doubtful meaning.

"Of course you do, my dear. If Wingfield got a wrong impression, — 'if he did,' mind you, — he must have got it from you. I think you might perhaps explain that to Katharine — when she's a little calmer. I can't allow her to think that her father, whom she's bound to respect, should have done such a thing. A man's actions carry much

more weight than a woman's. I couldn't allow
her to think that I'd taken her feelings for
granted. There's no immediate hurry, Emma, but
I should be glad if you would explain it to her.
It will help to restore peace. As for her reasons
for rejecting Wingfield," he continued, without
pausing for his wife's answer, "I regret them very
much. It's a miserable thing to see such a girl
wasting her chances of happiness on such a reprobate as Jack Ralston, and I do her the honour to
say that such an affection can't possibly be lasting.
As for her marrying him, of course that's altogether outside the question. I'm sure she clings
to the attachment far more out of a desire to oppose
my wishes in everything, than because she really
cares for that vagabond. I've not the slightest
fear that she'll ever marry him. I'm sure you
don't think so, either."

"Unless she runs away with him," suggested
Mrs. Lauderdale.

She was annoyed by the skill with which he, who
was ordinarily less keen, had passed from the main
subject in question to a side issue. She did not
know how a great passion like avarice can sharpen
wits under danger of discovery.

"Oh, well!" exclaimed Alexander, with much
dignity. "If she runs away with the fellow, that
puts her altogether beyond the pale of our love,
and we shall have done with her. We won't dis-

cuss that. The objection to this pretence of loving
Ralston — for I'm convinced that it's nothing else
— is that it keeps her from marrying a man
worthy of her, like Archibald Wingfield. Of
course there are people far richer than the Wingfields — uncle Robert, for instance, besides the
others who are so much richer even than he, and
count their millions by the hundred; but taking him
all in all, there's not a better match in society —
for looks, and education, and position, and health,
too, which I regard as a very important consideration. You must agree with me, my dear — Wingfield would have made an excellent husband."

"Of course I agree with you, Alexander. What
an unnecessary question!"

"My dear, when the very foundations of one's
life are being torn up and thrown out of the window by a silly girl, it becomes necessary to ask all
the simplest questions over again."

This extraordinary simile produced no very con-
vincing effect on Mrs. Lauderdale, who had listened
to phrase after phrase of his long tirades with
exemplary outward resignation, for the sake of
allowing peace to be restored by the overflow of
self-conscious virtue, but with little inward patience.

"I think the best thing to do is to let the whole
matter drop, and hope that Katharine will change
her mind," she said, sensibly.

"Yes. Let's hope that, at all events. Emma, we can't have any more scenes like this. If Katharine breaks out in this way again, I shall refuse to see her. You may, if you please. But I will not. When I'm at home she shall stay in her room."

"But that's impossible!" exclaimed Mrs. Lauderdale, in astonishment. "You wouldn't treat a child like that!"

"I would," answered Alexander, and his lips snapped on the words. "And I will, if there's any repetition of such conduct. That's a matter for me to judge, Emma, and I don't wish you to interfere. She has accused her own father of being a liar, of selling her, of being a miser, and of stealing his wife's money. You can't deny that, and I presume you've no intention of supporting the accusations. Yes, even as it is, I prefer that Katharine should not appear this evening. When she's begged my pardon for what she's done, I'll consent to see her. Not before. Pray tell her that this is my decision, Emma."

"But, Alexander, I never heard of such a thing! Of course she lost her temper and was awfully rude to you, and I'm very much displeased with her. But really — you can't treat a grown woman like a baby. It's too absurd."

"It's not absurd, my dear. You must excuse me if I adopt Katharine's method of contradiction.

The only way to treat her is to treat her as a child. If we consider her to be a grown woman, we must either resent what she's done — as though she were any other woman — or else take it for granted that she is temporarily insane, and drive her out to Bloomingdale Asylum to-morrow morning to be cured. But so long as we regard the whole thing as childish, it's sufficient to tell her that she's not to come to table until she's begged my pardon. Don't you see?"

Mrs. Lauderdale was aware that he was talking nonsense, approximately speaking, and she saw that he meant to do a very unwise thing. But as he put it, the only good argument against his course would have been to prove that Katharine was right and that he was wrong, which, with some allowance for undue and angry exaggeration, would be equivalent to proving him a miser and anything but a straightforward person. Mrs. Lauderdale's trouble was considerable at that moment.

"You may be right in theory," she said, almost despairingly, "but in practice I think you're quite wrong. One doesn't do that sort of thing nowadays. If we've all got to fight like mad people, let's keep it to ourselves —"

"That's precisely what I'm thinking of," interrupted Alexander, whose resolution was growing stronger every moment.

"Yes — but, my dear! The servants — and your father, too! I don't think he's very discreet — "

"Yes, exactly, my dear Emma. That's just how I look at it. I think I know Katharine quite as well as you do, and I'm sure that if she has an opportunity of attacking me, she will, before the servants and before my father. I should much rather let people know that I had told Katharine to stay in her room until she could treat me with proper respect, than have such a conversation as has just taken place here repeated all over New York. I'm sure you see that, don't you?"

"Yes," answered Mrs. Lauderdale, suddenly comprehending his point of view. "But it seems to me that if there's to be such an open break, it would be better to let Katharine go down to Washington for a few days and stay with Charlotte."

"Certainly not!" exclaimed Alexander. "You know what Charlotte is, and what trouble we have had with her. The two girls would make common cause. Not at all. Not at all, Emma. I shall be glad if you will go at once and tell Katharine what I've said — that I don't wish to see her until she has made amends for her outrageous conduct."

"But, Alexander," protested Mrs. Lauderdale, "it will be so inconvenient — sending her dinner upstairs!"

"I daresay it won't be for long. She'll understand in a day or two, I've no doubt."

"I can't do it," said Mrs. Lauderdale, trying to make a stand. "It's too utterly — extraordinary — "

"My dear, I'm the master in this house," answered Alexander, coldly. "I wish it to be so. But if you'd rather not speak to her, I'll go myself. She irritates me, but I'm glad to say she doesn't intimidate me. As for such domestic difficulties as serving Katharine in her own room, they can be got over. Let your maid take the child her dinner."

"Well — if you insist, I'll go," said Mrs. Lauderdale, weakly yielding. "I couldn't let you go — you'd quarrel again."

"I don't insist upon your going, my dear — I have no right to. But I insist upon the thing being done."

Mrs. Lauderdale went towards the door. She paused before she went out. "I think you're going too far, Alexander," she said. "I think you're tyrannical."

"I think not," he answered, coolly. "I should refuse to sit down to table with a man who had used such language to me. I don't see why I should submit to it from Katharine."

"Well — "

Mrs. Lauderdale closed the door behind her, and slowly went upstairs, feeling as though she had been driven from the field after a crushing defeat.

Yet she had made very little resistance. With her, the man's cold, arrogant personality was dominant. She had always submitted to it because there seemed to be no other course. She was conscious of wishing that during the last five minutes she might have possessed her daughter's character and fighting qualities, especially when her husband had quietly thrust all the blame about the treatment of Wingfield upon herself, without considering for a moment that his own words might have been misinterpreted.

She did not altogether sympathize with him against Katharine. For many years she had felt the galling of his miserable meanness, and had many times suspected that he was by no means as poor as he chose to declare himself to be.

CHAPTER IX.

MRS. LAUDERDALE went slowly upstairs, thinking over what she should say, as she climbed from one story to another. At the door she knocked softly, and Katharine's voice bade her enter.

Katharine was standing at the window, looking out, and did not turn round as her mother entered. The evening light was on the houses opposite, and the glow was gently sinking into the darker street. Katharine watched the horse-cars go by, and listened mechanically to the jingle of the bells, hardly conscious of either.

"What is it?" she asked, as she heard the door close.

Her voice had that peculiar reedy sound which comes of speaking through the closed teeth by the lips only. It seems to mean that the speaker is on the defensive and not to be trifled with.

"Your father — Katharine — he's so angry! He wanted me to speak to you."

"Oh — it's you, mother?" The girl's tone changed a very little, and she turned and came forward. "Well — I'm sorry," she said, after a short pause. "It can't be helped, I suppose."

Mrs. Lauderdale sat down in the one small arm-chair, by the toilet-table, and clasped her hands over her knee, leaning back, and looking up rather wistfully at Katharine.

"I think — in a way — it can be helped," said Mrs. Lauderdale, in a conciliatory manner. "If you would go downstairs now, and just say quietly that you're sorry, you know. Just as you said it now. I'm sure he'd be willing to accept that as an apology."

"Apology?" Katharine laughed bitterly. "I — make an apology to him? No, mother — I won't."

"You ought to — really," objected Mrs. Lauderdale, earnestly. "Why, my dear child! Have you any idea of what you've been saying downstairs? Some of the things you said were dreadful."

"They were all true, and he knows it," answered Katharine, stubbornly.

She leaned against the chest of drawers, and looked down into her mother's upturned face.

"Oh, no! they weren't all true, dear," protested the latter. "You exaggerated very much. It's quite possible that your father may have saved something in all these years — he's so careful! But as for having a million, as you said — "

"But, dear mother — there isn't a doubt of it! I didn't promise uncle Robert that I wouldn't tell that — "

"What? Did uncle Robert tell you?"

"Yes! Of course! Did you suppose I was inventing?"

"Well — not exactly. But I thought you might have heard some gossip — or something Jack Ralston said —"

"Not at all. Uncle Robert told me that he knew it to be a positive fact — a million, at least, he said. And he's quite as truthful as papa —"

"More so," said Mrs. Lauderdale, absently; "I mean," she added, very quickly, with a frightened look, for she had not realized what she was saying — "I mean — quite as truthful. They're both perfectly truthful —"

"Yes," answered Katharine in a doubtful tone, and smiling in spite of herself. "Not but that, if it came to believing, you know, I'd believe uncle Robert sooner than papa —"

"Hush, child — don't!"

Katharine said nothing, but still leaned back, resting both elbows on the high chest of drawers on each side behind her, and looking down thoughtfully at the points of her shoes. Mrs. Lauderdale was silent, too, for several seconds.

"Well?" Katharine uttered the convenient word interrogatively, without looking up.

"Well — yes," responded Mrs. Lauderdale. "I was going to say that —" She hesitated. "My dear," she continued, at last, "you'll have to say something to your father, after all this."

"Something like what I've said already?" asked Katharine, raising her black eyebrows and glancing at her mother.

"No, no! I'm serious, my dear."

"So am I — very. You began to talk of an apology. It's quite useless, mother — I can't and I won't apologize."

"But, Katharine, darling — he says he won't see you unless you do — he's dreadfully angry still!"

"Oh — he won't see me? What does that mean? That I'm to stay in my room?" She laughed a little.

"He's in earnest about it," said Mrs. Lauderdale. "That's what he said — he — I don't like to say it — but I must, I suppose. That's just it. He means you to stay in your room whenever he's in the house."

"How childish!" exclaimed Katharine, scornfully. "What do I care? I don't want to see him particularly. But, just for curiosity — if he happens to meet me on the stairs, for instance, what will he do? Throw things at me? Box my ears? He's quite capable of it — as you saw just now — "

"Please don't talk like that, dear," said Mrs. Lauderdale. "He was terribly angry — and you were saying the most dreadful things — he only meant to stop you from speaking."

"He hurt my mouth, and he hurt my arm — there'll be black and blue marks here to-morrow,

I'm sure, by the way it feels." She laid her left hand on her right forearm at the point where her father had seized it. "That's rather like violence, you know, mother."

Katharine turned perceptibly paler as she spoke of it. Mrs. Lauderdale was pained at the recollection, and looked away from her, clasping her hands a little more tightly over her knee.

"Did he ever touch you in that way, mother?" asked the young girl, slowly.

"Me?" cried Mrs. Lauderdale. "Oh — child! How can you think of such a thing! No, indeed! Fancy!"

"Well — I'm just as sensitive as you are," answered Katharine. "Put yourself in my place."

The unexpected answer silenced the elder woman.

"I think it's his place to apologize to me — and very humbly," added Katharine. "It was a cowardly piece of violence to a woman. I'm willing to believe — for the honour of the family, and men generally — that he didn't mean to strike, exactly. But it felt very much like it, and I told him so. I'll tell him so again, if he mentions the thing."

Mrs. Lauderdale was in great difficulties. Her husband and her daughter were both stronger than she, they had no intention of making up their quarrel, and yet, by her position, she was forced to act as intermediary. It was not easy. Her husband dominated her by his strong personality. Katharine had the better of her in argument. She turned away a little, in thought, resting one elbow on the toilet-table beside her, and covering her eyes with her hand for a moment. The beautiful, tired features were pale and drawn.

"It's very hard for me," she said, wearily. "You're both partly wrong and partly right."

"I think I'm altogether right," said Katharine.

"I know — so does he. But you're not — either of you — nor I, either, for that matter. Oh, dear! I wish I knew what to do!"

"There's nothing to be done, I'm afraid," answered the young girl, more gently, for she was somewhat pacified by her mother's owning a share in the blame. "Not that I'm going to make a fuss about it, if he doesn't. I'm not that kind. I won't come down to dinner to-night, because it would be unpleasant for everybody. As for to-morrow — we'll see what happens. The idea of shutting me up in my room so long as he's in the house, because the sight of me is disagreeable to him, it's silly — it's perfectly childish! Just like an angry man! I'm not sure that I should mind it very much, so far as not seeing him's concerned. I don't want to see him, any more than he wants to see me. But it's the principle of the thing that sticks in my throat. It's as though he had the right to treat me like a small child, to be sent to bed in a dark room at discretion, until I change my mind. It's the tyranny of the thing, the arrogance of it — and when I'm altogether right, as you both know."

"No — not altogether," objected Mrs. Lauderdale.

"I won't go over it again, mother. I'll sum it up in these words. He's rich, and he's told us that he was poor, and he's stood looking on and letting you work to give us small luxuries that amount to necessities. He's wilfully calumniated Jack for months. He's wilfully misled Archie Wingfield —"

"My dear — about that — he assures me that he only said you might ultimately accept him —"

"Well — he knew that I mightn't, and he had no business to say I might," interrupted Katharine, decidedly. "Besides, I can hear just his tone of voice, and his way of slurring over the 'might' till Mr. Wingfield felt it was 'may' — oh, it's abominable! As for his pestering me with questions about uncle Robert's will, it's natural enough, considering how he loves money, as a cat loves cream. Oh, I know! You're going to say it's disrespectful to say such things. Perhaps it is — I don't know — he seems to lap it up — with that smile of his — and it disappears, and we have to live on the drops. No — I don't feel respectful. Why should I? I've respected him for nineteen years, and I can't respect him any longer. It's over, once and for all. When a man deliberately sets to work to destroy his daughter's chances of being happy — oh, well! It isn't only that. It's the whole thing, the meanness, the miserliness, the Sunday-go-to-meeting-and-sit-up-straight sort of virtuous superiority outside — and all this other inside. It's revolting. It's upset all my ideas. I don't feel as though I could ever believe in anything again. I don't mean to shock you, mother, but I can't help saying it, just now."

"It's dreadful!" Mrs. Lauderdale spoke in a low voice and earnestly.

Katharine was silent for a few moments, and looked out of the window. It was almost dark by this time.

"You know, mother," she said, suddenly, "I used to admire papa — very much, in a certain way. I don't think you ever quite realized that. Of course I've been brought up in his church, though I've much more sympathy with yours. It always seems to me that his is a man's religion, and yours is a woman's. But then — Mr. Griggs says the world is a woman, in a sort of way, so yours ought to be the religion of the world. Never mind — I don't know enough to talk about these things. What I mean is this. I used to admire papa's uncompromising way of looking at life, and the way I thought he'd tell the truth and shame the devil at any price, and his cold, unreasoning, settled certainty about heaven and hell — and the way I thought that he took his flinty goodness down town with him, and did right, when one knows that ever so many business men don't. It all seemed so strong, and cool, and manly. I couldn't help admiring it. And I believed that he was poor, and that although he wouldn't say much, he'd fight for us, and die for us, if necessary. And then — he's handsome, too, and straight, and steely, and formal. I've always liked a little formality. Do you see what I mean?"

"Of course," answered Mrs. Lauderdale, thoughtfully, and nodding her head with a far-away look in her eyes.

Katharine had enumerated the very qualities that had once appealed so strongly to her mother.

"Well —" Katharine paused a second. "It's all a sham. That's all."

Mrs. Lauderdale started at the abrupt, rough words.

"Oh, Katharine, dear, don't say that!"

"It's true. It's broken to pieces. It began to crack just before Charlotte was married. It's all broken to bits. I can see the inside of it, and it's not what I thought. There's only one idea, and that's money. It would need a miracle to make me admire him again. It's broken to atoms, and what's so strange is, that it's taken everything

with it in the last few months — and it's taken
the last bit to-day. It's all gone. I can't help
it. It's dreadful — but it's a sort of confession,
like your confessions. I don't believe in God any
more."

"My child, my child!"

Mrs. Lauderdale looked up at her with scared
eyes and rising hands, which sought Katharine's,
found them, and gripped them in a frightened
way. The devout woman, good at heart with her
one big fault, felt as though the world were quak-
ing under her feet as she heard the last words.
Not that Katharine spoke them lightly, for she
was in earnest, and the declaration of unbelief was
more solemn from its strangeness than almost any
confession of rigid faith could have been.

"Yes, mother — I know — we won't talk about
it. I only want you to understand me — we've
been so much together in our lives."

She spoke sadly now.

"And we shall be, dear, I hope," answered Mrs.
Lauderdale.

"I don't know — perhaps. I don't believe we
shall ever be just as we used to be. You're not
the same — nor am I, I suppose."

"Oh, yes we are — in our hearts. But, Katharine, darling — what you said just now — if you
knew how it hurts me — "

"It's not your fault, mother. If anybody's to

blame, it's papa, and I think he is.   Oh, no!
You're different.   After all, we're only a pair of
women, you and I.   We can quarrel and make up,
and nobody will be hurt in the end.   We're not
each other's ideals — not that papa was mine, or
anything like it.   But you naturally believe in a
thing more when a strong man stands up and
asserts it and fights for it, than if it turns out
that he only says that he believes in it, out of
prejudice and family tradition and a sort of
impression that after all he may go to the wrong
place if he doesn't.   He's always talking about
setting an example — it seems to me that the
example lies in the effect of the thing upon the
person one's to imitate.   If this is the effect of
religion on him, I don't want it.   I'd rather talk
to Teddy Van De Water, who chatters about Dar-
win and Spencer without knowing anything particular about them, and sticks his glass in his eye
and makes bad jokes about the future state, but
who'd burn his hand to the wrist rather than do
anything he thought mean.   Men have done that
sort of thing before now — they're not the men
who talk about God over the soup, and try to sell
their daughters at dessert!"

"Katharine —"   Mrs. Lauderdale could not find
words.

"I know — but papa's not here — and then, I
don't mean to talk about it any longer.   You've

come up from him, I suppose, mother, to say that he doesn't want to see me. Very well. I don't want to see him. But how long is this state of things to last? I won't apologize, and I suppose he won't give in. It may go on for months, then. Supposing I refuse to be imprisoned in this way, is he going to lock me in and take the key with him? What's he going to do? I want to know what to expect."

"My dear, I don't know — he only said that. Just what I told you."

"Because if it's going to be a siege, I'll go away," said Katharine, calmly.

"I proposed that you should go to Washington and spend a fortnight with Charlotte. He wouldn't hear of it."

"Yes — but if I just go without asking his leave? What will happen? What do you think? Girls often go alone, and it's only five hours by the half-past eleven train that Charlotte always takes. She'd be glad to have me, too."

"Your father would be quite capable of going and bringing you back — on Sunday."

"On Sunday!" Katharine laughed hardly. "How you know him! He wouldn't lose a day at his office, to save you or me from drowning. That's what he calls duty. Yes — perhaps he'd come, as you say. Then we should have an opportunity of fighting it out on the way back. Five hours, side

by side — but I suppose we should turn our chairs
back to back and go to sleep or read. But he
might not come, after all. Do you know? I
should feel a sort of sense of security at the
Slaybacks'. I like him, though Charlotte makes
fun of him. There's something real about him.
I didn't mean to go to Washington, though."

"You couldn't go to the Ralstons'," observed
Mrs. Lauderdale. "With Jack at home — people
would talk."

"If I went there, I should stay," answered
Katharine, with a coolness that startled her
mother. "I should never come back at all.
Perhaps I shall some day. Who knows? No —
I thought I'd go and stop with uncle Robert.
That would terrify papa. He'd suppose, in the
first place, that I'd tell uncle Robert everything
that's happened, and then that uncle Robert would
tell me a great deal more about his intentions
with regard to the will. That would make papa
anxious to be nice to me when I came home again,
so as to get the secret out of me. I think it's a
very good plan; don't you? Uncle Robert would
be delighted. He's all alone and not at all strong.
The very last time I saw him, he begged me to
come and stay a few days. I think I will. Fancy
papa's rage! He'd scarcely dare to come and get
me there, I imagine."

Mrs. Lauderdale did not answer at once. She

saw the immense advantage Katharine would have
over her father if she carried out the plan, and
it seemed too great. Alexander would be almost
at his daughter's mercy. She could dictate her
own terms of peace. Incensed as she was against
him, she could easily use her influence against him
with his uncle, who had a lonely old man's fondness for the beautiful girl.

"Of course you could go — I couldn't prevent
you," said Mrs. Lauderdale, rather helplessly.

"Of course I could. I've only to walk there.
Uncle Robert will send for my things."

"I hope you won't, dear. It wouldn't make it
easier for me — he'll think it's been my fault, you
know — and then — "

Katharine looked at her mother in silence for
a moment, and pitied her too much, even after
what had passed between them, to leave her to
Alexander's temper.

"I won't go yet," said Katharine. "I won't
go unless he's perfectly intractable. Go and tell
him that it's all right, mother. I'll submit quietly
and stay in my room as long as he's in the house
— quite as much for my own sake as for his, you
can tell him. If he asks about my apologizing,
tell him that I won't, and that I expect an apology
from him. It can't last forever. One of us will
have to give in, at the end — but I won't. You
can put it all as mildly as you like, only don't

give him any impression that I'm submitting to him morally, even if I'm willing to keep out of his way."

"Couldn't you say something a little nicer than that, dear?" asked Mrs. Lauderdale, pleadingly, for she anticipated more trouble. "Couldn't you say that you'd let by-gones be by-gones — or something of that sort ?"

"It wouldn't be true. These are not by-gones. They're present things. The nice by-gones will never come back."

Mrs. Lauderdale rose slowly to the height of her still graceful figure, and stood before her daughter for a moment. In the emotion of the past hour she had forgotten for a time her envy of the girl's blossoming beauty. For a moment she was impelled to throw her arms round Katharine's neck in the old way, and kiss her, and try to make things again what they had been. But something hard in the young grey eyes stopped her. She felt that she herself was not forgiven yet and might never be, altogether.

"Very well," she said, quietly. "I'll do my best."

She turned and left the room, leaving Katharine still leaning back against the chest of drawers in the position she had not abandoned throughout the conversation.

When Katharine was alone, she stood up, turned

round and pulled out the upper drawer. Amongst her gloves and handkerchiefs lay a photograph of John Ralston. She took it out and looked at the keen, dark face, with its set lips, its prominent bony temples, and its nervous lines that would be furrows too soon.

"You're worth all the Lauderdales and the Wingfields put together!" she said, in a low voice.

She kissed the photograph, pressing it hard to her lips and closing her eyes.

"I wish you were here!" she said.

She looked at it again, and again kissed it. Then she put it back with an energetic movement that was almost rough, and shut the drawer. She sat down in the chair her mother had occupied, and gave herself up to thinking over all that had taken place.

Her instinct was to let John Ralston know as soon as possible what had happened, but she knew how foolish that would be. He would insist that the moment had come for declaring their marriage, and that she must go and live under his mother's roof. But she felt that something must be done soon. If she was willing to submit to her father's sentence, absurd as it was, she found a reason for doing so in her own disinclination to meet him. But the situation could not last. And yet, he was obstinate beyond ordinarily obstinate people, and it would be like him to insist upon banishing

her for a week. In such things he had no sense
of the ridiculous. Apart from the inconvenience
and constant annoyance of being expected to keep
out of his way, she was young enough to feel
humiliated. It was very like a punishment — this
order not to be seen when her father was in the
house. She had no intention of disregarding it,
however. To do so would have been to produce
an open war of which the rumour would fill
society. It was clear that her best course was to
be patient as long as possible, and then quietly to
go to uncle Robert's house. The world would
think it natural that she should pay him a visit.
She had done so before.

Alexander Junior seemed to be satisfied with
the answer his wife brought him. He felt that if
he could make Katharine stay in her own room
at his discretion, he was still master in his own
house, and his injured dignity began to hold up
its head again. The old philanthropist did not
even ask after Katharine at dinner, though he was
fond of her. She so often went out to dine alone
with intimate friends, that it did not occur to him
to remark upon her absence. But, as usual, when
she was not there, the family meal was dull and
silent. Alexander ate without speaking, and with
the methodical, grimly appreciative appetite of
very strong men. Mrs. Lauderdale was not hungry, and stared at the silver things on the table

most of the time. The old gentleman bolted his food in the anticipation of tobacco, which tasted best after eating. He was a cheerful old soul when he was not dreaming, an optimist and a professed maker of happiness by the ton, so to say, for those who had been forgotten in the distribution. He had big hands, shiny at the knuckles and pink where a young man's would be white, with horny, yellowish nails, and he was not very neat in his dress, though he had survived from the day when men used to wear dress coats and white ties in their offices all day. The Lauderdale tribe regarded him as a harmless member who had something wrong in his head, while his heart was almost too much in the right place. A certain amount of respect was shown him on account of his age, but though he was the oldest of them all, Robert the Rich was undisputedly the head of the family. It was generally believed, and, as has been seen, the belief was well founded, that he was not to have any large share of the money in case he survived his brother.

Early on the following morning Alexander Junior emerged from his dressing-room, equipped for the day. He wore the garments of civilization, but a very little power of imagination might have converted his dark grey trousers into greaves, his morning coat into a shirt of mail, and his stiff collar into a steel throat-piece. He had slept on his wrath, and had grown more obstinate with the grey of the morning. His voice was metallic and aggressive when he spoke to the serving-girl, demanding why his steak was overdone. When his wife appeared, he rose formally, as usual, and kissed her cheek with a little click, like the lock of a safe. He said little or nothing as he finished his breakfast, and then, without telling her what he meant to do, he went upstairs again and knocked at Katharine's door.

"Katharine!" he called to her. "I wish to speak to you."

"Well —" answered the young girl's voice — "I'm not dressed yet. What is it?"

"How long shall you be?" enquired Alexander, bending his brows as he leaned against the panel to catch her answer.

"About three quarters of an hour — I should think — at least — judging from the state of my hair. It's all tangled."

"Do you know what time it is?"

"No — I've not looked. Oh — my little clock has stopped. It's a quarter past four by my little clock."

"It's nine o'clock," said Alexander Junior, severely. "Three minutes to," he added, looking at his watch.

"Well — I can't help it now. It's only — no — it's sixteen minutes past four by my little clock."

"Never mind your little clock. I must be going down town at once, and I wish to speak to you. I can't wait three quarters of an hour."

"No — of course not."

"Well — can't I come in? Aren't you visible?"

"No. Certainly not. You can't come in. I'm brushing.— my hair. I always brush it — ten minutes."

"Katharine — this is absurd!" cried Alexander, becoming exasperated. "Put on something and open the door."

"No. I can't just — now." Her phrases were interrupted by the process of vigorous brushing. "Besides — you can talk through the door. I can hear — every word — you say. Can't you hear me?"

"Yes, I can hear you. But I don't wish to say what I have to say in the hearing of the whole house."

"Oh!" The soft sound of the brushing ceased. "In that case I'd rather not hear it at all."

"Katharine!" Alexander felt all his anger of the previous day rising again.

"Yes — what is it?" She seemed to have come nearer to the door.

"I told you. I wish to speak to you."

"Yes — I know. But you can't unless you'll say it through the door."

"Katharine! Don't exasperate me!"

"I'm not trying to. I understood that you didn't wish to see me for some days. If you'd sent me word, I should have been ready to receive you. As it is, I can't."

"You know perfectly well that you can, in ten minutes, if you please. I shall send your mother to you."

"Oh — very well. I've not seen her this morning. But you'd better not wait till I'm dressed. It will take a long time."

"Very well," answered Alexander Junior, who had completely lost his temper by this time.

A moment later Katharine heard the sharp click of the lock, and the rattle as the key was withdrawn. She never used it, having a bolt on the inside.

"You are at liberty to take all day if you please," said her father. "I have the key in my pocket. Good morning."

Katharine's lips parted in astonishment, as she turned her eyes towards the door, and she stood staring at it for a moment in speechless indignation, realizing that she was locked in for the day. Then, suddenly, her expression changed, and she laughed aloud. Alexander was already far down the stairs.

But presently she realized that the situation was serious, or, at all events, something more than annoying. She was to be shut up at least until after five o'clock in the afternoon, all alone, without food or drink, without the books she wanted, and without any one with whom to exchange a few words. Her face became grave as she finished dressing. She knew also that her father had lost his temper again, and she did not care to have all the servants know it.

She rang the bell, and waited by the door till she heard the maid's footsteps outside.

"Ask my mother to come here a moment, Jane," she said. "Say that it's important."

A few moments later Mrs. Lauderdale turned the handle of the lock.

"Is that you, mother?" asked Katharine.

"Yes. The door's locked. 1 can't open it."

"This is serious," said Katharine, speaking in a low voice, close to the panel. "Papa's locked it and taken the key down town with him. Didn't he tell you?"

"No — it's impossible, child! You must have slipped the bolt inside."

"But, mother, he said he meant to, and I heard him do it. He got angry because I wouldn't let him in. I couldn't then, for I wasn't dressed, and Jane's putting a new ribbon on my dressing-gown, so I haven't even got that. But I didn't want to. Never mind that — I'll tell you by and by. The question is how I'm to get out! Unless he didn't quite mean it, and has left the key on the table in the entry, with the latch-key. You might look."

Mrs. Lauderdale went downstairs and searched for the key, but in vain. Katharine was locked in.

CHAPTER X.

Mrs. Lauderdale was indignant. Katharine, at least, had been able to see the ludicrous side of the situation, and had laughed to herself on finding that she was locked in. Less conventional than either her father or mother, it had occurred to her for a moment that she was acting a part in an amusing comedy. The idea that by one or two absurd phrases she had so irritated Alexander as to make him forget his dignity and his common sense together, and do a thoroughly foolish thing such as a child in a passion might do, was funny in the extreme, she thought. But Mrs. Lauderdale, being called in, as it were, after the play, thought the result very poor fun indeed. In her opinion, her husband had done a senseless thing, in the worst possible taste.

Fortunately the house was an old one, and the simple, old-fashioned lock was amenable to keys which did not belong to it. In due time, Mrs. Lauderdale found one which served the purpose, and Katharine was set at liberty.

"This is just a little more than I can bear," she said, as her mother entered the room. "I didn't

expect this sort of thing last night when I said I
wouldn't go to uncle Robert's. Really — papa's
losing his head."

"I must say, it's going rather far," admitted
Mrs. Lauderdale.

"It's gone a great deal too far," Katharine answered. "I laughed when I found I was locked
in. It seemed so funny. But I won't let him do
it again."

"You two have a faculty for irritating each
other that's beyond anything," observed Mrs.
Lauderdale. "It really would be much better if
you could be separated for a little while. My
dear, what do you suppose could happen, if you
went to uncle Robert's?"

"Just what I told you yesterday. Papa would
be quite bland when I came home again. By that
time he could have got over his rage, and he'd
want to know things — oh, well! I won't talk
about all that. It only hurts you, and it can't do
any good, can it? Hadn't I better go up to
uncle Robert's and ask if he can have me? Meanwhile, Jane could pack a few things — just what I
need to-day — I can always come down, or send
down, and get anything I want at a moment's
notice. Shan't I, mother? What do you think?"

"Well — I don't quite know, child. Of course I
ought not to, but then if I don't — " She paused,
conscious of vagueness. "If I don't let you go,"

she continued, "there'll be worse trouble before long. This is an impossible position, we know, and if you went to Washington, I'm sure he'd go down on Sunday and bring you back. It was very clever of you to think of going to uncle Robert's."

"I could go to the Crowdies'," said Katharine, meditatively. "Of course, Hester's my best friend, but I do hate her husband so — I can't help it."

Walter Crowdie was a distinguished young painter, whose pale face and heavy, red mouth were unaccountably repulsive to Katharine, and, in a less degree, to her mother also. Mrs. Crowdie was Hamilton Bright's sister, and therefore a distant cousin.

"And papa might insist on bringing me back from there, too. There are lots of reasons against it. Besides — Hamilton — "

"What about Hamilton?" asked Mrs. Lauderdale.

"Oh, nothing! Mother — I don't want to do violent things and make a fuss, and all that, you know — but if you agree, and think it's sensible, I will go up and ask uncle Robert if I may stay a few days. You can see, yourself, that all this can't go on much longer."

In her resentment of her father's behaviour, she felt quite reconciled with her mother, and Mrs. Lauderdale was glad as she realized the fact. There was an underthought in her mind, too,

which was perhaps not altogether so creditable.
Though it was only to be for a few days, Katharine
was to be away from her. She was to have a
breathing space from the temptation which tormented her. For a little while she should be herself again, not contrasted, at every turn of her
daily life, with that terrible bloom which ever out-
shone the fading flower of her own beauty. That
was her dream. If she could but be supremely
beautiful still for one short month — that was all
she asked — after that, she would submit to time,
and give up the pride of life, and never complain
again. She would not have acknowledged to herself that this was a motive, for she honestly did
her best to fight her sin; but it was there, neverthee-
less, and influenced her to agree the more readily
to Katharine's absence. It counteracted, indeed,
the anxiety she felt about her husband's view of
the case when he should return from his office
late in the afternoon; but her instinct told her,
also, that he might very probably be a little
ashamed of what he had done, and be secretly glad
of the solution unexpectedly offered him.

Katharine got ready to go in a few minutes. As
she put on her hat and gloves, she glanced two or
three times at the bit of red ribbon that lay on her
toilet-table. She had taken down the signal from
the window on the previous evening, in order to
inform John Ralston that she could not come that

morning. On the whole, she was glad that she could not see him, for it would be hard to conceal from him what had happened. She would send him a message down town, and he could see her, undisturbed, at their uncle's house in the afternoon — more freely there than anywhere else, indeed, since Robert Lauderdale was in the secret of the clandestine marriage.

Before she left the house, Mrs. Lauderdale laid her hands upon the girl's shoulders and looked into her eyes with an anxious expression.

"Katharine, dear," she said, "don't ever let yourself think such things as you said yesterday afternoon."

"What things, mother?"

"About not believing — you know. You didn't mean what you said, darling, of course — and I'm not preaching to you. You know I promised long ago that I would never talk about religion to you children, nor influence you. I've kept my word. But this is different. Religion — well, we don't all agree in this world. But God — God's for everybody, just the same, dear. But then," she added, quickly, "I know you didn't really mean what you said. Only keep the thought away, when it comes."

Katharine said nothing, but she nodded gravely and kissed her mother on both cheeks. At the last moment, as she was going to the door, she stopped and turned back.

·"I'm awfully sorry to bother you, mother dear,"
she said, "but I've got no money — not even
twenty-five cents. Could you give me something?
I don't like to be out with nothing at all in my
pocket."

The deprecating tone, the real, earnest regret at
being obliged to ask for even such a trifle, told the
tale of what had gone on in the house, unknown to
the world, for years, far better than any words
could have done.

"Of course, child — I always have something,
you know," answered Mrs. Lauderdale, promptly.
"Here are ten dollars."

"Oh — I don't want so much!" cried Katharine.
"I'm not going to buy anything — it's only for
horse-cars, and things like that. Give me a dollar
and a little change, if you have it."

But Mrs. Lauderdale insisted that she should
take the note.

"I don't want you to go to uncle Robert's without a penny in your pocket. It looks like poor
relations."

"Well — you're always generous, mother," answered the young girl, with a little laugh. "But
it's papa's relation, and not yours."

"I know, dear — I know. But it makes no
difference."

As Katharine had anticipated, Robert Lauderdale was very glad to see her. He was sitting in

his library, into which the sun streamed through the high windows, one of which was partly opened to let in the spring freshness.

She thought he looked ill. He had not recovered from the effects of his illness so quickly as Doctor Routh had expected, owing to a certain weakness of the heart, natural enough at his age and after enduring so severe a strain. His appetite had never returned, and he was thin in the body and almost wasted in the face. If anything, Katharine thought he looked worse than when she had last seen him a few days previously. But he welcomed her with a cheery smile, and she sat down beside him.

"Come to pay me a little visit?" His voice was oddly hollow. "That's right! I wish you'd stay with me a few days again. But then, you're too gay, I suppose."

"Not at all too gay," laughed Katharine. "That's exactly what I want to do, and why I came at this hour. I wanted to ask if you'd have me for a week, and then, if you would, I was going to send for my things. And now you've spoken first, and I accept. My things are all ready," she added, still smiling. "You see, I knew you'd let me come."

"Of course, little girl!" answered the old man, his sunken eyes fixing themselves wistfully on her young face. "Ring for Leek and tell him to send a man down at once."

"Oh — there's no hurry about it. I made myself as beautiful as I could before starting — but I want to dazzle you at dinner. You sit up for dinner, don't you? How are you, uncle, dear? Better?"

"Yes — yes," he answered, slowly. "I suppose I'm better. But it's slow work. Yes, I sit up for dinner. It makes the days shorter. They're so long. You look pale, my dear. What's the matter? Too much dancing? Too much flirting? Or what?"

"I never flirt, uncle Robert!" Katharine laughed again.

"Well, then, it's time you began, and you'd better begin at once — with me."

And the old gentleman laughed, too, a queer hollow laugh that seemed to come from his backbone, with a rattle in it. And he laid two of his great bony fingers against the young girl's pale, fresh cheek — as though death played with life, and would like to kiss it.

So they chatted pleasantly together in the morning sunshine amongst the grand old books which the rich man had collected about him. Katharine had no intention of telling him what had happened in Clinton Place, if she could help it. Uncle Robert did not seem to require any reason for her sudden determination to pay him a visit, as she had done before on more than one occasion. He was glad enough to have her, whatever her reasons might be.

Katharine breathed the atmosphere of freedom and revived. The certainty that for several days, at least, the perpetual contest with her father was not to be renewed, brought colour to her cheeks and light to her eyes. But as the time wore on towards the hour for luncheon, and she came and went, and alternately talked with the old man and read aloud to him a little and sat in silence, watching his face, the conviction came over her that he could never get back his strength. The vitality was gone out of him, and he had grown listless. She could not tell whether he might live much longer, or not, but she felt that he had lost something which he could never regain.

"You feel stronger, don't you?" she asked, in an encouraging tone.

He did not answer at once, but looked at her affectionately and dreamily.

"Don't be worried about me, dear girl," he said, at last. "I'm doing very well."

"No, but really —" Katharine's face took an anxious expression.

"Really?" he repeated, looking at her still. Then his head fell back against the dark red cushion. "I'm not dead yet," he said, quietly. "But it's coming — it's coming by inches."

"Don't say that!"

But she knew it was true, and she began to talk of other things. He, however, seemed inclined to come back to the subject of his failing strength.

"I should be better if they didn't bother me," he said. "They keep coming to see whether I'm alive, and sending messages to enquire. Confound them!" he exclaimed, with a momentary return of energy. "They couldn't send more flowers if the undertaker were in the house! What does an old fellow like me want of flowers, I should like to know? They may turn my grave into a flower show if they like, when I'm tucked away in it, but I wish they'd leave me alone till I am!"

"Who are they?" asked Katharine, with some curiosity.

"The tribe, as you call the family. Your mother's one. Didn't she tell you she sent me flowers?"

"No — I'll tell her not to."

"Don't do that, little girl. You just let her alone. If she were the only one — I shouldn't care. I wouldn't hurt her feelings for anything, you know — and then, it means something when she sends them, because she works for them and earns the money. But why the dickens the three Miss Miners should think it necessary to send me American Beauties in cardboard boxes, I can't conceive. They're comfortably off enough, now, but that's no reason, and they can't stand the expense of that sort of thing long. Perhaps they think it won't last long. Of course it's well meant. I made Beman give them a lift with some little stocks they had lying round, and he took an interest in the thing, I suppose, for I hear that they're very comfortable — ten thousand a year amongst the four of them, with Frank — and I suppose he earns something with all his writings, doesn't he?"

"Oh, yes. *The Century* gave him a hundred and fifty dollars for an article the other day. He was so pleased! You have no idea!"

"I daresay," said the great millionaire, gravely. "Very nice, too — a hundred and fifty for one article. Well — he's another. He sends me all he writes — there's a heap of things on the table, there. That's his corner, you know, because he's the literary man of the family. And he scribbles me little notes with them. He's rather humble about his work — for he says he'd really be glad if anything he turned out could help to pass the time for me. Well — it's nice of him, I know. But it irritates me, somehow. As for that Crowdie, he's the worst of the lot — as he's the cleverest. By the bye, what day is to-day — Thursday, isn't it?"

"Yes — it's Thursday. Why?"

"Well — he's coming before luncheon to-day. It appears that he's painted a picture of you. I

think you said something about it last winter,
didn't you?"

"Yes. I told you I was sitting to him. He
painted it for Hester. She's my great friend, you
know."

"Oh, yes — so she is — so she is! Well — that's
a singular thing, too. He said in his last note
that it was for me."

"Did he?" Katharine laughed. "You'd better
take it, uncle dear — that is, if you want it. It's
a good picture."

"Everything the young scoundrel does is good!"
growled the old man. "Do you like him, child?"

"Like him! I perfectly loathe him — but I
can't tell why," she added, in quick apology.
"He's always very kind."

"I don't see how Walter Crowdie can be kind
to my niece," said Robert Lauderdale, with rough
pride. "Anyhow, he wants to get something out
of me. So he's bringing the picture to me this
morning. I told you what I meant to do for them
in my will. I don't see why I should do anything.
They're rich, those people. She had money and
he gets big prices, and I'll do him the credit to
say he's industrious, at all events. He seems to
be a good husband to Hester, too — isn't he?"

"She adores him," answered Katharine.

"Well — I suppose I'm like you. I can't tell
why I dislike the man, but I do. It's a case of

'Doctor Fell.' Yes — there's Crowdie, and the Miners — even Ham Bright — he's always enquiring and leaving cards! As for your father, he writes me long letters once a week, as though I were abroad, and he comes to see me every Sunday afternoon at four o'clock, rain or shine."

"Oh — that's where he goes!" cried Katharine. "I often wondered — he always disappears on Sunday afternoon."

"Yes — he comes here and tells me what a solid thing the Trust Company is, and how he's devoting his life to it, and sacrificing his chances of getting rich, so as to be useful. Oh, it's very fine, I admit. But then, he never says anything about that money of his which he keeps put away. And I never say anything about it, either. What's the use — it would only make him uncomfortable."

"But you're quite sure he has it, uncle Robert, aren't you?" asked Katharine. "You're not doing him an injustice?"

"Yes. I've seen it."

"What — the money? I don't understand."

"I've seen the value of a million of money in United States Bonds, which were the property of your father," answered the old man. "I won't tell you how it happened, because a banker accidentally betrayed your father's confidence. It was at the time of a conversion of bonds, two years ago. For some reason or other, Alexander — your

father — couldn't attend to it, or do it all himself.
I don't know why. Anyhow, he employed a
banker confidentially, and I came to know the fact,
and I saw the bonds. So that settles it. He's not
squandered a million on your clothes in the last
two years, has he, little girl?"

"Hardly!" Katharine laughed. "But mightn't
it have been trust money, or something like that?"

"No. His name was there. He's a careful
man — your father. So it couldn't have been
a trust. Well — I was going through the list,
wasn't I? I haven't half finished. There's your
grandfather. Sandy never had much sense when
he was a boy. He was all heart. I suppose he
knows I'm dying, and wants me to give my soul a
lift in the shape of some liberal contributions to
his charities. I wish you could see the piles of
reports he sends, and letters without end — in his
queer, shaky hand. 'Dear old Bob; what's a
million, more or less, to you, and it would make ten
thousand homes happy.' That's the sort of thing.
Ten thousand idiots! Give them all a hundred
dollars apiece — of course they'd be happy, for a
week or two. Sandy forgets the headaches they'd
have afterwards. He believes everything's good,
and everybody's an angel, more or less disguised,
but recognizable. Well — I suppose it's better to
be an optimist. They're the happy people, after
all."

"Do you think so? I don't know. People who are always happy can't ever feel how happy they are sometimes, as unhappy people do. That's what's so nice about being sad — now and then, when one feels gay, the world's a ball of sunshine. Haven't you felt like that sometimes? I do."

"Sometimes — sometimes," repeated the old man, with a faint smile. "Not lately. I've had so many cares. Great wealth complicates the end of life, Katharine. You'll be very rich. Remember that. Have your fortune settled so that it can be easily handled when you're old. That's what I've done, and it's something, at all events. If I had to be picking up odds and ends and loose threads now, it would be harder than it is. And perhaps I've made a mistake. Perhaps it's better to tell people just what they have to expect. People worry so! Now there are all the Miners' rich relations, you know — the Thirlwalls and the Van De Waters, and all that set. I don't know what they think, I'm sure. They've got heaps of money, and there's no reason on earth why I should leave them a dollar. But they worry. Ruth Van De Water comes and brings flowers — always flowers — I make Leek take them away — I suppose he decorates the pantry with them — and she says her mother would so much like to take me to drive when it's warmer. Why? What for? And one of the Thirlwalls sent me some cigars he'd

brought from Havana with him, and old Mrs.
Trehearne — the one who's 'old' Mrs. Trehearne
now, since her sister-in-law died — didn't she tod-
dle in the other day and say she wanted to talk
about old times! — she's another of those holy
scarecrows that hang round death-beds. Now,
she's nothing on earth to expect of me. It's sheer
love of worry, I believe."

"People may be fond of you for your own sake,"
suggested Katharine. "You don't know how nice
you are! That is — when you like!"

"Well — I don't know. It may be — but I
doubt it. You see, I've had a good deal of experience in the way of being liked."

"Has it been all a bad experience? You can't
tell me that nobody ever liked you for your own
sake — never, at all. I shouldn't believe it. The
world can't be all bad, right through."

"Oh, no! I didn't say that. And I suppose I
shouldn't say anything that looks like cynicism
to you, child. Still, I must say there's a good
deal of personal interest in the affection a rich
man gets. I used to hear that said when I was a
boy, and there's a good deal about it in old-fashioned books, but I didn't believe it. It's money
that makes the world go, Katharine, my dear.
It's love for one year, perhaps, but it's money all
the other sixty-nine out of the seventy. I've seen
a deal of money earned and squandered, and stolen

and wasted in my time, and there's no denying it
— money's the main object. It keeps the world
going, and when it gets stuck in one place, as
it has in my hands, there's an attempt — a natural
attempt, I suppose — to distribute it again. And
if it doesn't get distributed, there's a howl of pain
from all the relations. It's natural — it's natural
— but it doesn't make dying easier."

"Don't talk about dying, uncle dear — there's
no reason for —"

The door opened, and Leek, the butler, appeared.

"Mr. Crowdie asks if you'll see him, sir," he
said. "He says he wrote that he was coming this
morning, sir."

"Yes — yes. I know. Show him in, Leek."
The butler disappeared. "I'm sorry we don't like
him," added the old gentleman, with a rather
weary smile. "But I want to see your picture.
You said it was good?"

"Very."

There was the short silence of expectancy which
precedes the entry of a visitor, and then the door
opened again and Crowdie came in. He was of
average height, but ill made, slightly in-kneed and
weak-shouldered, neither thin nor stout; pale, with
a pear-shaped face and bright red lips, beautiful
brown eyes and silky brown hair which was a little
too long. His hands and feet were small — the

hands being very white, with pointed fingers, and they looked soft. He dressed well.

"It's so kind of you to let me come, sir," he said, as he shook hands. "I hope you're really better. Why, Miss Lauderdale, I didn't expect to see you! How do you do?"

"Thanks — how do you do? I'm staying here, you know."

Old Lauderdale pointed to a seat. He had shaken hands with the painter, but had not spoken.

"Yes," he said, as Crowdie sat down, "as my niece is here, we can compare her with her portrait. I'm very much obliged to you for thinking of giving it to me, I'm sure. I hope you've brought it."

Crowdie had grasped the situation at a glance.

"It was meant for my wife — she's Miss Lauderdale's most intimate friend, you know," he said, with fine frankness. "But we consulted about it, and we decided that I should offer you this one and do another for her from the sketches I have. May I have it brought in? It's rather a big thing, I'm afraid."

"By all means, let's see it," said the old man, touching the bell at his elbow as Crowdie rose. "The men will bring it in all right — you needn't go, Mr. Crowdie."

Crowdie went towards the door, however, with an artist's instinctive anxiety for the safety of his work, and while he was turned away Robert Lauderdale's eyes met Katharine's. They both smiled a little at the same moment, admiring the quick-witted ingenuity with which Crowdie had turned the difficulty of presenting the portrait to the old man while Katharine, to whom he had said that it was for her friend, — his wife, — sat looking on.

Two footmen, marshalled and directed by Leek, brought in the picture.

"Set it up on this arm-chair," said Crowdie. "It will be quite steady — so — a little more to the light — the least bit the other way — that'll do — thanks. Can you see it well?" he asked, turning to the other two.

"It's a good picture, isn't it?" asked Katharine, after they had both gazed at it in silence for a full minute.

"It's wonderful!" exclaimed the old man, in genuine admiration. "It's a great picture, Mr. Crowdie. I congratulate you — and myself — and the young lady here," he added, laying his hand on Katharine's arm as she sat beside him.

Crowdie was pleased. He knew very well, by long experience, when admiration was real and when it was feigned. Of late years, the true note had rarely failed in the chorus of approval. Whatever he might be as a man, he was a thorough artist, and a very good one, too.

"I'm so glad you like it yourself, Miss Lauderdale," he said, coming nearer to her as he spoke. "That's always a test."

"Yes — I do like it. But — I suppose I ought not to criticise — ought I? I don't know anything about it."

"Oh, yes, you do. I should like to hear what you think. You've not seen it for two or three weeks, and then it was in the studio. You've got a new impression of it now. Tell me — won't you?"

"Well — you don't mind? Really not? Then I'll tell you. I think you've put something of Hester into me. Look at it. Do you see it yourself?"

"No — frankly, I don't," answered Crowdie, but a change came over his face as he spoke — a mere shadow of amusement, a slight thickening of the heavy red lips.

"It's in the eyes and the mouth," continued Katharine. "I don't know exactly what it is, but it reminds me of Hester in such an odd way — as I've seen her look sometimes. There's a little sort of drawing down of the eyelids at the corners and up in the middle, with a kind of passionate, longing look she has now and then. Don't you see it? And the mouth — I don't know — it reminds me of her, too — the lips just parted a little — as though they wanted something — the way one looks at big strawberries on the table before they're served — " Katharine laughed.

"Yes — but that's just the way you looked," protested Crowdie. "Doesn't Miss Lauderdale raise her eyes just in that way, Mr. Lauderdale?" he asked, turning to the old gentleman.

"Oh, no!" laughed Katharine. "I never look like that. I keep my mouth shut and glare straight at people."

"It seems to me to be very like," said the old man, bending forward with his great head on one side and his hands on his knees, as he looked at the portrait.

"It's a great picture, anyway — whether it's like me or not," said Katharine.

She was too unaffected to make any foolish remarks about being flattered too much. She accepted the fact that she was good-looking, and said nothing about it. Crowdie reflected for a moment, wishing to turn a graceful compliment upon her last speech, but he could think of nothing new. His mind was preoccupied by the discovery she had made of a fact by no means new to himself nor, perhaps, wholly unintentional.

"Where shall we hang it, Mr. Crowdie?" asked the old gentleman, at last.

"Ah — that's an important question. Where should you like it, sir?"

Crowdie occasionally introduced a 'sir' when

he addressed the millionaire, by way of hinting, perhaps, that he considered him to be the head of the family, though his only connection was through his wife, and that was a distant one. Hester Crowdie's maternal great-grandfather had been Robert Lauderdale's uncle.

"I should like it near me," said the old man. "Couldn't we have it in this room?"

"Why not? Just where it is, if you like it there. I'll get you an easel and a bit of stuff to drape it with in an hour."

"An easel? H'm — that's not very neat, is it? An easel out in the middle of the room — I don't know how that would look."

"What difference does it make — if you'd like it here?" asked Katharine.

"That's true, child — why shouldn't I have what I like?" asked the old millionaire.

Crowdie laughed.

"If anybody has the right and the power to please himself, you have," he said. "Miss Lauderdale, would you mind sitting down beside the picture for a moment? I want to have a good look at it once more — I should just like to see if I can find that resemblance to Hester."

"Certainly."

Katharine sat down, assuming easily enough the attitude she had been accustomed to during a number of sittings. Crowdie drew back and looked at her. Then he came to her again and put out his hand towards her hair, but instantly withdrew it.

"I remember," he said, quickly, but in a low voice. "You don't like me to touch it. Would you raise your hair a little — on the sides? You know how it was."

She looked up into his face and saw the expression she detested — a sort of disagreeable smile on the heavy red lips. The feeling of repulsion was so strong that she almost shivered. Crowdie drew back and looked again.

"I can't see it — for the life of me!" said Crowdie, with a little laugh. "If you'll excuse me, Mr. Lauderdale, I'll go and get the easel at once."

"Yes — do!" said Katharine.

"Well — but — won't you stay to luncheon, Mr. Crowdie?" asked the old man.

"Thanks — I should like to — but I've got a sitter coming. You're very kind. I'll bring the easel myself."

"Thank you very much. See you by and by, then," answered Mr. Lauderdale.

When Crowdie was gone, the old man looked long and earnestly at the picture. Gradually what Katharine meant by the resemblance to Hester dawned upon him, and he knit his bushy white eyebrows.

"I'm sorry you told me," he said, at last. "I see it now — what you mean — and I don't like it."

"Somehow — I don't know — it looks like a woman who's been through something — I don't know exactly what. Perhaps it is like an older woman — a married woman."

"H'm — perhaps so. I think it is. Anyhow, I don't like it."

CHAPTER XI.

It was the habit of Robert Lauderdale, since he had been ill, to rest two hours before dinner, a fact of which Katharine was well aware, and she had sent a message to John Ralston begging him to come and see her when he came up town after business hours. But she did not mean to let him come without informing the old gentleman. Before he retired to his room late in the afternoon, she spoke to him about it.

"Of course, of course, my dear," he answered quickly, in his hollow voice. "He may spend the day here, if he likes — and if you like."

"Well, you see," said Katharine, "I've not seen him since yesterday morning. You know, since he's been going regularly to business, he's not free in the daytime as he used to be. And as for letting him come to Clinton Place when papa's at home, it's simply out of the question."

"Is it? Do you mean to say it's as bad as that?"

"Yes — it's pretty bad," Katharine answered, thoughtfully. "We've not been getting on very well, papa and I. That's why I came to you so suddenly to-day, without warning. My mother thought it would be better."

"Oh — she did, did she?" The old man closed his eyes, as though thinking it over. "And she's generally a peacemaker," he continued, after a moment. "That's a sign that she thinks the situation strained, as the politicians say. What's happened, little girl?"

"I don't want to tell you all the details. It's a long story, and wouldn't interest you. But they got it into their heads that I ought to marry Mr. Wingfield — you know — Archie Wingfield — the beauty — and of course I refused him. That was yesterday afternoon. And then — oh, I don't know — there was a scene, and papa got angry, and so this morning after he'd gone down town I consulted with my mother and came here. I only wanted you to know — that's all."

The old gentleman was silent for some time after she had finished speaking.

"I wish you'd induce Jack to stay here, and announce your marriage under my roof," he said at last, in a low voice. "I'd like to see it all settled before — Katharine, child, feel my pulse, will you?"

Katharine started a little, and leaned forward quickly, and laid her firm white fingers on the bony wrist.

"Can you find it?" he asked, rather anxiously.

"No — yes — wait a moment — don't speak!"
She held her breath, her eyes fixed upon his grey
face as she pressed the point where she thought
the pulse should be. "Yes — there it is!" she
exclaimed suddenly, in a tone of relief. "It's all
right, uncle Robert, only I couldn't find it at first.
I can feel it quite distinctly now. Does it always
go so fast as that?"

"It's going very fast, isn't it? I have a little
fluttering — at my heart."

"Shan't I send for Doctor Routh?" asked Katharine, with renewed anxiety.

"Oh, no — it's no use." His voice was growing
perceptibly more feeble. "I shall be better presently," he whispered, and closed his eyes again.
Then, as though fearing lest his whisper should
frighten her, he made an effort and spoke aloud
again. "It often happens," he said. "Don't be
afraid, little girl."

Katharine had no experience of sickness, and
did not know the danger of that fluttering at the
heart in such a case. She thought he knew better
than she whether he needed anything or not, and
that it would be wiser not to annoy him with
questions. She was used to manly men who said
what they wished and nothing more. He lay
back in his big chair, breathing with some difficulty. A deep furrow appeared between his eyebrows, which gave his face an expression of pain,

and his jaw dropped a little, making his cheeks look more hollow. Katharine sat quite still for several minutes.

"Are you suffering, uncle dear?" she asked at last, bending to his ear.

He shook his head slowly, opened his eyes a little and closed them again.

"I shall be better in a minute," he said, a moment later.

He revived very slowly, as she sat there watching him, and as the furrow disappeared from his brow and his mouth closed, the look of life came back to his face. He was a strong old man, and, though little attached to life, was to die hard. He opened his eyes at last and looked at Katharine, smiling a little.

"I think I'll go to my room," he said. "It's my time for resting, you know. Perhaps I've been up a little too long."

To Katharine's surprise, he was able to stand when Leek and the footman came to help him, and to walk without much difficulty. She followed the little procession to the door of his bedroom and saw Mrs. Deems come and take charge of him. He turned his head slowly towards Katharine and smiled before the door closed.

"It's all right, little girl," he said.

She went downstairs again and returned to the library. It faced the south and was still warm with the sunshine. She sat down again in the chair she had occupied before. Presently her eyes turned instinctively to her portrait. Crowdie had brought the easel while she and her uncle had been at luncheon, and had arranged it himself. He had come into the dining-room, and after exchanging a few more words, had gone away again.

She gazed at the beautiful features, now that she was alone with it, and the feeling of dislike and repulsion grew stronger, till she felt something like what she experienced when she looked at Crowdie's pale face and red mouth. She felt that he had put something into the painting which had no right there, which he had no right to imagine — yet she could not tell what it was. Presently she rose and glanced round the room in search of a looking-glass. But old Lauderdale did not like mirrors, and there was none in the library. On the table, however, stood a photograph of herself in a silver frame. She seized it as soon as she saw it and held it up in her hand, comparing it with the portrait. She found it hard to tell where the difference lay, unless it was in the eyelids and the slight parting of the lips, but she felt it and disliked it more and more.

At that moment the door was opened by one of the footmen.

"Mr. Ralston," said the man, announcing John, who entered immediately afterwards.

The door closed behind him as he came forward. Katharine's heart jumped, as she became conscious of his presence. It was as though a strong current of life had been turned upon her after having been long alone with death. Ralston moved easily, with the freedom that comes naturally of good proportions. His bright brown eyes gleamed with pleasure, and the hard, defiant lines of the lean face relaxed in a rare smile.

He kissed her tenderly, with a nervous, passionate lightness that belongs only to finely organized beings, twice or three times. And then she kissed him once with all her heart, and looked into the eyes she loved.

"How good it is to have this chance!" he exclaimed, happily. "This is better than South Fifth Avenue at nine o'clock in the morning — isn't it? Why didn't we think of it before?"

"I can't be always stopping with uncle Robert, you know," answered Katharine. "I wish I could."

Something in the tone of the last words attracted his attention. With a gentle touch he made her turn her face to the light, and looked at her.

"What's happened?" he asked, suddenly. "There's been some trouble, I know. Tell me — you've had more worry at home, haven't you?"

"Oh — it's nothing!" Katharine answered, lightly. "You see how easy it is for me to get away. What does it matter?"

"Yes — but there has been something," insisted John, shaking his head. "I don't like this, Katharine."

He turned away from her, and his eyes fell upon the portrait. It instantly fixed his attention.

"Holloa!" he exclaimed. "Why is it here? I thought it was for Hester."

Katharine laughed.

"He brought it this morning," she answered. "He's changed his mind, and has given it to uncle Robert. How do you like it?"

John looked at it long, his eyelids drooping a little. When he turned his head, he looked directly at Katharine's mouth critically.

"You haven't got a mouth like that," he said, suddenly. "And I never saw that expression in your eyes, either," he added, a moment later. "What's the fellow been doing?"

"I don't know, Jack. But I don't like it. I'm sure of that, at all events."

"Does uncle Robert like it?"

"No. He's anything but pleased, though he thought it splendid at first. Then he saw what you and I see. It wasn't so in the studio, it seems to me. He's done something to it since. Never mind the picture, Jack. Sit down, and let's talk, since we've got a chance at last."

John's eyes lingered on the portrait a moment longer, then he turned away with an impatient movement, and sat down beside Katharine. He stroked her hand gently two or three times, and neither said anything. Then he leaned back in his straight chair and crossed one knee over the other.

"Somebody's trying to get me out of Beman's," he said, and his face darkened. "I wish I knew who it was."

"Trying to get you out of the bank?" repeated Katharine, in surprise. "Oh, Jack, you must be mistaken."

Jack laughed a little without smiling.

"There's no mistake," he said. "Mr. Beman as good as told me so this morning. We came near having a row."

"Tell me all about it," said Katharine, anxiously, and leaning forward in sympathy. "It's outrageous — whoever has done it."

"Yes, I'll tell you," said John. "It was this way. In the first place, I went to the Vanbrughs' last night, after all."

"But you said you weren't asked! I'd have gone, too — why didn't you send me word? At least — I'd have tried to go," she added, recollecting that she had spent the evening in her room.

"I found a note when I came up town. It was very informal, you know."

"Yes — they only asked me the day before," said Katharine. "It must have been very amusing. They were going to do all sorts of things."

"If you'd been there, I should have enjoyed it," answered John. "Yes, they did all sorts of things — improvised charades and tableaux — Crowdie was there, and Griggs, and the set. The best thing was a tableau of Francesca da Rimini. Hester was Francesca — you know her eyes. There they are!" he exclaimed, looking at the portrait. "And they made me do Paolo, and Griggs murdered me — "

"Fancy your acting in a tableau!" exclaimed Katharine.

"I never did before — but it was all improvised. Griggs looked awfully dangerous with a black beard and a dagger. Of course I couldn't see myself, but they said I was dark and thin and would do; so I did it, just to make the thing go. It was rather fun — but I kept watching the door to see if you weren't coming. Well — the end of it was that we stayed very late. You know what a fellow Vanbrugh is — he's a criminal lawyer, of all things — and he knows all kinds of people. There was an actor and any number of musical people, and that Russian pianist — what's his name? — Bezpodobny, or something like that. And we had supper, and then we got to smoking — two or three of the women stayed. You know Dolly Vanbrugh likes smoke, and so does Hester. I smoked some horrible Caporal cigarettes, and they gave me a headache. But I didn't drink anything — "

"I know, dear," said Katharine, softly.

No one knew better than she what he had done for her sake, and how faithfully he was keeping his word.

"Well — I got a headache, much worse than if I'd had a lot of champagne and things. I shall have to live on milk and water and barley sugar if I get much worse. I'm so nervous since — since I gave up all those things. But it will go off — I've asked Routh, and he says it's natural — "

"You didn't tell me," said Katharine, anxiously. "Why didn't you?"

"Oh — why should I? He came to the house — he adores my mother, you know, dear old man — so I just asked him. Well — this morning I felt rather fuzzy in the head — woolly, don't you know. And of course I got up early, as usual, though it was awfully late when I got to bed. And then I saw no red ribbon in your window — and that put me into a bad temper, so that altogether I wasn't in the humour to be bothered much when I got to the bank. It happened that there wasn't much for me to do at first, and so I did it, and got it out of the way, and I sat doing nothing — just like this — look here!"

He rose, and went and sat down at the chair before the great writing-table, on the side away from Katharine. He planted his elbows on the big sheet of blotting paper, and bending down his head, clasped his hands over his forehead in the attitude of a man whose head hurts him.

"Do you see?" he asked, looking up at Katharine. "My head really ached, and I'd nothing to do for a quarter of an hour, so it was quite natural."

"Of course! Why not? Do you have to sit up straight at the bank, like school-children?"

"Well — old Beman seemed to think so. He came loping along — he has a funny walk, you know — and I didn't see him. He doesn't often come out. So he'd stopped right in front of me before I knew he was there. I looked up suddenly when I heard him speak, and I jumped up. He asked what the matter was, and I told him I had a headache, which was rash, I suppose, considering my reputation. Then he asked me why I was doing nothing, and I told him I'd finished what had been given me and was waiting for more. He grunted in a displeased sort of way, and went off. Then my head hurt me worse than ever, and I put my hands up to my forehead again. In about five minutes, back comes old Beman, and wants to see me in his room. What do you think he said? 'An old and valued friend had warned him that I had intemperate habits.' That was a pleasant way of opening the interview. Then he went on to say that he had paid no attention to the old and valued friend's

warning, but that I was so evidently suffering from
the effects of over-indulgence this morning that he
felt it his duty to say that he could not tolerate
dissipated idlers in his house — or words to that
purpose — and that as he had already convinced
himself by a previous trial — that was a year ago,
you know — that I had no taste for work, he
begged me to consider myself as free from any
engagement on the first of next month — which
struck me as unnecessary warning, considering that
I get no salary. That's what happened."

"It's abominable!" cried Katharine. "It's outrageous! But you didn't take it quietly, like that,
Jack? You said something?"

"Oh, yes — I said something — several things.
I told him quite frankly about myself — how I'd
been rather lively, but had given it all up months
ago. It's awful, how a thing like that sticks to
one, Katharine! He was virtuously civil — but I
can't help liking old Beman, all the same. He
didn't believe a word I said. So I told him to
ask Ham Bright, who's their junior partner and
is privileged to be believed. Unfortunately, Ham
didn't go to the Vanbrughs' last night and couldn't
have sworn to the facts. But that makes no difference. Of course, a year ago I'd have walked out
of Beman's then and there, if he'd said such
things to me, though I suppose they were true
then, more or less. It's different now — a good

deal depends on it, and I mean to convince the old gentleman and stay. I don't want him to bring any tales — lies, especially — to uncle Robert, who got me in. But it's a wonder we didn't throttle each other in his office this morning. I take some credit to myself for having behaved so well. But I confess I should like to know who the 'old and valued friend' is. I'd like to be alone with him for a few moments."

"Yes," said Katharine, thoughtfully. "I wish I knew. Oh, Jack, what a shame!" she cried, with sudden vehemence. "When you've been trying so hard, and have succeeded so well! Oh — those are the sins people are burned everlastingly for — those mean, back-biting, busy-body sins, dressed up in virtue and friendship!"

"I hadn't thought about the everlasting side of it. I should be quite satisfied to see the individual burn for three-quarters of an hour here."

"Jack — " Katharine's face changed suddenly, as though something that shocked her had been forced upon her mind.

"Yes — what is it? Have you guessed who it is? Do you know anything about it? Tell me!"

"I think I know," she answered, in a low voice, as though horrorstruck by the discovery. "I'm not sure — oh, Jack! It's awful!"

"What's awful? Who do you think it is?"

"No — I won't tell you. I may be wrong, you

know, and one has no right to condemn people on
a guess. But if it were —" She stopped.

"You mean your father?" asked Ralston.
"Don't you?"

Katharine was silent. She gave no sign of
assent or dissent, but looked straight into John's
eyes.

"Of course you do!" he exclaimed. "He was
in the bank the day before yesterday. Don't you
know? I told you I saw him. And he was alone
with Mr. Beman in his room. I say — Katharine
— if it is, you know —"

He did not complete the sentence, but his lower
jaw went out viciously as his lips closed. Not
knowing all that had passed between Katharine
and her father, he had not suspected the latter at
first. It was only when he remembered that he
had told Katharine of his appearance at the bank,
which she must remember, that he understood what
she meant.

"I'm not sure, Jack," she said. "Don't imagine that I'm sure."

"All right — I'll ask Mr. Beman —"

"Don't!" cried Katharine, in sudden anxiety.

"Why not? He's got no right to conceal the
name of a man who libels me. I shall tell him
that I wish to be confronted with his informant,
and that as a gentleman he's bound to give me the
chance of justifying myself. Of course he'll **say**

that he can't send for Mr. Lauderdale to discuss a clerk's character. Then I think I'll take Ham Bright with me and go round to the Trust Company. It won't take a quarter of an hour."

"Of course you have a right to, Jack," said Katharine. "Only, I hope you won't do that. I'm not cowardly, you know, am I? But if you knew what it meant to live in a permanent tempest—"

"Has he been tormenting you again?" asked Ralston, quickly, and forgetting his own troubles at the mention of hers.

She would have told him everything, and it might have been better if she had. But he had frightened her on the previous day by threatening to insist on announcing their marriage if she were further troubled at home. She thought it wiser to turn back to the original point.

"If I were sure that it was papa who spoke to Mr. Beman, I could never be civil to him again," she said. "Can you imagine anything much worse? I can't. But you're quite right to try and stay at Beman's. It means a great deal to uncle Robert—your sticking to regular work, don't you see?"

"I don't know what will happen when he dies," said Ralston, thoughtfully. "Nobody else will ever do anything for me, when he's gone."

"No," answered Katharine, suppressing a smile

at the thought of what she knew, "nobody else will do anything. Let's hope that uncle Robert will live long enough to see you succeed. But do you know, Jack, I'm anxious about him. Of course Doctor Routh tells him he'll get quite well again, and I daresay he will, but I can't help feeling sometimes, when I'm with him — " she hesitated. " He's very old, you know," she added.

They talked for some time of the old gentleman's condition, and he would have been pleased, could he have heard them, at their genuine hope for his recovery. It would have balanced the sentiments of some other members of the family as he had described them to Katharine that morning. They had much to say to one another, and as there was no especial reason why John should go away, he stayed, overjoyed at his good fortune in being able to talk with her at last without the fear of interruption and of exciting attention, which beset them when they met at parties.

It was growing late, and the sunshine had turned red and was fading from the splendid old books on the east wall of the room, when the door opened and Leek appeared.

"Mr. Alexander Lauderdale wishes to speak with you, Miss Katharine," he said, and then glanced discreetly at Ralston.

It is necessary to say that Leek was almost as thoroughly acquainted with the state of the family's affairs as any member of it, and that Alexander's dislike of John was perfectly well known to him.

Katharine stopped in the middle of a phrase, as though she had been struck. Ralston looked at the butler and then at Katharine, wondering what she would say. The library, constructed with a view to avoiding draughts, had only one door, which led into the hall, so that John could not go out without meeting Alexander. Katharine had not believed that her father would come to make trouble under his uncle's roof, but he was well acquainted with the old gentleman's habits, and knew that he would be resting at that hour. It was a difficult situation.

"I don't know what to do," said Katharine, in a low voice, helpless, at first. "I can't refuse to see him, since he knows I'm in. Can't you get out of the room, Jack?"

"There's no other door," answered Ralston, looking about. "Face it out. Let him come in!"

"I daren't — he'll make another scene —"

"Not before me — if he begins, I'll make him stop. You can't send him away," he lowered his voice to a whisper. "Imagine what that man would think, and what he'd tell the other servants. That settles it."

Leek stood motionless by the door during the colloquy, which he could not overhear, though he knew exactly what the two were saying. Katharine hesitated a moment longer, and then gave the order.

"Ask my father to go into the drawing-room," she said. "I'll come in a moment."

Ralston laughed softly as Leek disappeared.

"What idiots we were — of course!" he said. "As though there were only one room. Look here, Katharine," he continued, taking her hand as she rose, "I could slip out while you're in there, but I'm not going to. I want to see you afterwards. I'll wait here."

"Do!" answered Katharine. "I shall feel better if I know you're here. Not that I'm frightened — but — you understand."

"Perfectly," answered Ralston, looking at her.

She left the room and he closed the door behind her. She found her father standing in the middle of the great drawing-room, in the evening light, holding his hat, and still wearing his thin black overcoat, as though he did not mean to stay long — an observation which reassured her. But his face was dark and angry and his lips looked dry and cold. She stood still at a little distance from him.

"Katharine, what is the meaning of this?" he asked, sternly. "Why are you here?"

"You know why I'm here, papa," answered Katharine, quietly, for she was determined, if possible, to avoid an angry altercation.

"I suppose you mean that you've come here because I locked you in your room this morning. I don't consider that a reason."

"I think you'll admit that you acted hastily," said Katharine. "Besides, have you any objection to my paying uncle Robert a visit ? I've been here before in the same way, you know. You always seemed pleased. Won't you sit down?"

She was trying to be civil, but he was in no humour to court civility. He paid no attention to her invitation, but remained standing in the middle of the room.

"You understood perfectly well why I locked the door this morning," he said. "It's of no use to say that I acted hastily. I intended that you should feel my authority, and you shall. One of us two must be master. I'll not be browbeaten, and contradicted, and disobeyed by my own daughter, besides submitting to any language she chooses to apply to me."

"Do you propose to take me back by force?" asked Katharine, with a smile. "You know it's impossible. Or do you mean to argue with me? You won't convince me, and you ought to see that you can't."

"In other words, you've left your father's house without warning, and not meaning to come back," answered Alexander Junior, coldly.

"Not at all. I came here, with my mother's

consent, to make a visit. When you agree to treat me properly, I'll come back. I certainly won't stay where I'm liable to be locked up in my room by you at your discretion. It's not safe. You didn't even leave the key in the house, so that they might have brought me something to eat if I hadn't been able to get out."

"You did get out."

"By a mere chance. There happened to be a key which fitted the lock, or I might be there still."

"It's where you should be. How long is this state of war to last? Do you think I'll endure it much longer? You're mistaken."

"I don't see what you can do, if you won't treat me like a human being. Possibly you may get to the end of my patience, too."

"Do you mean to threaten me? Me!" Alexander's face darkened visibly, and he drew himself up to his full height.

"I don't know," answered Katharine, keeping her temper. "I might think it worth while to explain to uncle Robert, you know. I don't think that he'd be particularly pleased if he knew all you've done. I merely told him that it wasn't very peaceful in our house just now, as you wanted me to marry Mr. Wingfield, and I wouldn't. I've not told him anything else — but I might, you know. I'm likely to be with him most of the day. I imagine you'd rather not offend uncle Robert."

Katharine was not prepared for the effect produced by this speech, which was diametrically opposite to the result she had expected. She had imagined that a reference to the will would act directly upon her father's love of money and make him cautious. Instead of this, however, he grew more angry.

"If you insult me in this way again, I shall certainly use force," he said, in a harsh way. "You're not of age, and I believe that the law can constrain you to obey me, and the police will act with the law. How do you dare to tell me that you can frighten uncle Robert into changing his will! You're going a little further than yesterday. I've warned you to be careful. It's your own fault if you go too far. The nearest Justice of the Peace will give me an order to remove you to your home in an hour. Don't exasperate me! Put on your things and come quietly with me. If you refuse, I'll act at once. You shall come. I say it, and I won't be disobeyed."

"And I won't be threatened," answered Katharine, with a rising intonation. "As for your getting any order to remove me, as you call it, I doubt whether you could. I rather think that uncle Robert is a much more powerful person than you are, and that your policemen would think twice before trying to force their way into his house. Don't you think so yourself?"

Her anger was up, too, and her mother was not there to come between them. She forgot that the door of the drawing-room opened upon the same hall as the library, but that it was not closed except by a heavy curtain.

"And as for your saying that I've gone a little further than yesterday," she continued, her deep voice rising strong and clear in the big room, "you've gone further, too. You've been trying to hurt me by hurting the man I love. You've been to Mr. Beman, and you've told him that Jack is dissipated. Yes — I thought so — it was you who said it. You can't deny it."

"Certainly not!" exclaimed Alexander. "I was quite right to warn an old acquaintance against employing such a fellow. He's a discredit to the bank, he's a — "

"Stop, papa! I forbid you to say such things — "

Alexander's great voice suddenly broke out like thunder.

"You! You forbid me to say what I please! I say that John Ralston's a reprobate, a man not fit to be received in decent society, a low drunkard — "

"Oh! Is that what you say?" John Ralston

drew aside the curtain, and entered the room as he spoke.

Katharine turned pale, but her father was no coward. His steely eyes fixed themselves on John's face.

CHAPTER XII.

As Alexander Junior came towards him, John Ralston advanced from the door. Katharine placed herself between them, very much as her mother had come between her father and herself on the previous afternoon. But Ralston laid his hand gently on her arm, and drew her back.

"Please go into the library, Katharine," he said.

"No, no!" she cried, in answer. "I can't leave you together — so."

"Please go!" he repeated. "I'm angry — I must speak — I can't before you."

He pushed her with tender anxiety towards the door, and she felt his hand tremble on her arm. She yielded after a little hesitation, but paused as she reached the curtain, and looked back. John went on and faced Alexander, supposing that Katharine had left the room.

"So it was you who spoke to Mr. Beman about me," said Ralston, in a tone of menace.

"You're an eavesdropper, sir," answered Alexander Junior, with contempt.

"As you were shouting, and the door was open, I couldn't help hearing what you said, Mr. Lauderdale. I was anxious about Katharine, and had come into the hall."

"Then you've heard my opinion of you. You're not likely to change it by trying to browbeat me."

"I'm not browbeating you, as you call it. You've been saying things about me which are untrue. You've got to take them back."

Alexander Lauderdale drew himself up to his height, resting one clenched hand upon his hip. The other held his hat. He looked a dangerous adversary as he stood there, lean and steely, his firm face set like an angry mask, his broad shoulders square and black against the evening light.

"It occurs to me to ask how you propose to make me take back anything I've said," he answered.

Ralston looked at him quietly for several seconds, as a man looks who measures another's strength. Not that he had the slightest thought of violence, even then; but he was a born fighter as much as Alexander, if not more so. His instinct was always to strike rather than speak, in any quarrel. In a hand-to-hand encounter he would have been overmatched by the elder man, and he knew it. But that was not the reason why he lowered his voice and tried to speak more calmly, instead of growing hotter in altercation.

"You've done me a very great injustice, and

you've almost done me a serious injury — perhaps you really have, for Mr. Beman has turned me out," he said. "It's customary, I think, for people like us to repair such injuries as well as they can."

"You've injured yourself by your habits," answered Alexander. "I've a perfect right to say so. Don't contest it."

"It's contestable, at all events. I'm willing to admit that I've been what's called dissipated. More than most men, I daresay."

"That's undeniable, and that's precisely what I said, or words to the same effect."

"I think not. You were telling Katharine just now that I was a drunkard and a reprobate. I've not touched wine for months, and as for being a reprobate — it's a strong word, but rather vague. Since you've used it, please define what you mean by it."

"It's a general term of disapprobation which I applied to you because I think you're a bad character."

"Accusations of that sort have to be supported. You must go with me to Mr. Beman to-morrow, and repeat what you've said."

"Indeed? I shall do nothing of the kind."

"If Mr. Beman asks you to do it, you'll have to — at the risk of losing your character for truthfulness."

"Are you calling me a liar?" asked Alexander, and his voice rose angrily as he stepped forward.

"No," answered Ralston, calmly, but in a doubtful tone. "I'm not. But you've made an accusation, and if you fail to prove it, Mr. Beman will form his opinion about you. I formed mine long ago. I'm turning out to be right."

"I'm quite indifferent to your opinion," said Alexander, contemptuously. "And you're not in a position to influence that of lifelong friends like Mr. Beman. We'd better end this discussion at once. It can lead to nothing."

Katharine, who still stood by the door, her hand on the curtain, devoutly wished that in this, at least, John would follow her father's suggestion. She had a woman's instinctive fear of violence between men — a fear, strange to say, which has a fascination in it. If John had been inwardly as calm as he outwardly appeared to be, he would undoubtedly have seen that Alexander was right in this. But the insulting words which he had inevitably overheard rankled, as well they might, and against all probability of success, he still hoped that Alexander would make some acknowledgment of having been in the wrong. He thrust his hands into his pockets and made two or three steps, his head bent in thought. Then he turned upon his adversary suddenly again.

"Do you know — or don't you — that I've given up wine since last winter?" he enquired.

"I've heard it stated," answered Alexander. "I don't know it."

"Well — it's true. I tell you so now. I suppose you'll make no further difficulty about taking back what you said to Katharine just now — that I'm a drunkard?"

"If you have given up wine, you are certainly not a drunkard — at present. That's axiomatic." Alexander sneered.

"Will you remove the condition? I say that I have given up wine."

"I should hesitate to accept your unsupported evidence."

"In other words, you don't admit that I'm speaking the truth? Is that what you mean to say? Yes, or no."

"I don't accept your unsupported evidence," repeated Alexander, pleased with his own phrase.

"Do you know what you're saying? It's simply stating that I'm not to be believed. You can't put any other meaning upon your words."

"I don't wish to," answered Alexander, driven to stand by what he had said, but conscious that he had gone too far.

A pause followed. John was very pale. Alexander Lauderdale's face was dark with the blood that rose slowly under the grey olive skin. The hand that held his hat swung quickly by his side

once or twice. Ralston's fingers twitched nervously. By the door, Katharine held her breath.

"Look here, Mr. Lauderdale," said John, in a
low voice. "I'm not going to strike you here, but
when I meet you in the street I will."

"Jack! Jack!" cried Katharine, rushing forward and catching his arm, and throwing the other
of her own round his neck.

She knew how much stronger her father was
than he. At the sight of her, the deep red colour
appeared at last in Alexander's face, and his anger
got the better of him altogether.

"Take your arms from that man's neck!" he
cried, furiously. "Don't touch him, I say!"

But Katharine did not release her hold. A
woman's idea of protecting a man is to wind herself round him, so as to make him perfectly helpless to defend himself.

"Let me go, dear," said Ralston, in a voice suddenly tender, but trembling a little.

"Katharine! Go, I say!" The white of Alexander's eyes was bloodshot.

But Katharine tried to drag John back from him
as he advanced.

"Go! Leave the room!" cried Alexander,
roughly.

With a quick movement he seized her arm,
almost where he had grasped it on the previous
day, and he tried to pull her away from Ralston.
His strong hand hurt her. At the same time Rals-

ton, not seeing how tightly Alexander held her,
tried to disengage himself from her, as gently as
he could. The struggle was not apparently violent, yet Katharine was exerting all her strength
to cling to Ralston.

The floor, under the Persian rug, was highly
polished. As Katharine stood, overbalanced in
her strained position, the carpet slipped under her
feet. With a short, half-suppressed cry, more of
surprise than of fear, she relaxed her hands, fell
sideways, and swung downward, her arm still in
her father's iron grip. To tell the truth, he was
trying to hold her up, though in reality he had
thrown her down. Suddenly she uttered a pierc-
ing scream, and turned livid, as she fell upon the
floor, and her father let go her arm.

At the same instant John Ralston struck Alexander Lauderdale a violent blow on the mouth,
which sent the taller man staggering back two
paces. It all happened in an instant. Alexander
sprang forward again instinctively, and struck at
John, who dodged the blow and closed with him.
They were better matched at wrestling than with
fists, for Ralston, though less strong by far, was
the quicker, and had the advantage of youth.
They swayed and twisted upon each other, the two
lean, tough men, like tigers.

Katharine struggled to her feet. In getting up
she tried to use her right hand, and uttered another

cry of pain, as her weight rested on it a moment in making the effort. It was quite powerless.

In a few seconds the room was full of people. Katharine's scream had echoed through the open door all over the house. The butler, the footmen, and the housemaids flocked in. The cry was heard even in Robert Lauderdale's bedroom, and he was not asleep.

The old man started, listened, and raised himself on his elbow, at the same time touching the bell by which he called his nurse. She had gone out upon the landing, to try and find out what was the matter, but ran back at the sound of the bell.

"What is it? What's happened?" asked old Lauderdale, and there was an unwonted colour in his face.

"I don't know, Mr. Lauderdale," answered the nurse, a calm, ugly, middle-aged woman from New England. "It was a woman's voice. Shall I go and ask?"

"No—no!" he cried, huskily. "It was my niece—help me up, Mrs. Deems—help me up. I'll go as I am."

He was clad in loose garments of white velvet —the only luxurious fancy of his old age. He got up on his feet, steadying himself by the nurse's arm.

"Let me ring for the men, Mr. Lauderdale," she said, rather anxiously.

"No, no! I can go so, if you'll help me a little — oh, God! The child must be hurt! Quick, Mrs. Deems — I can walk quicker than this — hold your arm a little higher, please. Yes — we shall get along nicely so — why didn't I have a lift in the house! I was always so strong! Quickly, Mrs. Deems — quickly."

When Robert Lauderdale entered the drawing-room, he saw a crowd of people gathering together round something which they hid from him.

"Go away! Go away!" he cried, in his hollow, broken voice.

The servants fell back at the voice of the master, only the butler remaining at hand. Katharine was lying back in a deep arm-chair, her broken arm resting upon a little table which had been hastily pushed to her side. John Ralston was bending over it, and looking at it rather helplessly, as pale as death. Opposite him, on Katharine's left, stood her father, his face still darkly flushed, his lips swollen and purple from Ralston's blow.

"Clear the room — and send for Doctor Routh," said old Lauderdale, turning his head a little towards Leek as he passed him.

"Yes, sir."

"I'm afraid it's broken," Ralston was saying, and his hands trembled violently as he softly passed them over Katharine's arm.

Mrs. Deems was already undoing the buttons of

the tight sleeve which chanced to be the fashion at that time. Robert Lauderdale pushed Alexander aside, and bent down over the chair, supporting himself with his hands.

"Katharine — little girl — you're hurt, dear," he said, as gently as his hoarseness would let him speak. "How did it happen?"

"It won't be anything," she said, in answer, shaking her head and trying to smile.

"How did it happen?" repeated the old man, standing up again, and steadying himself, as he looked anxiously at Ralston.

But Ralston did not answer at once. Across the old gentleman's shoulder his eyes met Alexander's for an instant.

"Are you going to tell what you did, or shall I?" he asked, fiercely.

"What? What?" asked old Robert, in surprise. "What's this?" He looked from one to the other.

"Well —" Alexander began, "it's rather hard to explain —"

"You're mistaken," interrupted Ralston, promptly. "It's perfectly simple. You threw Katharine down, and she broke her arm."

"You — threw Katharine — down!" repeated the old man, the first words spoken in wonder, the last in wrath.

"Not at all, uncle Robert," protested Alexander.

"Do you suppose for a moment that I'm such a man as to —"

"I don't care what sort of man you are!" retorted Robert Lauderdale. "If you've laid hands on Katharine, you shall leave the house — for the last time. Tell me what happened, Jack — Katharine — both of you!"

"We quarrelled and didn't see Katharine," said John, his brown eyes on fire. "She thought we'd fight, and ran forward and held me round the neck to keep us apart. Her father dragged her away violently and she fell. Then I hit him."

"I didn't drag her violently —"

"Katharine — isn't that what happened?" asked Ralston.

Old Lauderdale bent down towards her again — but there was no need of looking into her eyes to find the truth there. Her only thought was for Ralston, and he was speaking the truth. She loved him as few women love. She had loved him through good and evil report, with all her soul. And she was ruthless of others, as loving women are. For his sake, she would have sent her father to the gallows, if he had done murder, and if the one word which might have saved him could have done Ralston the least hurt.

"It's exactly as Jack says," she answered, in clear tones. "He pulled me from Jack and threw me down."

Then the old man's wrath broke out like flame.
But there was a little pause first. The blood
rushed to his pale cheeks, his bony hands were
clenched, and the old veins swelled to bursting in
his throat and at his temples. The broken, harsh
voice thundered and crashed as he cursed his
nephew.

"God damn you, sir! Leave my house this
instant!"

Alexander Lauderdale Junior had got his deserts
and more also, and he knew it. But he stood still
where he was.

"It's useless to argue with a man in your
state —" he began.

"Are you going, you damned coward?" roared
old Robert. "Ring the bell, Jack — send for the
men — turn that brute out —"

He was beside himself with rage, but John
glanced at Alexander, and then walked slowly
towards the nearest bell. He was not inclined to
spare the man who had injured Katharine. Perhaps most men in his position would have carried
out the orders of the master of the house. Seeing
that he was in the act to press the button, Alexander yielded. It was not at all probable that the
millionaire's half dozen Englishmen would disobey
their master, and Robert was capable at the present moment of having him literally kicked into
the middle of the street. He had the temper that

ran through all the blood of the Lauderdale tribe, and it was up — the fierce, Lowland Scotch temper that is hard to rouse, and long controllable, but dangerous at the last. He had disliked and despised his nephew for years, but had not sought occasion against him. The occasion had come suddenly and by violence, and the wild beast in him was let loose.

Katharine's eyes followed her father's tall figure, as he stalked out of the room, with an odd expression. She was avenged for much in that moment.

"Brute!" growled Robert Lauderdale, as he disappeared behind the curtain.

"Infernal scoundrel!" answered Ralston, through his closed teeth.

"I'm so sorry I screamed, uncle Robert," said Katharine. "I waked you —"

Mrs. Deems interrupted her. She had ripped the seam of the tight sleeve, for she knew that it could not be drawn over the broken arm. On the white flesh there were two sets of marks — the one red, and evidently produced in the late struggle. The others were black and blue. They were side by side, the one set a little higher than the second. The arm was already much swollen. Mrs. Deems had listened in silence to what had been said, and her womanly heart had risen in sympathy for Katharine. She touched Robert Lauderdale's sleeve, and pointed to the old marks on Katharine's arm, calling his attention to them.

"Those weren't made now, Mr. Lauderdale," she said, in a low, matter-of-fact tone.

"No — it was last night," said Katharine, rather faintly. "Jack, dear — get me a cup of tea. I don't feel well."

Ralston hurried away, saying something to himself which was not audible to the others, and which may as well be omitted here. The black and white of paper and ink make youth's blood seem too red. Old Lauderdale's anger was still at the boiling-point, and broke out again.

"Do you mean to say that he's been maltreating you, child?" he asked, his face reddening again. "If he has —"

"No — not exactly, uncle dear — I'll tell you — but — I'm a little faint. Don't worry."

She sighed and closed her eyes, as she finished speaking. She was in great pain now that the arm was swelling.

"Best not talk, Mr. Lauderdale," said Mrs. Deems. "I'll get some ice and napkins."

And she also left the room. The old man, alone with Katharine, bent over her with difficulty, and kissed her white forehead. His old head trembled as he raised himself again and looked shyly round, as though he had done something to be ashamed of. The young girl opened her eyes, smiled a little, and closed them again at once.

"Do you feel very ill, little girl?" asked Robert Lauderdale.

There was something pathetic in the evident attempt to make his unnatural, hollow voice sound gentle and kind, and he stroked her thick black hair with one bony hand, while the other rested on the back of the chair.

"Oh, no — it's nothing — only the pain in my arm. Don't be frightened, uncle Robert — I'm not going to die!"

She tried to laugh to reassure him. Then a sharp twinge from the broken limb drew her face. The expression of her suffering was instantly reflected in the old man's features, and his bushy white eyebrows bent themselves.

"Routh will be here in a minute," he said, as though reassuring her. "I've sent for him."

She nodded her thanks, but said nothing. Then with her left hand she found one of his, and pressed it affectionately. He lifted hers, and pressed his bearded lips to it softly.

"It will be the worse for him," he said, consoling her, as many men console women, with the promise of vengeance.

In his mouth the words might mean much. There are few things which a just man, justly angry, cannot accomplish against an offender, with the aid of eighty millions of working capital, so to say. Moreover, Robert Lauderdale was not dead

yet, and could so change his will, if he pleased, as
to keep Alexander from ever receiving any share
whatsoever of the great fortune.

But Katharine was avenged already, and wished
no further evil to her father. She had seen him
humiliated and driven from the house, and she had
felt that he was not her father, but the man who
had insulted and cruelly wronged John Ralston,
her lawful husband. She had not seen the blow
Ralston had struck, for at that moment she had
just fallen to the floor. But all the rest had happened before her eyes, and she had neither spoken
word nor made sign to spare him. So far, she had
been utterly merciless.

Afterwards, she wondered how she could have
been so utterly hard and unforgiving, and tried to
remember what she had felt, but she found it impossible. It is hard to recall an old scald when
one is floating in cool water. Not that she ever
forgave her father for what he did and said during
those twenty-four hours — that is, in the sense of
forgiving entirely and thinking of him as though
nothing had happened. That would have been
impossible — perhaps it would have been scarcely
human. The virtue that turns the other cheek to
be smitten is in danger of having its head broken
by the second buffet, for cowardice takes arms of
charity. But they did not quarrel to the end of
their natural lives, and it seemed strange to Kath-

arine, at a later period, that she should have looked
on with a calm satisfaction that soothed her bodily
pain while Robert Lauderdale ordered her father
to be forcibly turned out of the house.   But that
is not strange, for humanity's hardest present
problem is almost always the problem of yesterday, which is in black and white, rather than the
expectation of to-morrow, confusedly shadowed
upon the mist of what is not yet, by the light of
the hope of what may be.

There was a sort of justice, too, in the fact that
Robert Lauderdale, who had once quarrelled with
John during the winter, should now be taking his
side, and be forced to take it by every conviction
of fairness.   The only thing which Katharine could
not understand was her father's own behaviour
towards his uncle.   It was in accordance with his
temper that he should behave to her as he had behaved, and to John Ralston also.   But it would
have seemed more natural that he should have
controlled himself, even by a great effort, rather
than have risked offending the possessor of the fortune.   On that afternoon he had seemed from the
first to be braving the old man's anger.   This was
a mystery to Katharine.   It seemed almost like
premeditation.   Yet she knew her father's limita-
tions, and was sure that he was not able to form a
deep scheme and carry it out, while mystifying
every one who looked on.   He was dull, he was

methodical, he was exact. He was also miserly, as
she had lately discovered. But he was a man to
keep a secret, rather than to produce one which
should need keeping, and she almost suspected
that he had lost his senses out of sheer anger,
though she knew that he was able to control his
temper longer than most men, when he pleased.

So far as the present was concerned, she felt, as
she might well feel, that she was amply avenged,
and when Robert Lauderdale seemed to be threatening further vengeance, she protested.

"Don't make it any worse, uncle Robert," she
said, with an effort, for she was growing very
faint. "But you must keep me here till I'm well,
if you will. I can't go home to him now."

"Of course, child — of course! Should you like
your mother to come and take care of you?"

"Oh, no — thank you — let me be with you.
We'll be invalids together, you know." She
smiled again, opening and closing her eyes.
"Don't forget yourself, now," she continued.
"You've had too much exertion — too much excitement — sit down and rest — here they come with
the tea and things."

John and Mrs. Deems entered in close succession. John had insisted upon bringing the tea-
tray himself, after overcoming Leek's objection
with the greatest difficulty. But Leek appeared,
nevertheless, playing footman to Ralston as butler,

so to say, and bearing a folding stand, which he set
down beside Katharine. Mrs. Deems had a bowl
of ice and a pile of napkins, with which she intended to cool Katharine's arm until Dr. Routh
arrived.

"Beg pardon, sir," said Leek to the old gentleman. "The old brougham was just in with the
bays, from exercise, William said, sir, so I sent
him as he was for Doctor Routh, sir. I hope I
did right, sir?"

"Quite right, Leek — very sensible of you," answered the old gentleman. "Just help me to a
chair, will you? I'm a little stiff from standing
so long. And get us some light. It's growing
dark."

Leek and Ralston installed him in a comfortable
chair on the other side of the tea-table. Mrs.
Deems was packing Katharine's arm in ice. The
young girl's face twitched nervously at first, but
grew calmer as the cold began to overcome the
inflammation.

Old Lauderdale watched the operation with
interest and sympathy. No one but Mrs. Deems
knew what Katharine must have suffered before she
began to feel the effects of the ice. Ralston stood
by in silence, looking at Katharine's face and ready
to help if he were needed, which was far from
probable. He was still pale, and the passions so
furiously roused were still at work within him.

He could not help dreaming of his next meeting with Alexander Junior, wondering when it would take place and what would happen; but he had the deep and incomparable satisfaction of an angry man who has dealt his enemy one successful blow. There had been nothing wrong about that blow — it had gone straight from the shoulder, it had not been parried, and it had crushed the mouth he hated. And even afterwards, in the struggle that had followed, Alexander had not thrown him, in spite of size and weight in his favour — these had been matched by youth and quickness. The moment the two men had seen that Katharine was hurt, they had loosed their hold on one another and gone to her, just as the servants had rushed into the room. But John was not satisfied, as Katharine was. He had tasted blood, and he thirsted for more — to have his fight out, and win or be beaten without interference. He meant to win, and he knew he could make even defeat dangerous, for he was quick of his hands and feet, and tough.

Of the three, old Robert was the first to regain his equanimity. Of all the Lauderdale tempers, his was the least hard to rouse and the soonest to expend itself, and therefore the least dangerous. It was commonly said among them that Katharine Ralston, John's mother, who had hardly ever been seen angry, had the most deadly temper in the family, though it was not easy to tell on what the tradition rested. John and Alexander had certainly not the best, and it was safe to predict that when they met again there would be war.

The old gentleman had made very unwonted exertions that afternoon, and before she had finished doing what she could for Katharine's arm, Mrs. Deems became anxious about him. His cheeks grew hollow, and as the blood sank away from them his face became almost ghastly. Ralston looked at him attentively and then glanced at the nurse. She nodded, and got a stimulant and gave it to him, and felt his pulse, and shook her head almost imperceptibly.

"How long is it since the doctor was sent for?" she asked of Ralston, in a low voice.

"It must be twenty minutes, I should think."

"Oh — longer than that, I'm sure!" exclaimed Katharine, whose suffering lengthened time.

"He'll be here presently, then," said Mrs. Deems, somewhat reassured. "How do you feel, Mr. Lauderdale? A little weak?"

"All right," growled the broken voice. "Take care of Katharine."

But he did not open his eyes, and spoke rather as though he were dreaming, than as if he were awake.

"Provided he's at home," said Ralston, half aloud and thinking of the doctor. "Hadn't we better send for some one else, too?"

He addressed the question to everybody, in a general way.

"Best wait till the carriage comes back," suggested Mrs. Deems.

This seemed sensible, and a silence followed which lasted some time. Ralston stood motionless beside the nurse. Katharine had swallowed some tea and lay quietly in her chair, while the skilful woman did her best with the ice and napkins. The old man's jaw had dropped a little, and he was breathing heavily, as though asleep. Mrs. Deems did not like the sound, for she glanced at him more and more uneasily.

"There, Miss Katharine," she said, at last, "that's the best we can do till the doctor comes. I think it's only the small bone that's broken, but I don't like to handle it. I guess it's better to leave it so till he comes. Best not try to move yourself."

Then she went round the table to old Lauderdale again, listened attentively to his breathing and felt his pulse.

"Are you asleep, Mr. Lauderdale?" she asked, almost in a whisper.

The jaw moved, and he spoke some unintelligible words.

"I can't hear what you say," said Mrs. Deems, bending down anxiously.

He cleared his throat, coughed a little and spoke louder.

"Take care of Katharine," he said, still without opening his eyes.

"Don't worry about me, uncle Robert," said Katharine, looking at him with anxiety.

Both she and Ralston turned enquiring glances to Mrs. Deems. She merely shook her head sadly and said nothing. Ralston beckoned to her to come and speak with him. She poured out another dose of the old man's stimulant and set it to his lips. He swallowed it rather eagerly and without difficulty. Then she glanced at Ralston and left the room. A moment later he followed her, and found her waiting for him on the other side of the curtain.

"You're very anxious, aren't you, Mrs. Deems?" he enquired, in a whisper.

"Well," she answered, "I suppose I am. I guess he's had a strain with this trouble. I do wish the doctor'd come, though. It's a long while since they went for him."

"Don't you think he's in danger now — that he might go off at any moment?" asked Ralston.

"Well — they do — with heart failure. That's the danger. But it's a strong family, Mr. Ralston, and he's been a strong man, old Mr. Lauderdale, though he's as weak as a babe now. You just can't tell, in these cases, and that's the fact."

There was a sound of wheels. A moment later Leek appeared.

"Doctor Routh can't be found, sir," he said. "They've been to his house and to two or three other places, but he can't be found, sir. So I've sent for Doctor Cheever. He's always on call, as they say in this country, sir."

"Quite right, Leek," answered Ralston.

He looked round for Mrs. Deems, but she had gone back into the drawing-room. She was evidently very anxious.

CHAPTER XIII.

ROBERT LAUDERDALE's condition was precarious, and Mrs. Deems was well aware of the fact as the minutes passed and neither of the doctors who had been sent for appeared. It was Doctor Routh's custom to come a few minutes before dinner time, as well as in the morning, and his visit at that hour was almost a certainty. As ill-luck would have it, Doctor Cheever was also out when the carriage reached his house, having been called away a few moments previously. Urgent messages were left for both, and the brougham returned empty a second time. So far as the old gentleman was concerned, Mrs. Deems knew well enough how to do what lay in her power, and she could do nothing more than she had done for Katharine already. But she knew how the least delay in setting a broken bone increased the difficulty and the pain when it came to be done at last, and her anxiety about Robert Lauderdale did not prevent her from feeling nervous about the young girl.

No one spoke in the great drawing-room where the old man and Katharine lay with closed eyes in their chairs, while the nurse and Ralston sat

274

watching them. But when Leek came with the news that Doctor Cheever could not be found, either, Mrs. Deems was roused almost to anger.

"You've got to get a surgeon, anyway," she said, sharply, to Ralston. "If you don't, they'll have a bad time when it comes to setting her arm. Mr. Lauderdale I can manage, perhaps, till the doctor comes, but I'm no bone-setter."

Ralston left the room, took the carriage, and went himself in search of a surgeon, and returned with one in less than a quarter of an hour. A few minutes later Doctor Routh appeared, and last of all came young Doctor Cheever. Then everything was done quickly and well. The three practitioners understood one another without words, and the machinery of the great house of the old millionaire did their bidding.

But Doctor Routh shook his head when he was alone with John Ralston half an hour later.

"I don't like the look of things," he said. "Of course, there's no telling about you Lauderdales. You're pretty strong people all round. I don't want any confidences. I don't want to know what's happened. I can see the results, and they're enough for me. You're a quarrelsome set, but you'd better have managed to fight somewhere else. I'm afraid you've killed him this time. However — there's no telling."

"How about Miss Lauderdale?" asked John, anxiously. "How long will she be laid up?"

"Oh — three or four weeks. But they must keep her quiet for a day or two, until the inflammation goes down. When the bone's begun to heal and the arm's immobilized, she can be about. It's no use your staying here. You can't see either of them. But if I were you — I don't say anything positive, I'm only giving you a hint — if I were you, I'd be at home this evening. If things get worse, I'll send for you."

"Are you going to stay yourself?" asked Ralston.

"Of course. Practically, as far as one can judge, your uncle's dying. You may just as well be here as any one else. He's very fond of you, in spite of your little tiff last winter. You're the only man in the family he'd like to see, and you won't be in the way."

It was his manner of putting it. At any other time Ralston would have smiled at the idea of being ' in the way ' of death.

"I suppose there's really no hope," he answered, gravely. "But the only person he'd really wish to have with him is Miss Lauderdale."

"Well — that's impossible, my dear boy. She can't be running about the house in the middle of the night with her arm just broken. It might be dangerous."

"You'd better not let her know if anything happens, then — or she will."

John Ralston left the house very reluctantly at
last, and returned to his home, feeling broken and
helpless, as people who have nervous organizations
do feel when they have been under great emotion
and are left in anxiety. Naturally enough, Katharine's present condition was uppermost in his
mind, and every step which took him further from
her was an added pain. But a multitude of other
considerations thrust themselves upon him at the
same time, and he asked himself what was to
happen on the morrow.

He had made up his mind, before Alexander
Junior had left the house, that it was absolutely
necessary to put an end to the present situation at
once, and to declare his marriage without delay.
He had never wished it to be kept a secret, and he
had now the best of reasons for insisting that it
should be made public. He might have been willing to believe that Katharine's fall had been an
accident, and that her father had not meant to hurt
her, but the fact remained that the accident had
occurred through his brutal roughness, with the
result that John had struck the elder man in the
face. It was not safe for Katharine to stay any
longer in her father's house.

On the other hand, it seemed clear that Robert
Lauderdale was near his end. It was hardly to be
hoped that he could survive the strain of his late
fit of passion, weakened as he was and old. Even

Doctor Routh thought it improbable. What would happen if he died that night? If Katharine had to be moved, — she could scarcely stay in the house after the old man was dead, — to whose house should she go? John swore, inwardly, that she should not return to her father's. And he thought, too, of his next meeting with the latter. Society would be amazed and horrified to hear that they had actually come to blows. Society, especially in our country, detests the idea of personal violence. Its verdict is against any use of such means to settle difficulties. Society, therefore, must be kept in ignorance of what had happened. No one had seen the blow, not even Katharine, who had just fallen to the floor. She alone had seen John and her father struggling, for they had loosed their hold on seeing that she was hurt, and the servants had found them bending over her. Consequently, a great part of what had happened would be kept secret. Robert Lauderdale would not speak of it, and Mrs. Deems was bound to secrecy by her profession. John wondered how Alexander Junior would meet him, however, and whether there was to be any renewal of hostilities.

Altogether, when he let himself into his own house, he was in need of counsel and advice. There was no one but his mother to whom he cared to appeal for either. She had known all along of his devotion to Katharine Lauderdale, though she knew nothing of the secret marriage. She knew how hard Katharine's life was made in the girl's own home, by her father's determined opposition to the match, and John had told her something of other matters — how old Robert had confided to Katharine what he meant to do with his money, and how her father had tried to force her to betray the confidence. Ralston was puzzled, too, by Alexander Junior's evident willingness to quarrel with his uncle, or at least by his determination to make no concessions whatever to him, and wondered whether his mother could not suggest some explanation.

Mrs. Ralston was, in some ways, very like her son, and the two understood one another perfectly. It would, perhaps, be more accurate to say that she had made him like herself, not intentionally, but by force of example, a result very unusual in the relations between mother and son. She was by no means a manlike woman, but she possessed many of the qualities which make the best men. She was fearless and truthful, and she was more than that — she had a man's sense of honour from a man's point of view, and admitted to herself that honour was the only religion in which she could believe. Like Katharine, she, the elder Katharine Lauderdale, had been brought up amidst contradictory influences, and had then married the Admiral, a brave officer, a man of considerable scientific

attainments, and a determined agnostic, of the
school of thirty years ago, when many people believed that science was to bring about a sort of
millennium within the next few years. In that
direction she went further than her son. Her
sense of fairness had shown her how unfair it would
be to make an unbeliever of him before he was old
enough to judge for himself, and in this idea she
had made him go to church like other boys, and
had persuaded his father not to talk atheism before
him. The result had been to produce, more or
less, the state of mind typical in these last years
of the century, amongst a certain class of people
who are collectively described as cultured, though
they cannot always be spoken of individually as
cultivated. John felt that he believed in something, but he had not the slightest idea what that
something might be, and did not take the smallest trouble to find out. In this respect he differed
from Katharine. Under very similar conditions,
the young girl vacillated between a set of undefinable but much discussed beliefs, which included
pseudo-Buddhism, Psychological Research, the
wreck of what was for a few years Theosophy, and
the latest discoveries in hypnotism, taken altogether and kneaded into an amorphous mass, on
the one hand, while, on the other, she was attracted by the rigid forms of actual Christianity,
widely opposed, but nearest in whole-heartedness,

which are found in the Presbyterian and the Roman Catholic churches. But John's mother was a peaceable agnostic, who had transferred the questions of right, wrong, and ultimate good before the tribunal of honour which held perpetual session in her heart.

She never discussed such points if she could avoid doing so, and if drawn into discussion against her will, she said frankly that she wished she might believe, but could not. In dealing with the world, her strength of character, her directness and her humanity stood her in good stead. In her heart's dealings with itself, she thought of Musset's famous lines — 'If Heaven be void, then we offend no God. But if God is, let God be pitiful!' And she offended no one, nor desired to offend any. She had in life the advantage, the only one, perhaps, which the agnostic has over the believer — the safety of her own soul was not in the balance when the humanity of others appealed to her own. He who believes that he has a soul to save can be unselfish only with his bodily safety.

Mrs. Ralston was eminently a woman of the world in the best sense of an expression which many think can mean no good. She had never been beautiful and had never been vain, but she had much which attracts as beauty does, and holds as no beauty can. Of the Lauderdales now living, she was undeniably the most gifted. Katharine might have rivalled her, had she developed under more favourable circumstances. But with the education she had received, good as it had been of its kind, it was not probable that the young girl would grow up into such a woman.

Yet Mrs. Ralston had no accomplishments, in the ordinary sense of the word. Her husband used to say that this was one of her chief attractions in his eyes — he hated women who played the piano, and sang little songs, and made little sketches, for the small price paid by cheap social admiration, and greedily accepted by the performer of such tricks. There were people who did such things well, and whose business it was to do them. Why should any one do them badly? Mrs. Ralston never attempted anything of the sort.

On the other hand, she was well acquainted with a number of modern languages, and knew enough of the classics not to talk about 'reading Horace in the original Greek,' which is as much knowledge in that direction, perhaps, as a woman needs, and as most men have occasion to use in daily life. She had read very widely, and her criticism, if not that of pure reason, was that of a clear judgment. She had found out early what most people never learn at all, that she could widen her experience of life vicariously by assimilating that of other people, in fact and even in fiction. Good fiction is very like reality. Bad fiction is generally made up of fragments of reality unskilfully patched together. She picked out truths wherever she found them, and set them in their places in the body of all truth.

She was, in a way, the least American of all the Lauderdales. She herself would have said, on the contrary, from her own point of view, that she was the most really American in the tribe. She loved the country, she especially loved New York, and she loved her own people better than any other with which she was acquainted. This strong attachment to everything American was in itself contrary to the ideas of most persons with whom she was brought into close relations. What calls itself society, pre-eminently, and numbers itself by hundreds, and shuts itself off as much as possible, requiring those who would be counted with it to pass a special examination in the subjects about which it happens to be mad at the time — Society with a capital letter, in fact, is tired of work, it associates home with hard labour and a bad climate, and Europe with fine weather, idleness, and amusement. 'They manage those things better in France,' expresses New York society's opinion of things in general apart from business. Mrs. Ralston differed from Society, and thought that many things were managed quite as well in America.

"That's because you've been abroad so much, my dear," said her friends. "Wait till you've

lived ten years at a stretch in New York. You'll
think just as we do. You won't like it half so
much. And besides — think of clothes and things!"

Now Mrs. Ralston did think of 'clothes and
things.' She had never been beautiful, but she
had in a high degree the strength and grace dis-
tinctive in many of the Lauderdales. She was
tall, long-limbed, slight as a girl, at five and forty
years of age, less strong than Katharine, perhaps,
though that might be doubted, and certainly lighter
and much thinner. She, too, was dark — a keen,
strong face, like her son's, with the same bright
brown eyes, and the same fine hair, though not
nearly so black, but her face was kindlier than his,
and far less sad. She had possessed the power
of enjoying things for their own sake as long
as Mrs. Lauderdale, Katharine's mother, who had
kept her faculty of enjoying the world subjec-
tively, with little interest in it for itself, but
with the intensely strong attachment of easily
satisfied personal vanity. The difference was, that
the one form of enjoyment was doomed to destruction with the beauty which was its source, while
the other increased with the ever broadening and
deepening humanity in which it found its dominant interest. If Mrs. Lauderdale had been shut
off from the gay side of social existence for a
time, as Mrs. Ralston had been in the first years
of her widowhood, she would have become sour and

discontented. Mrs. Ralston had seen where the
real bitterness of life lay, and the bitterness had
appealed to her heart almost as much as ever the
sweetness had. She had suffered in some ways
much, but not long; she had been disappointed
more than once, but had been repaid.

Above all, she was her son's friend. She had
lived a woman's life, and in him she was living
a man's life, too. She had felt a mother's fears
for him, a mother's sympathy in his failures, in
his downheartedness, in the love for Katharine
which had met with such bitter opposition. She
had almost known a mother's despair in believing
him lost and truly worthless, and when she had
found out her mistake, a mother's triumph had
made her heart beat fast. And little by little
through the last months she had seen the man's
real character coming to the surface in its strength
and boldness, outgrowing the boyish weakness, the
youthful faults that were not vices yet and never
would be now, and it was as though the growth
had been in her own heart, giving to herself new
interest, new life, and new vitality.

And John Ralston had forgotten that one hour
in which she had doubted him, though at the time
he had found it hard to say that he ever should.
She was his best friend and was becoming his
closest companion. Even Katharine could not
understand him so well, for she knew too little

of the world yet. She had given him her heart,
and her sympathy was all his, but neither the one
nor the other was yet quite grown.

John and his mother dined alone together that
evening, and afterwards went upstairs and sat in
a room which was called John's study, by courtesy,
as it had been called the Admiral's study when his
father was alive. It was a quiet, manlike room,
with a small bookcase and a large gun-rack, huge
chairs covered with brown leather, an unnecessarily
large writing-table, a certain number of trophies
of the chase, a well-worn carpet and curtains that
smelled of cigars. Mrs. Ralston had been accustomed all her life to the smell of tobacco, and
rather liked it than otherwise. She settled her
graceful figure comfortably in one of the chairs,
and Ralston sat down opposite to her in another
and began to smoke.

"There's been a row, mother," he began. "I
couldn't tell you before the servants, but I'm going
to tell you all about it now. I want your advice
and your help — all sorts of things of you. I'm
rather worried."

"Do you think I couldn't see that in your face,
Jack?" asked Mrs. Ralston, smiling as she met
his eyes. "There's a certain line in your forehead
that always comes when there's trouble. What is
it, boy?"

John told his story briefly and accurately, with-

out superfluous comment, and as much of what had
happened in Katharine's life as she had confided
to him. He made it clear enough that she was
being tormented to give up Robert Lauderdale's
secret, and if he dwelt unduly upon any point, it
was upon this. Mrs. Ralston listened attentively.
When he came to the scene which had taken place
on that afternoon, she leaned forward in her chair,
breathless with interest.

"Oh, Jack!" she cried. "You always seem to
be fighting somebody!"

"Yes — but wasn't I right, mother?" he asked,
quickly. "What could I do? He acted like a
madman, and he dragged Katharine from me and
whirled her off upon the floor as though he'd been
handling a man in a free fight. I couldn't stand
that."

"No — of course you couldn't," answered Mrs.
Ralston. "I don't see what you could have done
but hit him, I'm sure. And yet it's a shocking
affair — it is, really. I'm afraid it's cost uncle
Robert his life, poor, dear old man!"

"Poor man!" echoed Ralston, thoughtfully.
"Routh didn't seem to think he could live through
the night. We may get word at any moment."

"The wonder is that he didn't die then and
there. And there's no one with him, either —
Katharine laid up in her room — why didn't you
stay in the house, Jack?"

"Routh wouldn't let me. He's there. He told me I should only be in the way and that he'd send for me, if anything happened. It's an odd thing, mother — but there's no one to go to uncle Robert but you and I and cousin Emma. He'd have a fit if he saw cousin Alexander. And of course the old gentleman can't go." He meant Robert's brother.

"No — of course not."

A short silence followed, and Mrs. Ralston seemed to be thinking over the situation.

"Well, Jack," she said, at last, "what are we going to do? This state of things can't go on."

"No. It can't. It shan't. And I won't let it. Mother — you know we talked last winter — you said that if ever I wanted to marry Katharine — wanted to! Well — that we could manage to live here — "

It would be hard to give any adequate idea of the reluctance with which John approached the subject. Short of the consideration of Katharine's personal safety, which he believed to be endangered by the life she was made to lead, nothing could have induced him to think of laying the burden of his married life upon his mother's comparatively slender fortune. Although half of it was his, for she had made it over to him by a deed during the previous winter, out of a conviction that he should feel himself to be independent, yet he had never quite accepted the position, and still regarded all there was as being, morally speaking, her property. But now she met him more than half way.

"Jack," she said, almost authoritatively, "if Katharine will marry you, marry her to-morrow and bring her here."

"Thank you, mother," he answered, and was silent for a moment.

"We can live perfectly well — just as well as we do now. One person more — what difference does it make?"

"It would make a difference — more than you think," answered John. "But there's another thing about it, mother — there's a secret I've kept from you for a long time. I must tell you now. You must be the first to know it. But I want to ask you first not to judge what I've done until I've told you all about it."

"Is it anything bad, Jack?" asked Mrs. Ralston, with quick anxiety, bending far forward in her chair, while all her expression changed.

"No, mother — don't be frightened. It's this. Katharine and I were married last winter."

"Married!" cried Mrs. Ralston, in amazement. "Married!" she repeated in a tone which showed that she was deeply hurt. "And you did not tell me!"

She said nothing more for a few moments, and John was silent, too, giving her time to recover from her astonishment. She was the first to speak.

"Either Katharine made you marry her, or you must have had some very good reason for doing such a thing, Jack," she said. "It's not like you to get married secretly. When was it?"

"It was on that day when I was so unlucky. When I lost my way, and everybody thought I'd been drinking."

"Jack! Do you mean to say that you had that on your mind, too? Oh, Jack dear, why didn't you tell me?"

"In the first place, I'd said I wouldn't. The reasons seemed good then. They haven't seemed so good since. I'll tell you the idea in two words. We were to be privately married. Then we were to confide in uncle Robert, expecting that he would find me something to do, that I could do whatever he proposed well enough to earn a living without accepting money as a gift. There was where the disappointment came. I found out afterwards how true what he said was. Everybody's on the lookout for a congenial occupation that means living out of doors and enjoying oneself. He said there was nothing to be done but to go back to Beman's and work at a desk for a year. Then he'd push me on. He tried to make me take a lot of money, but I wouldn't. I'm glad of that, anyhow. So we've never said anything about it, except to him. But now something must be done."

"But you could have brought her here any time in these four months — at least, you might have told me and I would have helped you."

"I know — but then, it would have been a burden on you, as it's going to be now."

"A burden! Don't say such things."

"Only that now — well — I don't like to say it, but dear old uncle Robert isn't going to live long, and then you'll be rich, compared to what you are now, even if he only leaves you what he'd think a small legacy."

"Yes — that's true," answered Mrs. Ralston, thoughtfully. "Isn't life strange, Jack?" she continued, after a short pause. "We're both very fond of him. We shall miss him very much more than we realize. I think either you or I would do anything we could, and risk anything, to save his life — and yet we can't help counting on the money he's sure to leave us when he dies. I suppose most people would call it heartless to speak about it, though they'd think about it from morning till night. But I don't think we're heartless, do you?"

"No," answered John, "I don't. Not that it would be a crime if we were. People are born so, or they aren't. We can't all be rough plastered with goodness and stuccoed with virtue on top of

it. We're natural, that's all — and the majority
of people aren't. I don't wish uncle Robert to
die, any more than you do, or than any one does,
except cousin Alexander. It's only reasonable for
us who are young to think of what we may do
when he's gone, since he's so old."

"Yes, I suppose so," assented Mrs. Ralston.
"So you've been married all these months! It
hurts me a little to think that you shouldn't have
told me. I'd have helped you. I'm sure I could
have made it easier. But I see — you were afraid
that I should have to go without my toilet water
and have to wear ready made gloves, or some such
ridiculous thing as that! Married! Well — I'm
not exactly sentimental, but I'd rather looked forward to your wedding with Katharine. I always
knew you'd marry her in the end, and I liked to
think of it. I'm glad, though — I'm glad it's done
and can't be undone, in spite of her father. Tell
me all about it, since you've told me everything
else."

It was not a long story — how Katharine had
persuaded him, much against his will, how he had
found a clergyman willing to perform the ceremony, and how Katharine and he had gone to the
church early in the morning.

"And now she is Katharine Ralston, too, like
me — and I've got a daughter-in-law!" Mrs.
Ralston smiled dreamily.

After the first moment of surprise and after the first sharp pain she had felt for her son's want of confidence in her, as she regarded his secrecy, the news did not seem to disturb her much. For years she had been convinced that Katharine was destined to be her son's wife, and for many months she had felt sure that, with his nature, his happiness and success in life depended entirely upon his marrying her. She was heartily glad that it had come, though, as she said, she had often looked forward to the wedding as to something very bright in her own existence.

"Jack," she said, "leave it to me to set matters straight with the rest of the family, will you?"

"Why — mother — if you think you can — of course," answered Ralston, with some hesitation. "The difficulty will be with cousin Alexander. We're enemies for life, now."

"Yes. Until to-day you were only enemies by circumstance. You'll never be reconciled, now — not completely. You could never spend a night under his roof after what has happened, could you? Of course you can say to him that you acted under the impression that he was — well — what shall I say? — that he was treating Katharine brutally, but that if he wasn't, you apologize for striking him. But after all, that's only quibbling with honour. It wouldn't satisfy him and wouldn't be very dignified for you, it seems to me. And he's

not the man who would ever put out his hand and
forgive you frankly and say that by-gones should
be by-gones."

"Scarcely!" assented Ralston.   "Not at all that
kind of man.   By the bye, mother, — forgive me
for going off to something else, — what do you
think is the reason why he seems so ready to
offend uncle Robert, instead of bowing down to
him, as they all do?   He wants the money more
than any one.   He can't suppose that if uncle
Robert were to make a new will now, after what
has happened, he'd leave him anything.   You
should have heard the old gentleman swear at him,
and turn him out of the house!"

"I don't know," answered Mrs. Ralston,
thoughtfully, "unless he wants to irritate uncle
Robert, and drive him into making some extraordinary will that wouldn't hold.   Then he'd get it
broken.   You see, Jack, my uncle Alexander,
who's uncle Robert's own brother, and I, who am
the only child of uncle Robert's other brother, are
the next of kin.   If there were no will, or if the
will were broken, we two should get the whole
fortune, equally divided, half and half, and none
of the rest would get anything.   Mr. Brett told me
that a long time ago.   As it is, we don't know how
the money's left, though uncle Robert has often
told me that I should have a big share."

"Katharine knows," said John.   "That's the
reason her father leaves her no peace."

"And she's not told you, Jack?"

"Mother! Do you suppose Katharine would betray a confidence like that? You don't know her!"

"No, dear. I didn't seriously think she would. But then — she's your wife, Jack. She might tell you what she wouldn't tell any one else, and yet not think that she were giving away a secret. Most women would, I think."

"Katharine's not like most women," said Ralston, gravely.

A silence followed, during which his mother watched his face, and her own grew beautiful with mother's pride in man, and woman's gladness for woman's dignity.

When Ralston and his mother separated, they had come to a clear understanding about the future. They had decided to say nothing about the marriage until Katharine had recovered sufficiently to leave Robert Lauderdale's home, and then to establish her in their house, and tell the world that there had been a private wedding. If the old gentleman died, — and they were obliged to take this probability into consideration, — Katharine would have to be brought at once. If anything, this would make matters simpler. The household would be in mourning, Katharine would be unable to go out or to appear at all for some time, and society would easily believe that during the two or three weeks which must pass in this way, the marriage might have taken place.

CHAPTER XIV.

No one slept much during the early part of the night in the millionaire's home. Katharine lay long awake, prevented from sleeping partly by the painful numbness in her bandaged arm, and partly by the ever recurring picture of the day's doings which came back to her unceasingly in the stillness. Just as the picture was growing shadowy and dreamlike, some slight sound would break it and recall her to herself,— a distant foot-fall on the stairs, the opening and shutting of a door near her own, or even the occasional roll of a belated carriage in the street.

There was a soft light in the sick man's room. The white walls and hangings took up and distributed the whiteness, so that even the remotest corners were not dark. Robert Lauderdale lay in his bed, breathing softly, his eyes not quite closed, and his bony hands lying like knotty twigs upon the white Shetland wool that covered his body. For they were like wood or stone, yellowish in colour, rough in shape, and yet oddly polished by time, as some old men's hands are. His snowy beard and hair, too, were almost sandy again, as they

296

had been in youth, by contrast with the delicate linen and the snow-white, sheeny material that was everywhere.

He was not sleeping with his eyes open, as dying persons sometimes sleep a whole day. Nor was his mind wandering. Doctor Routh could see that well enough, as he sat there hour after hour, watching his old friend. The doctor wished that he might really fall asleep, and let his weary old heart gather strength to live a little longer. But even Routh was giving up hope. The machine was running down, and the game was played out. There was not one chance in a hundred that Robert Lauderdale could live another twelve hours. From time to time the doctor gave him a little stimulant, but the failing heart reacted less and less.

Between three and four o'clock in the morning, the old man turned his head slowly on the pillow, and his sunken eyes met Routh's in a long look — the look which those who have watched by the dying know very well.

"Routh," said the hoarse voice, with solemn slowness, "I'm going to give up the ghost."

Still for a few seconds the deep, mysterious, wondering look continued in the hollow eyes. Then he turned his head slowly back to the original position. The words struck the doctor as singular. He did not remember that he had ever heard a patient use just that phrase, though so many persons when near the point of death give warning of their end in some such expression.

"You're not going yet," the doctor answered, mechanically, and he held a glass to the old man's lips.

"I don't want any false hope. I know it's coming," answered the dying man, speaking against the rim of the little tumbler.

Routh stood up to his vast height, and then his nervous, emaciated frame bent like a birch sapling in a gale as he leaned over the bed, and listened to the fluttering beats of the heart that had almost done its work.

"Shall I call anybody?" he asked. "Is there anything you want done?"

"How long do you think it will be?" asked Robert Lauderdale, trying to speak more rapidly.

"Half an hour, perhaps," answered Routh.

In their voices there was that indescribable tone with which the words of brave men are uttered in the face of death. No one who has ever heard it can forget it.

"I'd like to say good-bye to Katharine." He paused and drew breath heavily. "Will it hurt her?" he asked, presently.

"No," answered the doctor, seeing the look of anxiety which accompanied the question.

A broken arm seemed a very slight matter to Routh, compared with the wish of his old friend.

He did not hesitate, but touched the bell for Mrs.
Deems, who appeared at the door.

"He wishes to see Miss Lauderdale," he whispered. "You must help her to wrap herself up,
and bring her here."

Mrs. Deems nodded, and looked at the doctor
with the grave glance of enquiry which means the
one question, 'Life or death?' And Routh answered with the other glance, which means
'Death.' Mrs. Deems nodded again, and left the
room. Routh returned to the bedside.

"When she comes — leave us alone — please,"
said the sick man.

There was silence again for a few minutes.
Again the lids were half closed, and the old eyes
stared out beneath them into the soft whiteness,
and perhaps beyond. But the beard moved a little
from time to time, as though the lips were fram-
ing words, and Routh knew that the end was near.

Then Katharine came, waxen pale, her raven
hair coiled loosely upon her shapely head, her
creamy throat collarless, her left arm and hand
free, the rest of her wrapped and draped in soft,
dark things. She, too, looked up into Routh's face
with the glance of the question, 'Life or death?'
And again the answer was, 'Death.'

But Mrs. Deems had told her. Her eyes said
that she knew, and her face told that she felt.
Robert Lauderdale's great head turned again,

slowly and painfully, towards her. She bent down to him, and the doctor left the room, taking the nurse with him. He did not quite close the door. He could almost hear, beforehand, the low cry the young girl would utter when the end came.

Katharine bent down and laid her hand softly upon the old man's brow.

"Uncle dear — you're not going," she said. "You'll get well, after all."

"I'm going to give up the ghost," he said, as he had said to Doctor Routh.

"No — no — " But she could not find anything to say, so she smoothed his forehead.

She had never seen any one die, but she was not afraid. That is a matter of temperament, and neither man nor woman should be blamed who can not bear to feel a soul parting and see a body left behind. Katharine felt only that she would keep him if she could. She knelt down and took one of his hands, his left. It was cold and hard to touch, with little warmth in it, like that of a statue in a garden when the sun has gone down.

"I want to say good-bye," said the hoarse voice, just above a whisper.

"Yes — I'm here," answered Katharine, and there was silence again, while she gently caressed the cold hand.

"Routh said half an hour."

The mysterious, dying eyes wandered a little,

and then sought the white clock on the mantel-piece.

"Can't see — what time it is," said the rough whisper.

"Twenty minutes to four," answered Katharine, glancing round quickly, and then looking again at his face.

"Poor child — little girl — ought to be in bed." The words came indistinctly, and the breathing grew more heavy.

Then the beard moved with unspoken words, and Katharine watched, hearing nothing. She had been a little confused at first, but now she recollected that she should ask if there were anything she could do. She could not tell whence the recollection came. She had perhaps got it from a book read long ago. He might want something. He might die unsatisfied. She made anxious haste to ask the question.

"Is there anything I can do? Any one else you want, uncle?" she enquired, speaking close to his ear.

The breathing, almost stertorous now, ceased for an instant. He seemed to be trying to collect strength to say something.

"Your father — tell him from me — bear no malice —" He could get no further.

"Yes — yes — don't think about it — don't distress yourself," said Katharine, quickly. "I'll tell him."

Again the heavy breathing blew the stiff white hairs of his beard and moustache, as his chin, raised in the effort of speaking, fell suddenly to his breast again. The breath raised the coarse white and sandy hairs and blew them to right and left. The eyelids drooped. Katharine wondered whether old men always died like that. Then the thought that he was really dying put on its reality for the first time, and struck her suddenly in the heart, and the pain she felt struck back instantly into her helpless, bandaged arm.

"Is it God?" asked the dying man, suddenly, in a louder voice and quite clearly.

Again, in the effort, his chin rose and fell. There was something awful in the question, asked with the strength of the death struggle. Then came more words, indistinct and broken.

"I shall be — a little boy again." So much Katharine understood of what she heard.

Her tears gathered. Some of them fell upon the yellow, branch-like hand. Then she bent close to his ear again.

"There is God," she said. "God will take you, dear — He is taking you now. Think of Him. You're dying."

Her tears broke her voice, as raindrops break the sighing of the breeze in summer. She wept, though she would not, and her pale face was wet. And his heavy breath filled her ears till it seemed

to roar like a furnace — the furnace of life burning itself out, where all was still and white.
She said prayers that took meaning in her heart
and lost it as they passed her lips, meeting the
great doubt on the threshold of her soul. She did
not know what she said. It was not much, nor
eloquent.

"I believe — God — " Then a great sigh blew
the white hairs to right and left.

The breathing grew more slow, longer, harder,
a great breathing of sighs. Death had life by the
throat. In awe, the girl looked into the ancient
face, and the stream of tears trickled and ran dry.
Once more the voice burst out, articulate but
rattling.

"Domine — quo — vadis?"

The great head was raised, and the mysterious
eyes were wide, gazing at her, waiting upon the
answer, waiting to die. She remembered the
answer.

"Tendit ad astra."

He heard it, and died.

Katharine had never seen death, but she knew
him, as we all know him. Twice, thrice, the
broad chest heaved under the soft, feathery woollen,
and the after-breath of the storm quivered in the
frost of his beard. But the girl knew he was
dead. Then came her low, trembling cry, the echo
of death's voice from living heartstrings.

It was not a great sorrow, though Katharine had been very fond of the old man and was very grateful to him, as well she might be. She was, perhaps, as closely attached to him as is possible in such a relationship between the very young and the very old. But although her tears flowed plentifully, it was not one of those deep-gripped wrenches that twist the heart and leave it shapeless and bruised for a time — or forever. Hearts, too, are less often broken by those who go than by those who stay with us. The young girl's grief was sincere, and hurt her, but it was not profound. They led her away, and when the door of her own room closed behind her, the tears were already drying on her cheeks.

Death brings confusion and leaves it in his path. Many hours passed before there was quiet in the great house, but Katharine slept, exhausted at last by all she had endured that day, beyond the possibility of being kept awake by mere bodily pain. Late in the morning her mother came to her bedside. Katharine had been awake a quarter of an hour, and had been hesitating as to whether she should ring or not. Her arm hurt her, and the hand that had been so white was purple against the tight white bandages. She longed to tear them off and have rest, if only for a moment.

"Poor uncle Robert!" said Mrs. Lauderdale, seating herself, after kissing the young girl's forehead.

She was a little pale with natural excitement, and she was certainly not looking her best in a black frock which was far from new, but which had to do duty until she could have mourning made. Katharine said nothing in answer, but nodded her head on the pillow. She wondered whether her mother knew that she had broken her arm. But in this she did her an injustice.

"Was your wrist much hurt?" asked Mrs. Lauderdale, almost immediately.

Then she caught sight of the splints and bandages and the purple fingers, as Katharine lifted the coverlet a little. Instantly her face changed.

"Heavens, child! What have you done to yourself?" she cried, springing to her feet and bending over to look.

"Papa broke my arm," answered Katharine, quietly.

"Your father — broke your arm?" Mrs. Lauderdale spoke with the utmost astonishment, mingled with unbelief.

"Why, yes. Didn't you know? It was last night — that — all the confusion and trouble have killed poor uncle Robert. Didn't papa tell you anything?" Katharine stared at her mother.

"He came home and said he had hurt his mouth. I could not get him to say what had happened to him. To tell the truth, I was rather worried. It's so unlike him to hurt himself, or have any

accident. He said it was a ridiculous affair, and
that he didn't choose to be laughed at, and begged
me to say nothing more about it. You know how
he is. But he never mentioned you."

Katharine said nothing for a few moments. She
wondered how wise it might turn to be to tell her
mother all that had happened. But the instinct of
child to mother overcame hesitation. Her mother
had begun to take her part again, and the broken
sympathy was being restored by bits and pieces, as
it were.

"There was a terrible scene yesterday afternoon
—late," said Katharine. "He came here, and
Jack was with me in the library."

"Jack! Oh, Katharine! I wish you wouldn't
see him in this way — "

"It's no use wishing, mother," answered the
young girl. "I made up my mind long ago.
Well, Jack was with me in the library, when Leek
came in and said that papa was here. I saw him
in the drawing-room, so that they shouldn't meet.
I forget all he said. The usual thing, about being disobedient and undutiful. He was awfully
angry because I got out yesterday morning. So I
just went over one or two of the things he had
done to hurt me. By the bye — I ought to say,
that just before he came Jack had been telling me
that some one had been to Mr. Beman, and had
said that Jack drank, and was dissipated, and was

altogether rather a good-for-nothing. And Mr. Beman had seen Jack the next day, doing nothing, because he had nothing to do just then, and with his head in his hand. So Mr. Beman took it into his foolish old head that Jack had been drinking, and told him to go at the end of the month. Now I knew it must be papa who had spoken, so I accused him of it, and he admitted that it was true, and began abusing Jack like a pick-pocket, at the top of his lungs. Jack heard what he said, for the door was open, and I don't blame him for coming in. They threatened each other, and got so angry, and I thought they'd kill each other, so, like a silly idiot as I was, I threw my arms round Jack's neck as though I meant to protect him. Papa's so much bigger, you know. Well, he — papa, I mean — lost his head and got me by the arm. He's horribly strong. He got me by the right arm a little above the wrist, and threw me half across the room, and when I tried to help myself up — "

"Do you mean to say that he threw you down? " cried Mrs. Lauderdale, really horrified.

"Yes — of course! With all his might, half across the room, so that I rolled on the floor. Well, when I tried to get up, my arm was broken, and Jack was wrestling with papa. I couldn't help screaming when I fell, and that roused the house, first the servants, and then uncle Robert, in those queer white velvet clothes he wears —

don't you know? Jack told what had happened, and uncle Robert was furious and ordered papa to leave the house — he swore awfully — I never saw him so angry. So papa went. But it was the rage, I suppose, and the exertion — they used up all the dear old man's strength —"

She stopped speaking suddenly as her thoughts went back to the dead man, and her expression changed. Her eyes filled very slowly with tears, that would not quite brim over, but dimmed her sight. When she turned her head again, she saw that her mother had hidden her face in her hands upon the edge of the bed. Katharine did not understand. A convulsive sob shook the shapely shoulders, and the golden hair trembled.

"Mother dear — don't cry so!" said Katharine, putting out her left hand and touching the fair head with a caress. "I know — you were very fond of him — of course —"

Mrs. Lauderdale looked up suddenly with streaming eyes and a face drawn in pain. She shook her head slowly.

"It's not that, child — it's not that! It's the other —"

"About me, dearest?" asked Katharine. "Don't cry about me. I'm all right. It hurts a little now, but it will soon be over."

"No — child — you — you don't understand!" answered Mrs. Lauderdale, with trembling lips.

A passionate burst of weeping hindered her from saying more. Katharine tried to soothe her with voice and hand, but it was of no use. Then she just let her hand rest there, touching her mother's cheek, and lay quite still, waiting till the storm should pass. It lasted long, for in the midst of her sorrow and indignation there was the acute consciousness of the part she herself had borne in all that had happened.

"It's my fault, it's all my fault!" she sobbed, at last.

"No, mother — why? I don't understand! Try and tell me what you mean."

Little by little the sobs subsided and Mrs. Lauderdale dried her eyes. Katharine really did not at all understand what was taking place. She thought her mother must be hysterical. Dark women rarely understand the moods of fair ones.

"You don't know how dreadful it seems to me," said Mrs. Lauderdale, as she grew calmer. "It seems — somehow — awful! There's no other word. Your father treating you in such a way — and fighting with Jack! But it isn't only that — it's deeper. I've done very wrong myself. I've been very bad — much worse than you know — "

"You, bad? Oh, mother! You're losing your head! Don't say such absurd things. You — well, you did go against Jack and me rather suddenly last winter, and I couldn't quite forgive you at the time. But it's going to be all right now."

Mrs. Lauderdale's face grew pale again. For a few moments she said nothing, and once or twice she bit her lip.

"I'm going to tell you what it was," she said, with a sudden impulse — unwise, perhaps, but generous and even noble in its way. "I envied you, dear. That's why I behaved as I did."

"Envied me? Envied — me?" Katharine repeated the words slowly and with a wondering emphasis. "Why? What for?"

Mrs. Lauderdale stared at her a moment in surprise at not being understood immediately.

"What for?" she repeated. "For your beauty — because you're young. Don't you know how beautiful you are?"

Katharine stared in her turn, in genuine astonishment. The idea that her mother could envy her had never crossed her mind.

"Yes — but —" she hesitated, and the rich young blood rose slowly under her white skin. "I know — at least —" she stammered, "people sometimes tell me I'm good-looking, of course. But — but the idea — of your envying — me! Why — it never occurred to me!"

"It's true," said Mrs. Lauderdale, looking down and pulling at the lace on the pillow, with a regretful smile.

"Oh, I don't believe it!" cried Katharine, suddenly. "It's impossible — you may have thought you did, once — "

"No, it's true," answered Mrs. Lauderdale, and the smile faded and was lost in the contrite expression which came into her face.

She had made her confession and wished to go to the end of it. She was trying to make a reparation, being a good woman, and she found it hard, especially as her daughter did not half understand what she meant.

"I'm losing my beauty, Katharine," she said, and every word of the acknowledgment cut her. "It's going, day by day, little by little. You don't know — it's as though my life-blood were being drained — it's worse — sometimes. I'd rather die than grow old and faded. You see, it's all I had. I know now how much I've cared for it — now that it's so hopeless to try and get it back. And one evening last winter — Crowdie was there — he kept looking at you while I was talking to him, and then I caught sight of my face in the little glass that hangs from the mantel-shelf. I shan't forget how I looked. I knew then."

Her face grew suddenly weary and half-desperate now, as she told the little story of the hardest moment in her life. Katharine listened in wondering silence, knowing that she was learning one of the secrets of the human heart. Mrs. Lauderdale paused a moment, and shivered a little, perhaps with the last after-sob of her convulsive weeping.

"Yes — I knew then," she continued, in a low voice and still looking down. "I knew how much it had all meant. And I began to hate you. Don't be horrified, child. I loved you just as much, but I hated you, too. How funny that sounds! But I can't say it any other way. It wasn't you I hated — at least it wasn't the same you that I loved. It was your face, and your freshness, and your youth — and that walk of yours. I wanted you to be all covered up, so that no one could see you — then I should have loved you just as much and in just the same way as ever. Do you understand? I want you to understand. You must, or I shall never be a happy woman again. What I suffered! So I made you suffer, too. Do you know what I thought? You must know everything now. I thought that if I could separate you and Jack and make you marry some one else — since you couldn't marry him — why, then you'd have been away somewhere else, and I could feel again that I was quite beautiful. Only for a month — one month! If I could only have that feeling of being perfectly beautiful again — just for one month."

She bowed her head again and hid her face in the pillow, for she was blushing with shame — the

good red shame that honest blood brings from a
sinful heart. The sight of the blush pained Katharine far more than the thought of what caused it.

"Mother dear —" she stroked the golden hair —
"it's all over now. What does it matter? You
don't hate me now!"

"Hate you! Ah, Katharine — I never hated
you without loving you just as much. I never
said those hateful things but what the loving ones
fought them and came out when I was all alone.
The moment you were gone, it was all different.
The moment I didn't have to look at you — and
think of myself, and the little wrinkles. Oh, the
vile, horrid little wrinkles — what they've cost
me! And what they've made me do! And they're
growing deeper — to punish me — pity me, dear,
if you can't forgive me —"

"Ah — don't talk like that! I never guessed it,
and now — why, I shall never think of it again.
Unless I have a daughter some day — and then I
daresay I shall feel just as you've felt. It seems
so natural, somehow — now that you've explained
it."

"Does it? Does it seem natural to you? Are
you sure you understand?" Mrs. Lauderdale looked
up anxiously.

"Of course I understand!" answered Katharine,
reassuring her. "You've always been the most
beautiful woman everywhere, and just for a little

while you thought you weren't, because you were
tired and not looking well. You remember how
tired you used to be last winter, mother, when you
were working so hard and then dancing every night,
into the bargain. It was no wonder! But you
are, you know — you're quite the most beautiful
creature I ever saw, and you always will be."

Yet Katharine in her heart, though she was
comforting her mother and really helping her with
every word she said, was by no means sure that
she quite understood it all. At least, it was very
strange to her, being altogether foreign to her own
nature. With all his faults, her father had scarcely
a trace of personal vanity, and she had inherited
much of her character from him. The absence of
avarice, as a mainspring which directed his life,
and the presence of a certain delicacy of human
feeling, together with a good share of her mother's
wit, were the chief causes of the wide difference
between her and Alexander. It was hard for one
so very proud and so little vain to understand
how, in her mother, vanity could so easily have
driven pride out. Yet she did her best to imagine
herself in a like position, and was quite willing to
believe that she might have acted in the same
way.

"Thank you, dear child," said Mrs. Lauderdale,
simply. "I don't know why I've told you all this
just this morning. I've been trying to for a long

time. But I hadn't the courage, I suppose. And now — somehow — we're more alone in the world than we were, since the dear old uncle has gone — and we shall be more to each other. I feel it. I don't know whether you do."

"Yes — I do." And Katharine's thoughts again went back to that strange death-scene in the night, in the white room with the soft, warm light. "We shall miss him more, by and by. He was a very live man. Do you know what I mean? Whatever one did, one always felt that he was there. It wasn't because he was so rich — though, of course, we all have had the sensation of a great power behind us — a sort of overwhelming reserve against fate, don't you know? But it really wasn't that. He was such a man! Do you know? I can't fancy that uncle Robert ever did a bad thing in his life. I don't mean starchy, stodgy goodness. He swore at papa most tremendously yesterday — only yesterday — just think!" She paused a moment sadly. "No," she continued, "I don't mean that. He always seemed to go straight when every one else went crooked — straight to the end, as well as he could. Oh, mother — I saw him die, you know! I didn't know death was like that!"

"It must have been dreadful for you, poor child — "

"Dreadful? No — it was strange — a sort of awe. He looked so grand, lying there amidst the white velvet! I see it now, but I didn't think of it then — the picture comes back — "

"Yes — I've seen him," said Mrs. Lauderdale, softly. "His face is beautiful now."

"It wasn't beautiful then — it was something else — I don't know. I felt that the greatest thing in the world was happening — the great thing that happens to us all some day. I didn't feel that he was dying exactly — nor that I should never hear him speak again after those last words."

"What did he say?" asked Mrs. Lauderdale. "No," she added, contradicting herself quickly. "If it's anything like a secret, I don't want to know."

"It wasn't. He looked at me very strangely, and then he said, quite loud, 'Domine quo vadis?'"

"Lord, whither goest Thou," said Mrs. Lauderdale, translating the familiar words to herself. "Did you say anything?"

"I answered, 'Tendit ad astra.' We had both said the same things once before, some time ago. He heard me, and then he died — that was all."

At this point some one knocked at the door. Mrs. Lauderdale rose and went to see who was there. Leek, the butler, clad in deep mourning already, stood outside. There was a puzzled look in his face.

"If you please, Mrs. Lauderdale, I don't know what to do, and I'd wish for your orders — "

"Yes — what is it?"

"There's Mr. Crowdie downstairs, madam, wanting the picture of Miss Lauderdale that he brought yesterday for poor Mr. Lauderdale, and desirin' to remove it. But the impression downstairs seems to be that Mr. Crowdie presented it to poor Mr. Lauderdale yesterday, in which case it appears to me, madam, to be part of poor Mr. Lauderdale's belongings."

"Oh! Well — wait a minute, please. I'll ask my daughter if she knows anything about it."

Mrs. Lauderdale re-entered the room.

"I heard what he was saying," said Katharine, before her mother could speak. "He distinctly said he gave the picture to uncle Robert. I was there when he brought it. Isn't that just like them — coming to get what they can when he's hardly dead!"

"Yes — but what shall we do?"

"I don't care. He'll give it to Hester, as he meant to do at first. Let him take it."

Mrs. Lauderdale went to the door again.

"Let Mr. Crowdie have his picture, Leek. I'll be responsible."

"Very good, madam."

CHAPTER XV.

THE death of Robert Lauderdale was the news of the day, and produced a profound impression everywhere. Even the city put on, here and there, an outward token of mourning, for on every building of the many which had belonged to him, the flag, if it were flying, was half-masted. New York is a city of many flags, and the eye is accustomed to attach meaning to their position.

And people spoke with respect of the dead man, which rarely happens when the very rich are suddenly gone. He had done well with his money, and every one said so. He had been more charitable than many had guessed until those who had been helped by him began to bemoan their loss. Stories went about of his having known, personally and by name, such men as the conductors on the Elevated Road, and of his having visited them in their homes — them and many others. His death made no difference to any one in Wall Street, and every one in Wall Street was therefore prepared to praise him.

Forthwith began the speculation and gossip in regard to the will. John Ralston heard much of

318

it, and he observed a curious tendency amongst
the men at the bank to treat him with greater
deference than usual.

The Ralstons had been informed of the final
catastrophe early in the morning. John had immediately gone to Robert Lauderdale's house,
rather to enquire about Katharine's condition than
for any other purpose, and had thence proceeded
down town. There was no reason why he should
not go to the bank as usual, he thought. The
dead man had only been his great-uncle, and he
had determined to make Mr. Beman change his
mind, and to counteract the influence of Alexander
Junior. The best way to do this was to go to work
as though nothing had happened. Before he had
been half an hour at his desk, his friend Hamilton Bright, the junior partner in the firm, came up
to him.

Hamilton Bright was a sturdy, heavily built
man, five and thirty years of age, with a prosperous air — what bankers call 'a lucky face.' He
was fair as a Saxon, pink and white of complexion, with clear, honest eyes, and quiet, resolute
features. In his early youth he had gone to the
West, and driven cattle in the Nacimiento Valley,
had made some fortunate investments with the
small fortune he had inherited, had returned to
New York, gone into Beman Brothers' bank, and
in the course of a few years had been taken into

the partnership. He was an extremely normal
man. His only peculiarity was a sort of almost
fatherly attachment to John Ralston, about which
he did not reason. The shadow in his life was his
love for Katharine Lauderdale, of which, for
John's sake, he had never spoken, but which he
was quite unable to conceal.

He came to John's desk and spoke to him in a
low voice.

"I say, Jack," he began, "is it true that cousin
Katharine has broken her arm?"

"Yes," answered Ralston, bending his black
brows. "How did you hear it?"

"It's got about and into the papers. There's a
paragraph about it. They say she fell downstairs."

"Some servant told, I suppose, and got a dollar
for the item. It's the small bone of her right
arm — she was staying with poor uncle Robert,
and she had a fall — somehow," added Ralston,
vaguely. "She must have been there when he
died. It was awfully sudden at the end. I saw
him yesterday afternoon. He seemed pretty
strong. I went this morning to enquire about
cousin Katharine — they say he died very peace-
fully. Failure of the heart, you know."

Bright nodded thoughtfully, as he leaned one
elbow upon Ralston's desk.

"What sort of a will is it going to turn out?"
he asked, after a moment's pause.

"I haven't the slightest idea," answered John, with perfect truth.

"It would be a good thing for you if he had died intestate. Your mother and old Alexander are the next of kin. They'd get something in the neighbourhood of thirty or forty millions apiece. You'd give up clerking, Jack."

"I don't know, I'm sure. If I were ever to have much money, a year in a bank wouldn't do me any harm. But I'm not likely to stay here. Cousin Alexander's a good enemy to me. He's been telling Mr. Beman that I drink, and that sort of thing, and Mr. Beman has requested me to leave on the first of the month."

"You don't mean that?" Hamilton Bright's fair Saxon face reddened in sudden anger for his friend.

"Of course I do."

Ralston told him exactly what had happened, and by the time he had finished, Alexander Lauderdale Junior had another enemy, and a dangerous one. Had Bright known all, and especially that Katharine owed her broken arm to her father's violence, something unexpected might have happened. Bright had for Katharine all the Quixotic devotion which a pure and totally unrequited love can inspire in a perfectly simple disposition, which has been brought into rather close contact with the uncompromising code of such a region as the Nacimiento Valley.

"And you wish to stay in the bank?" asked Bright, quietly, at last.

"Yes. And you know very well, Ham, that I'm not as bad as I used to be. I'm going to have a talk with Mr. Beman to-day."

"Don't you bother," answered Bright. "I'll talk to him — now."

Hamilton Bright's broad shoulders swung round, and he went straight to the senior partner's room. Mr. Beman was in his usual seat at his huge desk.

"I want to speak to you about Ralston, Mr. Beman," he said, briefly, laying one of his broad hands upon the shelf of the desk. "You've told him to go on the first of the month, because Mr. Alexander Lauderdale informed you that he drank."

"Yes," answered Mr. Beman, "I have, though I don't know how you heard that it was through Mr. Lauderdale."

"Well — it's a fact, or Ralston wouldn't have said so, in the first place, and I see you admit it. But there isn't a word of truth in the story. Ralston gave up wine altogether last winter."

"Do you mean to say that Mr. Lauderdale has told me — a deliberate falsehood, Mr. Bright?" asked the old banker.

"Yes."

Now Mr. Beman had a very high opinion of Hamilton Bright, but he looked long and earnestly

into the clear blue eyes before he made up his mind
what to say.

"I'd not considered the affair as of any importance," he said, at last. "But you've made it very
serious. Mr. Lauderdale is Ralston's cousin, and
might be supposed to know what he was talking
about."

"Yes. That doesn't make it any better for
him," observed Bright. "I know what I'm talking about, too. Mr. Lauderdale is a sort of cousin
of mine, and I know them all pretty well. I
haven't much opinion of Mr. Lauderdale, myself."

Again Mr. Beman stared and met the calm blue
eyes. He recalled Alexander Junior's steely grey
ones, and did not prefer them. But he said nothing. Bright continued.

"If you can get him to come here, Mr. Beman,
I'd like to repeat what I've said in his presence.
He's a liar, he's a sneak, and I'm inclined to think
he's a scoundrel, though I wouldn't say more."

But in this Bright did Alexander Junior an injustice. Mr. Beman, however, had not survived
fifty years of banking in New York without knowing that just such men as Alexander are sometimes
wrecked, morally and financially, after having
inspired confidence for half a lifetime.

"You use pretty strong language, Mr. Bright.
I've known Mr. Lauderdale a long time, but not
intimately, though I've always considered him a

valuable friend in business relations. I shall certainly not countenance any such proceedings as calling him to account for what he said. But if you are sure of Ralston, Mr. Bright, please ask him to step here for a moment. We'll keep him. Not that he's likely to stay long," added Mr. Beman, with a smile. "His mother and Mr. Lauderdale's father are next of kin to Mr. Robert Lauderdale, who died this morning, I'm told. I should certainly not wish to do an injustice to any near relation of my old acquaintance."

Hamilton Bright, who rarely wasted words, merely nodded and left the room. He went immediately to Ralston again.

"It's all right, Jack," he said. "Mr. Beman wants you to stay, and wants to tell you so. Go right in."

"Thank you, Ham," said Ralston, rising.

A moment later he was standing before Mr. Beman. The old gentleman looked up over his glasses.

"Mr. Ralston," he said, "I've reason to believe that I was hasty yesterday. I understand that my friend was mistaken in what he said of you. I regret what I said myself. I shall be very glad if you'll stay with us. I learn from other sources that you're very attentive to your work, and I must say — Mr. Ralston — " he smiled pleasantly — "it will be just as well for you to know something

about our business, considering the position — the
enviable position — which you'll probably some
day occupy."

John Ralston, the son of one of the next of kin,
was not quite the same person as Jack Ralston, the
grand-nephew of a millionaire.

"I don't know what position I'm to occupy," he
answered. "But I'm very glad to stay with you,
Mr. Beman — and I'm much obliged to you for
doing me this justice."

"Not at all, not at all. I should be very sorry
to do any one an injustice — especially a near relation of my old and valued acquaintance, Mr.
Robert Lauderdale."

Thereupon John Ralston withdrew, very well
satisfied. He had a sort of premonition to the
effect that things were to go better with him. It
was clear, at least, that Alexander Junior could
not prevail against him, since John had van-
quished him twice within twenty-four hours. He
wondered whether Alexander were sitting all alone
in his office at the Trust Company, nervously tap-
ping the table with his long, smooth fingers, and
wondering how soon he was to know the contents
of the will.

The morning wore on, and he could almost see
in the faces of his fellow-clerks how the impression was growing that he would turn out to be one
of the heirs. There was an indescribable some-

thing in their glances, a hardly perceptible change
in their manner, of which he was aware in spite of
himself. But no news came.

At half past twelve he went out and got his
luncheon at Sutherland's, as usual. When he came
back, he found a note on his desk from his mother.
He opened it in considerable excitement, for he
could not deny that he hoped a very large share of
the inheritance might come to Mrs. Ralston, if not
to himself. But the note contained no final news.
Mrs. Ralston said that, considering the enormous
value of the estate, the lawyers desired to make the
will public as soon as possible — a common measure in such cases, as the sudden demise of very
rich men has a tendency to affect public confidence,
until it is known who is to have the principal control of the fortune. Mrs. Ralston said that only
she herself and old Mr. Alexander Lauderdale, as
being the two next of kin, had been requested to
hear the will read that afternoon. She advised
him to come home and wait for her, as early as
he could conveniently leave the bank.

That was all, and he had to possess his soul in
patience during several hours more. His mother
had not yet seen Katharine, and did not mention
her. It was impossible to foresee what she would
do, but it was clear enough that she would not, and
could not, return to her father's house at once.

Before the afternoon was far advanced, the wisdom of the lawyers' advice about the reading of the will became apparent. Rumours were afloat that the whole fortune was to go to old Alexander, and rumour further stated that he was in his dotage, and would be capable of selling miles of real estate to found a refuge for escaped lunatics. Serious persons gave no credit to such talk, of course, but any one acquainted with New York knows how little, at a given moment, may upset the market and cause disaster. The reason of this appears to be that there are more undertakings unfinished yet, or just begun, in America, than there are elsewhere, which depend for their success altogether upon a period of comparative calm in financial affairs. To check them, though they might turn out well, is often to kill them, which means ruin to those who have backed them at the beginning.

But matters proceeded rapidly. Before Ralston left the bank, the newsboys were crying the evening papers, containing, as they avowed, 'the extraordinary will of Robert Lauderdale.' In five minutes every one in the bank had read the statement.

There was a paragraph in which, after giving the reasons for making the will public at once, its principal conditions were named. John, who knew nothing of what Katharine had heard, was neither surprised nor disappointed. The paragraph had evidently been written by one of the lawyers, and sent to all the papers for publication, and there was no account of any interview with any of the heirs. It was a plain account, as far as was possible.

Mr. Robert Lauderdale, it said, had never married; but he had numerous relations, who were all descended from the original Alexander Lauderdale, the grandfather of the deceased. In order to avoid all possible litigation after his death, Mr. Lauderdale had left his fortune as though it had been left by his grandfather, regularly distributed amongst all the heirs of the primeval Alexander, with no legacies whatsoever, excepting certain annuities to be bought of an insurance company before the distribution, for the benefit of the servants in his employ at the time of his death. The will, said the paragraph, bore a very recent date, and had been drawn up, strange to say, by a young lawyer of no particular standing. The names of the witnesses were also given, and, oddly enough, they were persons quite unknown to any one concerned. The paragraph went on to say that it was presumed that the will would not be contested by any one, and would be promptly admitted to probate. A list of the heirs followed. They were: Alexander Lauderdale Senior, Alexander Lauderdale Junior, Mrs. Benjamin Slayback, Robert Lauderdale Slayback, her infant son, Miss Katharine Lauderdale, Mrs. Admiral Ralston, John Ralston, Mrs.

Richard Bright, Hamilton Bright, Mrs. Walter Crowdie. In all, there were ten living persons. The property was to be divided precisely as though the primeval Alexander had left it to his two sons, and as though they, in turn, had divided it amongst their children, down to the youngest living heir, who was Benjamin Slayback's baby boy.

John Ralston pored over the paragraph till he knew it by heart. Then, as soon as he proceeded to apply the terms to actual circumstances, he saw that one-half of the whole fortune must go to Hamilton Bright, his mother, and his sister, Hester Crowdie. Of the remaining half, he and his mother would have half between them, or a quarter of the whole. The smallest share would go to those who actually bore the name of Lauderdale, for only the last quarter would remain to be distributed between the two Alexanders, Charlotte, Katharine, and Charlotte's child. Robert Lauderdale had thus provided a little more liberally for Katharine and himself than for most of the members of the family, since they were to have, ultimately, more than a quarter of the whole. And Alexander Junior would get one of the smallest shares. But it seemed strange that the Brights should have so much, though it was just possible that the old gentleman might have thought it wise to place a large share in the hands of a trained man of business who would keep it together.

On his side, Hamilton Bright had made the same calculations, and was as near to losing his head with delight as his calm nature made possible. He came up to Jack, and proposed that they should walk up town together and discuss matters.

"I can't," answered Ralston. "I'll go a bit of the way on foot, but my mother wants to see me as soon as possible."

They went out, followed by the envious eyes of many who had read the paragraphs. In a few days they were both to have millions.

"Well," said Ralston, when they were together on the pavement of Broad Street, "it's a queer will, isn't it? I suppose we ought to congratulate each other."

"Wait till it's all settled," answered Bright, cautiously. "Not that there's going to be any difficulty, as far as I can see," he added. "It seems to be all right, and properly witnessed."

"Oh — it's all right enough. But if Alexander Junior can fight it, he will. He's come out worse than he expected. The only odd thing, to my mind, is the name of the lawyer. Who is George W. Russell, anyway? Did you ever hear of him?"

"Oh, yes — I know who he is. He's a young chap who's lately set up for himself — real estate. I think I heard of his doing some work for uncle

Robert last year. He's all right. And he'd be careful about the witnessing and all that."

"Yes — well — but why did uncle Robert go to him? Why didn't he employ his own lawyer — his regular one, I mean — or Henry Brett, or somebody one's heard of? I should think it would be more natural."

"Probably he had made another will before, and didn't like to tell his own lawyer that he was making a new one. I've heard it said that old men are queer about that. They don't want any one to know that they've changed their minds. When they do, they're capable of going to any shyster to get the papers drawn up. That's probably what uncle Robert did."

"It's a very just will in principle," said Ralston. "I don't know what it will turn out in practice. I wonder what the estate is really worth."

"Over eighty millions, anyhow. I know that, because Mr. Beman said he had reason to be sure of it some time ago."

"That gives us two twenty and you forty amongst you three. You didn't expect all that, Ham."

"Expect it! I didn't expect anything. The old gentleman never said a word to me about it. Of course you were in a different position, your mother being next of kin with old Alexander. But if Alexander Junior broke the will — he can't

though, I'm certain — I shouldn't get anything.
Of course — I think any will's just that gives me
a lot of money. And if Alexander fights, I'll
fight, too."

"He will, if he has an inch of ground to stand
on. By the bye, if all goes smoothly, I suppose
you'll retire from business, and I shall stop clerking, and Crowdie will give up painting."

"I don't know," answered Bright. "As for me,
I think I shall stick to the bank. There'll be
more interest in the thing when I've got a lot of
money in it. Crowdie? Oh — he'll go on painting as long as he can see. He likes it — and it
isn't hard work."

They talked a little longer in the same strain,
and then Ralston left his friend and went up town
by the Elevated, pondering deeply on the situation.
One thing seemed clear enough. However matters
turned out, whether Alexander Junior fought the
will or not, Ralston and Katharine would be free
to declare their marriage as soon as they pleased.
That consideration outweighed all others with him
at the present moment, for he was tired of waiting.
It was four months since he had been married, and
in that time he had seldom had an opportunity
of talking freely with his wife. The perpetual
strain of secrecy was wearing upon his nervous
nature. He would at any time have preferred to
fight any one or anything, rather than have any-

thing to conceal, and concealment had been forced upon him as a daily necessity.

He said to himself with truth that he might as well have struck Alexander for one reason as for another; that he might just as well have faced him about the marriage as about the calumny upon his own character which Alexander had uttered. But circumstances had been against his doing so. At no moment yet, until the present, had he felt himself quite free to take Katharine from her home and to bring her to his mother's. Alexander's own violence had made it possible. And he had intended, or he and his mother had agreed, to take the step at once, when suddenly Robert Lauderdale's death had arrested everything. There were fifty reasons for not declaring the marriage now, or for several weeks to come — chief of all, perhaps, the mere question of good taste. To declare a marriage on the very morrow of a death in the family would surprise people; the world would find it easy to believe that the young couple had acted contrary to Robert Lauderdale's wishes, and had waited for his death, in fear of losing any part of the inheritance by offending him. Such haste would not be decent.

But there would be no need to wait long, John thought, and in the meantime Katharine could surely not go back to Clinton Place.

Wherever else she might be, he should have

plenty of opportunities of seeing her at his leisure. He reached his home and found his mother waiting for him in his study. She was pale and looked tired.

"I suppose you've heard?" she said, interrogatively, as he entered. "I see it's in all the papers."

"Yes," answered John, gravely. "I've been talking with Ham Bright — we left the bank together."

"I suppose he's in the seventh heaven," said Mrs. Ralston. "Who would ever have expected such a will?"

"I'm sure I didn't. May I smoke, mother? I haven't had a chance all day."

"Of course — always smoke. I like it. Jack — I've been there most of the day, you know. I went in twice to look at him. What a grand old man he was! I wish you could see him lying there on white velvet like an old king."

"I don't like to see dead people," answered Ralston, lighting a cigar. "Besides — I was fond of him."

"So was I. Don't think I wasn't, my dear — very fond of him. But you and I don't look at those things just in the same way, I know. I wish I could see them as you do — dream of something beyond, as you do. To me — feeling that it's all over, and that he is there, dead on his bed, and nowhere else, all there is of him now, or ever will be — well, I was glad to see him as I did. I shall always remember him as I saw him to-day. I wish I believed something. To me — the only hope is the hope of memory for good things and forgetfulness for bad things, as long as life lasts. I've got another good memory of a good man I was fond of — so I've got something."

"It's a depressing sort of creed," said Ralston, smoking thoughtfully. "Not that mine's worth much, I suppose. Still — "

He let the word imply what it might, and puffed slowly at his cigar. Mrs. Ralston passed her hand over her eyes, and said nothing in answer.

"I don't care!" exclaimed John, suddenly. "I can't believe it all ends here. I can't, and I won't. There's something — somewhere, I daresay I shall never get it, but there's something. I know it, because I feel there is. It's in me, and you, and everybody."

Mrs. Ralston smiled sadly. She had heard her husband triumphantly refute the ontological argument many a time.

"I wish I felt it in me, then," she answered, sincerely. "Jack — isn't there something strange about this will, though? An unknown lawyer, servants for witnesses — all that, as though it had been done in a hurry. It seems odd to me."

"Yes. Bright and I were talking about it."

He went on to tell her what Bright thought.

"He says he knows the lawyer, though," he concluded, "and that he's a straight man, so it must be all right."

"Mr. Allen said he'd only heard his name mentioned once or twice lately," said Mrs. Ralston. "It was a long, long will. Then every servant was mentioned by name. I had no idea there could be so many in the house."

"Who are the witnesses?" asked John.

"One was the secretary — you know? That nice young fellow who used to be about. I don't know who the others were — I've forgotten their names. Mr. Allen didn't seem to think there'd be any difficulty about finding them. He thought the property was all in this State — most of it's in the city, so that the will could be proved immediately."

"Well — I hope so. But I believe there'll be some trouble. Alexander only comes in for a small share. He'll do his best to break the will, so as to get the money divided between his father and you. The Brights would get nothing, in that case. We should get a lot more, of course — but then — I can't realize what twenty millions mean, can you? What difference will it make in our lives, whether we have twenty or forty? Those sums are mythological, anyhow. The more a man has, above ten millions, the more care and bother and worry and enemies he's got for the rest of his life."

"I'm glad to hear you talk in that way, Jack," said Mrs. Ralston. "It's just my feeling. But it's not everybody who thinks so. Most men — well, you know!"

"I think you're mistaken there, mother," answered Ralston. "I'm talking of private individuals, of course — not of men who are in big things, like railways, or banks — but just private persons who want to live on their income and enjoy themselves, and who haven't enormous families, of course. No reasonable being can spend more than five hundred thousand a year without trouble — at least, I don't think so. Uncle Robert didn't actually spend three hundred thousand, I've heard it said. He cared for nothing but white velvet and horses — of all things to go together! Of course he gave away a million a year or so. But that doesn't count as expenses. All the rest just rolled up, and he had to spend hours and hours every day in taking care of it. Now, I just ask you, what possible satisfaction can there be in that? And everybody thinks just the same who's not a born idiot — or a financier. Now Bright — he's different. He's a partner in Beman's and finance amuses him. He'd like to be the Astors and the Vanderbilts and the Rothschilds and all the rest of them, rolled into one. He'd like to ride Wall Street like a pony and direct millions, as he owns cattle out in the Nacimiento Valley. I wouldn't, for my part. Twenty thousand a year has always seemed wealth to me, though most people one knows say one can't more than live on it. Did you see Katharine, mother?"

"Of course. We had a long talk."

"You didn't tell her anything, I suppose? I mean, what we were talking about last night?"

"No. I thought you'd rather tell her that you'd told me. Besides — just now! But she can't stay there, Jack. It's rather a ghastly situation — alone in the house with the dead man, and only the servants. That nurse has stayed, though, to take care of her arm. But it's grim — all the shades down, and every one talking in whispers. She was in one of the back rooms, so that she could have the window open."

"Oh — she was up, then, was she? Dressed, and all that?"

"Yes — it's the small bone of the arm. She won't have to stay in bed. You can go and see her if you like. That is, if she's still there. I advised her to go and stay with the Crowdies.. She looked at me as though she wondered whether I knew anything. I suppose she expected that I'd advise her to go home. But that's impossible."

"Of course — but she hates Crowdie. We all do, for that matter. I don't believe she'll go. Didn't she say?"

"No. Why do we all hate Crowdie? We do — it's quite true. By the bye, he's distinguished himself to-day. You know that picture of Katharine?"

"Yes — he gave it to poor uncle Robert only yesterday."

"Well — he came and took it away this morning before ten o'clock. Katharine told me." Mrs. Ralston laughed without smiling.

"Upon my word! But it's rather curious, though. I didn't know he was mean. He never seemed to be, somehow."

"No — I know. It struck me as strange, too. A new light on his chai acter."

"I fancy he has some object. 1 hate him — I loathe him! But that isn't like him. I wonder whether Hester was angry because he gave it away. It was for her, you know, and she may not have liked his giving it away. I'll go and see Katharine. Was it late when you left there?"

"About half past four. I stayed with her a long · time after the lawyer had gone."

"Mother," said Ralston, suddenly, "why can't we just face it out and bring her here? Would it look too strange, do you think?"

"Yes. People would say we'd waited for poor uncle Robert to die. You must have a little more patience, dear boy."

"That's just what I thought at first," answered

Ralston. "I'll go and see her. If she hadn't left at half past four, I don't believe she'll leave to-day. When is the funeral to be?"

"Day after to-morrow, I think."

END OF VOL. I.

THE RALSTONS

THE RALSTONS.

CHAPTER XVI.

RALSTON was mistaken in supposing that Katharine had abandoned all idea of leaving the house on the Park because it was so late. Depressed as she was, and in almost constant pain from her arm, the atmosphere was altogether too melancholy for her to bear. Moreover, she saw how utterly unnatural her staying must seem in the eyes of the world, should her acquaintances ever find out that she had remained all alone in the great house after her uncle's death. After Mrs. Ralston had left her, she had made up her mind to leave in any case, had caused her belongings to be got ready, and had ordered a carriage. But she had not quite decided whither she would go, and Ralston found her in the library still turning the matter over.

"Oh, Jack!" she cried, "I'm so glad you've come, dear!"

"I came this morning," he answered. "But you weren't awake yet. You're dressed to go out —

1

surely you're not going to move at this hour? Tell
me — how's the arm? Does it hurt you much?"

"Oh — it hurts, of course," said Katharine,
almost indifferently. "That is — it's numb, don't
you know? But Doctor Routh says there's nothing to be done for a day or two, and he hasn't moved
the bandages. Now don't talk about it any more
— there are other things much more important.
Sit down, Jack — there, in uncle Robert's chair.
Poor uncle Robert!" she exclaimed, in a different
tone, realizing that the old man would never sit
beside her again.

"Poor man!" echoed Ralston, with real sorrow
in his voice.

There was silence for a moment while they both
thought of him. The stillness of the whole house
was oppressive. There was an odour of many
fresh flowers, and the peculiar smell of new black
stuffs which the disposers of the dead bring with
them. With a sort of instinct of sympathy, John
bent down and kissed the gloved wrist of Katharine's left hand as it lay on the arm of the easy-
chair. She looked at him quickly, moved her
hand a little towards him in thanks, and smiled
sadly before she spoke.

"Jack — I can't stay here," she said. "I'm not
nervous, you know, but I'm not quite myself after
all this. It's too awfully melancholy. Every
time I go to my room I have to pass the door of

the room where he's lying — and then I go in and look at him. It's got to be a fixed idea — if I go near the door I have to go in. And it brings it all back. Then all the people — they come in shoals. There have been ever so many who've wanted to look. It's that horrible curiosity about death. All the relations. Even the three Miss Miners came. I thought they'd never go. Of course I don't see them, so I have to be always dodging in here or into the drawing-room, or the gallery, or else I have to stay in my room. It will be worse to-morrow."

"Yes," answered Ralston. "You ought not to stay." He paused a moment. "Dear," he added, "I want you to know it at once — I've told my mother that we're married — "

"Oh, Jack!" exclaimed Katharine, taken by surprise.

"It was much better. I am not sure that it wouldn't have been better to tell her long ago. She was hurt, because I'd kept it from her — but she's very glad, all the same. You see, she would have had to know it all some day — don't you think I was right to tell her?"

"Yes — I suppose so. Do you know? I'm a little bit afraid of her — well — not exactly afraid, perhaps — I don't know how to express it — "

"You needn't be. She thinks there's nobody like you!"

"I'm glad she's fond of me," said Katharine. "I'm glad you've told her — I was a little surprised at first, that was all. Yes — I'm glad that she knows."

She was evidently thinking over the situation, wondering, perhaps, what her next meeting with her mother-in-law was to be like.

"She's been here with you, hasn't she?" asked John, resuming the conversation after a short pause.

"Yes, and my own mother, too — and then Mr. Allen, and dear old grandpapa. Poor old gentleman! He sat in a chair and cried like a baby when he went in. And then the reading of the will — and the endless people — the people who have to do with the funeral, you know. All those things jar on me. I must get away. I can't stand it another hour — at least — not alone. I think I shall go home, after all."

"Home?" repeated Ralston, in surprise. "But how can you, after all this? Just think how your father will behave! Especially since he's heard of the will. I'm sure he expected to divide everything with my mother, unless he managed to get it all for himself. I see why you promised not to tell after uncle Robert had told you —"

"No — you don't see, Jack," answered Katharine, thoughtfully. "I wonder whether it would be right for me to tell you now. I suppose so.

It may make a difference, though I suppose it can't, really."

"Do just as you feel, yourself," said Ralston. "You know what he said — I don't. I can't judge for you."

Katharine was silent for a few moments. Then it seemed best to confide in him, and she turned towards him suddenly.

"I'll tell you, Jack. This is not the will he told me of. It's quite different in every way. It was only made a few days ago."

"Well, then, this is the valid one."

"Yes — of course. The secretary knew where it was — in a drawer of this desk, here. Uncle Robert had told him it was there, only two days ago, in case of his death. The key was on his chain, on the dressing-table upstairs. You see the secretary was one of the witnesses."

"That's an advantage, anyway. Witnesses are often hard to find, I know. So this will is quite different from the old one?"

"Oh — quite! The one he told me about left everything to you and Charlotte and me — in three trusts, I think he said. We were all to give half our income to the parents — papa and my mother and your mother — and we were all to support grandpapa. The Brights were to have a million, and there was something for the Miners."

"Why, that would have given you and me two-thirds of the fortune! That would hardly have been fair."

"No — it seemed a great deal. But you see he changed his mind before he died. It's much more just, as it is — though it does seem as though grandpapa and papa ought to have more than the Brights."

"I don't see why, if you look at it logically — they're descended just as directly from our great-great-grandfather —"

"Yes — but what had he to do with it? The money didn't come from him."

"No — still — to avoid all quarrelling, there was no other way. Only — it's going to make the biggest family quarrel there's ever been since wills were invented. That's the real logic of events. Things always turn out like that. 'Better is the enemy of good,' you know. Now, let me see. Your father is going to try and break the will, of course. Your grandfather will go with him, because if there's no will, he'll get half — for his asylums and charities. Then I suppose I ought to advise my mother to go with him against the will, too, if there's any good ground for breaking it. Of course we don't want half of what he's left us, as it is — but still, if it's law, it's law, and there's no reason why we shouldn't have what belongs to us, if it does belong to us. The Crowdies are as prosperous as possible. Ham Bright's getting rich,

I know — and then — I say, Katharine, if this will breaks down, would the will he told you about be good, if we could find it? That's a curious question. I must ask a lawyer."

"I don't know anything about those things. But it's getting late, Jack. I must be going — somewhere, but where, I can't tell! I think I'd much better go home and face it out with papa. I'm right, and he's wrong, and he's got to give in sooner or later. I'd much better go, and put an end to all this — this tension."

"You're brave enough for anything!" exclaimed Ralston, with admiration. "Still, if I were you, I wouldn't go till after the funeral, at all events. Don't you think if my mother came here and stayed with you — "

"No, no, Jack! I can't stand it any longer. I can't help going to look at him — I should go in the night — and it's making me nervous."

"How funny! But if you don't want to go into the room, why do you go?"

"I can't help it — I don't know. I'm a woman, you know, and those things take hold of one so!"

"Somebody ought to stay. I think I will. But you'd much better go to the Crowdies'. I know you can't bear him, but it would only be for a couple of days. You'd be with Hester all the time, and you like her, and you needn't see much of him."

"I thought of going to the Brights'. Old Mrs. Bright and I are great friends."

"No — don't! It's hard on Ham. He's so awfully in love with you."

"Yes — perhaps he is. But he's down town all day — I should only see him at dinner, and a little in the evening."

"Don't be ruthless, Katharine!" exclaimed John, with almost involuntary reproach in his tone.

"Ruthless?" she repeated. "I don't understand. What is there that's ruthless in that? I could see you so much more freely."

"Why — don't you know how it hurts — that sort of thing? To go and stay under the same roof with a man who loves you, when you know, and he knows, that you can never possibly love him?"

"I suppose it does," answered Katharine, vaguely. "I hadn't thought of that. But then, you know, Ham would never say anything, any more than if he knew we were married."

"That just makes it so much the harder," replied Ralston, smiling at her woman's view of the case. "Don't you see?"

"Well — of course, if you don't want me to go, Jack, I won't. I believe you're jealous of Ham!" She laughed a little and looked at him lovingly.

"There's no fear of that," he said. "But he's always been a good friend to me. I know what

he'd suffer for those two or three days, though you
can't understand it, I suppose. I don't want him
to suffer on my account."

"Oh, very well. It seemed simpler, that's all.
I dislike Walter Crowdie so — I can't tell you! I
thought of going to your house. I suppose you
thought of it, too — but, of course, it wouldn't do
at all." She laughed again, a little nervously this
time.

"It's not to be thought of," answered Ralston,
gravely.

"Then there's nothing for it but to go to the
Crowdies'. Will you take me down there? I've
ordered the carriage, and I suppose it's ready by
this time. There can't be any harm in our driving
down together, can there?"

"Oh, no — I should think not. We'll pull the
shades half down. Is it one of uncle Robert's
carriages?"

"No — I sent to the livery stable. The men
have no mourning coats — and I thought it would
be odd if the carriage were seen driving about as
though nothing had happened."

Ralston could not help contrasting the tactful
foresight of this proceeding with Katharine's readiness to inflict any amount of pain upon Hamilton
Bright. It was quite true that he could see her
alone more easily at the Brights' than at the
Crowdies', but his own consideration for his friend

altogether outweighed the thought. Katharine saw that it did. She returned to the discussion when they were in the carriage.

"I should have thought you'd prefer to see me at the Brights', Jack," she said. "It would be so much nicer. Of course, at the Crowdies' I can't be always sending Hester off whenever you come. How strange you are sometimes! You don't seem to see things as I do."

"Not this, anyway," cried John, arranging the shades as the carriage turned into Fifth Avenue. "I'm sorry for Ham."

"I should think you'd sacrifice him a little for the sake of seeing me." Her tone showed that she was a little hurt.

"Oh — of course! That is —" he interrupted himself — "that is, you know, if it were very important."

"But isn't it important — as you call it? I wonder whether it means as much to you as it does to me?" She looked at him.

"What?" he asked.

"Our meeting just as often as we can, for a minute, for an hour, to be together as long as possible. You don't seem to care as much as I do?"

"Indeed I do!" protested John, laying his hand on hers. "How can you say such a thing, dear? You know how much I care!"

"Yes — but I sometimes wonder — " She hesitated. "You don't think that means that there is any difference in our love, do you?" she asked suddenly, as though she could not help it.

"Why, no! What difference should there be? We both care just the same — only each in our own way, I suppose."

Ralston's experience was limited, and he was not to be blamed for being a little obtuse and slow to understand. This was a new phase, too, and he was ready to reproach himself with having inadvertently been the cause of it.

"That's just it," answered Katharine. "You say, each in our own way — it seems to me that there's only one way — and that's the very most that can be. That's what I mean, dear. There mustn't be two ways. There's only one way of caring."

"Well — that's our way, isn't it?" asked Ralston, watching her tenderly.

"Not if it isn't just the same for both of us. Because you're a man and I'm a woman — that's not a reason for there being any difference — I'm sure it isn't, Jack!" she added, earnestly.

"Of course not!" he answered, not at all seeing what else he could say.

"Yes — but — " She stopped again and looked into his eyes.

John was not good at phrases. Under great emotion he could be eloquent in few words — with the short, burning syllables, trembling like fire-tongues from a furnace, which break through a man's outer self now and then. But at the present moment he felt no deep emotion — scarcely any emotion at all, in fact. For months he had been used to the idea that the beautiful young girl by his side was his lawful wife. For months he had been accustomed to short, half-clandestine meetings. The great thing, his real life with her, was as far off as ever, in his heart's sight, though his reason told him that the long period of probation was drawing to a close. A habit had formed itself in his heart of taking for granted, without words, that each loved the other truly, and that each was waiting for the other. He had won her long ago. His business . of late had been to overcome circumstances, and he felt that his actions might speak for him now, without language to help them. Yet he felt sorely at the present moment the need of the phrase, and the absence of the heart-beat that might prompt it. He saw that she missed it, but though he loved her so dearly he could not force it to come. She should have been thankful that he could not, and grateful to fate for his inexperience.

It is a long drive from the corner of the Park to Lafayette Place, where the Crowdies lived. The distance is fully two miles and a half, and John realized that in the twenty minutes before him there was time for many misunderstandings. With his natural directness, he spoke out.

"Darling," he said, "don't let's be foolish, and quarrel over nothings —"

"Quarrel? With you? Why — I'd rather die, Jack dear! It's not that. I was only think-ing —"

She stopped, evidently with no intention of com-pleting the sentence, which meant, doubtless, a great deal to her, though it was vague to him. But he had begun his explanation, and was not to be hindered from pursuing it to the end.

"Yes, I know," he replied, as though setting aside all her possible objections. "Let's look at it sensibly. It amounts to this. We both love each other with all our hearts. You always say 'care' instead of 'love.' I suppose it's a euphem-ism. But I say it just as it is. Do you think we should have gone through all we have for each other if we didn't love with all our hearts? I know we couldn't. And as for me, I'm perfectly sure I never cared two straws for any one else. Aren't you?"

"Jack!" exclaimed Katharine, almost offended at the idea.

"Yes — well," he continued, rapidly, "it isn't possible to say which has done the most, or said the most, for the other's sake. I think you've done more for me than I have for you, if you want

to know — but that's been the result of circumstances. You know I'd have done anything under
the sun, at any moment, don't you?"

"Of course I do! Do you think I'd have made
you marry me if I hadn't known that?"

"Well — that's all right. As for saying things
— I've said a great deal more than you have.
I've told you I love you several hundred thousand
times in the last year or two — haven't I?"

"Yes — I've not counted." Katharine smiled,
but Ralston did not see his advantage.

"I don't say that I've found many new words to
say it with," he pursued. "It doesn't always
seem to need new words, and if it did — well, I'm
not an author, you know. I'm not Frank Miner.
I can't go about with a dictionary in my pocket,
looking up new suits of clothes for my feelings
every time I want to air them. And sometimes
I've said it to please you, just because I knew
you wanted me to say it and would be disappointed
if I didn't. You see how frank I am."

"Yes — you're very frank!" She laughed a little, but rather hardly, as though something hurt her.

"Don't misunderstand me, dear," he said,
quickly. "You do — I see you do. It's just
because I won't be misunderstood that I'm talking as I am. What I'm driving at is this. It
isn't true that words never mean anything, as
some people say — "

"Who says so? What nonsense!"

"Oh — people say it — books do — when the authors can't find the words people really say when they mean things. But it's not true. Words mean a great deal, when they do — when they just come because they must, you know, in spite of everything and everybody — when they've strength enough to force themselves out, instead of being dragged out, like olives out of a bottle, and presented to you on a plate. But when they're real, they're very real, with all of one, like pain or pleasure. Actions always mean something. That's the point. There's no possible mistake when a man does things that need a lot of doing, and don't come easily. Then you know he's in earnest, if you'll only look at what he does. Don't you think that's true, Katharine?"

"Yes — oh, yes! That's true enough. But it needn't prevent a man from saying that he cares —"

"Of course not — but if he doesn't happen to want to say it just at that moment —"

"But you should always want to say it. Don't you always feel it?" She looked at him in an odd surprise.

"Feel it — yes — always," he answered, quickly. "But I don't always want to say just what I feel. Do you?"

"No. But that's different. It makes me so

happy when you say it, as you can say it sometimes."

"And don't you think it makes me happy when
you say it?" he retorted. "And you don't say
it half as often as I do, I'm sure."

"Don't I? But I feel it, Jack." Her eyes
sought his, and found them looking at her.

"Well — then — don't you understand?" he
asked.

But his voice was low, and it hardly reached her
ears as the carriage rumbled along, though she
knew that his lips moved, and she tried hard to
catch the sounds. For a few seconds longer they
looked into one another's eyes. Then, without
word or warning, Ralston took his wife in his arms
and kissed her passionately again and again.

No one in the street could have seen, for the
shades were half down and the evening light was
waning. The sun had just set, and the dark red
houses were floating in the afterglow, as everything seems to float when twilight lifts reality from
the earth into its dreamland. And the carriage
rolled and rumbled steadily along. But within it
there was silence for a while, as heart beat with
heart and breath breathed with breath.

"Jack — let me go to the Brights'," said Katharine, suddenly, after what had seemed a very long
time.

Her voice was quite changed. It sounded so soft

and touching that Ralston could not resist it, being taken unawares.

"Dear — if you'd so much rather," he answered, with hardly any hesitation.

"Then tell the coachman, please," she replied at once, without giving him time to change his mind.

It was instinctive, and she could not help it. He yielded almost without reluctance, and lowering the window in the front of the carriage, spoke to the coachman. Katharine breathed a sigh of relief.

"I'm so glad — oh, I'm so glad!" she cried, leaning far back in her seat. "I couldn't have stood Crowdie for a whole evening!"

Ralston said nothing in answer, for he was already repenting of his weakness, and the vision of his friend's face rose before him, with all its habitual calm cheerfulness suddenly twisted out of it.

"Thank you, dear," said Katharine, softly laying her sound hand upon his. "That was sweet of you. You don't know how I feel about it. And you'll come in this evening, won't you? Then perhaps Ham will go out. And Mrs. Bright always goes to bed early, so we can have an hour or two all to ourselves."

"Certainly," answered Ralston, a little absently, for he was thinking more of Bright than of himself just then.

Katharine withdrew her hand from his, not quickly, nor so that he should think she was hurt again by his tone. And she really suppressed the little sigh of disappointment which rose to her lips.

They had been already in Fourth Avenue when Ralston had given the new direction to the coachman, and he had turned his horses and was driving back. The Brights lived in a small but pretty house in Park Avenue, on Murray Hill. It was some distance to go back.

"Jack," said Katharine, quietly, "Hamilton Bright's your friend. Don't you think you'd better tell him that we're married, and put him out of his misery? Don't you think it would be much more kind? You can trust him, can't you?"

"Just as I'd trust myself," answered Ralston, without hesitation. "It's for your sake, dear — otherwise, I should have told him long ago. But you know what most people think of secret marriages, and Ham's full of queer prejudices. Even the West couldn't knock them out of him. He's the most terrific conservative about some things. That's the reason why I never thought of suggesting that I might tell him. Of course — if you'd rather. It would be a blow to him, I think, but at the same time it's much better that he should know, for his own sake. Only — I'd rather not tell him while you're in the house."

" Oh — if it's going to make any difference about
my staying there, we'd better wait," answered
Katharine. "Of course — I hadn't thought of
that. I suppose it would make it all the worse,
just at first. He wouldn't like to see me. But he
must have known, long ago, that we were engaged,
and that he had no chance."

"The one doesn't follow the other," answered
Ralston. "A man like Ham doesn't give up hope
until the girl he loves is married and done for."

"Married and done for! Jack! How you
talk!"

"Oh — it's a way of saying that she's out of
reach, that's all. I've heard you say it lots of
times. No," he continued, after a moment's
pause, "I think it would be kinder to wait till you
come away. But of course I could tell him any
day, down town."

"Do as you think best, dear. Whatever you do
will be right. Only —" She stopped, and looked
out of the window on her right, away from Ralston.

"Only what?" he asked.

"Only love me!" she cried, almost fiercely, and
turning upon him so quickly that she pressed her
injured right arm against the side of the carriage.
"Only love me as I want to be loved — as I must
be loved —"

The passion in her outran the pain of the physical hurt, that crept after it and reached her a moment later, so that she turned a little pale. Jack did not know of that, and in his eyes the pallor was of the heart, as the voice was, and the words. It made her more beautiful, and made love seem more true. Then his own heart beat hard, answering the call of hers, as wave answers wave, and his arms were around her again in an instant.

But at that moment the carriage stopped before the Brights' house. A smile came into the face of both of them as they drew back from one another. Then Ralston opened the door and got out.

It might not have been easy to explain to Mrs. Bright exactly why Katharine had arrived unexpectedly with a box and a valise to stay three or four days with her, instead of going to her own house at such a time. She knew, of course, that the young girl had been at Robert Lauderdale's during the last twenty-four hours. But Mrs. Bright wanted no explanations, and was overjoyed to have Katharine for any reason, or without any. She received her with open arms, ordered her things to be taken upstairs, asked Ralston to stay and have some tea, and at once began making many enquiries about Katharine's arm. Ralston went away immediately, however. After being alone with Katharine in the carriage, as he had been, he did not care to sit still and listen to the excellent Mrs. Bright's questions.

"Thank you, dear," said Katharine again, in an undertone, as he bade her good-bye. "Come this evening. May Jack come this evening, aunt Maggie?" she asked, turning to Mrs. Bright.

"Of course, my dear — whenever he likes," answered the cheerful lady.

Mrs. Bright was a great-granddaughter of the primeval Alexander. Her mother had been Margarate Lauderdale. By no possible interpretation of the relationship was she entitled to be considered the aunt of any member of the tribe. But they one and all called her aunt Maggie. Even the three Miss Miners, who were nieces of Mr. Bright's father, called her so, and the custom had become fixed and unchangeable in the course of many years. Of late, even grandpapa Lauderdale, the philanthropist, had fallen into the habit, much to the amusement of everybody.

Mrs. Bright was a huge, fair, happy-faced woman with an amazingly kind heart and a fresh face, peculiar from the apparent absence of eyebrows — which existed, indeed, but were almost white by nature. She had the busy manner peculiar to a certain type of very stout people. When she was not asleep she was doing good to somebody — but she slept a great deal. Her tastes were marvellously good, highly refined, and very fastidious. Cleanliness is a virtue next to godliness, according to the proverb — and since a number of persons

have relegated godliness to the catalogue of obsolete superstitions, cleanliness with them, at least,
should stand first of all.   But Mrs. Bright's mania
was specklessness surpassing all dreams of cleanliness, as pure spring water surpasses soap as a
symbol of purity. She took care to see that her
house was swept, and she garnished it herself.
She exhaled a faint suggestion of sprigs of
lavender.

Hamilton Bright inherited his fresh complexion,
sturdy build, and solid good humour from her, but a
certain shyness and reserve which were among his
characteristics had come to him from his father.

To Katharine's surprise, he was already at home,
and came down to see her as soon as he heard that
she was in the house. He sat down by the little
tea-table which stood between her and his mother,
and he wondered inwardly why she had come.   He
was pleased, however, and it seemed to him that
her coming crowned the day which had brought
him such vast and unexpected good fortune.   There
are men who love with all their hearts and who are
not loved in return, nor have any hope of such
love, whose greatest happiness is to see the vainly
worshipped object of their misplaced affections
under just such circumstances.   Bright was delighted that Katharine should be his guest and his
mother's — she was his guest first, in his thoughts,
and it gave him the keenest pleasure to see her

drinking his and his mother's tea out of his and his mother's old Dresden teacups, just as though it were her own, and thinking it just as good.

He asked no questions, and he thought of no answers which she might give if he asked any. He was simply pleased, and wished nothing to interfere with his satisfaction as long as it might last.

"It's awfully jolly to see you here," he said, after he had looked at her for nearly a minute.

"Well, you can't be half as pleased as I am," she answered. "I was there all last night, you know, and all to-day. It's grim. I couldn't stand it any longer. And I knew they didn't exactly expect me at home — and I didn't want to go to Hester's, so I thought I'd drop down upon you without warning, as I knew you had nobody staying with you. But it was rather a calm thing to do, now that I think of it — wasn't it, aunt Maggie?"

Mrs. Bright beamed, smiled, kissed her fingers to the young girl, and then did perfectly useless things with the silver tea-strainer, rinsing it again with boiling water, and touching it fastidiously, as though it might possibly soil her immaculate hands.

CHAPTER XVII.

KATHARINE had expected to spend a quiet evening with Ralston. She had counted upon Mrs. Bright's sleepiness, which was overpowering when it suddenly came upon her, and upon Hamilton Bright's tact. She thought that he would very probably go out soon after dinner and not appear again. But she was very much mistaken in her calculations.

When she came down to dinner she found Bright already in the library. He was bending over a low table and looking at a new book when she entered, and she saw a broad, flat expanse of black shoulders, just surmounted by a round, flaxen head. As he heard her step behind him he straightened himself and turned round to meet her. He put out his hand. She seemed a little surprised at this, since they had exchanged all the usual greetings when she had come, but she took it with her left, with an unconscious awkwardness which touched him. She laughed a little.

"It's not easy with my left," she said. "It doesn't come right — besides, we've shaken hands before."

24

"I know," he answered. "But it doesn't do any harm to do it again, you know."

It gave him pleasure to touch even the tips of her fingers.

"You have a sort of classic look," he said, glancing at her dress. "Toga — you know — that sort of thing."

"I don't know how I'm dressed, I'm sure," she answered. "It's such a bore to have one's arm in a sling."

She wore black. Her left side was fitted closely by the soft material, and she had a certain little silver pin at her throat, which had associations for her. She had worn it on the morning of her marriage with John Ralston, and seldom appeared without it, though it was a most insignificant little ornament. Over her right shoulder and arm she had draped a piece of black silk and some lace. Mrs. Bright had come to her room and arranged it for her with unerring skill and taste. It fell gracefully almost to her feet, whence Bright's remark about the toga.

"I should think it would be rather worse than a bore," he said. "It must hurt all the time. I wonder you keep up at all. But I'm glad you've come down before my mother. I wanted to say something to you about all that's happened. You don't mind, do you?"

"Why should I mind?" asked Katharine, smiling at the little timidity which had checked him with its question.

"Well — you know — it's about the will. There may be trouble about it. Your father may wish to break it if he can. It's not unnatural. But of course, if he does, there's going to be a most terrific row all round. We shall all be raging furiously together like the heathen in about a week, if he attacks the will. The Thirty Years' War wouldn't be in it, with the row there's going to be."

"You take a cheerful view, cousin Ham," said Katharine, with a smile. "Who's going to fight whom?"

"You and I are going to be on opposite sides," answered Bright, gravely, and fixing his clear blue eyes on her face.

"Well — what difference does that make?" she asked. "I mean, what personal difference? We shall be just as good friends, shan't we?"

"Ah — that's it! Shall we?" He continued to watch her earnestly.

"Why not?" she asked, returning his gaze quietly. "What earthly difference can it make to me? Of course, I hope papa won't do anything of the kind. We shall all have such heaps of money that I can't see why we should fight about a little, more or less —"

"No — but if he breaks the will, my mother and Hester and I shall get nothing at all, and of course

I shall fight it like anything. You understand that, don't you? It's rather a big thing, you know — it's forty millions or nothing, because we're not next of kin. You'll understand why I shall fight it, won't you?"

He asked the last question very anxiously, and in his broad face there was a curious struggle between the fighting instinct, expressed in the setting of the firm jaw, and the painful fear of being misunderstood, which showed itself in the entreating glance of the eyes.

"I understand perfectly," answered Katharine. "It's your duty to fight it — of course."

"I'm so glad you look at it in that way," he said. "Because if you didn't — " He paused in the middle of the sentence.

"If I didn't, I should be very stupid," observed Katharine.

"No, no! I mean — if I thought you couldn't understand it — well, I'll be hanged if I wouldn't pretty nearly let the millions go, rather than displease you!"

He blurted out the last words bluntly, as such men say wild but sincerely meant things. Katharine understood.

"Please don't say such foolish things, cousin Ham. You know it's perfectly absurd to talk of sacrificing a fortune in that way. Besides, you'd have no right not to fight your best. Two-thirds

of what you'll get will go to your mother and
sister. You haven't the slightest right even to
think of the possibility of sacrificing aunt Maggie
and Hester."

"No. I suppose I've not. And I know that it
isn't as though you weren't to have a big fortune
anyway, however it turns out. Perhaps I'm a
fool, but I simply can't bear to think of being
opposed to you in anything. That's the plain fact,
in two words."

Katharine heard a sort of unsteadiness in the
tone, and looked at him for a moment in silence.

"Thank you, cousin Ham," she said. "You're
a good friend. Thank you." She laid her hand
upon his arm for an instant.

"That's better than millions," answered Bright,
in an undertone, for his mother was just entering
the room.

Mrs. Bright might well be pardoned if she did
not assume a lugubrious and funereal expression
that evening. To her, Robert Lauderdale had been
a distant relation of enormous wealth, from whom
she had little or nothing to expect, and whom she
rarely saw. She had never needed his help, and
though he had occasionally remembered her and
sent her a jewel at Christmas, neither she nor her
son had ever felt very much indebted to him. The
surprise was therefore overwhelming, and the re-
joicing inevitable and natural. Knowing, how-

ever, how dearly the old man had loved Katharine,
and that she had been with him at the time of his
death and had been really fond of him, Mrs. Bright
avoided the subject altogether during dinner. It
would not keep out of her face, however, nor out
of her manner. Once or twice she and her son
exchanged glances, and both suppressed a happy
smile. Katharine saw, understood, and felt sad.
The conversation turned upon generalities and was
not very amusing.

. Katharine could not help thinking of what
Bright had said to her just before dinner. At
the moment, he had undoubtedly meant that he
would sacrifice the vast inheritance rather than
incur her momentary displeasure. Of course, she
said to herself, when the case arose he would not
really have done so, but she could not but appreciate the reckless generosity of the thought, and
wonder at the possible strength of the love that
had prompted it. He had spoken so earnestly and
there had been such a perceptible tremor in his
voice, that she had been glad when Mrs. Bright's
appearance had cut short the interview. While
she talked indifferently during dinner, her thoughts
dwelt on what Ralston had said about Bright's
feelings and then went back to Ralston himself,
who was almost always present in her reflections.
She felt that she should not have felt any surprise
if he had spoken as Bright had done. It would

have been quite natural. She might even have
thought of accepting the sacrifice.

Just then, after a little pause in the conversation,
Mrs. Bright suddenly asked her son whether he
meant to go out in the evening.

"No," he answered, promptly. "Not to-night.
I wouldn't go anywhere except to the club, and
even there — well, everybody would be talking and
asking questions, and that sort of thing. Besides,"
he added, "cousin Katharine's here."

The change of tone as he spoke of Katharine was
so apparent that Mrs. Bright smiled a little sadly.
Her woman's instinct had told her long ago that
her son had very little chance.

The three had not been long in the library when
a servant brought a card to Mrs. Bright. She
glanced at it, somewhat surprised by the coming
of an unexpected visitor, in these days when evening visit have disappeared from New York's
changeable civilization.

"It's Archie Wingfield," she said. "Funny!"
she exclaimed. "Show Mr. Wingfield in," she
said to the servant.

A moment later Archibald Wingfield entered the
room. In spite of himself, he paused a moment as
he caught sight of Katharine.

"Oh!" he ejaculated, awkwardly, in a low voice.

Then he came forward, resolutely keeping his
bold black eyes on Mrs. Bright's face as he went

up to her and shook hands. Katharine had understood the exclamation of astonishment, and felt
the awkwardness of the situation. But as she
had given up all hope of seeing Ralston alone that
evening, she thought it was as well, on the whole,
that some one else should have come to help the
general conversation. Nevertheless, she would
have chosen almost any one rather than her last
rejected suitor.

Both she and Hamilton Bright watched the
young fellow with involuntary admiration as he
crossed the room and stood exchanging first words
with Mrs. Bright. There is a fascination about
physical superiority when it far outdoes all its
surroundings and is altogether beyond competi-
tion which, perhaps, no other attraction exercises
in the same degree at first sight.

Wingfield came to Katharine next. The rich
blood rose in his brown cheeks.

"I didn't know you were here," he said, simply.

"Excuse my left hand," she answered, quietly,
as she extended it. "I've had a little accident."

Wingfield started perceptibly. The expression
in his black eyes changed to one of the deepest
anxiety, and the blush slowly ebbed from his
face.

"An accident?" he stammered.

"Oh — nothing serious," she answered, touched
by the evident strength of his feeling. "It's only

the small bone of my right arm. I fell down yesterday and broke it. It's in splints, of course, so
I have to use my left."

"And you're — you're not taking care of yourself? With a broken arm?" He seemed amazed,
not having had much experience of broken limbs
— his own were solid. "But you ought to be at
home — "

Katharine laughed a little.

"I'm staying here with aunt Maggie," she answered. "I could scarcely have any better care,
could I?"

"Oh — I see. Yes." But he did not seem
satisfied.

He turned to Bright, shook hands, and then sat
down.

"You must think it awfully funny — my dropping in, in this way," he said, recovering the self-
possession which naturally belonged to his character. "The fact is, I was going to dine out, and at
the last minute the people sent to tell me not to
come, because they've had a little fire in the
dining-room, and everything's flooded and uncomfortable, and they were going to picnic somewhere
— or something. So I dined at the club, and I'm
going to see the last act of that play with the
horses in it, you know — so I thought you wouldn't
mind if I asked leave to spend half an hour with
you on the way."

"Why, of course not!" cried Mrs. Bright. "I'm delighted. You must help us to amuse Katharine. She's rather gloomy, poor child — with her arm, and all she's been through. She was staying with poor Mr. Lauderdale when he died so suddenly."

"Yes — it's awfully sad," answered Wingfield, with appropriate solemnity, and wondering whether he should congratulate the Brights upon the inheritance. "As for amusing Miss Lauderdale," he continued, "I wish I could. But I'm not a very amusing person — not a bit."

"Perhaps we can amuse you, instead," suggested Katharine, by way of saying something.

"Oh, no · — thanks — you're very kind," answered the young man, confusedly. "You know my brothers always call me the family idiot. They're always chaffing me because I don't know languages and things. I say, Bright — you're clever — do you know a lot of languages?"

"I? No, indeed!" answered Bright, with a short laugh. "I don't know anything particular — except about cattle and horses, and something about banking. I've had a modern education! How should I know anything?"

"Oh, hang it all — I mean — I beg your pardon — but what a thing to say!"

"It's mere nonsense," observed Mrs. Bright. "Ham knows everything in a useful way. But he's always railing at modern education, and telling me that it's ruined his mind. He's not sensible about that. Really you're not, Ham," she added, with emphasis.

"Education's meant for the common herd, mother," answered Bright. "Fools are better without it, bankers don't need it, and geniuses can do better."

"That's rather good," said Katharine, thoughtfully. "With which do you class yourself?" she asked, with a laugh.

"Well — being neither a genius nor a fool, I have to be content with being a banker."

"I say — are lawyers part of the common herd, Bright?" enquired Wingfield.

"Not if you're going to be one, my dear boy," answered the elder man. "But I hope you're not going to nail me out on my statement like an owl over a stable door. It's not kind. It's much nicer to be misunderstood in a friendly way than to have all one's friends up on their hind legs trying to understand one, when one hasn't meant anything particular. By Jove! There goes the bell again! I wonder who it is?"

"What ears you have!" exclaimed Mrs. Bright. "I didn't hear anything. But it must be Jack Ralston. He'd come early, you know."

Katharine glanced surreptitiously at the two men, leaning back in her chair with half-closed eyes. Bright's expression became a little more set, and he moved one foot uneasily. Wingfield looked at Mrs. Bright as she spoke, and then straight at Katharine. Ralston entered in a dead silence, glanced quickly at Wingfield, greeted every one in turn, in the quiet, easy way peculiar to him, which was quite different from Bright's slow and rather heavy manner, and from Archibald Wingfield's physical style, so to say, which showed itself in long, swift, powerful movements, like the great stride of a magnificent hunter going along in the open.

"You'll be tired of the sight of me to-day," said Ralston, smiling as he sat down near Mrs. Bright.

"No fear of that, Jack," answered Bright, anxious to show Katharine that he was not displeased at Ralston's coming. "My mother always looks upon you as a sort of second son."

"The prodigal son," suggested John.

"Is that a hint to produce the fatted calf?" asked Bright. "Or have you dined? You don't look as though you had."

"Why? What's the matter with me? I've just come from dinner. I dined at home with my mother."

"You're rather lean for a man who dines every day," laughed Bright. "That's all. I believe you starve in secret. You're afraid of getting fat,

Jack — that's the truth. Confess it! You think
it wouldn't be romantic."

"I wish you would get a little fatter, Jack," said
Katharine. "You'd be much nicer, I'm sure."

The remark might have been natural enough
between two cousins, both young. But there was
a subtle suggestion of proprietorship, or at least of
belonging to one another, in the tone of her voice,
which jarred on Wingfield's ear. He was by no
means dull nor slow of perception, in spite of what
he had said of himself. As an athlete, however,
he took up the question.

"You'd be stronger if you were a little heavier,
Ralston," he said. "Do you go in for oatmeal
when you train?"

"Oh — I haven't trained since I was at college.
I never bothered much. But I don't like stodgy
things like porridge. I was a running man, you
know. I don't believe it makes a particle of difference what one eats."

"Oh, I do!" Katharine exclaimed, anxious to
make the conversation move. "I like some things
and I don't like others."

"What, for instance?" asked Bright. "What
do you like best to eat — and then afterwards, what
other things do you like best in the world? That's
interesting. If you'll tell us, we'll get them for
you right off."

"I should think you could, between you," said

Mrs. Bright, glancing round at the three goodly
men, and wondering whether Wingfield was as
much in love with Katharine as the other two.

"What I like? — let me see," said Katharine.
"I like simple things to eat. I hate peppermints,
for instance. My mother lives on them. I like
plain things, generally — fish and game. Truffles
— that's another thing I detest. Aunt Maggie
never can understand why. She says there's something mysterious in a truffle, that appeals to her."

"They're so good!" exclaimed Mrs. Bright.
"Big black ones in a napkin with fresh butter.
But it's quite true. There's a sort of mystery in
a truffle. It's like love, you know."

Everybody laughed at what seemed the fantastic
irrelevancy of the comparison — Bright laughing
louder than the rest.

"How do you make that out?" he asked. "It
would be rather a grimy, earthy sort of love, I
should think."

"Explain, aunt Maggie!" laughed Katharine.

"A truffle's a cryptogam," said Bright. "Nobody has ever explained about cryptogams."

"What is a cryptogam?" asked Katharine.
"I've always wanted to know."

"Cryptogam means secret marriage, or something of the sort," said Wingfield.

Katharine started a little and glanced at John
Ralston.

"Yes," said the latter. "It's equivalent to saying that nobody knows how they grow. But that doesn't at all explain what aunt Maggie means by what she said. Come, aunt Maggie, we're all waiting for you to tell us."

"Oh — I'm getting so sleepy, my dears, don't ask me to explain things! You know I'm always sleepy in the evening. It's taking an unfair advantage of me! Why is love like a truffle? Why, exactly for that reason — because nobody can possibly tell when it begins, or how, or why — or anything about it. Only, when you find it, you've found something worth having. As for secret marriages — wasn't it you who mentioned them just now, Mr. Wingfield? Yes — well, they're very romantic and unpractical and pretty, but I should think the people would find it a great nuisance. It's much better to run away, and be done with it."

Ralston's eyes met Katharine's, and he suppressed a smile, but in her pale face the colour was rising slowly. Again the door opened, and two men entered the room unannounced. The servant had taken it for granted that as two visitors had been admitted, he might admit as many more as came. Paul Griggs, the author, and Walter Crowdie, the artist, came forward into the bright light. Crowdie has been already described. Griggs was a lean, strong, grey-haired, plain-featured man of fifty, a gaunt, bony, weather-beaten man, who had lived in many countries and had seen many interesting sights — but none so interesting, people had been saying lately, as Katharine Lauderdale's face. It was commonly said that he was in love with the girl, and people added that at his age it was ridiculous, and that he was making a fool of himself.

Crowdie, as the son-in-law of the house, and one of the numerous persons who called Mrs. Bright 'aunt,' came forward first, to shake hands and explain the visit.

"I was going to make an apology for coming in without warning, aunt Maggie," he said. "Griggs dined with us, and we're going to see the last act of that play with the horses in it — you know — and as it's too early, we thought we'd ring the bell and call. But as you've got a party, I suppose you accept the apology. At least, I hope you will."

"You're very welcome, Walter — glad to see you, Mr. Griggs." Mrs. Bright beamed. "It is a party — isn't it? Why, there are five men in the room. Let's all go and see the last act of the play with the horses, and come back to supper! Oh — I forgot — and Katharine, too, with her broken arm. But Mr. Wingfield's going to it by and by."

"Yes," said Wingfield. "I'm going. We'll walk up together."

Both Griggs and Crowdie had already heard of Katharine's accident and were asking her about it, before Mrs. Bright had finished speaking. Presently the new-comers got seats, and the circle widened to admit them as they sat down.

"I'm sure we interrupted some delightful conversation," said Griggs, breaking the momentary silence. "Won't you go on?"

"My mother was explaining her views upon secret marriages," said Bright. "She'd just been comparing love to a truffle."

"Truffle — cryptogam — secret marriage — love," said Griggs, gravely. "Very natural sequence of ideas. The interesting link is the secret marriage."

"Yes, isn't it?" assented young Wingfield. "What do you think about it, Mr. Griggs?"

"What were you saying about it?" asked the man of letters, cautiously.

"No — what do you think about it?" insisted Mrs. Bright. "We hadn't said anything especial."

"Is anybody present secretly married?" enquired Griggs, with a pleasant laugh. "No — exactly — then I shouldn't advise any of you to try it. I did once — "

"You!" exclaimed two or three voices at once, and in surprise.

"Yes — on paper, in a book, with my paper dolls. I never want to do it again. It had awful consequences."

"Why, what do you mean?" asked Mrs. Bright.
"Oh — nothing! I fell in love with the heroine myself from writing about her, killed the hero out of jealousy, and blew out my brains in the end because she wouldn't have me. I suppose it was natural, considering what I'd done, but I took my revenge. I put her into a convent of Carmelite nuns. It was so awkward afterwards. I wanted her in another book — because I was in love with her — but as she was a Carmelite, she couldn't get out respectably, so she's there still. It's an awful bore."

Even Katharine, who had felt the blood rising again in her cheeks, laughed at the simple, natural regret expressed in Griggs' face as he spoke.

"Yes," said Bright. "That's all very well in a novel. But in real life it's quite different. I think a man who does that kind of thing is a cad, myself."

"So do I," said Archibald Wingfield, impetuously. "A howling cad, you know."

"It's an unnecessary piece of presumption to suppose that the world cares what one does," said Crowdie, who had not spoken yet. "And it complicates things abominably to be married and not married at the same time. Shouldn't you think so, Miss Lauderdale?" he asked, turning his head towards Katharine as he spoke.

"I? Oh — I've no opinion in the matter," answered Katharine, looking away, and feeling very uncomfortable.

"I don't agree with either of you," said Ralston, slowly. "It depends entirely on circumstances. There are cases where it's the only thing to do, if people really love each other. I don't think any one has a right to say that a man's a cad simply because he's married his wife secretly. A man's a much worse cad who marries a girl for her money, and doesn't care for her, than any man who gets secretly married for real love — and you all know it."

Ralston could not help speaking rather aggressively.

"Look out for the family temper!" laughed Walter Crowdie, in his exquisitely musical voice.

"We're all more or less of the family here," answered Ralston, "except Mr. Griggs and Wingfield. Not that we're likely to get angry about such a question," he added, with an attempt at indifference. "What I say is that it's a monstrous injustice to call a man a cad on such grounds."

"Oh — all right, Jack!" cried Bright. "If ever you get secretly married, we won't say you're a cad. But in most cases — well, I'd rather hear Griggs talk about it than talk myself. He's an expert in love affairs — on paper, as he says. Say what you really think, Griggs. Wingfield and I can hold Ralston between us if he shows signs of being dangerous."

"I think I could help myself, in a modest way," said Mr. Griggs, with a quiet smile. "I used to be pretty strong once."

He made the remark merely in the hope of turning the conversation. Wingfield, as an athlete and a young Hercules, could not hear any allusion made to physical strength without taking it up and discussing it.

"Were you a boating man, Mr. Griggs?" he enquired, with sudden interest.

"No. I never pulled in a race."

"I suppose you went in for long distance running, then. You're made for it," he added, rather patronizingly and glancing at the man's sinewy figure.

"No. I never ran in a race," answered the literary man.

"Oh — I supposed, when you spoke, that you'd gone in for athletics — formerly," said Wingfield, disappointed.

"No — I wasn't educated in places where athletics were the fashion at that time. I was strong — that's all. I could do things with my hands that other people couldn't."

"Could you?" Katharine saw that the original subject was dropping, and encouraged the dull conversation which had taken its place. "What

could you do with your hands?" she asked, with
an air of interest. "They look strong. Could
you roll up silver plates into holders for bouquets,
like Count Orloff?"

"I think I could do it," Griggs answered, quietly.
"But nobody ever wanted to waste a silver plate
on me."

"It's not easy, I should think," said young
Wingfield. "I know I couldn't do it."

"I'm sure you could," said Katharine, turning
to him. "You must be tremendously strong. But
can't you do something else with your hands, Mr.
Griggs? I like to see those things. They amuse
me."

Griggs was the last man in the world to wish
to show off his qualities, physical or mental, but
on the present occasion he could not resist the
temptation. He never knew afterwards why he
had yielded, and attributed his weakness to the
inborn desire to excel in the eyes of women, which
is in every man.

"Have you a pack of cards?" he asked, turning
to Bright. "If you have, I'll show you something
that may amuse you."

Bright was a whist player, and immediately
brought a pack from a remote corner of the room
and put it into Griggs' hands.

"Now — there's no deception, as the conjurers
say," he began, with a laugh, looking first at

Katharine, and then at Wingfield, as the strong
man of the party. "Perhaps you can do it, Mr.
Wingfield?" he added.

"What? Tricks with cards? No—I'm not
good at that sort of thing."

"Well—it isn't exactly a trick. I'm going to
tear the pack in two. Did you ever see it done?"

"No," answered Wingfield, incredulously. "I've
heard of it—but I don't believe it's possible, if
you tear it fairly."

"Is this fair? Have I got a fair hold on them?"

"Yes—that's all right. I don't believe anybody can do it that way."

"Well—look."

Griggs set his teeth a little as he made the
effort, and the furrows in the weather-beaten face
deepened a little, but that was all. The sinews
stood out on the backs of his hands for a few
seconds, and his hands moved, the one downwards,
the other up. The pack was torn clean in two.

"By Jove!" exclaimed Bright. "I never saw
that done."

"I wouldn't have believed it," said Wingfield.
"I've often tried. It's perfectly magnificent!"

"I'll avoid you in a fight," observed Ralston,
laughing.

Crowdie had looked on with curiosity, but he
had watched Griggs' face rather than his hands,
comparing it with a picture of Samson pulling

down the pillars, which rose in his memory. He
came to the conclusion that the man who had
painted the picture had never seen a great feat
of strength.

"It looks so easy," said Katharine. "But it
must be awfully hard."

"There's a good story the peasants tell in Russia
about Peter the Great," said Griggs. "He was
hunting. His horse lost a shoe, and he stopped at
a wayside smith's. The smith made a shoe while
Peter waited. Peter took it, tried it in his hands,
broke it and threw it into a corner, saying it was
bad. The smith made another, and the Czar broke
it again, and so on. But he could not break the
tenth. The blacksmith asked a rouble for the
shoe. Peter gave him one. He broke it in two
and threw it into a corner, saying it was bad —
and so he broke as many roubles as the Czar had
broken shoes, and said that the tenth was good.
Peter was so much pleased that he made the man
a general — or something."

"I suppose you could do that, too, couldn't
you?" asked Katharine, looking at the gaunt, grey
man with a strong admiration.

"Oh, yes — I've done it. But it's a strange
thing, isn't it, when you think that it's all an
illusion?"

"An illusion!" cried Wingfield, in disappointment. "What do you mean? It isn't a trick,
surely!"

"Oh, no! I don't mean that. But all matter is an illusion, isn't it? Nothing's real that isn't permanent."

"But if matter isn't permanent, what is?" asked Bright. "But I know — you have the most extraordinary ideas about those things."

"I don't think they're extraordinary. If matter were permanent in the sense you mean, then life would be permanent in the same sense, because we're matter, and we shouldn't die."

CHAPTER XVIII.

YOUNG Wingfield looked at Katharine with an air of entreaty, as though hoping that she, at least, might understand what Mr. Griggs meant. She smiled as she saw his expression, and understood what was passing in his mind. She was supposed to have seen far more of Griggs during the preceding month than she really had, and she got credit for comprehending, at least, the general drift of his ideas, beyond what she deserved. Wingfield looked at her in vain, and then broke the silence which had followed Griggs' last speech.

"I wish one knew what to believe," he said, formulating the nineteenth century's dying question. "It's not easy, you know, with all these theories about."

Of the seven persons present there was not one whose convictions really coincided, even approximately, with any established form of belief. Yet all belonged to some one of the few principal Christian churches, by birth, early associations and youthful teaching.

Wingfield's question was received in silence. His bold black eyes glanced from one to another of

48

his companions, and the blood mounted slowly in his healthy brown cheeks, for he was young enough to fancy that some of these might have thought his remark futile or trivial and he did not wish to seem dull before Katharine.

She found herself in a strange position. By a very natural train of circumstances she was accidentally set up as a sort of idol that evening before the five men who, of all others, each in his own way, most sincerely loved and admired her. Secretly married to the one of them she loved, two of the others — Hamilton Bright and Wingfield — wished to marry her. Of the other two, Crowdie, the painter, admired her more than any woman he had ever seen, though he was undoubtedly in love with his wife. Had she been able to understand his admiration, it would have repelled her. Fortunately it was beneath her understanding. And to Griggs, weather-beaten, overworked, disenchanted of all that the world held, by reason of having had much of it either too early or too late, with his hard head and his dreamy mind and his almost supernaturally strong hands — to Griggs she represented something he would not have told then, but something which Katharine need not have been ashamed to hear of, nor her husband to tolerate. Ralston might even have found sympathy for him.

They all worshipped her in one way or another,

though she was a very human girl of her time and place in the world. And somehow, in the silence which followed Griggs' speech, broken only by Wingfield's questioning remark, they all turned to her as he had done, as though in her face they sought the lost faith. Hard-headed men, some of them, too, and hard-fisted. The three eldest had each accomplished something. The two younger ones were perhaps on the way. They were rather typical men.

Katharine was vaguely conscious of their glances, and was the first to speak, after Wingfield.

"It's what we all feel — what half the people we know feel, though they haven't the courage to say it."

Wingfield looked at her gratefully, conscious that she had justified what he had feared had been a foolish observation.

"Katharine," said Mrs. Bright, who had not spoken for a long time, "if you're going to talk theology, I shall go to bed — like the baron in the Ingoldsby legends. 'There are no windows to break, and they can't get in' — do you remember? So he went to bed and slept soundly through the siege. It's exactly the same with theology, my dear. It's all been discussed a hundred thousand times, and yet nobody ever gets in. There's only one religion the whole world over, and that is, to do the best one can and help other people — because no one can do better than the best he can, according to what he thinks right. And there's a great deal in soap, my dear. I'm sure people feel like better people when they're clean, and as people do what they feel, why, they really are better people. I'd like to try free soap in the State of New York for a year, and see whether it didn't improve the criminal statistics."

"It's a splendid election cry, mother," said Bright. " 'Soap — Something — and Stability.' We'll try it some day."

"No, but there's truth in it," protested Mrs. Bright. "Isn't there, Mr. Griggs?"

"Of course," answered Griggs, gravely. "Every religion that ever existed has some rules of ablution. And there's a lot of truth in the other things you said, Mrs. Bright. Only the trouble is, a code of action — what you call doing the best one can — doesn't satisfy humanity. The average human being won't do anything for its own sake. He must do it for his own advantage here — or hereafter, since people will insist on using that idiotic word."

"Why idiotic?" asked Wingfield, very naturally.

"Hereafter means a future, and there isn't any such thing, except in a small way, for matter-worlds and such little trifles, which go to pieces every two or three thousand million years."

"Yes, but the soul — if we've got one."

Wingfield added the last conditional expression
rather sheepishly, as though he suspected that the
highly intellectual beings amongst whom he found
himself might have done away with such old-fashioned nonsense as the soul.

"Of course you've got a soul," said Griggs,
rather impatiently. "But if it's a real soul, it
has no weight and no size, and no shape and no
colour, nor anything resembling matter — nor anything with which to resemble anything, except
other souls. Well, of course you know that time
is only conceivable in relation to matter in motion,
so that where there isn't any matter, there isn't
any time. And where there's no time there can't
be portions of time, which are past, present, and
future. So the soul has no time, doesn't exist in
relation to time, and consequently can't be said to
have a hereafter. The body has a hereafter — oh,
yes — it's absorbed into the elements and lives
over again thousands of millions of times. But
the soul hasn't. It's eternal. If it always is to
be, as we say, comparing it to matter, why, then, it
always was, by the same comparison. But the
fact is, that 'it is' — and there's no more to be
said. 'It is,' and as it's indestructible, not being
matter, by the hypothesis, nothing can be said of
it in that respect except that 'it is.' You can't
say that an axiom, for instance, has a past, present,
and future, can you ? Well — if the soul's any-

thing, it's axiomatic. There, I've bored you to death — shall I tear another pack of cards for you, or break silver dollars to amuse you? I'll do anything I'm told, now that I've had my say."

Griggs laughed quietly and crossed one leg over the other, as he looked at Katharine.

" You're not a comforting person when one feels religious," she said.

" No — by Jove!" exclaimed Bright. "You wouldn't have converted the cowboys in the Naci-miento Valley, Griggs. They'd have tried their own idea of a hereafter on you — quick. That's the trouble with all that metaphysical stuff, or whatever you call it — it doesn't say anything to mankind — it only talks to professorkind. Unless a fellow's passed a sort of higher standard in terminations, he hasn't the ghost of a chance of spiritual comfort. He couldn't understand the first word of what you talk about."

"Did I use long words?" asked Griggs, blandly. "I thought I didn't."

"Well, not exactly long words. I don't mean literally terminations. But you talk another language, somehow. I know I'm what they call an educated man, because I once learned some Latin and Greek at a sinful expense of time. But I can't half follow you, even when you use good plain English. The policeman at the corner would march you off and clap you in jug like a shot if you talked to him that way for five minutes. That is, unless you tied him up in a hard knot with those hands of yours, and set him down by the railings to cool. I wouldn't try it, though. I suppose there's a limit to the number of policemen you could strangle with each finger. No — joking apart — that sort of thing isn't going to take the place of Christianity, you know — even as people like us look at what we call Christianity. You've got to have something to pray for and somebody to pray to, you know, after all."

" Well," answered Griggs, "there's God to pray to and salvation to pray for."

" Not in your system — without any future," retorted Bright.

" Oh, yes, there is," replied the other. " You seem to think I'm an atheist, or a freethinker, at least — though I can't see why, I'm sure."

" Why — because — " Bright stopped, trying to formulate his accusation.

Katharine laughed a little, and Wingfield looked from one to the other with a puzzled expression, as though he should have liked to understand better. Griggs proceeded to defend himself.

"Did I say that there was no soul?" he enquired. " On the contrary, I said that the soul was eternal. Did I say that there was no God? I said nothing about it. The soul is a part of God, and, therefore, since the part exists, the Whole, of which it is a part, exists also. It's my belief, and, therefore, so far as I'm concerned, it's fact. Belief is knowledge — the ultimate possible knowledge of every man at the moment of asking him what he believes. Did I deny that the soul is happy or unhappy according to its rule of itself? Not at all, though I didn't try to explain the way in which it strikes me. You might not understand it. But I believe that its happiness or unhappiness is exactly inversely relative to the amount of alloy it gets from the things of which it is conscious. As I see them all in my own way, I believe all the articles of faith of my church, and I'm a Roman Catholic."

" Well — I don't see how you can," said Bright, discontentedly.

" You're our dear Buddhist!" put in Mrs. Bright, with a breadth of toleration peculiar to her, and becoming. " You've often told me the most delightful things about Buddhism, and I shall never think of you as anything but a Buddhist."

"That's a thoroughly logical position, mother!" laughed Bright. " Stick to it!"

" I can't help it if my Christianity seems like Buddhism to you," answered Griggs. "If you knew more about Buddhism, you'd see the difference very soon. But religion's like love. It affects different people differently. It isn't often that any two people see it in precisely the same light. When they do — "

He paused, interrupting himself. His tired eyes
became suddenly dreamy, as he stared at the Persian embroidery that hung before the disused fireplace around which they were all sitting.

"What happens when they do?" asked Katharine.

"What happens, Miss Lauderdale? How should
I know what happens when people who are in love
see love in the same light? I'm an old bachelor,
you know." He laughed drily, being roused again.

"You're right about one thing at all events," said
Crowdie. "It's not often that two people love
in the same way. There are five of us men here,
about as radically different from each other as five
men could be, I should think. It's quite possible
that we may all be more or less in love at the
present moment. I'm willing to confess that I am.
Don't jump, Ham! I'm in love with my wife, and
as we're in the family I suppose I may say so,
mayn't I?"

"You needn't be ashamed of loving Hester, my
dear Walter!" cried Mrs. Bright.

Bright himself said nothing, but looked curiously
at his brother-in-law, whom he disliked in an unaccountable way. He had never been able to understand Griggs' apparent attachment to the man.
He had heard that when Crowdie had been a young
art student in Paris, twelve or fourteen years
earlier, Griggs had nursed him through an illness,

and had otherwise taken care of him. There was a mystery about it which Hamilton Bright had always wished to solve. According to him, the best thing about Crowdie was his friendship for the literary man. Bright could not fathom its mystery, any more than he could understand his sister's passionate, all-devouring love for Crowdie. The husband and wife were almost inseparable. Such a state of things should have seemed admirable to the wife's brother, but for some mysterious reason it did not. Bright had almost resented his sister's ardent devotion to a man who seemed to him so unmanly. He always thought that Crowdie, with his soft, pale face and vividly red lips, was like a poisonous tropical flower that would ultimately harm Hester in some unimaginable way.

"No — I'm not ashamed of it," said the painter, in answer to his mother-in-law's remark. "But that isn't the question. What I mean is, that we all love, or should love, in different ways — all five of us. Look at us — how different we are! There's Griggs, now. I've known him half my life and a good bit of his. If he's in love, he's picked out a soul, and then a face, and then a set of ideas out of his extensive collection, and he's sublimated the whole in that old retort of a brain of his, and he's living on the perfume of the essence. Poor old Griggs!"

"Don't pity me, and don't patronize me, Crowdie!" laughed Griggs. "If you offend me, I'll pay you off, you know."

"I'm not frightened — but I've done with you. I'll go on. There's Ralston — he's dangerous. He'd love like Othello, and lose his temper like Hotspur. As for Bright, he has permanent qualities. When he's once made up his mind, it makes up him for the rest of his life. Faithful Johnnie, don't you know? He's a do or die sort of man — and with his constitution it means doing and not dying. Wingfield — oh, Wingfield's Achilles. An Achilles with black hair — only rather more so. With his size, it's lucky for the Trojans that he hasn't got your Lauderdale temper that you're always talking about. Schliemann wouldn't even find the foundations of Troy. Wingfield would pulverize the whole place and use it up for polishing his weapons. Briseis, or nothing — while the mood lasts. I don't mean to say that you're fickle, Wingfield, but you're much too human for an undying passion, you know."

"How about yourself?" enquired young Wingfield. "We've each had our turn. Don't forget yourself."

"Oh — as for myself — I don't know. I'll leave that to you. You can all take your revenge, and define me, if you like. I'll be patient. I'm not aggressive by nature. Besides, I'm quite different — I mustn't be judged like you other men."

"And why not ? " enquired Katharine.

"Why — I'm an artist. The foundations of my nature are different from yours. I'm a skilled workman. It's your business to be more or less skilled thinkers. I do things with my hands, you do things with your brains. The beginning of art is manual, mechanical skill. Any one who's got it enough to be an artist must be something of a materialist. He can't help it, any more than a surgeon can. What's subject to you is object to me — so we can't possibly look at the same things in the same way."

"That's why you're such a confounded materialist ! " exclaimed Griggs.

"Nonsense !" retorted Crowdie. "You're always saying that matter's an illusion and an idea. I'm the real idealist because I go in for matter, which is nothing but a dream, according to you."

"Of all the consummately impertinent arguments ! " laughed the man of letters. " You're an arrant humbug, my dear Crowdie."

"Since matter's only humbug, I don't mind," rejoined the painter. " That's unanswerable unless you throw up your theory — which you won't, for I know you. So you'd better leave me and my art to do the best they can together."

"It seems to me that Crowdie's got rather the better of you," observed Bright.

"Oh—he has. I always admit that the children

of light haven't a chance against the children of
darkness."

"That's an argument 'ad hominem,'" observed
Crowdie. "It's your way of throwing up the
sponge."

"Hit him again!" laughed Bright. "Turn the
other theoretical cheek to the smiter, Griggs!"

"He's afraid of me, all the same," retorted
Griggs. "These materialists are the most superstitious people alive. He believes that I learned
all sorts of queer things in the East, and that I
could roll up his shadow, like Peter Schlemil's, and
destroy his Totem, and generally make his life a
burden to him by translating 'The Owl and the
Pussy Cat' into Arabic, and pouring ink into my
hand, and all that. You know you do."

"Yes," answered Crowdie. "I confess that I'm
what you call superstitious. I'm inclined to believe
in things like magic and spells — like John Welling-
ton Wells. Since your matter's all a dream, it
can't take much to blur it, and make it move about
and change and behave oddly. Oh, yes — I believe
in the spirits of the four elements, and all that —
or if I don't, I'd like to."

"What good would it do you?" asked Wingfield,
bluntly.

"Good? It isn't a question of good, it's a
question of beauty. I want to believe that beautiful things have a consciousness and a sort of

power of their own, a special perishable soul —
the sort of soul that Lucretius talks about. I'm
quite willing to think that they may have an
immortal soul, too, but what concerns me is the
perishable one, that suffers and enjoys and speaks
in the eyes and sighs in the voice."

Crowdie knew what he was talking about. In
painting, his talent lay chiefly in expressing that
perishable, passionate animation which is in every
human face. And so far as the voice was concerned, his own was remarkable, and the few who
ever heard him sing were almost inclined to ask
whether he had not mistaken his vocation and
erred in not becoming a public singer. It is not
an uncommon thing to find painters who have
beautiful voices. Gustave Doré, for instance,
might have earned both reputation and fortune
as a tenor.

"I'm afraid you're an incorrigible heathen,
Walter," said Mrs. Bright. "I wonder you
haven't set up gods and goddesses all over your
house — you and Hester — with little tripods before them, and garlands and perfumes — like Tade-
ma's pictures, you know."

"You can't symbolize matter, aunt Maggie,"
laughed Crowdie. "If you do, you get entangled
with the ideal again, and your symbol turns into
an idol. The Greek statues were meant for portraits of gods and goddesses, not for symbols. So

were the pictures and the images of the early
church — portraits of divine and holy personages.
The moment such things become symbols, there's
a revulsion, and they turn into idols."

"That's a profound thought, Crowdie," said
Griggs. "I don't believe you ever hit on it by
yourself."

"Well — it's in my consciousness, anyhow, and
I don't know where it comes from," answered the
painter. "I suppose it's part of my set of ideas
about matter."

"It all seems to me very abstruse," said Wingfield, who was considerably bored by the discussion, to Katharine, who was listening.

"No," she answered, quickly. "I like it. It
interests me."

She had only glanced at him, but she had realized at once that he was still wholly occupied with
herself. There was a wistful, longing regret in
his black eyes just then which she understood well
enough. She was sincerely sorry for him, and
would have done anything reasonable in her power
to comfort him. As he turned from her she looked
at him again with an expression which might have
been interpreted to mean an affectionate pity,
though she had certainly never got so far as to
feel anything approaching to affection for the
magnificent youth. Almost immediately she was
conscious that both Ralston and Bright were

watching her during the momentary pause in the conversation.

"Why are you both looking at me like that?" she asked, innocently glancing from one to the other.

"Oh — nothing!" answered Bright, colouring suddenly and turning his eyes away. "I didn't know I was staring."

Ralston said nothing in reply to her question, but transferred his gaze from her to Wingfield, with something not unlike envy in his look. Few men could look at Wingfield without feeling a little envious of his outward being, and Ralston was a man singularly devoid of personal vanity, like his mother.

"I wish I could paint you all!" exclaimed Crowdie, suddenly.

"That's a large order," observed Bright, with a smile.

"You've all got such lots in your faces to-night," continued the artist, with an odd enthusiasm. "There must be something in the air — well, that doesn't mean anything, of course — but it's very strange."

"What's strange?" asked Katharine.

"Oh — I can't exactly explain. There's an unusual air about us all, as though we were under pressure and rather inclined to do eccentric things. I could paint it, but I can't possibly put it in words."

"I suppose I'm not sensitive," said Wingfield to Katharine. "I don't notice anything particular, do you? At least — not outside, you know," he added, quickly, being all at once conscious of something he had not been aware of a moment earlier.

"I know what he means," answered Katharine. "I feel it myself. But then — I'm tired and I suppose I'm nervous."

"There's a queer, mythological atmosphere about," Crowdie was saying.

"It's what we've been talking about," said Mrs. Bright. "We're all so completely mixed on the subject of time and space and things like that, that we're just ready to believe in ghosts, and turn tables, and make idiots of ourselves."

"What a barbarian you are, aunt Maggie!" cried Crowdie, looking round at his mother-in-law. "You'd take the poetry out of the Nine Muses. Not that I meant anything poetical. It's much more a sort of creepy, dreamy, undefinable sensation. Yes — perhaps you're right after all. I shouldn't be surprised if one of us saw a ghost to-night."

"What will you bet?" enquired Ham, with the slow, western emphasis he could assume when he chose.

"You're insufferable!" exclaimed Crowdie. "Fancy betting on seeing ghosts! You're worse than aunt Maggie. The only man who understands me is Griggs. Griggs, you do understand, don't you ? "

There was something petulant and almost womanish in his tone, which struck all four men disagreeably, though perhaps none of them could or would have told why.

" Don't talk ! " answered Griggs. " When you want people to understand you, paint or sing. You only make a mess of it when you try to explain what you feel in English. You're a good painter and you sing like an angel, but you're a bad talker."

" That's said because I got the better of you in talking just now," retorted Crowdie, who did not seem in the least annoyed.

"Oh, don't begin sparring again, for heaven's sake ! " exclaimed Bright. " Cousin Katharine's tired to death of hearing you two fighting. Sing something, Walter. It's much better."

" Oh, no ! " answered Crowdie. " Oh, no ! I can't sing, thank you. I never sing at parties — as they call it."

" You don't call this a party, do you ? " enquired Bright. "Don't be silly. We all want to hear you. You're not the common amateur who has to be begged and flattered and cajoled, and praised afterwards. You can sing when you choose, and we all want you to."

" No. I'd rather not," said the painter, with a

change of tone, as though he were very much in earnest.

"I wish you would!" Katharine, for the moment, really longed to hear the wonderful voice.

"Do you?" asked Crowdie.

There was a hesitation in his tone which suggested the idea that he had perhaps been waiting for Katharine to ask him, in order to yield to the request. Instantly the young girl was aware that the eyes of Ralston and Bright were upon her. Griggs had turned his head and was watching Crowdie curiously. Mrs. Bright looked at him, too, hesitated, and then spoke.

"I really think that promise you made Hester was too absurd, Walter!" she said.

"What promise?" asked Katharine, quickly.

"Not to sing for any one but her," said Mrs. Bright, before Crowdie could interrupt her. "Hester told me."

Everybody looked at Crowdie and smiled at the sentimentality. His soft eyes glanced disagreeably at his mother-in-law for a moment, and the smile on his red lips did not conceal his annoyance.

"Besides," continued Mrs. Bright, "if Katharine asks you, I think you might — really, it's too silly of Hester."

"Oh!" exclaimed Katharine, "I don't want you to break any promise, Mr. Crowdie — especially

one you've made to Hester. She'd never forgive
me. Please don't sing — some time when she's
here — perhaps — "

But at once she again felt Ralston's glance and
Bright's. She wondered why they looked at her
so often.

"Well then, it isn't Katharine who asks you,"
said Mrs. Bright. "I do. I'll be responsible to
Hester. I know she won't mind, if it's for me.
Now, Walter, do! Just to please me!"

Crowdie said nothing. He turned his eyes upon
her and then to Katharine's face. But, feeling
uncomfortably as though she were being watched
for some reason which she could not understand,
Katharine was looking down, nervously pulling
at a thread in the lace which covered her right
arm.

Wingfield was sitting on one side of her, in one
of those naturally graceful attitudes which athletes
assume without thought or care, one elbow on his
knee as he bent forward, supporting his chin upon
his in-turned hand, his resolute young face turned
towards Crowdie, his black eyes somewhat sad and
shadowy. On Katharine's other side sat Ralston,
nervous, moody, ready to spring, as it were, for he
had not yet recovered from his anger at what had
been said about secret marriages. Next to him
was Bright, upright in his straight-backed chair,
his heavy arms folded on his full chest, his round

head thrown back, his clear blue eyes fixed on Katharine's face.

As she looked up again, she had a strong impression of being surrounded by splendid wild animals. Wingfield was the tiger, colossally lithe, brown, black, and golden; Ralston the panther, less in strength, but lighter to spring, quicker to see, perhaps more cruel; Bright the lion, fair, massive, dominant, silent in his strength. Griggs was a wolf, grey, old, tough, destined to die hard some day without a cry. And Crowdie — with his woman's eyes, his soft, clear voice, his delicate white hands, his repellent pallor, and wound-like lips — Katharine thought of neither man nor beast. Even in the midst of her dream of wild animals, he was Crowdie still, with a mysterious, indescribable, poisonous something in all his being which made it a suffering for her to touch his hand. To this something, whatever it might be, she preferred her father's cruel avarice, her mother's envy, heartless as it had been while it lasted. To it she would have preferred a drunkard's trembling hand and lip. John Ralston's ungovernable temper was immeasurably preferable to that, or her sister's mean pride and petty vanity. There was no weakness or sin, scarcely any crime of which her maiden heart had dreamed with horror, which she would not have met and faced and seen in its bare ugliness, rather than that unknown something of which the existence was a certainty when Crowdie was near her.

In the dead silence of the moment the very faintest sound would have been loud. Whether they admitted it or not, they were none of them just then in a natural or normal state of nerves, except perhaps Mrs. Bright, whose supernal calm was not easily disturbed. Each one of the five men was thinking in his own way of Katharine, and of all she might be to him. The great passion was there, five-fold, and it made itself felt in the very air of the quiet room.

Then a soft vibration, as of a soul far off, murmuring to itself, just trembled and felt its way amongst them, like the promise of a caress. And again it came, more strongly, more clear, floating in the soft air and taking life in it, and stealing to the heart with a tender, backward-reaching regret, with a low, passionate looking forward to things of love yet to come.

Crowdie was singing. He had not changed his position as he sat in his chair, and he had scarcely raised his face. There was no effort, no outward striving for art, no searching for effect. The notes floated from his lips as though he thought them rather than as though they were produced by any human means, rising, sinking, with ever varying colour, tone, and meaning, ringing, as he sang, like an angel's clarion tones, sighing, as he breathed them, like the whole world's love-dream.

Then time, too, sank away into dreamland. Before Katharine's closed eyes rose Lohengrin, silver-armed — floated the mystic swan — clashed the clanging swords. And then, moonbeams, the passionate, great, spell-ruled love — the question and its horror of endless parting — the rush of the destroyers to the bridal chamber, the last, the very last farewell, and out through the misty portals of the dream floated again the fatal, lordly swan, with arching neck, bearing away, spirit-like, the last breath of love from Elsa's life.

None of them could have told how long he sang, for time was away in dreamland, and passion's weary eyes drooped and saw not the pain.

CHAPTER XIX.

KATHARINE felt considerable hesitation about going to see Mrs. Ralston after John had told her that he had confided the secret of their marriage to his mother. She knew very well that they must meet before long, as they often did, and she felt that, since Mrs. Ralston knew the truth, it would be very disagreeable if the meeting took place in the presence of other persons. So far as any formality was concerned, too, it would naturally have been her duty to go and see her mother-in-law, though, in consideration of the young girl's broken arm, any such questions of courtesy could well be overlooked.

Katharine's sensations as she looked forward to the interview could not easily be described. She was, as usual, in a very exceptional position, for she was so placed that she should have to make something like an apology to Mrs. Ralston for having married John against his will. There was something absurd in the idea, and Katharine smiled, alone in her room, as she thought of it.

She was tired with all she had been through, and she put off the difficult moment rather weakly, telling herself that she would surely write and make an appointment on the following day, when she had collected herself and thought it all over. She was fond of Mrs. Ralston, and knew that her liking was returned. Mrs. Ralston had made her understand that well enough, and John had taken pleasure in telling her that his mother never wished him to marry any one else. Nevertheless Katharine felt shy and awkward, and was afraid of saying too much or too little.

Mrs. Ralston herself cut short all hesitation and came to see Katharine at the Brights', and found her in her little sitting-room upstairs. The young girl was taken by surprise, as the elder woman had followed the servant and entered almost as soon as she had been announced.

"Oh — Mrs. Ralston!" she cried, sitting up on the lounge on which she had been lying after luncheon.

They exchanged greetings. Mrs. Ralston made her lie down again and sat beside her. There was a moment's silence.

"I'm so glad you've come," said Katharine, breaking the ice.

"Of course I've come!" answered Mrs. Ralston. "If you'd not had this dreadful accident, you'd have come to me; but as it is, I've come to you, since we wanted to see each other."

There was not much in what she said, but it gave

Katharine courage, which was precisely what the elder woman wished to do. That was one of her few secrets. She knew how to make what was the best thing to be done seem altogether natural, and even easy, for those who had to do it, while avoiding the appearance of ever giving advice unless it were asked of her. That is the rare gift of those who really influence others in the world. Their art lies in going so straight as to make any way but their own seem crooked by comparison.

"Yes," said Katharine, "I wanted to see you very much. The fact is —" she hesitated and she felt the colour rising in her cheeks, though Mrs. Ralston could not see it. "The truth is that I —" she broke off again. "Oh, what's the use of making phrases, cousin Katharine?" she exclaimed. "Jack and I are married — and you know it — and you must forgive me — that's what I want to say!"

"And that's the best and the simplest way of saying it, my dear," answered Mrs. Ralston, smiling — for she was happy. "And now that it's said, let's talk about it."

"How good you are!" Katharine put out her left hand, and turned, bending a little, so that her face was near her companion's shoulder.

"I don't know whether I'm good to be glad," said Mrs. Ralston. "As for forgiving you — that's for your father and mother, not for me. The only thing I didn't like was that Jack shouldn't have told me at once. I was hurt by that. We've been good friends, he and I, and he ought to have known that he could trust me."

"We were afraid to trust anybody — except uncle Robert," answered Katharine, simply. "And we had to trust him. That was the object of our getting married as we did."

"Of course you could trust him perfectly, my dear. But it did no good. Jack told me all about that. If he had come to me and said it all before-hand, I could have helped a good deal. But that wasn't your fault."

"Yes, it was," protested the young girl, anxious lest Ralston should be blamed unjustly. "It was altogether my idea from beginning to end — "

"Jack didn't tell me that — "

"No?" Katharine's face lightened softly. "No," she repeated, in another tone. "He wouldn't have told you that. He would have thought that it would be like blaming me. He left that out of the truth. But it's true, and you ought to know it. You don't know how hard it was for me to per-suade him to marry me secretly. I used every sort of argument before he would promise. It was I who thought that if we went straight to uncle Robert with our secret, he would find it so easy to give Jack just what he wanted. But Jack was right. He knew more about it than I did. How-

ever, he yielded at last. But I want you to know
how hard it was. He said it was like a begging
speculation. He would rather have died than have
accepted money from uncle Robert. I'd have taken
it, and uncle Robert offered it to me, but Jack
wouldn't let me accept it."

"Of course not, my dear," answered Mrs. Ralston. "That's exactly what it would have been —
a begging speculation. There's only one thing
that can excuse a secret marriage, and that's
love."

"Well — in that case — " Katharine did not
finish her sentence, but smiled happily as she
turned her face away.

"Yes — exactly!" And Mrs. Ralston laughed
softly. "That's the reason why I say that I've
nothing to forgive you," she continued, after a
little pause. "You see, you've loved each other a
long time — "

"Ages!" exclaimed Katharine, energetically.

"And your father objected. Of course he had
a right to object, if he saw fit. And you couldn't
have told him what you had done unless you were
prepared to leave him and come to me — which you
wouldn't do — no! I know what you're going to
say — that it would have been putting a burden
upon me — and all that. But it wouldn't. That's
what hurt me, that taking it for granted that I
should not be ready — much more than ready — to

make a sacrifice for Jack's sake. Do you know what he is to me — that boy — your husband ?"

Her face changed suddenly, and the even lips set themselves in a look that was almost fierce, as she asked the question.

"I can imagine," said Katharine, in a low voice. "I know what he is to me."

"Yes. I know you love him. But it's not the same thing. You'll know some day. I hope you may. There's another kind of love besides that of men and women."

She spoke with a suppressed energy that Katharine hardly understood. The young girl mentally compared this woman's love for her son with Alexander Junior's parental affection for his daughter. It seemed to be a very different thing.

"No," continued Mrs. Ralston. "You can't guess what Jack is to me, and always has been. I don't think he knows it himself. If he did, he'd have trusted me more when he was in trouble. I'd do a good deal to make him happy."

As usual with her, there were no big words nor harmonious phrases. What she said was very simple. But at that moment she looked as though Katharine Ralston would have trampled on Katharine Lauderdale's body, if it could have contributed to Jack's happiness.

"You love him very much," said the young girl. "So do I."

"I know you do. I don't mean to say that in your way you may not love him as much as I do. We shan't quarrel about that. I only want you to understand why I was hurt because he wouldn't tell me what he'd done. Since he was a boy I've thought his thoughts, I've lived his life, I've done his deeds — I've been sorry for the foolish ones and proud of the good ones — I've been his other self. It was hard that I shouldn't have a share in the happiest moment he ever had — when he married you. It hurt me. I'd give my body and my soul — if I had one — for him. He had no right to leave me out and hide what he was doing."

"It was my fault," said Katharine. "It was foolish of me to make him marry me at all, as things were then. I've thought of it since. Suppose that we had changed our minds, after it was done — we were married, you know — we couldn't have got out of it."

"If you changed your mind, as you call it, I wouldn't forgive you," said Mrs. Ralston, as sternly as a man could have spoken.

Katharine looked at her in silence for a moment.

"Yes," she answered, gravely. "I think that if I changed my mind now, you'd try and kill me. You needn't be afraid."

Mrs. Ralston returned her gaze, and her features gradually relaxed into a peaceful smile.

"In old times I should," she said. "I believe I'm that kind of woman. But we're not going to quarrel about which loves him best, my dear — though I believe we're both capable of committing any folly for him," she added.

"Yes. We are," said Katharine. "And I don't suppose that we could say so to any one else but each other in the world."

"I'm glad you feel that. So do I. And Jack knows it all without our telling him. At least, he should, by this time."

"Do men ever know?" asked Katharine.

"That's hard to say. I think there are men who know what the women who love them would do for them. I'm sure there are. But I don't think that any man that ever lived can understand what a mother's love can be like, when it's strongest. It belongs to us women — and to animals. Men can only understand what they can feel themselves, and they can never feel that. They understand anything that's founded on passion, but nothing else."

"Isn't a mother's love a passion, then?" asked Katharine.

"No — it can't be jealous."

Katharine wondered whether the saying were true, and whether Mrs. Ralston's own words and looks had not disproved her proposition before she had stated it.

CHAPTER XX.

It is not long since, upon the death of a well-known lawyer, it was found that he had made a long and elaborate will for himself, duly signed and witnessed, but no single clause of which was good in law, though he had been in the habit of drawing up wills for others during all his professional life. It is not an easy matter to dispose of property amongst a number of persons in such a way that no one shall be able to find a flaw which may invalidate the whole document, even if the signing and witnessing be in order and unassailable.

For a long time past Alexander Junior had been much interested in the subject, and he believed that he had mastered it unaided, in all its details, so as to be able to detect any technical illegality at a glance. Being quite unable to foresee the nature of Robert Lauderdale's intentions, he had done his best to prepare himself at all points, in case the will should turn out contrary to his hopes and wishes, as had actually occurred. At first sight, however, his anticipations were disappointed. So far as he could judge, the will was unassailable, though it contained very unusual provisions. If it were admitted to probate, it looked as though it would be unassailable.

It had of course been in the power of the testator to leave the whole property to whom he pleased, irrespective of relationship, or to divide it amongst such of the living relations as he chose to favour. But, in theory, he had favoured no one. He had willed as though the whole portion had belonged to his grandfather, and had descended from the first Lauderdale who had emigrated, to all the members of his family in its present ramifications. It was not easy to assail the justice of the idea upon which the will had thus been founded, and there could be no question of attacking it on the ground that the testator was not of perfectly sound mind.

Clearly, however, it would be vastly to Alexander Junior's advantage if the will were not allowed to stand. Katharine Ralston would get half the fortune, indeed, but Alexander Senior would get the other half. This, in the estimation of Alexander Junior, would be tantamount to getting it himself. It would be more easy, considering his father's age and infirmities, and especially in consideration of the old gentleman's known tendency to give away everything he possessed, to have a trust constituted, at his own request, so far as the world should know, which trust should manage the property and pay him the income arising from it during the remaining years of his life. In the ordinary course of human events, Alexander Senior could not be expected to live many years longer, and his son believed it would be very easy to influence him in the making of his will, or to prove that he had been of unsound mind in case the will were not satisfactory. Then the whole fortune would come to his son as next of kin.

But Alexander Junior was met at the outset by the difficulty of finding any fault with the will of Robert Lauderdale. It was clear from the date that it had been made during his last illness, in the interval between the day when he had first been very near death, on which Alexander had met Katharine in the house, and his ultimate demise. Several weeks had passed, during which it had been expected that he might recover, and he had found ample time to reconsider his last wishes. It was immediately clear to Alexander that this was probably not the will of which his uncle had spoken to his daughter. It might be. It was possible that he had told her what he intended to do, and had then done it. But it was improbable; for when she had seen him that first time, he had not been expected to live, and it was not likely that he then looked forward to the possibility of drawing up a document requiring considerable thought and great care.

It was quite clear that Alexander must put the

matter into the hands of a keen and experienced
man without delay, and he lost no time in doing
so. If he had not acted quickly, the will might
have been proved and administered in a few days,
and his chance would be gone. Within twenty-
four hours it was known that the will would be
contested by Alexander Lauderdale Junior on be-
half of the next of kin, being his father and
Katharine Ralston.

At this news there was a great commotion in
all the Lauderdale tribe, and sides and parties
declared themselves immediately. The prediction
that there would be a tremendous disturbance of
the family elements was immediately realized, for
the interests at stake on all sides were very large.
The ranks were marshalled and the battle began.

Clearly it was to the interest of the Lauderdales
and the Ralstons to invalidate the will if possible,
while it was that of the Brights to sustain it, and
the heads of the opposing parties were actually
Alexander Lauderdale Junior and Hamilton Bright.
It should have followed that the Brights should
have stood alone against all the others, a state of
things which Alexander believed should influence
the court in his favour, since in common opinion
it would not seem exactly fair that a small family
of distant relations should get as much as all the
nephews and nieces of the deceased together. In
the matter of wills, the courts often have a con-

siderable latitude within which to exercise discretion, and no circumstance which bears upon the
equity of the case is insignificant.

Though Alexander Junior had neither a very
profound nor a very diplomatic intelligence, he saw
at once, and his lawyer dwelt upon the point, that
it would be greatly to his advantage if he could
establish an evident solidarity amongst the next of
kin as against the Brights, who would profit by
the will as it stood. It became his object therefore to assure the coöperation of the Ralstons.

At first sight it seemed to him that Mrs. Ralston
should without doubt support him. He could not
easily conceive that she should hesitate between
accepting a quarter of thé fortune to be divided between her son and herself, and the half of it to be
held in her own right. He judged her by himself,
as people of strong passions judge others. He threw
out of consideration any sentiment she might have
in regard to the fulfilment of Robert Lauderdale's
wishes, and made it purely a question of money
for her, as it was for himself. He did not believe
that any enmity which her son might, and undoubtedly did, feel for him, could stand in the way of
such a power as twenty millions of money to influence her. His lawyer, who did not know her well,
agreed with him.

But when it became necessary to find out what
Mrs. Ralston meant to do, Alexander was conscious

that he might be wrong in his calculations. Much
against his will he secretly admitted that there
might be other motives at work besides the love
of money, especially in a case where a large fortune
was a certainty, whatever happened, and where the
choice lay not between much and nothing, but
between much and more. Mrs. Ralston returned
answer that she desired to consider the matter and
wished to know how soon she must make a definite
reply.

Then she consulted John.

"I don't know what to do, Jack," she said, seating herself in her favourite chair in his study.

It was late in the afternoon, and it was raining.
But it was warm, and one of the windows was
raised a little. The smell of the wet pavement
and the soft swish of the shower came up from the
street.

"Why should you do anything, mother?" asked
Ralston. "However — I don't know — " he checked
himself suddenly and became thoughtful.

"What is it, Jack? Why do you hesitate?"
asked his mother. "I hesitate, too. I want to
know what you think about it."

Ralston reflected in silence for a few minutes,
before he spoke.

"There are so many ways of looking at it," he
said at last. "In the first place, you and I should
naturally like to carry out the dear old man's

wishes, shouldn't we? That's our first instinct, I suppose. Isn't it?"

"Of course it is. There can be no question of that."

"Yes. You and I always agree. We were both fond of him, and we're both grateful to him. We both want things to be done as he wished. He's tried to be just all round, and if he hasn't been quite fair in leaving the Brights so much, it's because justice isn't always exactly fair. Law is one thing and equity's another, all the world over. His general idea was to make litigation impossible, and in carrying it out the principle happened to favour the Brights. It might have happened to favour us instead."

"Yes. That's plain," said Mrs. Ralston. "That's one side of the case. But there's the other."

"More than one other, perhaps. In the first place, if poor uncle Robert did anything that's not good in law, I've no business to advise you to support his mistake out of sentiment, and to lose twenty millions by it."

"Put that out of the question, Jack."

"No — I can't. It's a first-rate reason against my giving you any advice at all. I ought not to influence you. You should act for yourself. Only, as we agree about things generally, we're talking it over."

"No," answered Mrs. Ralston. "It's not that.

It's your children. If I should stand out against
Alexander on the ground of sentiment, I may be
keeping money from your children, or their children, which they have much more claim to have than
the Crowdies' descendants, for instance. And you
must think of that, too. Hamilton Bright's getting on towards forty. I suppose he doesn't marry
because he's still in love with Katharine, poor
fellow. But if he doesn't marry soon, he probably
nèver will. At his age men get into grooves. He's
devoted to his mother, and with all her good qualities I don't believe she'd be a pleasant mother-in-
law, if Hamilton brought his wife to the house.
He'll see that, and unless he falls in love rather
late, he won't marry for any other reason. Well
— he and aunt Maggie will leave their money to
Hester's children, if she has any. There's no
reason why they should have such an enormous
amount. They're very distant relations, anyhow.
I wonder how uncle Robert didn't see that.
There'll be an accumulation of money enough for
twenty ordinary fortunes, if things turn out in
that way."

"Yes — but you wouldn't leave the Brights out
altogether, mother, would you ? That's what will
happen, if the will won't hold."

"We'll make a compromise and give them
enough."

"A few millions," suggested Ralston, with a

little laugh. "Isn't it funny that we should be talking about such sums in real earnest? But Alexander can't see it in that light."

"Well — if he doesn't? We can do it alone in that case. What's a million in forty?"

"Two and a half per cent," answered Ralston, promptly, from sheer force of the new habit he had acquired at the bank.

"You're turning into a business man," laughed his mother. "I didn't mean that. I meant it would be little enough."

"Yes — but Ham wouldn't take it. You know him as well as I do. He'll have his rights or nothing. Honestly, there's no reason on earth why you should make him a present of a million, if the law doesn't give it to him. And there can't be any comparison in this case, because Alexander means to have everything for his father, and then lock him up in Bloomingdale and manage the fortune in his own Trust Company. For the Brights it means forty millions or nothing — not a red cent."

"I suppose you're right about that. And Hamilton's your friend, Jack."

"He's been a good friend to me. But he's not the sort of fellow to turn on me because I'm opposed to him in a suit. Still — he couldn't help feeling that it must make a difference. He wouldn't be human if he didn't. You mustn't blame him for it."

"Blame him! Of course not! Who would? He's the one who has everything at stake. Well, Jack, what shall we do? We've got to decide."

"It's not easy. Mother — why don't you send for Harry Brett and put the whole thing in his hands? He's a perfectly honourable man — there aren't many like him. Tell him what your position is, and then wash your hands of the matter. That seems to me to be by far the best thing to do. Tell him just how far you feel that you should like to carry out uncle Robert's wishes, and all you've told me. He's absolutely honest, and he's a gentleman. If the law is plainly for us, and there's no question about it, then let him take it. But if Alexander's going to try and get round it by quibbling, Brett will stand up against him like a man. He's a fine fellow, Brett. I like him. You can be sure that he'll do the right thing."

"I think that's very good advice. I'll see him and get him to answer the letter. I suppose the next thing will be that Alexander will come to see me and want to persuade me, especially if Brett's for upholding the will. If he does, I won't say anything. What I hate is the uncertainty of it all. Until it's settled you and Katharine can't consider yourselves married. At least, you could — but I suppose you won't."

"She shan't go back to Clinton Place, at all events," said Ralston. "The next time she goes through that door, she shall go as my wife. That brute has ill-treated her enough, and he shan't have another chance. Of course, she can't go on staying at the Brights' through all this. That's another thing. It won't be pleasant for her to feel that her father's trying his best to keep them out of the fortune, and to have to sit down to dinner with them every day and hear it discussed. Besides — poor Ham's deadly in love still, in his dear old heavy way. I wish she'd go to the Crowdies'. I tried to make her go the other day — "

"But that would be just as bad," said Mrs. Ralston. "Worse, in fact. Crowdie wouldn't be half so careful how he talked as Bright would be."

"That's true. Well — she'll just have to go and stay with the three Miss Miners, then. It won't be gay, but it won't be unpleasant, at all events."

"Upon my word, Jack, you'd better let me ask her here. At all events, we can keep her father away. Go and see her and try to persuade her to come. Or I'll go. I can manage it better. If you'll let me tell her that you've told me about your marriage, it will be easier. Otherwise she'll have that on her mind as a reason for not coming. After all, there's no especial reason why she should not know, is there? And then, Jack — you don't know how I should like to feel as though she were really your wife! I've always wanted her for you."

Ralston kissed his mother's hand affectionately, and held it in his own a moment.

"There's no reason," he said, presently. "I think you'll love each other as I love you both."

"If she loves you, I shall," answered Mrs. Ralston, and her face set itself oddly. "If she doesn't — I think I could kill her."

In this way they agreed as far as possible upon the position they would assume in the great family quarrel which was imminent, and, on the whole, they seemed to have chosen wisely.

CHAPTER XXI.

In each household there was rumour of war and discussion of plans, and the nervous tension was already great. In Lafayette Place, the exceedingly unfashionable and somewhat remote corner where the Crowdies dwelt in one of the half-dozen habitable houses there situated, there was considerable disturbance. Walter Crowdie and his wife were in the studio, alone together, talking about it all. Crowdie had received a communication from his brother-in-law, telling him of Alexander's contemplated attack and enquiring as to Crowdie's opinion, more as a matter of form than because he expected any interference or needed any help.

Hester Crowdie was a nervously organized woman, almost insanely in love with her husband. She had one of those pale, delicate, passionate faces which are not easily forgotten, and which seem to bear the sign of an unusual destiny in each line and shade of expression. She had much of the hereditary beauty of the Lauderdales, but the regularity of her features was not what struck the eye first. She was slight, but graceful as a doe, alternately quick and then indolent as an

91

Oriental woman, strong, yet liable to what seemed inexplicable fatigue and weakness which overtook her without warning, and often sensitive as a fine instrument to every changing influence about her, yet constant as steel in her idolizing love for her husband.

To do him justice, he seemed to return all she felt for him in an almost like degree. They were well-nigh inseparable, and she spent every moment of the day with him which she could spare from her very slight social and household duties, when he himself was not occupied with a sitter.

The studio was a vast room occupying the whole upper story of the house, and lighted from above as well as by windows, the latter being generally closed. It contained a barbaric wealth of rich Eastern carpets, stuffs, and embroideries, which covered the walls and the huge divans, and were draped about the chimney-piece. There was an old-fashioned high-backed chair for Crowdie's sitters, and there were generally at least two easels in the room, having unfinished canvases upon them. But there was nothing else — not a sketch, not a bit of a plaster cast, not the least object of metal. There were none of those more or less cheap weapons with which artists are fond of decorating their studios, there were no vases, no plants, no objects, in short, but the easels, the one chair, and the rich materials hung upon the walls, spread upon the divans, covering the heaps of soft cushions. Even the high door which gave access to the room from the narrow landing was masked by a great embroidery. Crowdie kept all his paints and brushes in a large closet, cut off by a curtain, and built out, balcony-like, over the yard at the back of the house.

Hester Crowdie lay among the cushions on one of the enormous divans. She was dressed in black, and the garment — which was neither gown nor tea-gown, nor yet a frock — followed closely the lines of grace in which her bodily beauty ran, from her throat to her slender feet. One blood-less hand lay upon the dark folds, the other was pressed almost out of sight in the yielding coils of her rich brown hair; she supported her head, resting upon her elbow, and watching her husband.

Crowdie was standing before an easel near by, palette and brushes in hand, touching the canvas from time to time, mechanically rather than with any serious intention of doing anything to the picture.

"I don't see why your brother takes the trouble to write," he said. "It may be a sort of formality. He must know that I'd be dead against the Lauder-dales in anything. They all detest me, and I hate them every one, with all my heart."

"So do I," answered Hester. "I hate them all

— except Katharine. But you don't hate her, either, Walter."

"Oh — Katharine? No — not exactly. She's too good-looking to be hated. But she can't bear me."

"It's not so bad as that. If it were, she shouldn't be my friend for a day. You know that. But she's with the enemy in the present case. It can't be helped. I hope we shan't quarrel. But if we must — why, we must, that's all."

Crowdie touched his picture, looked at it, then glanced at his wife and smiled.

"After all," he said, "what does that sort of friendship amount to?"

"Well — perhaps you're right," she answered, and she smiled, too, as her eyes met his, and lingered a moment in the meeting. "I don't know — perhaps it fills up the little empty places in life — when you've got a sister, for instance. Besides — I'm fond of Katharine. We've always been a good deal together. Not that I think she's perfection either, you know. I don't like the way she's gone and installed herself with mamma, as though she didn't know perfectly well that Ham was in love with her, and that she was making him miserable."

"Ham will survive a considerable amount of that sort of misery. Still, it must be unpleasant, especially just now. After all, it's her father who's attacking you and your mother and brother. They can't talk freely before her any more than you and I should."

"No." Hester paused a moment, and her face was thoughtful. "Walter," she began again, presently, "I want to ask you a question."

"Do you?" he asked, softly. "I have all the answers ready to all the possible questions you can ever ask of me. What is it?"

"Walter — weren't you just a little tiny bit in love with Katharine, ever so long ago, before we were married? Tell me. I shan't mind — that is, if it was very long ago."

"In love with Katharine Lauderdale? No — never. That's a very easy question to answer."

He stood looking at her, and the hand which held the palette hung down by his side.

"Weren't you? I sometimes think that you must have been. You look at her sometimes — as though she pleased you."

Crowdie laughed, a low, golden laugh, and glanced at his picture again, but said nothing. Then, in the silence, he went and put away his paints and brushes behind the curtain on one side of the fire-place at the other end of the great room. Hester lay back among the cushions and watched him till he disappeared, and kept her eyes upon the curtain until he came out again. She watched him as a wild animal watches her mate when she fears that he is going to leave her, with earnest, glistening eyes.

But he came back, bringing with him a small Japanese vase of that rare old bronze that rings under the touch like far-off chimes. He set it down upon the tiles before the fireplace, and poured something into it, and set fire to the liquid with a match. It blazed with a misty blue flame, and he threw a few grains of something upon it. A soft, white smoke rose in little clouds, and an intoxicating perfume filled the air.

Hester's delicate nostrils quivered, as she lay back amongst her cushions. She delighted in rare perfumes which could be burned. The faint colour rose in her pale cheeks, and her eyelids drooped. Crowdie drove the white smoke with his hands, wafting it towards her.

"What a strange question that was of yours," he said, suddenly, seating himself upon the edge of the divan, and touching the back of her hand softly with the tips of his fingers.

She withdrew her hand and laid it upon his as soon as he had spoken, caressing his in her turn.

"Was it?" she asked, in a dreamy voice. "It seemed so natural. I couldn't help asking you. After all, there are days when she's very beautiful. But that wasn't it, exactly. It was something — oh, Walter! why did you sing to her the other night? You know you promised that you'd never

sing if I wasn't there. It hurt me — it hurt me all
over when I heard of it. Why did you do it?
And then, why didn't you tell me?"

"And who did tell you?" asked Crowdie, gently,
but his eyelids contracted with curiosity as he
asked the question. "Not Griggs?"

"Oh, no! Mamma told me, yesterday. Why
did you do it? And she said dreadfully hard
things to me about trying to keep you all to myself,
and locking up what gives people so much pleasure
— and all that."

"I'm sorry she told you. Why will people interfere and tell tales?"

"Yes — but, Walter darling — do I lock you up
and try to keep you from other people? Am I
jealous and horrid, as she says I am? If you
think so, tell me. Have I ever interfered with
your pleasure? Am I always getting in your
way?"

"Darling! What nonsense you talk sometimes!"

"No, but seriously, would you like me any better
if I were like Katharine Lauderdale?"

The passionate eyes sought his, and there was a
quick breath, half suppressed, as her hand ceased
to caress his passive fingers.

"I couldn't like you better — as you call it,
sweetest," answered Crowdie.

And again his soft laugh rippled up through

perfumed air. With a movement that was almost girlish he dropped upon one elbow, and raising her diaphanous hand in his, tapped his own pale cheek with it. Hester laughed a little, too.

"Because if I thought you cared for Katharine Lauderdale — I'd —" She paused, and her fingers stroked his silky hair.

"What would you do to Katharine Lauderdale if you thought I cared for her?"

"I won't tell you," answered Hester, very low. "It would be something bad. Why did you sing for her if you don't care for her?"

"I sang for everybody. Besides, it was so dull there. They'd been talking metaphysics and such rubbish, and there was a long pause, and aunt Maggie wanted me to. And then, when she said that I'd promised never to sing except for you, I didn't choose to let them all believe it was true. Katharine begged me not to, I remember — when she was told that I'd made you a promise."

"Did she?" Hester's eyelids opened and then drooped again. "She knew that would be the way to make you sing, or she wouldn't have said it. How mean women are! I'm beginning to hate her, too. Are you sorry?"

"Sorry? No. Why should I be sorry? Sweet — you've got this idea that I've a fancy for her — it's foolish."

"Is it? You look a little sorry, though, because

I said I should hate her. She's better looking than I am."

" She!" Crowdie laughed again, the same gentle, lulling, golden laugh. "Besides — I told you — she can't bear me."

"I hate her for that, too — for loving your voice as she does, and not liking you. And I shall hate her if her father gets all the money that ought to come to us, because if I ever get it, I'm going to make you do all you've ever dreamed of doing with it. You shall build your palace like the one at Agra — Griggs will help you, for he knows everything — you shall do all you've ever dreamed — we'll have the alabaster room with the light shining through the walls — you shall sing to me there, by the fountain — but you shan't sing to Katharine Lauderdale — there, nor anywhere else — Walter, you shan't — "

"She's got into your head, love — " Crowdie's red lips kissed the bloodless hand, and his beautiful eyes looked up to Hester's face. " It's a foolish thought, sweet! Let me kiss it away."

Hester said nothing, but her own eyes burned, and her nostrils quivered like white rose leaves in the breeze, delicate, diaphanous, passionate. A little shiver ran through her, and she sighed.

" Sing to me," she said. " Sing what you sang to her the other night. Make the song mine again. Make it forget her. Sing softly, very softly — soft, soft — you know how I love the notes — "

She closed her burning eyes, but not so wholly but what she could see him, as she threw back her head upon the cushions.

Crowdie sat motionless beside her, watching her. His lips were parted as though he were just about to sing, but no sound escaped them. In the heavy, perfumed air the stillness was intense, and it was warm.

"Sing," said Hester, just above a whisper, as though she were murmuring in her sleep.

But still no single note came from his lips, and still his eyes rested on her face.

"I can't!" he exclaimed, suddenly, as though his own breath oppressed him.

Slowly she raised her lids, and her eyes met his, wild, dark, almost speaking with a voice of their own.

"Why did you sing for her?" she asked, whispering, as he gradually bent down towards her. "Do you love me?"

"Like death," he answered, bending still.

"Do you hate Katharine Lauderdale?" she asked, very near his face.

"I hate everything but you, sweet —"

The two transparent hands were suddenly raised and framed his eyes, and held him a moment.

"Say you hate her!" The whisper was short, fierce, and hot.

"Yes — I hate her."

Then the hands dropped.

Far off before the great chimney-piece, the little cloud of white smoke curled slowly from the censer upwards through the soft, love-laden air — and the perfume stole silently everywhere, in and out, half poisonous with aromatic sweetness, all through the great still room.

CHAPTER XXII.

KATHARINE found herself in a very difficult position. During the next few days she realized clearly that she could not continue to stay with the Brights indefinitely, both on account of their attitude in the matter of the will, and because Hamilton Bright was in love with her. She felt that the friendships to which she had been accustomed all her life were slipping away under the pressure of circumstances, and that some of her friends were becoming her enemies. Reflections she had never known before now rose in her mind, and in a few days she had reached that state of exaggerated cynicism and unbelief which overtakes the very young when those with whom they closely associate change their minds upon very important points. In the meantime, Katharine went every day to see her mother in Clinton Place while her father was down town.

The bond between mother and daughter, which had been so violently strained during the previous winter, and again within the past few weeks, was growing stronger again. The events which were breaking up Katharine's intimacy with Hester

Crowdie and the Brights had the effect of drawing her and her mother together. So far as Hester
Crowdie was concerned, Katharine's friendship for
her had existed upon a false basis, as has been
seen. The elder woman's ardent and sensitive
nature reflected itself in her minor actions and
relations, lending them an appearance of depth
which she herself was far from feeling. Katharine
was indeed sympathetic to her, and there had been
much confidence between the two, which had not
been wholly misplaced on either side. But Hester
did not wish the young girl to see too much of
Crowdie. How far she understood him it is impossible to say, but that she loved him desperately
and was jealous of every glance he bestowed on
any passing figure that pleased him, there could
be no doubt. Her vanity was not proof against
that jealousy, and she feared comparison. That
Crowdie should have broken his promise about
singing, and should have sung to please Katharine,
had hurt her even more deeply than she herself
realized.

On the other hand, Mrs. Lauderdale's confession
to her daughter on the morning after Robert Lauderdale's death had produced a profound impression
upon the young girl. Being quite unable to realize
a state of mind in which her mother could really be
envious of her, Katharine readily believed that Mrs.
Lauderdale had greatly exaggerated in her own

judgment the fault of which she had been guilty, and that much of what had seemed to be her unkindness and heartlessness toward Katharine had really been the result of her unjust self-accusation, leading her to avoid the person whom she believed that she had injured. All that was a little vague, but that did not matter. The two had always been allies in family questions, and had been devotedly attached to one another until this year. And after the first violent scene with Alexander Junior, the mother had taken the daughter's side again, had released her from imprisonment in her own room, and had approved of her taking shelter with uncle Robert. The confession she had made on that morning had been in reality a complete reconciliation. Katharine did not understand how much her absence from home during twenty-four hours had to do with the subsidence of her mother's unnatural envy.

The result was that at the present juncture Katharine desired earnestly to return to her home, and would have done so in spite of Ralston's objections, had she been assured of finding any condition approaching even to an armed peace. But of this she had little hope. She learned that her father was morose and silent, and that he never referred to her. His attention was naturally preoccupied by the uncommon interests at stake in the approaching conflict, and he grew daily more

taciturn. His old father watched events with that
apparent indifference of old age, which often con-
ceals a curiosity not without cunning in finding
means of satisfying itself. Mrs. Lauderdale also
told Katharine that Charlotte and her husband
were coming up from Washington for a few days,
in order that Slayback and Alexander might talk
matters over. Contrary to the latter's expecta-
tions, Slayback did not seem inclined to agree with
the Lauderdales about the attempt to break the
will, though his wife and his children would ultimately profit largely by the result, if it proved
successful.

Katharine returned one afternoon from Clinton
Place, after discussing these matters with her
mother, and found Hamilton Bright in the library
in Park Avenue. She always avoided as much as
possible being alone with him, and when she
caught sight of his flaxen head bending over the
writing-table, she was about to withdraw quietly
and go to her own room. But he looked up quickly
and spoke to her.

"Don't run away, cousin Katharine," he said.
"And you always do run. You know it's not safe,
with your arm in a sling."

"But I wasn't running," answered the young
girl. "Of course I'll stay if you want me. I
thought you were busy."

"Oh, no — I was only writing a note. I've fin-

ished — and — and I should be awfully glad if
you'd stay a little while."

Katharine glanced at his face and saw that he
was embarrassed. She wondered what was in his
mind as she sat down. He had risen from his seat
and seemed to hesitate about taking another.
When a man hesitates to sit down in order to talk
to a woman, only two suppositions are possible.
Either he does not wish to be caught and obliged
to stay with her, or he has something important
to say, and thinks that he can talk better on his
legs than seated, which is true for nine men out of
ten. Bright at last decided in favour of standing
by the fireplace, resting one elbow upon the shelf
and thrusting one hand into his pocket. Katharine could hear the soft jingle of his little bunch of
keys. She expected that he meant to say something about the difficulty of their relative positions
in regard to the will, which must lead to her putting an end to her visit immediately. So long as
the subject had not been mentioned the position
had been tenable, but if it were once discussed, she
felt that she should be obliged to go away at once.
She could not well accept the hospitality of her
father's bitterest opponents, though they were her
friends and relations, if once the position were
clearly defined.

"What is it?" she asked, after a short pause, by
way of helping him, for by this time she was sure
that he had something to say to her.

"Oh — nothing — " He hesitated. "That is —
I only wanted to talk to you a little — that is, if
you don't mind."

"Oh, I don't mind at all!" answered Katharine,
with a smile in which she tried to turn her amusement into encouragement.

Except at great moments, almost all women are
wickedly amused when a man is embarrassed in
attacking a difficult subject. The more kind-
hearted ones, like Katharine, will often help a
man. The cynical ones get all the diversion they
can out of the situation and give a graphic account
of it to the first intimate friend who turns up
afterwards. Katharine really thought he meant to
speak of the will, and the position struck her as
absurd. She was in the position of having forced
herself upon the hospitality of her father's enemies.
She wondered how Bright would put the matter,
and, woman-like, at the same moment she cata-
logued her belongings as they lay about her room
upstairs and calculated roughly that it might take
her as much as an hour to pack all her things if
she decided to go that evening. Still Bright said
nothing.

"It seems to be rather a serious matter," she
said, assuming that he had not asked her to stay
in order to talk about the weather.

"Well — it is pretty serious for me," he answered. "It amounts to this. I don't know

whether you've ever noticed anything, so I'm not sure just how to begin. I'd like to make a straight statement if you wouldn't mind — that is — if I were sure of not offending you."

"I don't exactly see how you can offend me," answered Katharine, gravely. "If it's about the will, I suppose we think alike, only I'd hoped that we might not bring it up and talk about it just yet. But if you're going to do that, I'd rather you'd let me speak first. I think I should antici- pate what you were going to say. I'd rather — and it would be less trouble for you."

"Well," replied Bright, doubtfully. "I don't know that I meant to talk about that exactly. But there's a certain connection. If you've any- thing on your mind to say about it, why, go ahead, cousin Katharine — go ahead: I daresay you'll put it much better than I shall."

"I'm not so sure of that. But it may seem to come better from me. I'll say it, at all events, and if you don't think as I do, tell me so. Of course I know how strange it must have seemed to you and aunt Maggie that I should have come here, out of a clear sky, the other day, without so much as giving you half an hour's warning. No amount of charity and hospitality can make that look natural to you, — to either of you, — and I dare- say you've wondered about it. And then, to stay on in this way, after my father has behaved in the way he has — it's not exactly delicate, you know — "

"Nonsense!" exclaimed Bright, emphatically. "You're mistaken if you think that's my view of the case."

"I don't think I'm mistaken, cousin Ham. I daresay you may like to have me, but that doesn't explain my coming, does it? But I'm in an awfully hard position just now, and the other day — do you know? I was driving to the Crowdies', and then I changed my mind and came here instead."

"I'm glad you did. So's my mother. As for not thinking it natural, when your father's tearing about like wild and rooting up everything like a mad rhinoceros — oh, I say! I beg your pardon — "

Katharine did not smile, for there was good blood in her veins, of the kind that does not play false at such moments. But the temptation to laugh was strong, and she looked fixedly at her left hand.

"No," she said. "Please don't speak of my father like that. I suppose you both think you're right in this horrible question of money. I myself don't know what I think. He's wrong in one way, of course. Whether there's a flaw in the will or not, it represents poor uncle Robert's last wish about his fortune. If he changed his mind, that's none of our business — "

"How do you mean?" said Bright, quickly, and

forgetting his embarrassment. "Did you say he changed his mind?"

"I didn't mean to say that, positively," answered Katharine, who had forgotten herself for a moment. "As the will was made almost at the last moment, perhaps there had been — others, before it. People often make several wills, don't they? That's all I meant. My own feeling would be to carry out his wishes. But I suppose men feel differently — and it's an enormous fortune, of course. The main point is that you and your mother are legally my father's enemies — well, call it opponents — and I've no business to be eating your bread while it lasts. That's what it comes to, in plain language."

"I wish you wouldn't talk in that way, cousin Katharine," said Bright, in a low voice. "I don't think it's exactly kind."

"It's true, at all events," answered Katharine. "As for being kind — it's not a case of kindness on my part. It's gratitude I feel, because you and aunt Maggie have been so awfully kind to me, just when I was in trouble."

"Oh — if you're going to look at it in that way!" Bright paused, but Katharine said nothing. "Well, I don't see where the kindness lies," he continued. "Of course, if you choose to put it so — but it's a long way on the other side. It's a pretty considerable kindness of you to come and stop in my house. If that's what you've got to

say about the will business, cousin Katharine, I
hope you won't say any more, because I don't like
it. I appreciate—I suppose that's the word—I
appreciate your motives in trying to twist things
inside out and to make martyrs of us because
we've accepted your company without saying,
'Look here, cousin Katharine, this is our bread,
and you're eating it, and we don't exactly mind,
but we'd rather you'd go and eat your own.' I
suppose that's what you make out that we're thinking all the time. I don't know whether you call
that being kind to me, exactly, but I know pretty
well what it feels like. It feels as if you'd slapped
my face."

"Ham! Cousin Ham!" cried Katharine. "You
know how I meant it — please, please don't
think — "

"No; I know I'm an idiot. I suppose it's just
as well you should know it, too. It may make
things more comfortable. But I'll tell you. Don't
talk that way, please, because we don't feel that
way, and we're not going to. I'd rather have you
know that this is just as much your home as Clinton Place is than — well, than lots of things. And
since we're saying everything right out, like this,
and we're either going to be friends — or not — I'd
like to ask you one question, if you don't mind.
You may be offended, but you'll know I didn't mean
to be offensive, because I've said so. May I?"

He spoke roughly, relapsing under excitement and emotion to habits of speech which had been formed and strengthened in his early years in the West. Katharine had occasionally heard him talk in that way with men, losing all at once the refinements of accent and speech which had been familiar in childhood and again in maturity, but which ten years of California and Nevada had lined, so to say, with something rougher and stronger that occasionally broke through the shell. Katharine was by no means sure of what he meant to say, and would very much have preferred that he should not ask his question just then, whatever it might prove to be. But she saw well enough that in his present mood it would not be easy to control him.

"Yes," she said. "Ask me anything you like, if you think I can answer. I will if I can."

"Well — are you going to marry Jack Ralston or not, cousin Katharine? It would make a difference to me if you'd tell me."

Katharine was taken unawares, both by the question and its form. Not to answer it was very difficult, under the circumstances. She had risked trouble in letting him speak, and it would not be true either to say that she was going to marry Ralston or that she was not, since she was married already. But she had never contemplated the possibility of telling Bright the secret, and she did not wish to do so now. She was very truthful and also very reticent — qualities which she inherited, and which were therefore the foundation of her impulses and not acquired virtues from which there was at least a chance of escape under very trying circumstances. She hesitated a moment, and then made up her mind.

"I'd rather not answer the question just now," she said, but she felt the blush slowly rising to her cheeks.

Bright glanced at her with a look almost expressing fear. Then he turned his eyes away, and grew red. He jingled his little bunch of keys in his pocket, in his emotion. Once or twice he opened his lips and drew breath, but checked himself and kept silence. Seeing that he said nothing, Katharine rose to her feet, hoping to put an end to the situation. He pretended not to see her, at first. She felt that she should not go away in silence, for she did not wish to seem unkind, so she stood still for a moment, keeping herself in countenance by adjusting the little cape she wore over her injured arm. Still he said nothing, and at last she made a step as though she were going away, purposely trying to put on a kindly and natural expression.

"Where are you going?" he asked, almost roughly.

"I was going to my room," she answered, quietly. "I haven't even taken off my hat, yet, you see. I'm just as I came in."

She lengthened the short explanation unnecessarily in order to seem kind, and then regretted it. She made another step.

"Don't go just yet!" he exclaimed.

His throat was dry, and the words came with difficulty. Katharine knew that there was nothing to be done now but to face the situation. She stopped just as she was about to take another step, and came back to him as he stood by the fireplace.

"Please don't say anything more," she said. "I hadn't any idea what question you were going to ask. Please don't —"

"Just hear me, please," he answered, paying no attention to what she said. "It isn't going to take long. You know what I meant. Well — I've thought for some time that things had cooled off between you and Jack, and that you'd settled down to be friends. So I thought I'd ask you. Of course, if you said right out that you were going to marry him or you weren't — well, that would rather simplify things. But of course, if you can't, or won't, I've just got to be satisfied, that's all. You've got a doubt, anyhow. And Jack's my friend. He had the first right, and he has it until you say 'no' and send him off. I don't want you to think that I'm not acting squarely by him."

For a moment Katharine hesitated. She was much tempted to tell him of her marriage, seeing how he spoke, but again her natural impulse kept her silent on that point.

"There'll never be any chance for any one else, Ham," she said gently. "Put it out of your mind — and I'm grateful, indeed I am!"

"Never?" he asked, looking at her — and a nervous smile that meant nothing came into his face.

She shook her head in answer.

"There'll never be any chance for any one else," she repeated gravely.

He looked at her a moment longer, his face growing rather pale. Once more he jingled his keys in his pocket, as he turned his head away.

"Well — I'm sorry," he said. "Excuse me if I spoke — you see I didn't know."

There was a tone with the commonplace words that took them straight to Katharine's heart. She saw how the strong, simple, uneloquent man was suffering, and she knew that she should never have come to the house.

"I'm more sorry — and more ashamed — than you can guess," she said, and with bent head she left him standing by the fireplace, and went to her room.

He did not move for a long time after she had gone, but stood still, his face changing, though little, from time to time, with his thoughts. He jingled his keys meditatively in his pocket every now and then. At last he sighed and uttered one monosyllable, solemnly and without undue emphasis.

"Damn."

Then he shook his big shoulders, and got his hat and went for a solitary stroll, eastwards in the direction of the river.

But Katharine had not such powerful monosyllables at her command, and she suddenly felt very much ashamed of herself, as she shut the door of her room and looked about, with a vague idea that she ought to go away at once. It was not as though she had not been warned of what might happen, nor as though she had been forced into the situation against her will. She had deliberately chosen to come to the Brights' rather than to go anywhere else, and had obliged John Ralston to let her do so when she had been with him in the carriage. If she ever told him what had just happened he would have in his power one of those weapons which, in a small way, humanity keenly dreads, to wit, the power to say "I told you so." It is not easy to explain the sense of utter humiliation which most of us feel — though we jest about it — when the warning of another proves to have been well founded.

Katharine saw, however, that her wandering existence could continue no longer, and that if she left the Brights' she must go home. She could not continue to transfer herself from the home of one

relation to that of another, with her box and her
valise, for an indefinite period. In the first place,
she was inconveniencing people, and secondly, they
would ultimately begin to wonder what had happened in Clinton Place to make it impossible for
her to stay in her father's house. On the other
hand, she was not prepared to go there at a
moment's notice. She could hardly expect a very
hearty welcome from her father, considering how
they had parted on that afternoon at Robert Lauderdale's house more than a week earlier.

She hesitated as to whether she should not pretend to be ill and stay in her room until the next
morning, when she could go back quietly to Clinton
Place. But she knew that Mrs. Bright would come
and sit with her and would very soon find out that
there was nothing the matter. She might have
saved herself the trouble of thinking of that, for
Bright himself did not wish to meet her, and went
out and dined at his club as the surest way of
avoiding her. It was as well, at all events, that
she did not attempt to go to the Crowdies', for her
appearance there just then would not have pleased
Hester, and would have considerably disturbed
Crowdie's own peace of mind.

She was immensely relieved to find herself alone
at dinner with Mrs. Bright, who made Hamilton's
excuses, and she looked forward to spending a quiet
evening and going to bed early, unless Ralston

came. This, however, was not probable, for he had come on the previous evening, and he hesitated to come every day on account of the Brights.

He came, however, not long after dinner. Katharine did not understand his expression. He smiled like a man in possession of an amusing secret which he was anxious to communicate as soon as an opportunity offered. At last Mrs. Bright left the room.

"Look here," said Ralston. "I've got this thing —I wish you'd look at it and tell me what you think."

He produced a letter and handed it to her, with a short laugh. She saw that it was in her father's handwriting.

"Read it," said John. "It will make you open your eyes. He has a most — peculiar character. It's coming to the surface rapidly."

Katharine held out the envelope to him.

"You must take it out," she said. "I've only got one hand, and that's my left."

"Poor dear!" he exclaimed. "I suppose you'll have at least ten days more of this."

He had opened the letter while speaking and handed it to her.

"Why don't you read it to me yourself?" she asked.

"Because — I'd rather you should read it. It's a very extraordinary production. He's not diplomatic — your father. It's lucky he's not an ambas-

sador or one of those creatures. He wouldn't
cover his country with glory in making treaties."

Katharine was already running her eye over the
page, and her face expressed her surprise. She
even turned the sheet over and looked at the signature to persuade herself that her father had really
written what she was reading, ·for it was hard to
believe. As she proceeded, her brows bent, and her
lip curled scornfully. Then all at once she laughed
with genuine, though bitter, amusement—the laugh
that comes from the head, not from the heart.
Then she grew grave again and read on to the
end. When she had finished, her hand with the
letter in it fell upon her knee and she looked into
Ralston's face with parted lips, as though helpless
to express her astonishment.

In any jury of honour the communication would
have been accepted as a formal apology for everything her father had done, and for anything he
might have done inadvertently. Ralston was
wrong in saying that Alexander Junior had no
talent for diplomacy. Consciously or unconsciously, he had succeeded in writing a letter in
which he took back every insulting word he had
spoken of Ralston, either to his face or behind his
back, without exactly saying that he meant to do
so. He took the position of considering it a
matter of the highest importance to sift the truth
out of what he called the labyrinth of evil speak-

ing, lying, and slandering, by which he was
assailed on every side. The confusion of similes
at this point was almost grand in its chaotic incoherence, and it was here that Katharine had
laughed, as well she might. The honour of the
family, said Alexander, was at stake, and he had
accordingly performed the operation of sifting the
attacking and mendacious labyrinth. The result
of his labour of love for Ralston's reputation, in
the interests of the family honour, was much simpler than his alleged mode of getting at it. For
he did not hesitate to say that he had ascertained,
beyond the possibility of doubt that the stories
concerning John's intemperance were lies — and
the word was written with conscientious calli-
graphy. There was to be no mistake there. Alexander thought it due to Ralston, as indeed it
was, to make the statement at once, as the ultimate
expression of a carefully formed opinion. With
regards to any other differences which there might
have been between them, he thought that amicable
settlements were always more Christian, and generally more satisfactory in the end. He should
never forget that he had parted from his dear
uncle in wrath. Here Katharine's lip curled as
she remembered what the nature of that parting
had been. He was sure that the wish of the
dear departed would have been that all parties
should seek peace and ensue it. "To ensue" was

a verb which Katharine had never understood, and she had always suspected that it was a mistake in the printing, but the quotation sounded well, and brought up the rear with a clang of armour of righteousness, so to say. The phrase appeared to be thrown out as a suggestion — as a very broad hint, in fact, seeing that it came from him who had received the blow, and not from him who had dealt it.

There was much more to the same effect. It was a very long letter, covering two sheets of the Trust Company's foolscap — very fine bond paper with a heading in excellent good taste. But the most remarkable point of all had been reserved for the last paragraph. Therein Alexander Lauderdale said that he did not abandon all hope, even after what had occurred, of cementing a union between the two surviving branches of the Lauderdales, upon the worldly advantages of which his delicacy would not allow him to dwell, but in which he thought it possible and even probable, that all family differences might be forgotten on earth. Whether he expected that they should afterwards be revived in heaven, or in a place more appropriate, he did not add. But he signed himself sincerely John Ralston's cousin, Alexander Lauderdale Junior, and it was quite clear that he wished all he had said to be believed.

"Now isn't that the most remarkable production

of human genius that you've ever seen?" asked
John, as Katharine dropped her hand.

She slowly nodded her head, her lips still parted
in wonder, and her eyes looked far away.

"It came over to the bank by a messenger of the
Trust Company," said John.   "So I wrote an answer on the bank paper —"

"What did you say?" asked Katharine, with
sudden anxiety, dreading lest he had given way to
some new outburst of temper.

"What should I say?   I said it was all right.
That I was glad he had found that I wasn't quite
so bad as he'd thought.   And I added at the end
— because he'd put it there — that if there was any
thing that I hankered for and believed I was fitted
for, it was to be used up as cement for the family
union — 'apply while fresh' — that sort of thing.
Only of course I put it nicely.   Oh — you needn't
be afraid!   I wasn't going to do anything idiotic.
Besides, I see what he's driving at.   It's as plain
as day."

"What?   I can't understand it, myself — it all
seems so strange and unexpected, and unlike him."

"It's as clear as day, dear.   He knows he must
come round some day, and he's doing it now, so that
we may be all patched up and peaceful before the
hearing about the will — that's it.   You know if
all the next of kin appear together against the distant relations, it influences the court's opinion,

when the court has a choice of opinions, as it very likely will have in this case."

"Then you think the will is likely to be broken?"

"I don't know. They're saying to-day that one of the witnesses is mentioned in the will — in the list of servants who get annuities, and that if the witnessing's wrong, the will can't be probated, as they call it. I don't understand those things."

"And the Brights will get nothing."

"Nothing."

"Poor Ham!"

"Yes — well — he's got enough to live on without forty millions more."

"It would have been a consolation to him — oh Jack! You were right — don't say, 'I told you so' — please! This afternoon he wanted to — well he did ask me — he thought it was off between you and me."

"I told you — no, darling, I won't say it," answered Ralston. "Give me a kiss, and I won't say it."

He did not say it.

CHAPTER XXIII.

Love, Mrs. Lauderdale had said in her absent-minded way, was not at all like other passions. The words remained in Katharine's memory and pleased her and comforted her in a manner which would have surprised the elder woman, had she guessed that she had unintentionally drawn music from a human soul with one of those dull and stereotyped phrases which people fall back upon when they cannot or will not explain themselves.

But that was precisely what Katharine wished to believe — that love was not at all like other passions, that it bore not the slightest resemblance in its nature to those which she had seen asserting themselves so strongly around her, and of which she was beginning to understand something by proxy, as it were. For though she had said that her love for John Ralston was like her father's love of money, she did not in the least wish to believe it. She attached to love the highest interpretation of which it is capable; she attributed to it the purest and most disinterested motives; she gave it in her thoughts the strongest and best qualities which anything can have.

She had a right to do so, and though she sought
an explanation of her right, she was not disturbed
because she found none. She dreamed of theories
vague, but as beautiful as they were untenable, as
men of ancient times imagined impossible, but
deeply poetic, interpretations of nature and her
doings. Her soul, and the soul of the man she
loved had elected one another of old from amongst
myriads; neither could give light without the other,
nor could either live without the other's life. Together they were one immortal; separate they must
perish. The good of each was the triumphant
enemy of evil in the other, and the evil in both was
gradually to be driven out and forgotten in the perfection of the whole.

All that was contemplative in her nature was
entranced before the exquisite beauty of her imagined deity. Little by little, as other attachments
were rudely shaken, broken, and destroyed, the one
of all others which she most valued grew stronger
and fairer in the wreck of the rest; the one passion
which she saw was good towered in her soul's field
as an archangel among devils, spotless, severe, and
invincible. The angel was not John Ralston, nor
were the devils those persons with whom her life
had to do. They all had other features, immortal
natures, and transcendent reasoning. At that time
there was in her the foundation of a great mythol-
ogy of ideals, good and bad, personified and almost

named, among which love was king over all the
rest, endowed with divine attributes, with knowledge
of the human soul, and power to move the human
heart, knowing all motives and divining all impulses, — a being to whom a prayer might be said in
trouble, and whose beneficent hand would be swift
and strong to help.   Love, in her theory of the
world, was the prime cause, the intelligent director,
and at the same time the ultimate end.   She and
her husband were under his immediate and especial
protection.   If they were faithful to him, he would
shield them from harm, and make them immortal
with himself beyond the stars.   If they denied
him — that is, if they ceased to love one another —
his face would grow dark, his right hand would be
full of semi-biblical terrors, and he would abandon
them to the wicked will of the devils, — which were
the bad passions the girl saw in others, — to be tormented until they themselves should be extinguished
in eternal night.

Practically, Katharine had constructed a religion
for herself out of the most human thing in her
nature, since she had lost the bearings of anything
higher in the storms through which she had passed.
It was by no means an unassailable religion, nor a
very logical one, being derived altogether from the
exaltation of the most human of all passions, and
having its details deduced from the one-sided experience of an innocent child.   But that very inno-

cence, that very impossibility of conceiving that there should be anything not good in love that was true, gave it an enormous force against the powers which were evidently evil. There was an appearance of inexorably sound reason, too, in the conclusion that all human motive was passion of one kind or another, and that all passions but love were bad and self-destructive in the end, having their foundation in selfishness, and not in the other self that fills love-dreams.

Since passion and motive were one and the same, thought Katharine, there could be no question as to which of them all was the best, since true love such as hers was the only passion that had no one of the seven capital sins attached to it. Such an argument was manifestly unanswerable when it came from her, and she rejoiced in the security of knowing herself to be right in the midst of many wrongs, which is one of the highest satisfactions of human vanity for the young or the old. Day by day, through the changing events of the past year, the conviction had grown, until it was now the dominant cause and mover of her being, and was assuming superhuman proportions in her estimated values of things transcendent.

Paul Griggs, with his vaguely expressed explanations of things which meant much, and meant it clearly, to himself, had unconsciously helped Katharine to deify love at the expense, and to the ruin, of any form of religious belief to which she might have been inclined. He was assuredly not one of those men who seem to make it their business to destroy the convictions of others, and to give them nothing in exchange for what was consolation, if not salvation. He was, at least, a man who believed in belief, so to say, and who, perhaps, believed many things which must have seemed utterly incredible to ordinary beings of ordinary experience. But he was fond of stating the results he had reached, in a careless way, which seemed less than half-serious, without giving the smallest hint as to the means by which he had obtained them. The statements themselves were fragmentary: here a hand, there a head, now a foot, and next a bit of the shoulders. He was not conscious of his fault. To him the image was always present and complete. It seemed to him that he was but calling attention to one point or another of the visible whole, when it seemed to others as though he were offering them broken bits, often unrecognizable as belonging to any possible image whatsoever. Others sometimes put the bits together in their own way.

He was not in any sense an ordinary being, nor one to be judged by ordinary standards, though he rarely claimed the right to be treated as an exception. The difference between him and the average man lay not in any very unusual gifts, and many might have been found who, knowing him well,

would have denied that there was any radical difference at all. He would certainly have taken little
pains to persuade these of the contrary. Outwardly,
he was a man of letters who had met with considerable success in his career — about as much as justifies
good-natured people in making a lion of an author
or an artist, but no more. He had written many
books, and had learned his business in the bitter
struggles which attend the commencement of an
average literary man's life, when the fight for bare
existence forces the slender talent to bear burdens
too heavy for its narrow shoulders, along paths not
easy to tread for those most sure of foot. He had
some valuable gifts, however, which had stood him in
good stead. He possessed almost incredible physical strength in certain ways, without the heavy,
sanguine temperament which requires regular exercise and perpetual nourishment. His endurance
was beyond all comparison greater than that of men
usually considered very strong, and he had been
able to bear the strain of excessive labour which
would have killed or paralyzed most people. That
was one of the secrets of his success. Secondly, he
had acquired an unusual mechanical facility in the
handling of language and the arrangement of the
matter he produced, so as to give it the most
favourable appearance possible. His imagination
was not abundant, but he did the best he could with
it under all circumstances, and answered all critics

with the unassailable statement that he wrote for a
living and did the best he could, and sincerely regretted that he was not Walter Scott, nor Goethe,
nor Thackeray, nor any of the great ones. That
was his misfortune, and not his fault. People
flattered him, he said, by telling him that he could
do better if he tried. It was not true. He could
not do better.

But in all these points he did not differ very
widely from the average man who attains to a
certain permanent and generally admitted success
by driving his faculties to their utmost in the
struggle for a living. The chief difference between him and other men had been produced by
an experience of life under varying circumstances,
such as an ordinary individual rarely gets, and
possibly by the long-continued action of unusual
emotions with which this study, or history, of
Katharine Lauderdale can have nothing to do, and
which did not directly concern his literary career
nor his relations with the world at large, though
the outward result was to make unthinking people
say that there was something mysterious about
him, which either attracted them or repelled them,
according to their temperaments and tastes. At all
events, his life had tended to the creation of a form
of belief and a mode of judgment which seemed
very simple to himself, and perfectly incomprehensible to almost every one else. He showed

other people fragments and bits of it, when he was in the humour, and sometimes seemed surprised that those who heard him should not also understand him. One of his fundamental articles of faith seemed to be that life as a possession was of no value whatsoever: a doctrine which attracted very few. But those who knew him and watched him were sure that there was no affectation in that part of his creed, though they might hesitate in finding reasons for his belief in it. It was strongly contrasted with his immovable faith — not in a life to come, for he despised the expression — but in the present fact of immortality. The mere fact that he laughed at the idea of 'past' and 'future' in their relation to the soul, sufficiently confused most of those who had heard him talk of such things.

Katharine Lauderdale had neither the man's experience to help her in following him, nor any superior genius of insight to lead her to his conclusions by what one might call the shorthand of reason — intuition. She was simply attracted without understanding, as so many people are nowadays, by everything which promises a glimpse at the unknown, if not a knowledge of the unknowable. She took the longing for the power of comprehension, the fragments for the whole, and the crumbs for the bread of life. It was not unnatural, considering the tendencies of modern culture, but it was unfortunate.

She halved her soul, and gave John Ralston his
share of it, though he had a very good one of his
own. She elaborated a theory of interchangeable
and interdependent selves for herself and him,
which momentarily satisfied all her wants. She
took his self with her own into the temple of
love, and bade it bow·down and worship with her
the glorious deification of human passion which
she had set up there. And his imaginary self,
being really but that part of her own being which
she called his, consented and obeyed, and did as
she did. And the incense rose before the shrine,
and the love-angels chanted love's litany of praise,
while Love himself smiled down upon her, and
told her that he was immortal, and would make
her deathless for her belief in him. The temple
was beautiful beyond compare ; the deity was
spotless, fair of form, and noble of feature ; the
heart that worshipped was fresh, unsullied, and
sincere.   There had never been anything more
perfect than it all was in Katharine's imagination ;
and there could never, in all the long life that was
before her, be anything so perfect again. John
Ralston, single-hearted and deeply loving as he
was, could never have any conception of the
divinity his maiden wife adored in secret. Her
instinct told her that though he was with her, the
manliness in him looked at the world from another
point of view ; and in all their many exchanges of

thought she never spoke of her visions of blessed-
ness. The fact that she kept them to herself gave
them more strength, and preserved their intact
beauty in all its splendid strength and all its infinite delicacy.

In a certain way she owed to Paul Griggs some
of her sweetest and most exquisite thoughts, of
which the memory must be with her all her life,
long after the humanity of truth supplanted the
dignity of the ideal. Not that he had taught her
anything of what he believed and thought that he
knew. She, like the rest, had received only fragments of his meaning; but out of them she had
constructed a whole which was beautiful in itself,
if nothing else — as lovers of art have dreamed an
unbroken ideal of perfection upon bits of marble
unearthed from the grave of a great thing destroyed, moulding theories upon it, and satisfying
their tastes through it, each in his own way, though
perhaps all very far from what was once the truth.

But, on the other hand, Griggs was partly responsible for the eclipse of what, in her nature,
as in all, was essentially necessary. She did not
at the present time feel the loss, if it were really
a loss, and not a mere temporary shutting off
of all higher possibilities from her mental sight.
She did not, perhaps, fully realize the distance to
which she had gone in unbelief in substituting one
ideal for another; and she would have been pro-

foundly shocked had any one told her that she
had at the present time wholly abandoned anything approaching to a form of Christianity. She
would have reasoned that she said prayers, as she
supposed other people did; but she would have
found it hard to say what she thought when she
said them. Nine-tenths of them were for John
Ralston, and were in reality addressed to the
divinity in the love temple — the remaining ones
were mere words, and said in a perfunctory way,
with a sort of sincerity of manner, but with no
devotion whatever, and no attempt to strengthen
them with a belief that they might be answered.
She had been taught to say them, and continued
to say them with the conscientiousness which is
born of habit, before there can be any thought
connected with the thing done.

Griggs and his talk had only contributed to this
result. The quick and noiseless destruction of
Katharine's beliefs had been chiefly brought about
by the actions of the persons with whom she had
to do, and by the collapse of their principles in
the face of difficulties, temptations and tests. It
was natural that she should ask herself of what
use her father's blind faith and rigid practice
could be, when neither the one nor the other could
diminish his avarice nor check his cruelty when
anything or any one stood between him and money.
She was not to be blamed if she doubted the

efficacy of the true faith, when she saw her religious
mother half mad with envy of her own daughter's
youth and beauty. As for the rest of them all,
they did not pretend to be religious people. Their
misdeeds killed her faith in human nature, which
is, perhaps, the ordinary key to that state of mind
which believes in God, though it is by no means
the only one.

Had she been able to discern and analyze what
was going on in her own heart, she would have
seen that her difficulty was the old one. The
existence of evil in the world disproved to her
the existence of a Supreme Power which was all
good. But she neither analyzed nor discerned.
It was sufficient for her that the earthly evil facts
existed to assure her that the heavenly, transcendent Power was an impossibility. She never made
the statement to herself, but she unconsciously took
it for granted in substituting one divinity for the
other. John Ralston said that he 'believed in
things' — and did, vaguely. But she had never
found it possible to bring him to any concise statement of what his beliefs were. And yet he was,
in her loving opinion, by far the morally best of
all the men and women she had ever known. He
did not go to church every Sunday, as her father
did. She believed that he never went to church
at all, in fact. But there was no denying the
superiority of a man who had bravely overcome

such temptation as John Ralston had formerly
had to deal with, over one who, like her father,
believed, trembled, and nevertheless gave himself
up wholly to his evil passion.

So she had lost her belief in human nature.
But as she could not afford to lose her belief in
the man she loved, she had taken him out of the
rest of humanity, and made him the half of herself,
so that they two stood quite alone in the world,
and had their temple to themselves, and their little
god to themselves, and their faith and belief and
religious practice altogether to themselves, though
John Ralston was quite ignorant of the fact. But
that made no difference to Katharine. He was in
her earthly paradise, though he did not know it,
and was as sincere a worshipper of the divinity as
she herself.

In this way she excepted both him and her from
common humanity, and was sure that she had
found the true path which leads to the fields of
the blessed. Love was the centre of hope and
the circumference of life; it was the air she
breathed, the thoughts she thought, and the actions
she performed. There was nothing else. And since
eternity was the present, as Griggs said, there was
no hereafter, and so there could never be anything
but love, even after men ceased to count time.
In the midst of the prosaic surroundings of a
society life, as in the midst of the great and evil

passions which do devilish deeds just below the calm, luxurious and dull surface, there was one true idealist, one maiden soul that dreamed of love's immortality, and placed hers in love's heart of hearts.

CHAPTER XXIV.

THE letter Alexander Lauderdale Junior had written to Ralston will have given some idea of what he was willing to sacrifice for the sake of having the will annulled. A moral degeneration had begun in him, which might go far in the end. The passion he had so long tried to conceal, with considerable success, and which had fed for many years on a small object, was stirred up and set at large by the enormous wealth now at stake. The man's pride shrank away before it, and even his rigid principles wavered. He began to make those compromises with his conscience which circumstances suggested, and he forced his religious habits to help in doing the dirty work of his greed. In a lower walk of life, perhaps, such a man, in such a situation, would have committed crimes to obtain the money. Alexander Junior robbed his own soul, and murdered his own conscience. We shall know some day what difference there is between that and murder in the first degree.

It was not an affair of a few days. Such a character could not change easily nor quickly, either for better or for worse. For years the thought of

his uncle's money had been constantly present
with him, and for many years he had dreamt the
miser's dream of endless gold. There was nothing
new in it, nor, of itself, had it ever disturbed the
equanimity of his well-practised righteousness. It
had never even occurred to him that in not spending
his hoarded income he was wronging any one. He
had regarded his wife's painting and selling her
miniatures as a wholesome occupation, and as what
certain persons call a moral discipline. The principles of economy which he forced his household to practise were agreeable to the ascetic
disposition which in a greater or less degree
showed itself in the Scotch blood of the Lauderdales. Economy was a means of feeling that he
was better than other people, and, axiomatically, it
cost nothing, and helped to satisfy his main passion.
Only his sense of social importance, which was
strong and hereditary, had hindered him from
actually reducing his establishment to a condition
of positive penury. But that would have been impossible, because it would have been impossible to
conceal it. He preserved the limits so carefully
that, while every one said that the Lauderdales
lived very quietly, no one ever thought of saying
that they lived poorly. Then, too, Mrs. Lauderdale was herself an excellent manager, and had
long been deceived by her husband's assurance that
he was poor and wholly dependent upon the salary

he received from the Trust Company, in which he
held no interest, as he could always easily prove.
As a matter of fact, though he practically directed
the affairs of the Company himself, he considered
United States' bonds as a safer investment. He
did not consider that he was deceiving his wife,
either. In his own opinion he was poor. What
was a million? There were some who had nearly
two hundred millions. Scores, perhaps hundreds,
in the country had more than fifty millions. What
was a million? Was not a man poor who had but
one dollar when his neighbour had two hundred?
It was no business of his wife's, nor of any one else,
if he had something put away. It had always
been possible, within the limits of the law, that his
uncle might leave him nothing. So he had practised
economy, and grown rich secretly.

But all his hardly hoarded savings were but as a
drop to the sea of gold which surged upon the
horizon of his hopes when he thought of Robert
Lauderdale's death, and which rushed forward all
at once to his very feet, as soon as the old man
was really dead. It washed away his elaborately
drawn pattern of morality, as the tide obliterates
the figures a child has scrawled upon the sand; it
rose by quick degrees, and flowed higher than the
rigid landmarks which he had driven like stakes
into the flat expanses of his soul; it boiled up and
sucked back the earth from beneath the very foun-

dations of the chapel of ease he had built for his conscience, over his own little spring of wealth, when all the shore had been dry and arid, and the golden ocean very far off.

The long cherished hope had prepared the circumstances for the reality. He meant now to have at least half the fortune, or perish in the attempt to get it. That is, he was ready to spend even what he had saved, in order to get possession of the greater sum. And he was far more ready to spend other things, such as his pride and his manliness. He was ready and willing to lay the shears to his garment of righteousness, and to clip and cut it to the very limits of moral decency, leaving but enough to cover the nakedness of his miserly soul.

Therefore he had written that letter to John Ralston, and one something like it to John's mother, believing it probable that she had been told by her son of much that had taken place. His lawyer had told him that if the will were probated, and if it became necessary to attack it on other grounds, it would be of the highest importance that the next of kin should act in concert against the distant relations who had been so highly favoured. It became his business, therefore, to make sure of having the Ralstons on his side.

He distrusted them, after what had happened. He knew that they cared little for money, and much for a certain kind of sentiment which was

quite foreign to him, and he believed them capable
of opposing him, merely in order that the dead
man's wishes might be carried out. The situation
in which he found himself was an unexpected one,
too. He had been taken by surprise and obliged
to act at short notice, and he was no diplomatist.
He merely took the first means which offered for
carrying out his lawyer's idea. The will itself was
of an unusual character. He had expected that his
uncle would either divide the fortune between the
next of kin, in trusts for their children, with a
legacy to the Brights, or that he would make something like an equal distribution amongst all the
living members of the family. He had long cherished, however, the secret hope that as his own
branch of the family was the most numerous, and
as he himself had such an unassailable character
for uprightness and economy, the largest share
might be placed in his hands for administration, if
not actually as his own property. He had been
disappointed, and he considered the will a piece of
flagrant injustice.

Many outsiders shared his opinion, and asked
one another why the Brights should have so much,
and Alexander Junior had the satisfaction of feeling that his action would be approved by a large
number of hard-headed business men amongst his
acquaintances. His lawyer, too, was encouraged by
this fact, and looked forward confidently to pocket-

ing an enormous fee. He was a man as hard headed, as upright, and as spotless in reputation as his client, and the high morality of their united forces was imposing.

If Alexander had conceived it possible that Mrs. Ralston and her son could agree to have no opinion in the matter, but to abide by their lawyer's judgment, and let him act as he thought best, he might have spared himself the trouble and humiliation of writing the letter to John. He would have known that Mr. Henry Brett was not the man to advise his clients against taking their rights without any regard to sentiment, and Alexander's joy was great when he found that Brett was with him — a much younger man than his own lawyer, but keen, business-like, and of excellent standing. Brett had married the widow of the notorious forger and defaulter, John Darche, and had diminished neither his popularity nor his credit by so doing.

Alexander reproached himself in a way that would have surprised his former virtue, for having so bitterly opposed Katharine's marriage with John Ralston. He really could not conceive how he could ever have attached so much importance to the young fellow's youthful follies. It was the most natural thing in the world, as it seemed to him now, that with the prospect of boundless wealth the boy should have idled away his time and amused himself as other boys did. His mind was full of excuses for Ralston. What he could not pardon, he allowed to be swamped by the gold-flood as soon as it presented itself. That one unpardonable thing was the blow he had received. When he could not help thinking of it, and when it stung his manliness — for he was a brave man — he took pains to recollect that he had at once got John by the throat, and would probably have broken some of his bones for him, if Katharine's hurt had not interrupted the struggle. It was not as though he had received a blow tamely, without retaliation. His blood had been up, and Ralston must have got the worst of it if circumstances had not obliged him to pause in his vengeance. Nothing can equal the unconscious sophistry of a man whose main passion requires that he shall not feel that he has been insulted.

And so matters proceeded. The Brights' lawyer did his best to force the will to probate. The Lauderdales' and Ralstons' legal advisers created delays, and as they were in possession of the will, they were able to prolong the situation, and prepare for action. Old Robert Lauderdale's lawyer, Mr. Allen, was moreover their ally. He did not believe that the will was good, and resented the way in which his deceased client had surreptitiously employed a young fellow like Russell, before mentioned, to draw it up, after he, Allen, had drawn up one which had been irreproachable. The first point that arose was in connection with one of the witnesses, who was unluckily not forthcoming. The signature was that of one 'John Simons.' In the list of servants who were to receive annuities appeared the name of one 'J. Simmons,' a groom, who, strange to say, was not to be found either. The Lauderdale lawyers maintained that the witness and the servant were the same person, and that there had been a mistake in spelling the name in the list; a fact which would have debarred the will from probate, as no legatee can be a witness. This forced the Bright lawyers to ask time in order to find either the witness or the groom, or both, and meanwhile the other side looked into the will itself in search of irregularities connected with the suspension of the power of alienation, and the like. Mr. George W. Russell, who had drawn up the will, looked on with his hands in his pockets, and was 'interested in the show' from a purely artistic point of view.

The parties began to rage furiously together. Alexander Junior did not hesitate to say that he remembered the groom Simmons, and that his name was John. He assuredly believed that he did remember the fact, or he would not have said so. But Hamilton Bright remembered, with equal certainty, that the man had more than once gone with him when he had been consulted, as an authority, about the buying of horses for old Robert, and that his name was James. He had called him James, and the man had answered to his name. That was proof positive. The servants of the accused did not know anything about it. The man had always been called Persimmons, because he lisped a little. He had been badly kicked by a horse during Mr. Lauderdale's last days, and had been sent to St. Luke's Hospital. At the hospital it was ascertained that he had been discharged in a few days. He had not come back to Mr. Lauderdale's. He probably had some good reason for not coming back. It had been one of his duties to buy certain things for the stables. Possibly he had been dishonest and feared discovery. Mr. Russell, privately questioned, said that the man who had signed the will as a witness might have been a servant, and added, a few seconds later, that as he had not been present when the will was signed, he did not know. He was young enough to laugh to himself at his own pretended hesitation. He had drawn up the will. When or where it had been signed and witnessed was beyond his knowledge.

The other witnesses said that from his appearance the man might have been a respectable servant. He was clean shaven, and might have been a groom. They had not heard him speak, so that they did not know whether he lisped or not. They had never seen him before, and he had been in the room when they had been called in. They had seen him write his name, and were prepared to swear to it. They should also recognize him if they saw him. Mr. Russell, privately questioned, said that he had copied the name 'J. Simmons' with a list of names given him by Mr. Lauderdale for the purpose. It had not struck him that it was informal to insert only the initial, since there was no other Simmons, a servant, in the house at the time. He was told severely, by the Brights' lawyer, that it was. He said he regretted the fact, and put his hands into his pockets and looked on again.

Crowdie, who never swore, anathematized Alexander Junior in the dialect of the Paris studios, a language which Alexander could not have understood. Bright, who had driven cattle in the Nacimiento Valley, spoke differently. Aunt Maggie's charity suddenly ceased to be universal, and excluded both Lauderdales and Ralstons from its benefits. From Washington, Charlotte Slayback wrote an unusually affectionate letter to her sister Katharine, in which she playfully compared the fair-haired aunt Maggie and Hamilton Bright to a lioness and her whelp, and all the tribe of Lauderdales to poor little innocent lambs with blue ribbons round their necks. Benjamin Slayback of Nevada, Member of Congress, said nothing. He was a singular man, having mines of silver of his own, and his solitary pleasure was in giving his wife much money, because she had none of her own. He reflected that if she were suddenly made rich in her own right, his pleasure would be greatly diminished. But on the whole, he believed in respecting dead men's wishes, in spite of legal formalities. He had known wills made by word of mouth by men who had bullets in them before witnesses who had put the bullets there, but who were scrupulous in carrying out the instructions of the departed. He was a lawyer himself, however, and took an interest in the case. He talked of running up to New York, from Friday to Monday, to have a look at things, and a guess at which way the cat would jump.

Then Leek, the butler, who was anxious about his annuity, found Persimmons, the groom, in a down-town stable, and showed him how important it was for them both that he should at once go and swear that he was not the John Simons who had signed the will, which he immediately did. But on being confronted with the other witnesses, they said that the signer had been clean shaven, and about of the same height; that the room had been dimly lighted, and that they were not prepared to swear that Persimmons was not the signer. Then Persimmons, being indignant, and having had two goes of whiskey with Leek, lifted up his voice, and swore to his own identity, and gave an account of himself, and declared that his name was not and never had been John Simons, nor J. Simmons, nor

Persimmons, because he was not a Simmons at all, but one James Thwaite, and had changed his name when he left England, because he had been unjustly disqualified as a jockey, for roping Mr. Cranstoun's mare in the Thousand Guineas. All of which further complicated matters, while the other witnesses grew more and more conscientiously sure that he was the man who had signed with them, and wished to see him in a brown jacket. Persimmons owned that he possessed such a garment, but refused to put it on to play Punch and Judy for a couple of noodles, which almost produced a free fight in Mr. Brett's private office, and did not improve things at all, for the two witnesses promptly swore that this was the same Persimmons who had signed with them, and they should have liked to know whether a disqualified jockey were a proper person to sign with respectable persons like themselves — they should like to know that, once for all. And they departed, much ruffled. Privately questioned, Mr. Russell said that he had given Mr. Lauderdale no advice as to the selection of his witnesses. He supposed that Mr. Lauderdale, who had made at least two other wills in the course of his life, might have been expected to understand what was required of witnesses. The Brights' legal adviser told him that it was the duty of a lawyer to tell his client how to make the signatures on a will legal. Mr. Russell thrust his hands

into his pockets and looked on. But the Brights'
lawyer began to think that things looked queer,
and that he might not get the will through probate
after all. He had not expected such a check at
the outset. He had anticipated a fight over much
more complicated questions.

The Brights tried to ascertain whether the court
would admit the will to probate on the testimony
of the two reliable witnesses. It seemed pretty
clear that the court would not hear of it. There
had been a recent case, argued the Brights, in which
the testimony of one witness had been held to be
sufficient to establish the signatures of the others,
though at least one of the others was living at the
time in a remote part of the world. They were
told that this was all very well, but that in the case
quoted there had been no question of any one of the
witnesses being a legatee, still less of that one having given an assumed name and not being an American citizen, and that furthermore, in that case,
there had been no prospect of any litigation arising
between the heirs, because there had been only
one heir, and excepting two small legacies, he
would have got the fortune just as surely if the
deceased had died intestate; and finally, that the
Brights had better not come into court with any
such trumped-up case, which was unkind to the
Brights, because the will was in their favour, and
they were not trumping up a case, but defending
one.

Then Persimmons, finding that eighty millions of money depended upon his having signed or not signed the will, and that no one had, as yet, offered him so much as a drink, save Leek, the butler, went privately to Alexander Lauderdale Junior, and made certain propositions which immediately resulted in his being kicked into the middle of Broad Street by an unfeeling person in brass buttons, who answered to the name of Donald McCracken, having red hair, large bones, and a Scotch accent — very terrible.

On the advice of friends, Persimmons attempted to recover damages for indignities and bruises received on the premises of the Trust Company, and the popular feeling in the stables was with him. But he got nothing but the promise of more kicks, payable at sight, by Donald McCracken, and the hexecrations of Mister Leek who perceived that 'is hannuity was vanishing before 'is very heyes.

And now no lawyer would make bold to say in his heart whether Persimmons had signed or had not signed, and the war raged furiously, and the Lauderdales, being in possession of the will, swore that they would bring it to probate without delay, and that the Brights ought to be very much pleased at this, as they had been so anxious to get the will probated without delay. But the Brights were less anxious to do so than they had been a few days earlier, and looked about them for means

of strengthening testimony.   Also, the whole story
was well ventilated in the newspapers.

Then came a man privately to Hamilton Bright
and said that he was John Simons, who spelled his
name in the right way, and had been the witness of
the will.   He was in difficulties, and was obliged
to hide from his creditors ; but if a small sum of
money were forthcoming — and so forth.   Bright
looked at him, and he was clean-shaven, and of
average height, and wore a brown jacket.   Bright
hesitated, and then called the other witnesses, who
unhesitatingly swore that the man who had signed
was Persimmons and not this Simons.   And nothing more was heard of the man in the brown
jacket to this day.   But another clean-shaven man
of average height with another sort of brown
jacket appeared the next morning, and many more
after him, very much alike.   But the departure
of them from the office was much more precipitate
than that of the first.   And this also was in the
morning and evening papers, and still the will was
unprobated, and lay in Mr. Allen's safe.   After
that the lawyers on each side began to accuse one
another of causing delay, and while they were
quarrelling about it the delay continued, and the
public jeered, and the actors at Harrigan and
Hart's introduced jokes about the Lauderdale will
which brought the house down, until Teddy Van
De Water, chancing to be in the audience, took

friendly action, and requested that the name should not be introduced in future. At this the public of the theatre took offence, and called all the Lauderdales gilt-edged galoots, and by other similar epithets commonly applied to the Four Hundred by a godless population which has not the fear of millions before its eyes, but rather a desire for the same.

About this time the quality of the cigars smoked by Alexander Lauderdale Senior suddenly improved at a wonderful and miraculous rate, so that in a few days he was brought by successive stages of delight from the 'Old Virginia Cheroot,' at ten cents for a package of five, to the refinement of Havanas, at thirty cents apiece, after which of his own accord he returned to what are known as Eden Bouquets from Park and Tilford's. He smoked in silent surprise, not unmixed with an old man's cunning curiosity, and not without much internal amusement. Reporters also came often to see him, ostensibly to make enquiries about the vast charities in which he was chiefly interested; but in reality they came cynically to have a look at him, and to tell the public what probabilities of life remained to him in which to enjoy his half of the Lauderdale fortune. Most of them came to the conclusion that he might live many years longer.

In the Lauderdale household there was peace

during these days. Katharine had returned, and
had been received by her father with reticent
affection, and nothing more had been said about
her offering an apology for her hasty speeches.
From time to time the Ralstons were spoken of in
connection with the family affairs, and then Alexander suggested to his wife that they might be
asked to dinner. It would, in his favourite phrase,
tend to cement the union between the two branches
of the family which stood together in the great
contention, pitted against the Brights and the
Crowdies.

They came, and their coming was an event.
Even the servants took an interest in it. Ralston
and Lauderdale shook hands rather spasmodically,
and each looked at Katharine's arm a moment
later, recalling the words they had exchanged when
they had last met, and the blow and the struggle
after it, and many other things of a similar nature.
The Ralstons were very quiet, but behaved naturally and made conversation, avoiding the subject
of the will as much as possible. After dinner
John and Katharine sat in a corner for nearly half
an hour, as they used to do long ago in the early
days of their love-making, and Alexander Junior
seemed well satisfied, and resolutely turned his
back on them and talked with Mrs. Ralston.

John remembered having told his mother, when
Katharine was still at the Brights', that the next

time Katharine entered her father's house she should go as his wife; but fate had managed matters otherwise. Until the question of the fortune was settled, it would be as well to keep the marriage a secret. It could only be a question of days now. That was clear enough from Alexander's face, which expressed his certainty of triumph as clearly as his cold features could express anything. His electric smile flashed more frequently than it had done for many years, and his steely eyes glittered in the light. But he had grown thin of late, for it was hard to wait so long before realizing the miser's dream.

In the night, when he lay awake, he had a wild idea which haunted him in the dark hours, though it never crossed his brain during the daylight. He thought of realizing a whole million in gold coin, and of revelling in the delight of pouring it from one hand to another. He had a million of his own, in a very realizable shape, but somehow he would not have risked that, so long as he had not a second. Some one might rob him — one could never tell. He should like to be alone with the gold in his own room for one hour, and then know that it was safe. He considered whether the gas-light in his dressing-room were strong enough to make the metal glitter. Electric light would be better.

It was a childish thought, and in the daytime he paid no attention to it, but at night it came upon him like hunger or thirst, drying his lips and driving away sleep. Then, in order to quiet his brain, he had to promise himself that he would really do the thing he longed to do as soon as it lay in his power. But in the morning, when he stood before his shaving-glass, and looked into his own hard eyes, he laughed scornfully.

So things went on for a few days more. Then Alexander arose and said that there should be no more delay, but that the will should be brought to probate at the next session of the court, which does not sit every day. And then the excitement grew more intense, and the Brights and the Lauderdales avoided one another in the street. Ralston still went regularly to the bank and saw Hamilton Bright every day. But though they were friends still, and there had been no unfriendly word spoken between them, they met as little as possible and merely nodded quickly when a meeting was unavoidable. But Ralston was displeased by the notice he attracted whenever he got up from his seat or sat down again. Occasionally an acquaintance of one of the numerous young gentlemen in the bank came in, and it was rarely that, after exchanging a few words with his friend, the stranger did not turn and glance at John, where he sat. Ralston did not like it, but he could do nothing against it.

Then came the day of judgment. Without

warning the Brights produced a man whom they believed to be the real John Simons, and who swore that he had signed the will in the presence of the testators and in the presence of the other witnesses.

This was a terrible blow to the Lauderdale side. But the other witnesses had previously sworn to and signed a statement, extracted from them by the Lauderdales, to the effect that Persimmons was the man who had signed with them; and whether the John Simons now present, who was a genuine John Simons of some kind, were the right one or not, they had no intention of laying themselves open to a possible action for perjury, and stuck to their original testimony, regardless of the fact that the witness now confronted with them, being also clean shaven, of average height, and possibly the possessor of a brown jacket, was a perfectly respectable citizen of New York. At this the legal advisers of the Brights were thunderstruck, and the court was surprised. But with the fear of prosecution by the Lauderdales before their eyes, the other two would not budge, though the real John Simons, whether he had signed or not, immediately threatened to prosecute them for perjury on his own account. But he did not look imposing enough, and they preferred that risk to the other.

In the face of such conflicting evidence the court

ruled that, the witnesses not agreeing, the will could not be admitted to probate, and there was clearly nothing to be done but to give judgment that the deceased had died intestate, and that administrators must dispose of the property between the next of kin, Alexander Lauderdale Senior, and Katharine Lauderdale, widow of the late Admiral Ralston of the United States Navy.

When Alexander Junior heard the judgment he laughed hysterically, and showed his brilliant teeth. Hamilton Bright said nothing, but he, who generally reddened under emotion, turned white to his neck and under his ears.

"That's all very well," said Mr. Allen to Mr. Henry Brett, as they walked away together. "But if he didn't happen to destroy the will I made for him, there may be trouble yet. I wonder where it is!"

But nobody seemed to know.

CHAPTER XXV.

It is not very easy to conceive of the disappointment felt by persons to whom a gigantic fortune has been left by a will which is then entirely set aside, so that they receive absolutely nothing. It would be useless to attempt an analysis of the state of mind which prevailed in the households of the Brights and the Crowdies after judgment had been given against them in the court of probate. The blow was sudden and stunning. Though they were all very well-to-do, even rich, in the ordinary acceptation of that word, their joint imagination had of late so completely outrun their present circumstances, that they felt impoverished when the hope of millions was removed beyond their reach. They could not realize that the will was absolutely valueless, and they still felt sure that something might be done.

Unfortunately for them the matter had been finally settled. In the presence of witnesses who denied one another's identity, and threatened one another reciprocally with actions for perjury, the court could hardly have done otherwise than it had done. To this day it is still doubtful — from

a legal point of view — which of the John Si-
monses signed as a witness, though everything
goes to show that the last one produced was the
right one, in spite of the fact that the others
denied having known him. Persimmons had, from
the first, denied having had anything to do with
the matter, but he had subsequently sworn to all
manner of statements. The confusion was complete. There was no doubt that the respectable
John Simons who appeared last was a tenant of
one of the Lauderdale houses in MacDougal Street,
and he said that he had found himself at Robert
Lauderdale's house, having gone to complain of
a leak in his roof to old Robert himself, after
having vainly laid his grievance before the agent
a number of times. The story was probably true,
but the other witnesses remained firm in their
assertion that he was not the man. They were,
perhaps, telling the truth to the best of their abil-
ity. Neither Persimmons nor John Simons were
men who had anything unusual about them to impress itself upon their memory. They themselves,
somewhat awed by the presence of the great millionaire, had looked at him much more than at
their insignificant fellow-witness. The room had
not been light, for the signing had taken place
late in the afternoon, as all agreed in stating, and
they had not remained in one another's presence
more than three minutes altogether. Simons, said

the other two, had stayed behind, whereas they had left the room immediately. It was not surprising that their memory of the man's face should be indistinct.

The Brights, however, threw the whole blame upon the Lauderdales and their legal advisers. The latter had not the right, they said, to make the two witnesses sign an affidavit beforehand to the effect that they recognized the third. The Lauderdales answered that there was no law to hinder them from requesting any individual with whom they had to do, to swear to any statement he made. The two need not have signed unless they pleased. There had been no pressure brought to bear upon them. They had said that they recognized Persimmons. The Lauderdale lawyers wished to make sure that they did, so as to avoid any subsequent trouble, because Persimmons denied that he was the man, and might disappear before the hearing. What was more natural than that, out of pure caution, they should have wished to file an affidavit of the man's identity? The Brights, amongst themselves, were obliged to admit that they did not really know who had signed, and that the only person who could have settled the dispute was dead, so that they could not blame the court for its decision.

After the judgment John Simons quarrelled with the other two, who turned upon him in defence of their own reputations. They swore out warrants against one another which were not served, and they pottered amongst shysters and legal small fry, until they had spent most of their money, and disappeared from the horizon with their quarrel. The private opinion of the judge who had settled the question was that there had been an unfortunate mistake, and that all three had originally intended to be perfectly honest. But he also thought it far more just that the fortune should go to the next of kin, in spite of Robert Lauderdale's wishes.

Alexander Lauderdale did his best to conceal his delight in his triumph. It had been a far more easy victory than he had expected, and it was practically complete. The only drawback was that the fortune had come into his old father's hands instead of into his own, but he anticipated no difficulty in ruling the old gentleman according to his own judgment, nor in getting control of the whole estate. He intended to treat it as he had treated his own comparatively small possessions, and he had hopes of seeing it doubled in his lifetime. He could make it double itself in twenty years at the utmost, and he was but fifty years of age, or thereabouts. He should live as long as that, with his iron constitution and careful habits.

His father received the news with an old man's chuckle of pleasure, and one heavy hand fell into

the other with a loud slap of satisfaction. He had
but one idea, which was to extend the scope and
efficiency of his charitable institutions, and he saw
at last that he had boundless power to do so.

"I always knew I should live to build that other
asylum myself!" he cried, referring to one of his
favourite schemes. "It will only cost a million or
so, and another million as a foundation will run it.
I'll send for the architects at once."

Alexander Junior smiled, for he believed that
he was quite able to prevent any such extravagance
by getting himself appointed his father's guardian,
on the ground that the old gentleman would squan-
der everything in senseless charities. But in the
meanwhile it would take some time to make the
division of the property, which was almost wholly
in real estate, as has been seen, and could not be
so readily apportioned as though it had been held
in bond and mortgage. Of course the administrators would allow either of the heirs to draw a large
amount on credit before the settling, if they desired
to do so.

Alexander Senior said that he meant to live in
Clinton Place for the rest of his life, and his son
considered this a very wise decision. The people
who lived opposite began to watch the old gentleman, who had inherited over forty millions, when he
went out on foot in his shabby coat for his airing
on fine days. They wondered why he did not buy

a new one, as they did, when their overcoats were worn out.

Mrs. Lauderdale was indignant at the idea of continuing to inhabit the old house. In her mind it was associated with a quarter of a century of penurious economy, and she longed at last for the luxury she enjoyed so thoroughly in the houses of others.

"It's perfectly absurd," she said to Katharine, indignantly. "I've stood it all these years because I had to — but I won't stand it any longer. If ever I paint another miniature! But I'd made up my mind that I wouldn't do that, even if we didn't get all the money."

"I should think so!" laughed Katharine. "Put away your paints and your brushes, mother, and say that you'll never use them any more. You'll be at it again as hard as ever in a week, because you really like it, you know!"

"I suppose so." And Mrs. Lauderdale laughed, too. "Let's go out, child. Let's take a long drive — somewhere. I suppose we can drive as much as we like now."

"From morning till night," answered Katharine; "why don't we use the horses and carriages? They're all there, you know, and all the grooms and coachmen and everything, just as though nothing had happened."

"Do you think we could just go there and order

a carriage?" asked Mrs. Lauderdale, rather doubtfully.

"Why, of course! Whose are they all, if they're
not ours and the Ralstons'? We have a perfect
right—"

"Yes—but if we were to meet people—don't
you know?"

"Well—they're our carriages, not theirs."
Katharine laughed again. "The only question
is whether they'll belong to the Ralstons or to
us. I suppose they'll all be sold and we shall
buy new ones."

"I don't see why," answered Mrs. Lauderdale.
"They're perfectly good carriages, and there are
some splendid horses—"

Twenty-five years of rigid economy were not to
be forgotten in a day, and Alexander Junior saw
with satisfaction that his wife showed no signs of
developing any very reprehensible extravagance.
But she enjoyed that first drive, lying back in the
luxurious carriage with her daughter by her side,
and feeling that it all belonged to her, or, at least,
that she was privileged to consider that it did, as
much as though she had inherited the fortune
herself.

Aunt Maggie Bright saw the two in the Park
and bent her head rather stiffly. She recognized
the carriage and spoke of the meeting to her son
that evening.

"They've a right to do as they please," answered Hamilton gravely. "As for the carriages and all the personal belongings, they'd have had them anyway. I should like to know where that other will is, though. If he didn't destroy it, it's good now."

"If it's in existence, it will turn up amongst the papers one of these days."

"Unless Alexander gets at them — then it won't," said Bright, savagely.

"Perhaps that isn't quite just, Ham. I don't think Alexander's capable of destroying such a thing."

"Oh — isn't he! You don't know him, mother. If you think anything would stand in the way of his defending his millions, you're very much mistaken. There's been something very queer about the whole affair. That affidavit wasn't straight."

They argued the case and talked over it, as they had done many times already, without coming to any conclusion, except that they should have had the money and Alexander should not. They always considered that he had got the property, though it was really his father's. But they both knew how futile discussion was, and they abandoned it at last, as they always did, with a hopeless conviction that the truth could never be known.

Katharine on her side was much disturbed by what she knew of the previous will, and she took counsel with John Ralston, as to how she should

act. There was not much to be done, since the
will itself had not been found up to the present
date, though the administrators had been already
some time engaged in examining the papers. Of
these there was no end, though the agent of the
estate was acquainted with most of them. They
consisted chiefly of title deeds and leases.

By this time Alexander had practically admitted
that Katharine was engaged to be married to
Ralston, but like every one else concerned, he
thought it better to wait until the summer, before
announcing the fact. To do so now would look as
though the family had only waited for Robert
Lauderdale's death. Moreover, though it is so
little the custom to wear mourning for any but the
very nearest nowadays, the inheritance of wealth
requires a corresponding show of grief on the part
of the heirs. There is a sort of tacit understanding about that. When an uncle leaves a fortune,
the particular nephew who gets it must acknowledge the fact and propitiate the shade of the dear
departed with a decently broad hatband. The
position of the Brights caused some amusement.
They had worn something approaching to mourning after old Lauderdale's death, but they did not
think it necessary to continue to do so after the
court had set aside the will. The Lauderdales
and the Ralstons wore half mourning.

As has been said, Katharine's engagement was

accepted as a fact in the family, and she had no difficulty in seeing Ralston as often as she pleased, when he was free from his work. He had told Mr. Beman that he should prefer to stay in the bank for a time and learn something about business, and Beman had been delighted, especially when he saw that John came as regularly as ever.

CHAPTER XXVI.

' In the late spring John and Katharine often
walked together of an afternoon, between half
past five and sunset.

It was during one of these walks that Katharine
consulted him seriously. They went about together
in unfrequented places, as a rule, not caring to
meet acquaintances at every turn. Neither of
them had any social duties to perform, and they
were as free to do as they pleased as though they
had not represented the rising generation of Lauderdales.

The spring had fairly come at last. It had
rained, and the pavement dried in white patches,
the willow trees in the square were a blur of green,
and the Virginia creeper on the houses here and
there was all rough with little stubby brown buds.
It had come with a rush. The hyacinths were
sticking their green curved beaks up through the
park beds, and the little cock-sparrows were scrap-
ing their wings along the ground.

There was a bright youthfulness in everything,
— in the air, in the sky, in the old houses, in the
faces of the people in the streets. The Italians

with their fruit carts sunned themselves, and
turned up their dark rough faces to the warmth.
The lame boy who lived in the house at the corner
of Clinton Place was out on the pavement, with a
single roller skate on his better foot, pushing himself along with his crutch, and laughing all to
himself, pale but happy. The old woman in grey,
who hangs about that region and begs, had at last
taken the dilapidated woollen shawl from her head,
and had replaced it by a very, very poor apology
for a hat, with a crumpled paper cherry and a green
leaf in it, and only one string. And the other
woman, who wants her car-fare to Harlem, seemed
more anxious to get there than ever. Moreover the
organ-grinders expressed great joy, and the children danced together to the cheerful discords, in
Washington Square, under the blur of the green
willows — slim American children, who talked
through their noses, and funny little French children with ribbons in their hair, from South Fifth
Avenue, and bright-eyed darkey children with one
baby amongst them. And they took turns in holding it while the others danced.

Now also the patriotic Italians took occasion to
bury a dead comrade or two, and a whole platoon
of them, who had been riflemen in their own army
at home, turned out in their smart, theatrical uni-
forms of green and red, with plumes of gleaming
cock's feathers lying over one side of their flat

waterproof hats. And they had a band of their
own which played a funeral march, as their little
legs moved with doll-like slowness to the solemn
measure.

But Katharine and John Ralston followed less
frequented paths, crossing Broadway from Clinton
Place east, and striking past Astor Place and
Lafayette Place — where the Crowdies lived —
by Stuyvesant Street eastwards to Avenue A and
Tompkins Square. And there, too, the spring was
busy, blurring everything with green. Men were
getting the benches out of the kiosk on the north
side, where they are stacked away all winter, and
others were repairing the band stand with its
shabby white dome, and everywhere there were
children, rising as it were from the earth to meet
the soft air — rising as the sparkling little air
bubbles rise in champagne, to be free at last —
hundreds of children, perhaps a thousand, in the
vast area which many a New Yorker has not seen
twice in his life, out at play in the light of the
westering sun. They stared innocently as Katharine and Ralston passed through their midst, and
held their breath a moment at the sight of a real
lady and gentleman. All the little girls over ten
years old looked at Katharine's clothes and approved of them, and all the boys looked at John
Ralston's face to see whether he would be the
right sort of young person to whom to address an
ironical remark, but decided that he was not.

"There goes a son of a gamboleer," observed one small chap on roller skates, as he looked after John. "He's fly."

"You bet! And his girl, she knows it," replied his companion, sharing in his admiration.

"Your dad's new coat's that shape," said the first. "But 'taint made that way. Fifth Av'nue, that is! Bet?"

"Lemme be!" retorted the other. "Botherin' me 'bout dad's coat. Mine's better'n yours, anyhow."

"Take a reef in your lip, Johnny, or I'll sit on it!"

Thereupon they fought without the slightest hesitation. But Katharine and John Ralston went on, and crossed the great square and left it by the southeast corner, from which a quiet street leads across the remaining lettered avenues to an enormous timber yard at the water's edge, a bad neighbourhood at night, and the haunt of the class generically termed dock rats, a place of murder and sudden death by no means unfrequently, but by day as quiet and safe as any one could wish.

"I don't know what to do, Jack," Katharine said, as they walked along. "The idea of that other will haunts me, and I lie awake thinking of it at night."

"Don't do that," laughed Ralston. "It isn't

worth while. Besides, it wouldn't make so much difference if it were found."

"The Brights would get their share — as much as they ought to expect — instead of getting nothing. That's the principal thing. But papa wouldn't like it at all. As things are now, he'll probably have all grandpapa's share when grandpapa dies. I suppose he'll have the management of it as it is. But if the old will were found, and were legal, you know — why then papa never could possibly have anything but the income of half my share. He wouldn't like that."

"What in the world does he want with so much?" asked Ralston, impatiently. "I do think you Lauderdales are the strangest people! If the will —"

"Don't say 'you Lauderdales' to me like that, Jack!" interrupted Katharine, with a little laugh. "You're every bit as much one as I am, you know —"

"Well — yes. I didn't want to say disagreeable things about your father —"

"So you jumbled us all up together! That's logical, at all events. Well — don't!" she laughed again.

"No, I won't. So I'll say that your father is the strangest person I ever heard of. As it is now, he's practically got half the fortune. If the old will turned up and were proved, he and your mother would get two-thirds of the income — "

"No they wouldn't, Jack. The two-thirds would be divided equally between them and Charlotte and me."

"Oh — I see! Then they'd only get one-third between them. Well — what difference does it make, after all? There's such a lot of money, anyhow — "

"You don't understand papa, Jack. I'm not sure that I do — quite. But I think what he wants is not the income, for he'll never spend it. I believe if he had the whole eighty-two millions locked up in the Safe Deposit, he'd be quite happy, and would prefer to go on living in Clinton Place on ten or eleven thousand a year — or whatever it costs — just as he's always lived. It's the money he wants, I think, not the income of it. That's the reason why I'm sure he wouldn't like the other will. He'd fight it just as he fought this one. For my part I never could understand what made uncle Robert change his mind at the last minute, just after he'd spoken to me."

"He did, anyhow. That's the main point."

"Yes. You know he was very much troubled in his mind about the money. I believe he's been thinking for years how to divide it fairly. I could see, when he spoke to me, that he wasn't satisfied with what he'd done. It was worrying him still.

But now — about this other will — ought I to say anything? I mean, is it my duty to tell papa what was in it?"

"No, indeed! How could it be your duty? Everybody knows that uncle Robert had made a previous will. Mr. Allen drew it up, though of course he's bound to say nothing about what was in it. It is always taken for granted that when a man makes a new will he burns his old one. That's probably what uncle Robert did, like a sensible man. What's the use of telling anybody about it? Besides — frankly — I wouldn't trust your father, if he knew what was in it. He'd go out of his mind and do something foolish."

"What, for instance? What could he do?"

"Well — it might fall into his hands by accident. One never knows. And he might say nothing about it. Of course, I don't mean to say exactly that he would —"

"No, dear — please don't say it. He's my father, you know — and I don't think you understand him as I do. He never would do anything like that — never! I don't think it's quite fair even to suggest such a thing."

"I'm sorry I spoke," answered Ralston, in a contrite voice, for he saw that she was really hurt. "You know what I mean — "

"Yes —" she replied in a doubtful tone. "But you don't understand him, quite. It's the view

of right and wrong, it isn't the real right and
wrong. He's violent, and he's been cruelly unkind
to me, and — well — he loves money. I can't deny
it."

"Hardly!" exclaimed Ralston, feeling that she
was justifying him with every word.

"No. It's much too clear. Nobody could deny
it. But you're very much mistaken if you think
that papa would do anything which he knew to
be dishonest. With all his faults he's got that
good point. He's honest in the letter, and I
think he means to be in the spirit."

"How awfully charitable women are!" Ralston
laughed rather scornfully.

"No," answered Katharine. "I don't go in for
being charitable. I'm not telling you that I love
him, nor that I can ever forgive some of the things
he's said and done. I suppose I ought to. But
I'm just as human as other people. I can't turn
the other cheek, and that sort of thing, you know.
I never mean to give him another chance of hurting me, if I can help it, because I don't know
what he might do. We're very different, he and
I, though we're so much alike in some ways. But
all the same, I say that papa's not a bad man,
and I won't let any one else say it — not even
you. He's very limited. He's fond of money.
He's got a cruel streak — I believe it's his New
England blood, for none of the other Lauderdales
have it — "

"Except Hester Crowdie," observed Ralston. "I'm sure she's cruel."

"Hester!" exclaimed Katharine, in surprise. "How absurd! She's the kindest woman living."

"I may be mistaken — I judge from her face, that's all, and from her eyes when she sees Crowdie talking to any other woman."

"Oh — she's infatuated about him," laughed Katharine. "She's mad on that point, but as they love each other so tremendously, I think it's rather nice of them both — don't you?"

"Oh yes," answered Ralston, indifferently. "Go on with what you were saying. You were talking about your father."

"Yes. He has a cruel streak. In a small way, Charlotte has it, too. She can say the most horrid things sometimes, that give pain, and she seems to enjoy it. But you're wrong about Hester — she's kind-hearted. As for papa — it's just that. His religion and his love of money are always fighting in him. His religion gets the better of it whenever he's tempted to do anything that's plainly wrong. But his love of money drives him up to the very edge of what's fair. Now, for instance, he's always told us that he was poor, and yet uncle Robert knew that he had a million put away somewhere. That's fifty thousand a year, isn't it? Yes, I've heard him say so. Yet, I'm quite sure that he really considered that

very little, much too little to have divided it
between us girls. So he's made us live on a
quarter of it all our lives. He felt poor, and he
said he was. Those things are relative, Jack.
Uncle Robert would have felt as poor as a church
mouse with only a million to dispose of. As papa
looked at it, it was true, though it didn't seem
so to us. Do you see what I mean?"

"Dear — if you wish to defend your father,
defend him as much as you please. But let's
differ in our opinion of some of his peculiarities.
It's better to agree about differing, you know.
We've both got the most awful tempers, you and
I, and unless we label the disagreeable things, we
shall quarrel over them. That's one of them —
your father. Put him away and lock up the idea.
It's safer."

"But you and I wouldn't really quarrel — even
about him, Jack," said Katharine, with sudden
earnestness.

"Well — I don't know. Not for long, of course."

"Not for one minute," said Katharine, in a tone
of absolute certainty. "When have we quarrelled,
Jack? Except last winter, over that wretched
misunderstanding — and that was all my fault.
You don't think I'm angry about what you said of
papa, do you? I'm not, and I'm sorry if you
thought I was. But how could two people love
each other as we do, and quarrel? You didn't

mean what you said, dear, or you don't understand by quarrelling what I understand by it. Perhaps that's it. I've grown up in an atmosphere of perpetual fighting, and I hate it. You've not. You don't understand, as I said. You've never quarrelled with your mother, have you?"

"Never but once — at the same time, you know, when they were all against me. It didn't last long."

"Exactly. You've had your fights with men, I suppose, and all that. It's quite different. But I've lived all my life in the most especial garden of our family tempers. Four of us — grandpapa, papa, Charlotte, and I — and my mother as the only peacemaker, with her Kentucky blood! But she's always done her best, and we love each other dearly, she and I, though we've been tearing each other's hair out for the last four months — until the other day. Now we're friends again, Jack; she's been splendid, you know, or rather, you don't half know!"

"And what happened the other day, to save your remaining locks?" enquired Ralston, with a smile.

"Oh, I can't tell you. Perhaps she will, some day. But as I was saying, you can't imagine what my life at home has been all these years. I'm not sure whether it hasn't been worse since Charlotte was married. You know what we are — we're so awfully polite when we fight. Ham Bright's the only one who gets rough when he's excited. That's

California and Nevada, I suppose. But we! we quarrel with all solemnity. A family of undertakers couldn't do it more gravely. It always seems to me that papa ought to have a band on his hat and black gloves when he begins. Yes, it's funny to talk about. But it's not pleasant to live in the middle of it. We're all used to being on the defensive. Charlotte didn't mind what she said to papa, but she used to pick her words and arrange her phrases — like knives all stuck up in a neat row for him to fall upon. And he generally fell, and hurt himself badly — poor papa! He's not very clever, though he's so precise about what he knows. And every now and then mother would strike out with one of her dashing southern sentiments, and then I'd say something, and when nobody thought that grandpapa had heard a word of the conversation, he'd suddenly make a remark — a regular Lauderdale remark that set everybody by the ears again. But it's only since you and papa had that awful scene — you know, when you first wanted to marry me — it's only since then that he's got into the habit of raising his voice and being angry, and — " She stopped short.

"And generally behaving like a fiend incarnate," suggested Ralston, by way of ending the sentence.

"Oh, well — let's leave them alone, dear," answered Katharine. "It's all going to be so different now. I only wanted to explain to you what I meant by quarrelling, that's all. I want to forget all about it, and live with you forever and ever, and ever, and be perfectly peaceful and happy — as we shall be. Look at the sunset. That's much better than talking about those horrid old times, isn't it?"

They stood by the edge of the river, on the road that runs along from pier to pier. Katharine laid her hand upon Ralston's arm, and felt how it drew her gently close to him, and glancing at his face she loved it better than ever in the red evening light.

The sun was going down between two clouds, the one above him, the other below, grey and golden, behind Brooklyn bridge, and behind the close-crossing pencil masts and needle yards of many vessels. From the river rose the white plumes of twenty little puffing tugs and ferry-boats far down in the distance. Between the sun's great flattened disk and the lovers' eyes passed a great three-masted schooner, her vast main and mizzen set, her foresail and jib hauled down, being towed outward. It was very still, for the dock hands had gone home.

"I love you, dear," said Katharine, softly.

But Ralston answered nothing. Only his right hand drew her left more closely to his side.

CHAPTER XXVII.

KATHARINE had been intimate with Hester
Crowdie from the time when they had both been
children, though Hester was several years older
than she. Possibly the friendship had been one
of Katharine's mistakes. For his part, Ralston,
as has been seen, did not place great confidence
in the married woman's nature, and if he did not
tell Katharine exactly what he thought, it was not
from lack of conviction but because he felt that the
conviction itself was intuitive rather than logical.
Men, as well as women, have intuitions which they
cannot explain, but they are much more inclined to
conceal them than women are, because they have
been taught not to trust to them. They judge
others, and especially they judge women, from
small facts which they are often ashamed of seeming to value so highly. At least, when they analyze
their feelings about any given woman, it often happens that their reasoning leads up to some detail
which, standing alone, must and does appear altogether insignificant. It is not easy to decide
whether such very small causes among the realities actually produce the whole consequence which

182

affects the mind, or whether man's view of woman and woman's view of man, as distinguished from the judgments each forms upon his and her own sex, is not dependent upon a very subtle sense of truth, acting by paths shorter than logical deduction.

In illustration and as an example it may be noticed that the eyes of the majority of persons convey the consciousness of numbers precisely, up to a certain point, without any operation of counting. Most people can say at a glance, of any small group of objects, that there are two, three, four, or even seven. With almost all individuals, counting, and counting from the beginning, becomes necessary when there are eight or more objects together. For though the eye embraces seven, as seven, it cannot embrace seven out of eight and count one more to make up the number. If there is any counting it must be done from the very beginning.

Similarly, in reading rapidly, there are many who do not read every word. Their eyes and intelligence seize upon and comprehend blocks of words and even of lines, by a series of spasmodic leaps, as it were, after each one of which there is a pause of very short and hardly perceptible duration. Those who have been obliged to read very quickly, such as readers of manuscripts, and especially professional critics of second-class literature, are perfectly well aware of this faculty. Such men often read through and judge several volumes in a day, a fact which would not be possible if they had to read each word of every sentence. It is not well done, as Dr. Johnson would have said, but we are surprised to see it done at all. The result, in the modern phrase, is not judgment, but tasting. But it is a result, all the same. By force of a habit which cannot by any means be acquired by every one, words and even blocks of words to a great number have become to such a reader as symbols, which convey to his mind an idea all at once. There is no doubt but that by easy stages real symbols could, in our ordinary books, take the place of long sentences, and convey meaning without words at all. All forms of religion have made use of such symbols, and there is no reason why they could not be used in printing, though there may be excellent reasons why they should not be adopted. But in reading, as in counting, when the meaning of a whole sentence is not understood at a glance, it becomes necessary to read it from the beginning, word by word, or by shorter blocks of words, just as it is necessary to spell out a single word, such as a name, if it is not familiar at first sight, and is not made up of familiar syllables.

And in this way, perhaps, the mind of one individual judges the whole personality of another, without going through any form of analysis or any enumeration of qualities and defects. The instinctive attraction of opposite sexes for one

another sharpens the faculties of all living creatures, and hence it may possibly be, that men generally understand women better than men, and the
converse, that women are better judges of men
than they are of other women. It is often true
that the combined judgment passed by a man and
woman in consultation upon any individual is
vague and worthless, though in rare cases where a
profound and wide-reaching sympathy really exists,
such joint judgment is the best in the world.

This may be a mere theory, or it may be the
truth, but at all events it seems simpler to believe
that what we call intuition is founded upon some
such appreciation of each individual as a symbol
representing a set of thoughts, than to suppose that
it is a sort of sixth sense, sometimes amounting to
second sight. Every one may judge of that out
of his own experience.

Ralston, who was familiar enough with the character of his family in all its branches, thought that
he saw in Hester Crowdie a sort of modification of
the same love of possession which made a miser of
Alexander Junior, and which, if opposed, would be
as ruthless and as dangerous. He might have been
willing to admit that he had a share of the same
peculiarity, quality, or defect, himself. The tenac-
ity of his love for Katharine proved that he had it.
But as he disliked Crowdie so sincerely, Hester's
passion for her husband seemed abnormal in his

eyes. He fancied that if it were crossed or thwarted
she would be capable of going to any extremity for
its sake. Her friendship for Katharine, in his
opinion, might be turned to hatred at a moment's
notice.

The friendship of a passionate woman who seeks
an outlet for the confidences of her overflowing
nature, rather than the companionship and mutual
respect which friendship means, if it means anything, is always selfish and generally dangerous.
It has no elements of stability in it. When she
has no more confidences to make she is silent, not
companionable. When she has exhausted sympathy by the often repeated tale of her own minor
experiences or of her woes, real or imaginary, and
when the response of the worn-out listener grows
more dull or slow, she believes that she has exhausted also her friend's heart, that it is shallow
and arid, and she turns away in disgust and disappointment, seeking a kindred soul. And that is
the end of many friendships between women. As
often as not, they are founded upon the irresistible
desire to make confidences, experienced by one or
both of the fancied friends, and they come to an
end when confidence no longer elicits sympathy.
There is neither the simple delight in companionship which requires no emotion, nor the active
intellectual principle on both sides which finds
pleasure in the free trade of thought without sub-

jection to the exigent tariff which exacts the duty
of pity or admiration and unhesitatingly excludes
those who have neither to pay, from intellectual
commerce.

The less impulsive, the less passionate woman of
the two, she who receives all this outpouring of
the shallow but easily agitated soul, is the one who
is imposed upon. Until she has had experience,
she believes in sufferings and joys commensurate
with the words which express both, and even
greater. Her pity is really excited; her admiration is genuine; she sheds tears sympathetic, and
glows with pride vicarious. Her slow nature is
roused, and its activity continues after the truth
begins to dawn upon her. Then, all at once, she
finds out that truth, and suffers the rude shock
which a less stable being would scarcely feel. She
is the one who suffers. The other merely wonders
why her confidences no longer interest her friend,
and lets them boil over in a new direction. Not
knowing what real friendship means, she who loses
it loses nothing. What she misses is the pity and
also the admiration which helped her to pity and
admire herself, and she can get both elsewhere.
But the stronger, more silent woman, broods over
her disenchantment and loses her belief in human
nature, which is the key to human happiness, as
faith in God is the key to heaven. She will not
easily be drawn into such friendship again, and is
quick to scoff at it in others.

For the disenchantment of broken friendship is less violent but more deep-reaching than the disenchantment of broken love-faith. Love is for the one, friendship is, or may be, for the many. There is no natural reason why any man or woman whom we meet, should never become our friend. To lose faith in human nature may sometimes render love impossible. But though one woman have betrayed us, and though we say in our heart that men and women are faithless in love, yet we have not therefore said that all humanity is faithless in all that which makes up friendship.

Friendship is more composite than love, and becomes more and more so with advancing years, as the whole of life, which made such a hugely noble impression upon our young sight, is dissected, bit by bit, before the weary eyes that have seen it too long, and before the tribunal of a heart that has known bitterness. Friendship, like charity, covers a multitude of sins. The rending of it shows them as they are, and they are not beautiful.

Katharine had of late gone through events which had tended to destroy the whole-heartedness of her view of the world and its people. Within the past six months her character had developed, if it had not changed, and if she was more in earnest about her realities, she was harder in judging her imaginings and in testing anything in the nature of an ideal which presented itself to her moral vision. She would have made a firmer friend now, than formerly, but her friendship was also much harder to obtain.

She was, doubtless, quite truthful to herself in what she thought of her own mother, for instance. They were altogether reconciled for the present, and outwardly their intercourse was what it had been before Mrs. Lauderdale's unreasoning envy had almost brought about a permanent estrangement. But the fact remained that the estrangement had come, though it had also gone again, and Katharine felt that it might possibly some day return. The childlike faith, the belief that her mother could do nothing wrong, which is one of childhood's happiest tenets, was destroyed forever. Her mother, henceforth, was as other women were in her eyes, nearer to her, by the natural bonds that bound the two together and by the necessary intercourse of daily life, but not in heart nor in real sympathy. Katharine asked herself coldly what an affection could be worth which could hate its object out of pure vanity; and the answer was that it could not be worth much. But she never underrated its true value in the newly discovered proof of its fallibility.

Evidently, she was going far — too far, perhaps, for justice and certainly too far for happiness. And she applied her conclusion not only to her own mother, but to all handsome mothers who had pretty daughters. The first breath of envy would poison any mother's love she thought, and the memories of her own childhood were poisoned retrospectively by the bitterness of the present. She was at that stage of growth when generalities have a force which they have never acquired before and which they soon lose, as life's hailstorm of exceptions batters them out of shape. Out of isolated facts she made them, and made of them rules, and of rules, laws.

As for her father's conduct, it had been less unexpected, though it had hurt her even more, because it had crossed her own path so much more rudely and directly. But it had helped to destroy other illusions, and in a way to undermine something which was not an illusion at all. She had always believed in his courage and manliness, and both had, in her opinion, broken down. No man could be brave, she felt, who treated any woman as her father had treated her, and the mere thought of the past scenes of violence sent a thrill of pain to her injured arm. No man could be manly who could wish to sacrifice his daughter as she considered that he had wished to sacrifice her — to sell her, as she said in her anger.

There was injustice in this. Archibald Wingfield was one of the most desirable and desired young men in New York. Having made up his mind that Katharine should not marry Ralston,

Alexander Junior could hardly have done better for her than he did in trying to bring about a match with Wingfield. But there Katharine was influenced by her love for John, which made her look upon the mere suggestion of a rival as an insult hardly to be forgiven.

The deeper and less apparent wound in her belief was the more dangerous, though she did not know it. Alexander Junior had always professed to act upon the most rigid religious principles, and though Katharine did not sympathize with the form of worship in which she had been brought up, and had at one time been strongly inclined to become a Roman Catholic, as her mother was, she had, nevertheless, accorded a certain degree of admiration to her father's unbending and uncompromising consistency. There was no gentleness and no consolation in such religion, she thought, but she could not help admiring its strength and directness. She had said, too, that her father was faithful in his love for her mother, a fact which seemed suddenly to have lost its weight in her eyes at present. But of late he had done many things which Katharine was sure could not be justified by any religion whatsoever, and had shown tendencies which, if his religion had ever been real, should, in her view, have been stamped out or wholly destroyed long ago. His avarice was one of them, his cruelty to herself another, his attempt to injure John Ralston in Mr. Beman's opinion was a third. And all these tendencies were as strong as himself and could not be easily hidden nor charitably overlooked. Not knowing the real strength of any great passion, she could not realize that there might have been a conflict in her father's heart. To children, real sin seems as monstrous as real virtue seems to those who have sinned often, and in respect of real sin, Katharine was yet but a child. She saw a man doing wrong, who said that he acted in accordance with the principles of his religion. She overlooked his temptations, she ignored his struggles, she said that he was bad and called his religion a fiction.

The direct consequence was that such convictions as she had herself were undermined and shaken and almost ruined, and the moral disturbance affected her in all the relations of life, except, perhaps, in her love for John Ralston, which grew stronger as other things failed.

With regard to her friendship for Hester, however, it had not, as yet, suffered any rude shock.

CHAPTER XXVIII.

KATHARINE and Hester had seen but little of
one another during the battle of the will, and a
certain awkwardness and reticence had appeared
between them, which Katharine attributed altogether to the question of the fortune. As has been
seen, however, it had another source on Hester's
side, and one much more likely to produce results
that might hurt one or the other or both of them.
As for Katharine, it was characteristic of her that
she attempted to return to the former cordiality of
their relations as soon as the matter of the inheritance had been settled.

She found Hester cold and unsympathetic, but
she excused her on the ground of the family dispute, and of the very great disappointment the
Crowdies must have suffered from the decision of
the court. The conversation turned upon indifferent matters and languished, as they sat together in
the pretty little room at the front of the house. It
was l te in the afternoon, and the smell of the
spring came in through the open windows.

"T's getting very dull in New York," said

198

Hester, after a long pause. "I think we shall go out of town soon, this year."

She suppressed a yawn with her diaphanous hand, as she leaned back in her corner of the sofa, staring vacantly at an etching which hung on the opposite wall, and wishing that Katharine would go. Then she rang the bell, having thought of tea as a possible antidote to dulness.

"I suppose we shall go away, too," said Katharine, wondering what the summer was to be like.

The servant came, and got his orders, and went out, and Hester almost yawned again.

"I don't know what's the matter with me," she said, half apologetically. "I'm so sleepy."

"You'll be all right after you've had some tea," answered Katharine, trying to think of something pleasant to say, and finding nothing.

"I hope so," observed the elder woman. "This is awful. I'm conscious of being dreadfully dull."

"It's probably the reaction," suggested Katharine.

There was another long pause. The sound of a carriage passing along the street came in through the windows, but scarcely seemed to break the silence. Presently the servant returned — a highly respectable, elderly butler with very white hair, answering to the name of Fletcher. He set down the tea and departed noiselessly and with dignity. He had formerly been butler at the Ralstons' for a number of years, but Mrs. Ralston had reduced her establishment after her husband's death.

"What reaction did you mean?" asked Hester, idly, as she made the tea.

"Oh — I meant the natural reaction after the tremendous excitement we've all been living in for so long."

"Oh!" ejaculated her companion, rather coldly. "I see," she continued after a pause, during which she had made a busy little clatter with the tea things, "you mean because we hoped to get the money and didn't — therefore, I'm sleepy. That doesn't sound very sensible."

"Well — not as you put it," answered Katharine, with a short laugh of embarrassment.

She had determined to attack the subject boldly, so as to break the ice once and for always. Hester's aggressive answer put her out.

"How would you put it?" enquired the latter, leaning back again and waiting for the tea to draw. "Explain! I'm awfully dull to-day."

"Don't you think it's natural?" asked Katharine. "It's of no use to deny that we've all been tremendously excited during the last fortnight, and now the excitement has stopped. One's nerves run down — that sort of thing, you know — and then one's tired and feels depressed."

"The depression's natural — in our case," answered Hester, lifting the cover and looking into the teapot in a futile way, as though she would see whether the tea were strong enough.

"Yes," said Katharine, thoughtfully. "Do you know, dear? It seems to me as though you were thinking that it was my fault, in a way."

"What? That I'm depressed? Don't be silly! Do you like it strong? I've forgotten. It's about right now, I should think."

"A little water, please—no cream—one lump of sugar—thanks. No," she continued, a little impatiently, "you know perfectly well what I mean, if you'll only understand. I suppose that's rather Irish—" she laughed again.

"It's Greek to me!" replied Hester, smartly, as she poured out her own cup of tea. "You're trying to say something—why don't you say it?"

It began to be clear to Katharine that there were more difficulties in the way of what she was attempting to do, than she had dreamt of. She had expected that Hester would be quite ready to meet her half way, instead of intrenching herself behind an absurd and pretended misunderstanding, as she was doing. The best way seemed to be to enter into an explanation at once. She sipped her tea thoughtfully and then began again.

"I'll tell you exactly what I mean," she said; "so that you'll see it as I do. I'm afraid that this question of money has come between you and me.

And if it has, I'm very sorry, because I'm very fond of you, Hester."

" Well — I'm fond of you," answered Hester, in a matter-of-fact tone. " I don't see why the money should make any difference."

"I hope it doesn't. Only — I'm afraid it does, in spite of what you say. I don't feel as though we could ever be again exactly what we've always been until now. But it's not fair, Hester. It's not just. You know very well that if I could have done anything to make the will good, I would have done it. I couldn't. What could I do? It's simply a misfortune that we were on opposite sides of the fight — or our people were. I'm not exactly what you'd call gushing, I suppose — indeed, I know I'm not. But it hurts me to think that we're to be like strangers, because three men couldn't agree about a signature. It's unnatural. It's not right. I came here to-day, meaning to say so — and I'm glad I've had the courage to say it without waiting any longer. But if we're only to know each other — in a general way like distant cousins — why, it's better to acknowledge it at once. It shan't come from me — that's all. But I'd rather be prepared for it, you know."

"So far as I'm concerned, I don't want to fight," said Hester, coolly. " I don't see any reason why we should. Of course we don't throw ourselves into each other's arms and cry with delight every

time we meet, like schoolgirls. We've outgrown
that. But as for my quarrelling with you because
your father's inherited a fortune when I ought to
have had a part of it — it's too ridiculous. You
would have had a share, too, under the will. Then
you ought to quarrel with your own father, much
more than with me. Isn't that common sense?"

"Yes — I suppose it is. But you don't say it
exactly as though — "

Katharine stopped short. She was afraid of
seeming impulsive, as many people of self-con-
tained natures are. She knew that she was not
herself very expansive, as a rule, in her expressions
of affection. But Hester was, and the change from
her former manner to her present coldness was
startling. One may miss in others what one would
not have in oneself, and one may resent another's
refusal to give it. The regret of missing anything
is not measured by its value, but by the strength
of the habit its presence has created. Men lib-
erated after years of captivity have missed their
chains. The Irish woman in the typical story
complained that her husband no longer beat her.
She missed it.

"I'll say it in any way you like," answered
Hester, hardly. "It seems to me that we're just
as good friends as ever. I see no difference."

"I do," answered Katharine. "And there's
always going to be a difference, now," she added,
regretfully.

She was conscious that in some unaccountable
way the positions had been reversed with regard
to her character and her friend's. It should naturally have been the more passionate, expansive,
sensitive woman who should be almost begging
that the old friendship might not be forgotten, and
Katharine herself, the colder of the two, the one by
far less easily carried away by passing emotions,
should have been giving the assurance that nothing was changed. It was incomprehensible to her,
as well it might be, since there was a cause for
Hester's behaviour which lay very far from the
question of money, though the coldness which the
latter had caused was helping to make matters
worse.

"I suppose we're outgrowing each other," suggested Hester, who was more or less anxious to
account for the change, since Katharine was laying such great stress upon it. "You know that's
the way of the world," she added, tritely. "People
are ever so fond of each other for a long time, and
then all at once they find out that they're not what
they were, you know, and that they don't really
care."

"Oh — do you look at it in that way?" Katharine's voice and manner changed, for she was hurt.
"But don't you think this outgrowing, as you call
it, has been rather sudden? It's only about three
weeks since we were talking quite differently. It
can't be more, I'm sure."

"Isn't it?" asked Hester, indifferently. "Really, it seems ever so long since we sat here and told each other things."

There is a beautiful vagueness about the language of a woman when she wishes to have something forgotten.

"It seems long to me, too, — in another way," answered Katharine. "It's far off — like a good many things that happened then."

Hester made no answer to this remark, but leaned back against her cushion and meditatively nibbled the edge of a ginger-snap.

"Of course," said Katharine, "if you want it all to end here, I'm not going to cry and behave like the schoolgirl you talked about — "

"No," interrupted Hester, munching her biscuit audibly; "it isn't worth it."

"Once upon a time we should both have thought it was," answered the young girl. "But when a thing like friendship's gone — it's gone, that's all, and there's nothing more to be said about it."

"I wish you wouldn't be so silly, my dear!" exclaimed Hester, who, having swallowed the remains of the ginger-snap, suddenly realized that she might at least bury her intimacy with a protest to the effect that it was not dead. "You really go on as though we were lovers, and I had betrayed you. In the first place it doesn't follow, because we're grown up and not exactly what we used to be, that there's no friendship between us. We can go on just the same as ever, even if we talk differently and gush less, and we can see just as much of each other as we always did. You've got some idea or other into your head about my being cold, because I'm sleepy and dull to-day. Probably the next time we meet it will be just the opposite, and you'll think me too gushing."

So long as Hester had made no serious pretence of anything more than she felt, confining herself more or less to generalities and vaguely saying that she desired no break, Katharine had remained calm, but something in the last speech seemed to ring outrageously false, and the blood slowly rose to her throat and ebbed again without reaching her cheeks.

"Don't pretend!" she exclaimed. "We've got to get at the truth to-day, if we're ever to get at it at all."

Hester raised her beautiful eyebrows, as delicately and finely marked as though they had been drawn with pen and ink.

"My dear child!" she answered, with real or affected surprise. "Don't fly into little pink rages like that."

"I'm not in a rage," protested Katharine. "And if I were, I shouldn't be pink — I never am. But I don't want you to pretend things you don't feel. We've never pretended much with each other, and

I don't want to begin now. It's over and done for. Let's make up our minds to it and be sensible. I don't see that there's anything else to be done. But don't let's pretend things. I hate that."

"Not half so much as I do, my dear," said Hester, airily, as though to close the discussion. "I don't see the slightest good in talking about it any more. You've got it into your head that I've changed. If you believe it, you know it, for Mr. Griggs says that—"

"Do leave Mr. Griggs alone!" cried Katharine, irritably. "It isn't a mere idea, either. You said we'd outgrown each other. I'm not conscious of having grown a head taller in the last three weeks. But so far as talking about it goes, you're quite right. Only—" her voice changed again and took a gentler tone—"let's part friends, Hester, for the sake of all that has been."

"Why, of course!" exclaimed Hester, with insincere frankness. "That is, if you insist upon parting, as you call it. But I declare! we might just as well be a pair of lovers quarrelling, you know. It's just about as sensible, on the whole."

"I suppose things mean more to me than they do to you," answered Katharine, with sudden coldness. "Friendship—like everything else—like—"

She was going to say 'like love,' but checked herself. In that at least she felt that she must have been mistaken. Whatever else she might think of

Hester, she knew that she was almost insanely in love with her husband. At the very moment when the words were on her lips the thought flashed through her mind, that with Hester it might be the half-desperate, all-absorbing passion which was draining her of all capacity for any other attachment. Katharine thought of herself and of her love for Ralston, and felt more real sympathy for her friend just then than she had felt for many a day.

As she ceased speaking she heard the hall door opened and shut again, just outside the sitting-room, and a moment later she heard Crowdie's soft voice, low and sweet, humming to himself as he began to ascend the stairs. As she turned to Hester, as though to continue speaking, she saw how the pale face had changed in a moment. Every faculty was strained to catch the faint echo of the melody, the deep eyes gleamed, there was colour in the transparent cheeks, the dewy lips were just parted. There was nothing unreal nor affected in that.

CHAPTER XXIX.

KATHARINE could not keep the expression of curiosity out of her eyes as she watched Hester Crowdie. The woman's whole manner had changed in an instant, and she seemed to be another person. She seemed trying to hold her breath to catch the distant and ever retreating sound of her husband's voice. The colour in her pale cheeks heightened and paled and heightened again in visible variations. Her slender throat fluttered with quick pulsations like that of a singing bird or a chameleon, and her deep eyes were filled with light. Katharine even fancied that the little ringlets of soft brown hair trembled and waved like the leaves of a sensitive plant, impossible as it was. Hester's whole being was all at once intensely alive, intensely sensitive, intensely brilliant. A few minutes earlier she had been leaning back against her cushion, suppressing a yawn from time to time, saying cold and disagreeable things, pale, cool, diaphanous.

Katharine moved slightly, and the white hand was upon hers instantly, with a light touch of warning, as though to silence her, lest a single faint echo of Crowdie's voice should fail to reach Hester's ears.

The young girl wondered whether she herself ever behaved so strangely when John Ralston was near, and whether any one sitting beside her could see his presence reflected in her eyes. She did not know, though she believed herself, as she really was, colder and less quick to show what she felt. The last note died away as Crowdie ascended the staircase and got out of hearing, and Hester sank back against her cushion again. The colour faded from her cheek, the light died in her eyes, and her throat was quiet. The bloodless hands just met on her knees, and the tips of the slight fingers tapped one another nervously two or three times, and then lay quite still.

There had been something in the quickly succeeding changes which struck Katharine as not exactly human, though she could have found no other word with which to describe better the phases of the passing sensitiveness she had witnessed. But it had been more like the infinitive sensitiveness of nature than the ordinary responses of an impressionable woman. Katharine had thought of the sensitive plant, for she had seen many in hothouses and had often played with them, softly stroking the fern-like plumes made by the two rows of tiny oval leaves, and delighting to see how they rose and waved, and tried to find and

follow her finger. And she thought, too, of stories
she had heard about the behaviour of animals
before an earthquake, a great storm, or any terrible convulsion of nature. She had never before
quite understood that, but it was clear to her now.

At the same time she felt a strong sympathy for
Hester, and for the love which was so unmistakable and real. It was impossible for her to comprehend how such love could exist for such a man
as Crowdie, whom she herself thought so strangely
repulsive, though she could find nothing to say
against him. It could only be explained on the
ground of an elective affinity, mysterious in its
source, but most manifest in its results. She had
never been allowed to read Goethe's great book,
but the title of it had always meant something to
her, and represented a set of ideas which she used
in order to explain the inexplicable. It was true,
also, so far as she could see, that between Hester
and Crowdie the affinity was mutual and almost
equally strong, and Katharine thought with an
unpleasant sensation of the way Crowdie sometimes smiled at his wife. Of course, she thought,
if one did not object to a certain amount of woman-
liness in a man's looks and manner, nor to a pale,
pear-shaped face with intensely red lips, nor to a
figure which altogether lacked masculine dignity —
if one could forget all those things and consider
what Crowdie must seem to a blind woman, for

instance, and if one could forgive a certain insolent softness of speech which now and then was his, why, then, Crowdie was one of the most charming of men. There was no word but that one. Take him all in all,—his remarkable power as a portrait painter, developed by study and real industry, his exquisite voice and perfect taste in singing—so perfect that there was not a trace of that art which it is art's mission to conceal—his conversation, which was often brilliant and almost always interesting,—taking him all in all, thought Katharine, and quite apart from his appearance he was a marvellously gifted man. She had never known a man like him. Paul Griggs was not to be despised as a judge of men, for he had seen and known many who were worth knowing, and Paul Griggs liked Crowdie and was intimate with him. It was true that no other man of Katharine's acquaintance liked him, but Griggs' opinion might outweigh that of many just men. But when she thought of Crowdie's appearance, she marvelled how any woman could love him. There was something about it which thrilled her painfully, like a strong, bad taste—yet not so as to hinder her from feeling sympathy for Hester, in spite of all the latter had said during the past half hour.

"How you love him!" she exclaimed, when the voice had died away, and Hester leaned back again in her seat.

The words were spoken impulsively and half unconsciously — the natural expression of the young girl's wonder. But Hester's eyes turned quickly, with a suspicious glance which Katharine did not see and could not have understood.

"Well — is there any harm in my loving my husband?" asked Hester, in a tone of unmistakable resentment.

Katharine turned and looked at her in surprise, not realizing that she could possibly have given offence.

"Harm! why no — no more harm than there is in my saying so — nor than I meant, when I spoke. Why, are you angry?"

"I'm not angry. Why did you say it, though — and just then? I want to know."

She fixed her eyes on Katharine, and a little colour came back suddenly to her cheeks, just where it had been while Crowdie was singing — as a transparent glass, that has been heated red in the flame and has cooled, flushes where it had flushed before, almost as soon as it is brought to the fire.

"Why did I say it?" repeated Katharine, surprised. "I don't know, I'm sure. It was a very natural remark. Everybody knows that you love your husband very much. I suppose it struck me particularly at that moment. How strange of you to take offence!"

" I'm not offended. I only want to know why
you said it just then. Did I change colour — or
what ? "

" A little colour came into your face — yes. It's
very becoming," added Katharine, by way of pro-
pitiation.

" Yes — I know. You needn't tell me that I'm
generally too pale. Were my eyes different from
usual ? "

" They were very bright, with a far-away look at
the same time — as though you saw him through
the wall."

" Do you think any one would have noticed how
I looked? I mean — any one sitting near me, as
you are ? "

" I should think so — yes," answered Katharine,
without much hesitation. " I only said what any
one would have thought who happened to see you
just then. I didn't think there was any harm in
it. I shall certainly never say it again, since you're
displeased."

" Oh — that doesn't matter ! " exclaimed Hester,
with a little scornful laugh. " As we're not to be
friends any more, you can displease me as much as
you like now. It doesn't matter in the least ! "

" How strange you are, Hester ! " Katharine
said, thoughtfully. " I don't in the least understand you."

" We never really understood each other," replied

Hester.   "We only thought we did.   But — as I say — since we're not to be friends any more, it's of no consequence."

"You can't say that — that we never understood each other," said Katharine.   "It's not true."

"Oh yes, it is!   We never understood — never, what I mean by understanding.   So I blush, and stare, and behave like a schoolgirl, when Walter comes in singing!   I didn't know it.   I am glad you've told me, for I don't like to do foolish things in public."

"I don't think it's always foolish to show what one feels.   It's better to feel something, and show it, than to feel nothing at all."

"I should think so!"   Hester laughed rather contemptuously again, and glanced at Katharine's face.

The young girl moved, as though she were about to rise, — the little preliminary movement which most women make, as a clock gives warning five minutes before it strikes.   It is often a tentative measure, and there is some expectation on the part of her who moves that her friend will make at least a show of detaining her.   When she does not mean to do so, she herself generally moves a little, which precipitates matters.   If men could understand this, they would more often be able to understand whether they are wanted any longer or not.   But, instead, they rarely give warning, but

seize their hats, in countries where it is manners
to carry them, and rise with one movement, giving
the lady no choice about detaining them or not.

On the present occasion, as soon as Katharine
moved, Hester did likewise, sitting up straight,
and pushing the small tea-table a little away from
her, in order to make room for herself to rise.
Katharine did not fail to notice the fact, and got
up at once.

"I'm sorry we can't make it up, Hester," she
said, regretfully. "I'm sorry if we're both changed
so much in such a short time. I shouldn't have
thought it possible."

"The world's full of surprises," observed Hester,
rising and slipping out from behind the tea-table.

"Oh — really, Hester!" exclaimed Katharine,
impatiently. "You needn't make it worse by saying such things as that, you know!"

"What things? Isn't it true, my dear? I'm
sure I've found the world a very surprising place
to live in. Haven't you?"

Katharine said nothing, but turned her face
away a little, and made haste over her gloves,
which she had forgotten to put on before rising,
in her sudden haste to get away. Hester looked
down at the tea-table, and absently took up a
teaspoon and moved a little leaf that lay in the
bottom of the empty cup. Katharine was only
just beginning to use her right hand a little, and

had difficulty in buttoning the glove on her left. She tried once or twice, and then turned to Hester.

"I wish you'd button it for me," she said. "I can't do anything with my right hand, it's so weak."

She held out her left, and Hester bent over it. But before she had fastened two buttons, she started, and looked at the door. Her quick ear had caught her husband's footfall as he came downstairs again, doubtless in search of her. She paused, and held her breath, listening, though he was not singing now. The footsteps came nearer, the handle of the door turned, and Crowdie entered the room.

"Oh — Miss Lauderdale!" he exclaimed. Then he smiled at Hester, who held out her hand, and he touched it with his lips, in a foreign fashion. "You're not going away?" he asked, turning to Katharine again. "Just as I've come in. Do sit down again! Now, please give me a cup of tea, Hester — I'm tired and thirsty — and I've been awfully bored. Do sit down, Miss Lauderdale! Just a minute, to please me!"

"Well — I would," answered Katharine, affecting a hesitation she did not feel, in order not to seem ungracious. "I would — but I really must be going. I've been here ever so long, already."

"Yes — but you've got another welcome to wear out — mine," he said, letting his voice soften and dwell on the last word.

"I really think Katharine's in a hurry," said Hester, who was pale.

Katharine glanced at her in some surprise. She had never in her life been so plainly told to go away, and she was inclined to resent the rudeness. She might never enter the house again, but she did not choose to be turned out of it by a woman who a few weeks earlier had professed with pro- testations that she was her dearest and closest friend.

"You can't be in such a hurry as all that," objected Crowdie, who supposed that Katharine had really said that she was pressed for time. "Besides, I've got something to show you."

"Have you?" asked Katharine, suddenly glad of an excuse for staying a few moments, in spite of Hester's anxiety to get rid of her.

Hester looked at her husband in surprise, and her finely chiselled lips moved and almost trem- bled.

"What do you mean, Walter?" she asked, in an uncertain tone.

"Oh — don't you know? That head of poor uncle Robert, I did last night. I want to show it to Miss Lauderdale — she knew his face better than any of us."

Katharine tried to detect a shade of irony in the words; but they were spoken quite naturally, without the least underthought.

"I should like to see it," she answered, quietly, after an instant's silence.

"I'll get it," said Crowdie, "if you don't mind waiting a minute. It's in your dressing-room, isn't it, Hester?" he asked, turning to his wife. "You were looking at it last night, just before you went to bed. I did it late in the evening," he added, explaining to Katharine.

"Certainly," she replied. "I'll wait while you get it. I should really like to see it."

Crowdie left the room, and her eyes followed him, and she disliked the undulating, feminine swing of his walk. He was badly made, having low, sloping shoulders, and being heavy about the waist, though he was not stout. He left the door open, and the two women waited in silence, not looking at one another. A moment later they heard Crowdie moving about overhead, where Hester's dressing-room was situated, corresponding with the sitting-room in which they were. Hester listened intently, her eyes turned upwards towards the ceiling, as though they could help her to hear.

"He can't find it," she said. "I'd better go and help him — he'll never find it alone."

She made a step towards the door, paused, and listened again. The wrathful instinct grew stronger in Katharine. She imagined that Hester had thought of going upstairs in order to escape from the unpleasantness of being alone with her a little longer.

"If you'd finish buttoning my glove," she said, calmly, "I'll go without waiting. I'm very sorry, but I can't do it myself."

Hester's eyebrows twitched irritably, but she bent over the outstretched hand, for she could not do otherwise. A moment later Crowdie's footstep was heard on the stairs again, and he came in through the open door.

"I've hunted everywhere!" he exclaimed. "I can't think where you've put it. I wish you'd go and find it for me, dear. It's awfully stupid of me, I know!"

"Oh — I know just where it is," answered Hester. "You must have seen it — why, I set it up on the toilet-table, on one side of the looking-glass, turned to the light."

"Well — it's not there now," said Crowdie, "because I've just looked."

"I'm sure it's there," replied Hester, going towards the door. "Nobody could have moved it."

"Go and see, darling — I assure you I've looked everywhere for it, and I don't believe it's in the room at all."

It was one of those absurd little discussions which occur between two people, the one who has seen, and the other who believes. Hester left the room rather impetuously, being absolutely sure that she was right. She, also, left the door open behind her.

"Can't I button your glove for you?" asked Crowdie. "I saw that Hester was doing it when I came in."

Crowdie's touch was intensely disagreeable to Katharine, but she held out her hand to him, in spite of the fact. Just then, she felt that she should almost prefer to let him do it, rather than let Hester help her. She was standing in the middle of the room, half turned away from the door.

"I thought you would like to see the sketch," said Crowdie, fastening the button nearest to her wrist with his deft, pointed fingers, skilful as any woman's. "I did it on a board last night — just a crayon thing from memory, with an old photograph to help me. Hester thought it was very like. If you approve of it, I'll paint a picture from it."

"I wish you would!" answered Katharine. "There never was anything good of him — I should so like to have something — "

She checked herself, having momentarily forgotten that Crowdie had been a very heavy loser, through his wife, by the decision in the case of the will, and that he could hardly be expected to make a present to one of her family, under the circumstances.

"Why do you hesitate?" he asked, pausing at the last button and looking into her face.

"Oh — because — I don't know!" She was a
little embarrassed. "I was afraid I'd spoken as
though I meant to ask for the sketch."

"You didn't!" laughed Crowdie, softly. "You're
going to have it anyway. I made it for you."

"I don't believe that," answered Katharine,
quickly, but smiling. "You're only trying to help
me out of my rudeness. But it's very generous of
you to think of giving me anything, after all that's
happened."

"Why? Do you mean about the will? Really,
Miss Lauderdale, if you think I'm that sort of
person —"

He stopped and laughed again, so naturally and
easily that she hardly doubted his sincerity. His
womanish eyes looked innocently into hers. He
held her left wrist in both his hands, just as he
had paused in the act of buttoning the glove.

Overhead, Hester's light footstep was audible in
the short silence that followed, as she moved about
the room, searching for the sketch, which had
evidently not been in the place where she had
left it.

"Besides," added Crowdie, after a short pause,
"you're not your father. And if you were," he
continued, lightly, "that wouldn't be a reason for
being horrid. The law decided it, and I suppose
the law was right. Mr. Lauderdale didn't make
the law, and it gave him his rights. Hester and I

shall get along just as well on what we've always had. I don't complain. Of course it would be nice to buy Greek islands, and play with marble palaces and Oriental luxury. But after all, I'm a painter. I suppose it's an assumption, or a boast, or something. But I don't care — before you — I like painting, and I should always paint, and I should always want to sell my pictures, if I had a hundred millions. What could Hester and I do with five or six hundred thousand a year? That would have been about our share. I shouldn't feel like myself, if I didn't earn money by what I do. I suppose you can't understand that, can you?"

"Oh yes, I can," answered Katharine, quickly. "I understand it, and I like it in you. It's because you're not an amateur that you feel like that."

"I'm not exactly an amateur," said Crowdie, with a smile. "As for the sketch, or the picture, if I paint it, they're yours. You were the old gentleman's favourite, and it's right that you should have a portrait of him — that is — if you'll accept it."

"Thank you very much. I don't know about taking it, exactly — it's much too generous of you."

She knew what Crowdie's work was worth, for he was a very successful man at portrait painting, and he had never seemed to care much for any other variety of the art. He was more or less of

a specialist in his own department, but so far as he
went, he brought an amount of experience and a
richness of conception to bear upon what he did,
which had carried him beyond most rivals. Possibly he had not in him the stuff which makes the
greatest artists — the manly, ascetic, devoted nature
which has in it a touch of the fanatic, the absolute
concentration of all faculties upon a single but
many-sided task. He was, in a way, the product of
the age, an artist and a good one, but a specialist
— an expert in the painting of portraits. All his
gifts favoured and strengthened the tendency.

"I don't see anything generous in offering you
one of my daubs!" he laughed, in answer to what
Katharine had said last. "Hester can't find it —
I knew it wasn't where she said it was," he added,
after a short pause, during which he listened for
his wife's footstep.

"Please button the last button, too," said Katharine, who had listened also, but had heard nothing.
"You're so awfully clever at it."

"Am I?" he asked, still smiling. "This is
evidently my day of grace and favour in your royal
eyes."

His beautiful voice had an inflection of something like tenderness in it, which displeased Katharine. She pushed his hands lightly with hers as
he held it, to remind him of what he was doing.

"Please button it!" she said, a little imperiously, and looking at the button in question as she spoke, but quite conscious of his eyes.

He inclined his head dutifully, after gazing at her an instant longer, and then bent over the hand again and quietly slipped the button through the button-hole, touching it very delicately and in evident fear of tightening the glove so as to pinch her arm. Gloves with buttons chanced to be the fashion just then, in an interval between two fits of the Biarritz gauntlet. When he had performed the little operation, he glanced at each of the others in turn, touching each with his finger, while Katharine watched him carelessly. Then, before she could withdraw her hand, he bent his head a little more and lightly kissed the button at her wrist, releasing it instantly.

Katharine drew it back almost before he had let it go, with a quick movement of displeasure.

"Don't do that!" she cried, in a low voice.

But as he raised his head Crowdie turned ashy pale. Even his lips lost some of their over-brilliant colour, and his eyes lost their light. Hester had descended the stairs noiselessly and stood in the open door, her face whiter than his. As their glances met, she dropped the sheet of pasteboard she held in one hand by her side, and steadied herself against the door-post. Katharine turned quickly and saw her. It did not strike the young girl that such agitation could be due to having

seen what Crowdie had done. Katharine herself
had been annoyed, but, after all, it was an innocent
offence, she thought, especially for a man who had
lived long abroad, and could not be supposed to
attach much importance to the act of touching a
glove with his lips, when he had been long familiar
with the custom of kissing a lady's hand instead
of shaking it at meeting and parting, if the hand
were offered to him.

"Why, Hester!" she exclaimed. "What's the
matter? Are you ill?"

"No — it's nothing," answered Hester, twisting
her lips to form the words. "Here's the drawing.
I ran — I'm out of breath."

She held it out as she spoke, and Crowdie took
it from her mechanically. His hand trembled as
he did so, for he was a coward. Hester turned
from them both and went to the open window.
She lifted one hand and rested it on the sash at
the level of her head. They could not see that the
other was pressed to her heart, for she kept the
elbow close to her side. Crowdie was still pale
and trembling, and he glanced uneasily towards
her, as he held up the drawing to Katharine to
look at.

"Give it to me," said the young girl, unconsciously speaking in a low voice. "Your hand
shakes."

She began to wonder exactly what had taken

place, and could find no explanation except Crowdie's small offence.   Instantly, she understood that Hester was desperately jealous of her.   It sometimes takes longer to understand such things in real life, when they are very far from one's thoughts, than to guess them from the most meagre description of what has taken place.   Katharine almost laughed when she realized the truth.   She looked intently at the drawing.

"It's wonderfully like!" she exclaimed, feeling that matters would be worse if she did not express some admiration of the work, though she found it hard to concentrate her attention upon the familiar features.   "Especially the"—she did not know what she was saying—"the beard," she added, completing her sentence.

"Ah, yes—the beard—as you say," responded Crowdie, in a rather tremulous tone, and glancing at his wife's figure.   Then he laughed very nervously.   "Yes—the beard's like, isn't it?" he said.

"Oh, very!" answered Katharine, looking quickly at Hester and then intently at the pasteboard again.   "Every hair—"

"Yes."   And Crowdie tried to laugh again, as though it would help him.   "There are hairs in the pasteboard, too—sticking up here and there —it helps the illusion, doesn't it?"

"Why, so there are!"   Katharine looked at the

drawing in silence for a moment and collected herself. "The expression's very good," she said. "I like a picture when the eyes look right at you."

She raised her own mechanically as she spoke, and she realized how white he was. She held out the drawing to him.

"Thanks, so much," she said. "I'm glad to have seen it. It was so good of you. I really must be going now. It's getting late."

He took the drawing and laid it carefully upon the table, with the instinctive forethought of the artist for the safety of his work.

"Good-bye, Hester," said Katharine, moving a step towards the window.

Hester turned abruptly. There were deep shadows under her eyes, and there was a bright colour in her face now, but not like that which had come to it when her husband had passed the door, singing. As she stood with her back against the bright light of the window, however, Katharine could hardly distinguish her features.

"Oh — good-bye," said Hester in a strange, cold voice, not moving and not holding out her hand.

But Katharine extended her own, for she entirely refused to be treated as though she had injured her friend, just as a little while earlier, she had chosen to stay a few minutes rather than to take a hint so broad that it sounded like an order to go. She went nearer to the window.

"Good-bye, Hester," she repeated, holding out
her hand in such a way that Hester could not
refuse to take it.

And Hester took it, but dropped it again instantly. Katharine nodded quietly, turned, nodded
again to Crowdie in exactly the same way, and passed
out through the open door, calmly and proudly, being
quite sure that she had done nothing to be ashamed
of. She knew, at the moment, that all hope of ever
renewing her friendship was gone, at least for the
present, and she regretted the fact to the last
minute, and was willing to show that she did.
Hester's behaviour had been incomprehensible from
the first, and it was still a mystery to Katharine
when she left the house. One thing only was
clear, and that was the woman's uncontrollable
jealousy during the little scene which had taken
place. The idea of connecting that jealousy with
former events never crossed the young girl's mind,
and of finding an original cause for it in the fact
of Crowdie's having sung at Mrs. Bright's on a
certain evening three weeks earlier. Still less
could she have guessed that it had begun long ago,
during the preceding winter, when she had sat for
her portrait in Crowdie's studio, while Hester lay
extended upon the divan where she could watch
her husband's face, and note every passing look of
admiration that crossed it, as he of necessity studied
the features of his model. Such an idea was alto-

gether too far removed from Katharine, in her ignorance of human nature — as far as Hester's passion for her husband, which went beyond the limits of what the young girl had ever dreamed of in its excessive sensitiveness.

Katharine closed the front door behind her and went out into the street. As she descended the neat white stone steps she was close to the open windows of the little sitting-room and could have heard anything which might have been said within. But no sound of voices reached her. She could not help glancing over her shoulder towards the window, as she turned away, and she could see that Hester was still standing with her back to it, as she had stood when Katharine had insisted upon taking leave of her.

She walked slowly homewards, wondering what was taking place since she had left the two together, and going over in her mind the details of the scene. She remembered Crowdie's face very distinctly. She was not sure that she had ever in her life seen a man badly frightened before, and it had produced a very vivid impression upon her at the time. And she recalled the picture of Hester, standing in the doorway, the pasteboard at her feet, and her hand raised to support herself against the doorway. She had heard of 'domestic tragedies,' as they are called in the newspapers, and she wondered whether they ever began in that way.

CHAPTER XXX.

HESTER CROWDIE heard Katharine's footfall outside, and did not move from her position at the window until she had listened to the last retreating echo of the young girl's light step upon the pavement. It was very still after that, for Lafayette Place is an unfrequented corner — a quiet island, as it were, round which the great rivers of traffic flow in all directions. Only now and then a lumbering van thunders through it, to draw up at the great printing establishment at the southeast corner, or a private carriage rolls along and stops, with a discreet clatter, at the Bishop's House, on the west side, almost opposite the Crowdies' dwelling.

But as Hester stood in silence, with her back to the window, her eyes rested with a fixed look on her husband's face. He was pale, and his own beautiful eyes had lost their self-possessed calm. He looked at her, but his glance shifted quickly from one point to another — from her throat to her shoulder, from her hair to the window behind her — in a frightened and anxious way, avoiding her steady gaze.

226

What he had done was harmless enough, if not altogether innocent, in itself. That there had been something not exactly right about it, or about the way in which he had done it, was indirectly proved by Katharine's own quick displeasure. But he knew, himself, how much it had meant to Hester, over, above and beyond any commonly simple interpretation which might be put upon it. His face and manner showed that he knew it, long before she spoke the first word of what was to come.

" Walter ! "

She uttered his name in a low tone that quivered with the pain she felt, full of suffering, and reproach, and disappointment. Instantly his eyes fell before hers, but he answered nothing. He looked at his own white hand as it rested on the back of a chair.

"Look at me!" she said, almost sharply, with a rising intonation.

He looked up timidly, and a slight flush appeared on his pale forehead, but not in his cheeks.

" I don't know why you make such a fuss about nothing," he said, in the colourless voice of a frightened boy, caught in mischief before he has had time to invent an excuse.

" Don't use such absurd words!" cried Hester, with sudden energy. " It's bad enough as it is. You love her. Say so! Be a man — be done with it ! "

"I certainly won't say that," answered Crowdie, regaining a little self-possession under the exaggerated accusation. "It wouldn't be true."

"I've seen — I know!" She turned from him again and rested her forehead on her hands against the raised sash of the window.

He gained courage, when he no longer felt her eyes upon him, and he found words.

"You've no right to say that I love Katharine Lauderdale," he said. "You saw what I did, and all I did. Well — what harm was there in kissing her hand — not her hand, her glove, when I had fastened it?"

"What harm!" she repeated, in a low voice, without turning to him, and moving her head a little against her hands.

"Yes — what harm was there, I ask? Wasn't it a perfectly natural thing to do? Haven't you seen me — "

"Natural!" Hester turned again very quickly and came forward two steps into the room. "Natural!" she repeated. "Yes — that's it — it was natural — oh, too natural! What else could you do? Buttoning her glove — her hand in yours — and you, loving her — you kissed it! Ah, yes, — I know how natural it was! And you tell me there was no harm in it! What's harm, then? What does the word mean to you? Nothing? Is there no harm in hurting me?"

"But Hester, love — "

"And as though you did not know it — as though you had not turned white when you saw me at the door there, looking at you! If there were no harm, you needn't have been afraid of me. You'd have smiled instead of getting pale; you'd have held her hand still, instead of dropping it, and you'd have kissed it again, to show me how little it meant. No harm, indeed!"

"Your face was enough to scare any one, sweetheart. I thought you were ill and were going to faint."

He spoke softly now, in his golden voice, and threw more persuasion into the thin excuse than its words held.

"Don't — don't!" she cried. "You're tearing love to pieces with every word you say — if you know what you're saying! I tell you I've seen, and I know! This is the end — not the beginning. I saw it beginning long ago — last winter, when she sat to you day after day, and I lay in my corner and watched you watching her, and your eyes lighting up, and that smile of yours that was only for me — "

"But I was painting her portrait — I had to look at her — "

"Not like that! Oh, no, not like that! There's no reason, there never was any reason, why you should look at any woman like that — as you've

looked at me.   What a fool I was to let it go on,
to trust myself, to believe that I could be the only
woman in the world for you!   And then, the other
day, when you sang to her before all those people;
do you remember what you once promised me?
Do you remember at all that you swore to me
by all you held sacred that you'd never, never
sing, unless I were there to hear you?   How you
told me that your voice was mine, and only for me,
and for no one else, because that at least you could
keep for me, though you couldn't keep your art
and make that all mine, too?   And then you sang
to her — I know, for they told me — you sang my
song, the one I loved, from Lohengrin!   Why did
you do that ? "

"Why — I told you the other day — we talked of
it, don't you remember?   Why do you go back to
it now, dear ? "

"Because it's part of it all," she cried, passionately.   "Because it was only one of so many
things that have all led up to this that you've done
now.   I told you how I hated her, the other day,
and I made you say that you hated her, too, though
you didn't want to say it.   But you did, and you
meant it for a little minute — just while it lasted.
But you can't hate her when she's here — you
can't because you love her, and one can't hate and
love at the same time, though I do — but that's different.   You love **her, Walter!** You love her —
you love her — "

"You're beside yourself, darling," said Crowdie, softly. "Don't talk like this! Be reasonable! Listen to me, sweet!"

He knelt down beside her as she threw herself into a low chair, and he tried to take her hands. But she drew them away, wringing them as though to shake something from her fingers, and turning her face from him, as she clasped the back of the chair on the opposite side.

"No, no!" she cried, quivering all over. "I'm not mad. I know what I'm saying — God knows, I wish I didn't."

Her voice sank to a whisper, and her head fell against her hands. Crowdie laid one of his upon her arm, and she quivered again, like a nervous thoroughbred. Crowdie's own voice was full of soft pleading as he spoke to her.

"My sweet — my precious! Listen to me, love; don't think I don't love you, not even for one instant, nor that I ever loved you even a little less. Hester, look at me, darling — don't turn your face away as though you were always going to be angry — it's all a wretched mistake, dear! Won't you try and believe me?"

But Hester would not turn to him.

"What has she got that I haven't?" she asked, in a low monotonous tone, as though speaking to herself.

"Nothing, beloved — not half of all you have, not a quarter nor a hundredth part —"

" Yes — she's more beautiful, I suppose," continued Hester, speaking into the chair as she buried her face. " But surely that's all — oh, what is it? What else is it that she has, and that I haven't, and that you love in her? "

"But I don't love her — I don't care for her — I don't even like her — I hate her since she's come between you and me, dear."

"No — you love her. I've seen it in your eyes — you can't hide it in your eyes. You do! You love her!" she cried, suddenly raising her face and turning upon him for a moment, then looking away again almost instantly. " Oh, what has she got that I haven't? What's her secret — oh, what is it ? "

Crowdie bent over her shoulder and kissed the stuff of her frock softly.

"Darling! Don't make so much of so very little!" he whispered, close to her ear. "I tell you I love you, sweet — you must believe me — you shall believe me! I'll kiss you till you do."

"No!" she exclaimed, almost fiercely. "You shan't kiss me! "

And she rose with a spring, and left him kneeling beside the empty chair. He struggled to his feet, cut by the ridicule of his own attitude. But he could not move easily and swiftly as she could, being badly made. She stood back, looking at him over the chair, and her eyes flashed angrily. He moved towards her, but she drew further back.

"Don't come near me!" she cried. "I won't let you touch me!"

"Hester!" His voice trembled as he uttered her name.

"No — I know what you can do with your voice! I don't believe you any longer — you've spoken to her just like that — you've called her Katharine, just as you call me Hester! Oh no, no! It's all false — it doesn't ring true any more. Go — I don't want to see you — I don't want to know you're here — "

But still he tried to get nearer to her with pleading eyes that were beginning to light up as he moved, making his feet slide upon the carpet, rather than walking.

"Don't!" she cried. "Don't come near me! If you touch me — I'll kill you!"

Her hands went out to resist him, and her low, passionate cry of warning vibrated in the little room. Crowdie was startled, even then, and he paused, checked as though cold water had been thrown in his face. Then, very much discomfited, he turned and, thrusting his hands into the pockets of his jacket, began to walk up and down, passing and repassing her as she stood back against the fireplace. Her eyes followed him fiercely, and she breathed audibly with a quick, sob-like breath, with parted lips, between her teeth.

"I don't know what to say to you," he said, in

a tone of a man who is at his wit's end and is debating with himself.

"Say nothing — go — what could you say?"

"I could say a great many things," he answered, growing calm again in the attempt to argue the case. "In the first place, it's all a piece of the most extraordinary exaggeration on your part — the whole thing — pretending that a man can't kiss a girl's glove without being in love with her! As though there had been any secret about it! Why, the door was wide open — of course you might have come in at any moment, just as you did. And then — the way you talk! You couldn't be more angry if I'd run away with the girl. Besides — she can't abide me. I only did it to tease her, and she didn't like it a bit — upon my word, you're making a crime out of the merest chaff. It's not like you to be so unreasonable."

He stopped in his walk and stood opposite to her, near the chair in which she had sat.

"I'm not unreasonable," she answered. "And you know I'm not. You know what you meant —"

"I meant nothing!" cried Crowdie, with sudden energy. "You've got an absolutely wrong idea of the whole thing from beginning to end. You began by saying that I stared at her last winter, when I was painting her. Of course I did. Do you expect me to turn my back on my sitter, and imagine a face I can't see? It's perfectly absurd. I

looked at her, and stared at her, just as you've
seen me stare at Mrs. Brett, who's young and
quite as handsome as your cousin, and at Mrs.
Trehearne, who's old and hideous. You're out of
your mind, I tell you! You're ill, or something!
How in the world am I to paint people if I don't
look at them? As for having sung the other
night, I couldn't help it. It was aunt Maggie's
fault, and Katharine told me not to, when she
heard I'd made a promise —"

"I know — the little snake!" exclaimed Hester.
"She knew well enough that was the best way —"

"She didn't know anything of the kind. She
spoke perfectly naturally, and merely didn't want
me to displease you —"

"Then why did you do it?" asked Hester,
fiercely. "It wasn't to delight poor dear old
mamma, nor to charm four or five men, most of
whom you hate — was it? Then it was for Katharine, and for no one else —"

"It was not for Katharine," answered Crowdie,
with emphasis. "It wasn't for any one of them.
I sang to please myself, because I didn't choose
to have them laugh at me, as though I were a boy
out of school —"

"You mean that you didn't choose to let them
think that you cared enough for me to give such a
promise — to keep your voice for me, instead of
singing about in other people's houses like a mere

amateur, who pays for his supper with a song.
You were afraid they'd laugh at you if you said
you cared for me, and for what I'd asked of you
— and you were really afraid, because you didn't
really care. Oh, I know now — I see it all, and I
know! You can't deceive me any longer."

"I tell you, you're utterly and entirely mistaken!" cried Crowdie, angrily. "You're making
a mountain out of a mole hill. You're losing your
temper over it, and working yourself into a passion,
till you don't know what's true and what isn't.
It's madness in you, and it isn't fair to me. When
have I ever looked at another woman — "

"It had to begin some time — so it's begun now
— in the worst way it could begin, with Katharine
Lauderdale!"

"I hate Katharine Lauderdale — her and the
sound of her name! How often must I say it
before you'll believe me?"

"Oh — saying it won't make it true! Do you
think I didn't see your face — just now?"

"I don't know what you thought you saw — but
I know what there was to be seen, and if you
weren't beside yourself with jealousy you wouldn't
have thought twice about it. I never knew what
jealousy meant before — "

"And you don't now. I'm not jealous of her — I
hate her. I despise her for trying to steal you from
me, but since she's got you — since you love her

so that you'll lie for her, and be a coward for her, and be angry for her — just as it suits you — oh no, indeed! I'm not jealous of Katharine. That's quite another thing. Jealous! And you reproach me, and cast it in my teeth, because I say I hate her, when she's taken everything I cared for in this earth, everything I had! Ah — I could kill her! But I'm not jealous. One must care for oneself to be jealous; one must be wounded, hurt, insulted, to be jealous! Do you think I want you, if you don't want me? How little you've ever understood me!"

She drew herself up, leaning back against the shelf of the mantelpiece, and her lips curled scornfully, though they trembled a little, and she fixed her eyes upon his face with a strange, frightened fierceness, like that of a delicate wild animal driven to bay, but determined to resist. Crowdie met her glance steadily now, leaning with both hands upon the back of the chair between them and bending his body a little, in the attitude of a man who means to speak very earnestly.

"I don't think any one could understand you now," he began, in a quiet, but determined tone. "I can't, I confess. But I know you're not yourself, and you don't know what you're saying. I'm not going to argue as to whether you're jealous of Katharine Lauderdale, or not. It's too absurd! You've no right to be, at all events —"

"No right!" cried Hester, with a half hysterical laugh. "If ever a woman had a right to be jealous of another —"

"No, you've not — not the shadow of a right. You know how I've loved you for years — well — you know how, and what sort of love there's been between us. You're mad to think that anything I've done —"

"That's all your argument — that I'm mad! You say it again and again, as though it comforted you! Yes — I am mad in one way — I'm mad not to hate you ten thousand times more than I do — and I do hate you — for what you've done! You've torn up my heart by the roots and thrown it to that wretched girl — you've twisted, and wrenched, and broken everything that was tender in me, everything that was for you, and was yours — and it won't grow again! You've taken everything — have I ever refused you anything? You've taken it all, and I thought that you'd never had it before, and that for its sake you loved me, because I loved you so — that you'd wear me in your heart, and carry me in your hands, and love me all your life — and for that girl, that creature with her grey eyes — oh, what is it? What has she got that I haven't, and that makes you love her — what? What?"

She covered her eyes with a desperate gesture, and her voice almost broke as she repeated the last word. Below her hand her lips trembled, and Crowdie watched them. Then before she looked at him again, he had passed the chair and was trying to take her in his arms. For an instant she struggled with him, holding her face back from him and thrusting him away. But his small white hands had more strength in them than hers.

"Walter — don't!" she cried, pushing against him with all her might. "Don't! Don't!" she repeated.

But in spite of her, he got near to her face, and kissed her on the cheek. She started violently, and then wrenched herself free.

"How dare you?" she exclaimed, angrily, retreating half across the room with the rush of the effort she had made.

Crowdie laughed, not naturally, and not at all musically. There was a curious hoarseness in the tone, and his eyes glittered.

"And how dare you laugh at me?" she asked, moving still further back, towards the door, as he advanced. "Have you no heart, no feeling — no sense? Can't you understand how it hurts when you touch me?"

"I don't want to understand anything so foolish," answered Crowdie, suddenly growing coldly angry again. "If you're afraid of me — well, I won't go near you until you see how silly you are. There's no other word — it's silly."

"Silly! When it's all my life." Her voice shook. "Oh, Walter, Walter! You're breaking my heart!"

A passionate sob struggled with the words, and she fell into a chair by the door, covering her face with her hands again. Then came another sob, and the convulsion of her strength as she tried to choke it down, and it broke the barrier and burst out with a wild storm of scalding tears.

Crowdie was a very sensitively organized man in one direction, but singularly hard to move in another. So long as the passions of others appealed to his own, the response was ready and impulsive. But in him mere sympathy was not easily roused. Once freed from self, his faculties were critical, comparative, quick to seek causes and explain their connection with effects. Hester's words wakened his love, roused his anger, called out his powers of opposition, and touched him to the quick by turns; but her tears said nothing to him at first, except that she was suffering. He was only with her in happiness, never in unhappiness. He stood still for a moment watching her, and asking himself with considerable calmness what was best to be done.

It is not always easy to judge and decide exactly how far a woman could control herself if she thought it wise to do so, and for that reason the genuineness of her tears often seems doubtful.

It would be as fair to doubt that a tortured man suffers if he does not groan in his agony, or because he does.

But although at that moment he felt no sympathy with her, though he loved her in his own way, yet his instinct and experience of women told him that with the tears there must come a change of mood. He went slowly to her side, and though she did not look up he knew that she felt his presence, and would not drive him from her again just then. He bent over her, laying his arm upon her shoulders, and looking at the hands that covered her eyes. He did not speak at once, but waited for her to look up. She was sobbing as though her heart would really break. At last, between the sobs, words began to come at last.

" Oh, Walter, Walter ! " she wailed, repeating his name.

"Yes — sweetheart — look at me, dear," he answered, pressing her to him.

Her head rested against him as she sobbed. Then one hand left her eyes and sought his hand, but was instantly withdrawn again. He found it and brought it, resisting but a little, to his lips. In all such actions he had the gentleness, almost boyish, which some women love so well, and which is so kingly in the very strong — for they say that it is sweeter to be caressed by the hand that could kill, than by one that at its worst and strongest could only scratch.

Presently she uncovered her eyes and looked up to his face, and the sobbing almost stopped. Her cheeks were flushed through their whiteness and were wet, and her eyes were dark and shadowy, but the light in them was not hard. The tide of anger had ebbed as the tears flowed, and its wave was far off.

"Tell me you really love me, dear," she said, still tearfully.

"Ah, sweet! You know I do — I love you — so! Is that right? Doesn't it ring true now?" He laughed softly, looking into her face. "When did I ever sing false?"

A shade of returning annoyance passed over her features, as her brow contracted at the allusion to his singing, and though she still allowed her head to rest against his side, her face was turned away once more.

"Don't speak of singing, dear," she said, trying to smile, though he could not see whether she did or not.

"No, darling — forgive me. I'll never speak of it again. I'll never sing again as long as I live, if you don't want me to."

"I didn't mean that," she answered. "It's only now — till I forget. And, Walter, dear — I don't want you to promise it any more — I'd rather not, really."

Still she turned away, but he bent over, drawing

her closer to him, and he lifted her face with his
hand under her chin. The eyelids drooped as she
suffered her head to fall back over his arm, and
she shut out the sight of his eyes from her own.
He murmured soft words in his low voice, in
golden tones.

"Darling — precious — sweet one !"

And he repeated the words and others, as her
features softened, and her parted lips smiled at his.
And still he pressed her to him, and spoke to her,
and looked at her with burning eyes. So they
might have been reconciled then and there, had
Fate willed it. But Fate was there with her
little creeping hand full of the tiny mischief that
decides between life and death when no one knows.

Fate willed that at that moment Crowdie should
be irritated by something in his throat. Just as
he was speaking so softly, so sweetly that the
exquisite sound almost lulled her to sleep, while
the passionate tears still wet her cheek, — just as
his face was near hers, he felt it coming, insignificant in itself, ridiculous by reason of the moment
at which it came, yet irresistible in its littleness.
He struggled against it, and grew conscious of
what he was saying, and his voice lost its passionate tenderness. He strove to fight it down, that
horrible little tickling spasm just in the vocal
chords, for he knew how much it might mean both
to her and to him, that her forgiving mood should

carry them both to the kiss of peace. But Fate
was there, irresistible and little, as surely as though
she had stalked gigantic, sword in hand, through
the door, to smite them both. In the midst of
the very sweetest word of all, it came — the word
rang false, he turned his face away and coughed to
clear his throat. But the false note had rung.

Hester sprang to her feet, and thrust him from
her. To her it had all been false, — the words, the
tone, the caresses. How could a man in the
earnestness of passion, midway in love's eloquence,
wish to stop — and cough? She did not think
nor reason, as she turned upon him in the anguish
of her disappointment.

"How could I believe you — even for a moment?" she cried, standing back from him. "Oh,
what an actor you are!"

But he had not been acting, save that he had
done what his instinct had at first told him was
wisest, in beginning to speak to her when she had
burst into tears. With the first word, the first
caress, with the touch of her, and the sweet,
unscented, living air of her, the passion that had
truly ruled his faultful life for years took hold of
him with strength and main, and rang the leading
changes of his being. And then she broke it
short.

As he stood up before her, he shook with emotion stronger than hers, such as women rarely feel,

and such as even strong men dread. Unconsciously he held out his hands towards her and uttered a half articulate cry, trying once more to catch her in his arms.

"Kiss me — love me — oh, Hester !"

But he met her angry eyes, for she had lost the hand of reality in the labyrinth of her own imaginings and disappointments and jealousies, and she knew no longer the good from the evil, nor the truth from the acted lie.

" No — you're acting," she answered, cruelly — trying to be as cruel as the hurt she felt.

And she stared hardly at him. But even as she looked, a deep, purple flush rose in his white cheeks, and overspread his face, even to his forehead, and darkened all his features. And his eyes turned upwards in their sockets, as he fell forward against her, with wet, twisted lips and limp limbs — a hideous sight for woman or man to look upon.

She uttered a low, broken cry as she caught him in her arms, and he dragged her down to the floor by his weight. There he lay, almost black in the face, contorted and stiffened, yet not quite motionless, but far more repulsive by the spasmodic and writhing motion of his body than if he had lain stiff and stark as a dead body.

She had seen him thus once before now, on a winter's night, upstairs in the studio. She did not know that it was epilepsy. She knelt beside him, horror-struck, now, for a few moments. It seemed worse in the evening glow than it had looked to her before, under the soft, artificial light in the great room.

She only hesitated a few seconds. Then she got a cushion and thrust it under his head, using all her strength to lift him a little with one arm as she did so. But she knew by experience that the unconsciousness would last a long time, and she was glad that it had come at once. On the first occasion the convulsion that preceded it had been horrible. Her own face was drawn with the anguish of intense sympathy, and she felt all the horror of her last cruel words still ringing in her ears.

She did not rise from her knees, but bent over him, and looked at him, seeing himself, as she dreamed him, through the mask of his hideous face. She touched his hands, and tried to draw them out of their contortion, but the inturned thumbs and stiffened joints were too rigid for her to move. But she lifted his body again, straining her strength till she thought his weight must tear the slight sinews of her arms at the elbow, and she tried to turn his head to a comfortable position on the silken pillow, and stroked his silk-fine hair with gentle hands. As she did her best for him, her throat was parched, and she felt her dry lips cleaving to her teeth, and the sight of her eyes was almost failing, being burned out with horror. But no tears came to put out the fire.

At last she rose to her feet, steadying herself against the chair in which she had last sat, for she was dizzy with pain and with bending down. She gazed at him an instant; then turned and went and closed the open windows, and pulled down the shades and drew the thick curtains together. After that, groping, she found matches and lit one candle, and set it so that the light should not fall upon his eyes, if by any chance their conscious sight returned. Then she looked at him once more and left the room, softly closing the door behind her, and turning the key with infinite pains, lest any servant in the house should hear the sound. She took the key with her and went upstairs.

CHAPTER XXXI.

KATHARINE was sincerely distressed by the result of her interview with Hester, and she walked slowly homeward, thinking it all over and asking herself whether she had left undone anything which she ought to have done. But as she thought, it was always the last scene which rose before her eyes, and she saw distinctly before her Hester's white face staring at her through the open doorway. There was a great satisfaction in feeling sure that she had been wholly innocent in the matter of Crowdie's kissing her hand; yet felt that the resentment Hester had shown on re-entering the room had not been anything different in its essential nature from the coldness she had already shown when Katharine had spoken of renewing their friendship. But the young girl could not understand either, though the supposition that Hester must be jealous of her thrust itself upon her forcibly.

Ralston helped her. He had asked for her at the house in Clinton Place, and having been told that she was still out, he had hung about the neighbourhood in the hope of meeting her, and had been at last rewarded by seeing her coming towards him from the other side of Fifth Avenue. In a moment they met.

"Oh, I'm so glad to see you, Jack, dear!" she cried as she took his hand. "I've got such lots to tell you!"

"So have I," answered Ralston. "Where shall we go? Should you like to walk?"

"Yes — in some quiet place, where we can talk, and not meet people, and not be run over too often."

"All right," answered John. "Let's go west. There are lots of quiet streets on that side, and it's awfully respectable. The worst that can happen to us will be to meet Teddy Van De Water looking after his tenants, or Russell Vanbrugh going to administer consolation to the relations of his favourite criminal. Something's happened, Katharine," he added suddenly, as they turned westward, and the strong evening light illuminated her features through her veil. "I can see it in your face."

"Yes," answered Katharine. "I want to tell you. I've had such a time with Hester! You don't know!"

"Tell me all about it."

They walked along, and Katharine told her story with all the details she could remember, doing her best to make clear to him what was by no means clear to herself. When she had finished, she looked at John interrogatively.

"That fellow Crowdie's a brute!" he exclaimed, with energy.

"Well — I don't like him, you know. But was it so very bad? Tell me, Jack — you're my natural protector." She laughed happily. "It's your business to tell me what's right and what's wrong. Was it so very bad of him to kiss my glove after he'd buttoned it? I almost boxed his ears at the time — I was so angry! But I want to be fair. Was it exactly — wrong? I wish you'd tell me."

"Wrong? No; it wasn't exactly wrong." Ralston paused thoughtfully. "Kissing women's hands is one of those relative things," he continued. "It's right in one part of the world, it's indifferent in another, and it's positively the wrong thing to do somewhere else — whatever it's meant to mean. We don't do that sort of thing much over here. As he did it, I suppose it was simply the wrong thing to do. At least, I want to suppose so, but I can't. The man's half in love with you, you know."

"Oh, nonsense, Jack! It's only because we dislike him so. If ever a man was in love with his wife, he is."

"Yes, I know," answered Ralston, in the same thoughtful tone. "That's quite true. But it doesn't prevent him from being half in love with lots of other women at the same time. It's not the same thing. Oh, yes! he loves Hester. She's quite mad about him, of course. We all know that, in the family. But Crowdie's peculiar — and it's not a nice peculiarity, either. One sees it in his manner somehow, and in his eyes. I can't exactly explain it to you. He admires every woman who's beautiful, and it's a little more than admiration. He has a way with him which we men don't like. And when he does such things as he did to-day there's always a suggestion of something disagreeable in his way of doing them, so that if they're not positively wrong, they're not positively innocent. They're on the ragged edge between the two, as Frank Miner says."

"I think it's more in the way he looks at one than in anything else," said Katharine. "He has such a horrid mouth! But it's absurd to say that he's in love with me, Jack."

"Oh, no, it's not! That night at aunt Maggie's, when he sang, you know — it was for you and nobody else. What a queer evening that was, by the way! There were five of us men there, all in love with you in one way or another."

"Jack! It's positively ridiculous! The idea of such a thing!"

"Not at all. There was Ham, in the first place. You admit that he's one, don't you?"

"I suppose I must, since he proposed," answered Katharine, reluctantly, and turning her face away.

"And you're not going to deny Archie Wingfield?" Ralston tried to see her eyes. "I'm sure he's offered himself."

Katharine said nothing, but John saw through her veil and was sure that a little colour rose in her face.

"Of course!" he said. "That's two of them. And Crowdie's three. I count him. And you mustn't forget me. I'm what they call in love with you, I suppose. That's four."

Katharine smiled, and glanced at him, looking away again immediately.

"At least," she said, "you'll leave me dear old Mr. Griggs —"

"Griggs!" laughed Ralston. "He's the worst of the lot. He's madly, fearfully, desperately, fantastically in love with you."

"Jack! What do you mean?" Katharine laughed, but her face expressed genuine surprise. "Not that I should mind," she added. "Dear old man! I'm so fond of him!"

"Well — he returns your fondness with interest. He makes no secret of it to anybody, because he's old, or says he is, — but he's old like an old wolf. I like him, too. He goes about saying that you're his ideal of beauty and cleverness and soul — and good taste. Oh, Griggs!" He laughed again.

"He's quite off his head about you! He'll put you into one of his books if you're not careful. I should like to see your father's expression if he did."

"Don't be a goose, Jack!" suggested Katharine, by way of good advice. "Of course, I understand what a dear old silly idiot you are, you know. But don't talk such nonsense to other people. They'll laugh at you."

"No, I'm not going to. I let Griggs do the talking, and people laugh at him. But there's nothing silly in it, as a matter of fact. Everybody loves you — except some of the people who should. And I must say, with the exception of Crowdie, we were a very presentable lot the other night. And even Crowdie — well, he's a celebrity, if he's nothing else, and that counts for something with some women. I say, Katharine — are you and Hester going to quarrel for the rest of your lives?"

"I'm afraid so, — at least, we shan't quarrel exactly. But we can never be just as we were."

"I'm rather glad," said Ralston. "I never believed much in that friendship between you two."

"Oh, Jack! We loved each other so dearly! And it was so nice — we told each other everything, you know."

"Yes — but you've outgrown each other."

Katharine looked at him quickly, in surprise.

"That's exactly what Hester said to-day," she answered. "It seemed to me to be such nonsense."

"Well — you have, and she's quite right if she says so. That sort of school-girlish friendship doesn't amount to anything when you begin to grow up. I've seen lots of them in society. They always break up as soon as one of the two marries and has other things to think about. Besides, between you and Hester, there's Crowdie. It's perfectly clear from what you've told me that she's jealous. If you're not careful she'll try and do you some mischief or other. She's jealous, and she has a streak of cruelty in her. She'll make you suffer somehow — trust the ingenuity of a woman like that! She'd burn her most intimate friend at a slow fire for Crowdie any day."

"Well — isn't she right?" asked Katharine. "I would, for you, I'm sure — if it would do you any good."

"It wouldn't," laughed Ralston. "Those cases don't arise nowadays. Sometimes one wishes they might. We've all got a lot of cruelty and romance in us somewhere. We all believe in the immutability of the affections, more or less."

"Don't laugh, Jack!" said Katharine. "Love has nothing to do with friendship. Besides, you and I aren't like other people. We're always going to care — just as we always have. We're faithful people, you and L."

"Yes. I think we are." He spoke quietly, as though from a long and familiar conviction.

A short silence followed, and they walked along side by side in the soft evening air, so close that their elbows touched, as they kept step together — a mode of courtship not usually practised by their kind, and which they would have been ashamed of in a more frequented quarter of the city. They would probably have noticed it unfavourably in another couple, and would have set the pair down as a dry-goods clerk and a shopgirl. But when the 'stiff and proud' Four Hundred are very much in love, and when they are quite sure that none of the remaining Three Hundred and Ninety-eight are looking, they behave precisely like human beings, which is really to their credit, though they would be so much ashamed to have it generally known.

"But then, we're married, you know," said Katharine, as though she had solved a difficult problem.

Ralston glanced at the face he loved and smiled happily.

"There's a good deal besides that," he said. "There are a great many things that tie us together. You've made a man of me. That's one thing. But for you, I don't know where I should have been now — in a bad way, I fancy."

"No, you wouldn't," protested Katharine. "A

man who can do the things you've done doesn't come to grief."

"It isn't anything I've done," Ralston answered. "It's what you've made me feel. If I've done anything at all, it's been for your sake. You know that as well as I do. And if there were big things to be done, it would be the same."

"You've done the biggest thing that any man can do. You don't need to have me tell you that."

"Oh — about reforming my ways, you mean?" He affected to laugh. "That wasn't anything. You made it nice and easy."

"Especially when I didn't believe in you, and treated you like a brute," said Katharine, with an expression of pain at the recollection. "Don't talk about it, Jack. I've never forgiven myself — I never shall."

"But it was so nice when it was over!" This time the little laugh was genuine. "I'd go through it all again, just to see your face when you found out that you'd been mistaken — and afterwards, when we sat behind the piano at the Van De Waters' — do you remember? Oh, yes! I'd like to have it all over again."

"Jack — you're an angel, dear! But don't talk about that night. I suppose, though, that those things have helped to bind us together and make us more each other's. Yes — of course they have. And then — we're such good friends, you know.

Doesn't that make a difference? I'm sure there are people who care very much, but who are never good friends. Look at papa and my mother. They're like that. They're not at all good friends. They never tell each other anything if they can help it. But they care all the same. We could never be like that together, could we? Jack — where does friendship end and love begin?"

"What a beautiful question!" exclaimed Ralston, very much amused. "Of all the impossible ones to answer!"

"I know it is. I've often wondered about it. You know, I can't at all remember when I began to care for you in this way. Can you? It must have been ever so long ago, before we ever said anything — because, when we did, it seemed quite natural, you know. And it always grows. It goes on growing like a thing that's planted in good earth and that has lots of life in it and is going to last forever. But it really does grow. I know, that I'm ever so much more glad to see you when we meet now than I was a month ago. If it goes on like this I don't know where it's going to end. Hester and her husband won't be anywhere, compared with us, will they?"

"They're not, as it is. They're quite different. When they're old, they'll quarrel — if not sooner."

"Oh, Jack — I don't believe it's quite fair to say that!"

"Well — wait and see. We're warranted to wear, you and I. They're not. There's no staying power in that sort of thing. Not but what they're in earnest. Even Crowdie is, though he's half in love with you, at the same time."

"I wish you wouldn't keep saying that," said Katharine. "It makes me feel so uncomfortable when we meet. Besides, it's absurd, as I told you. A man can't be madly in love with his wife and care for any one else at the same time."

"That depends on the man — and the way of caring," answered Ralston. "Crowdie's a brute. I hate him. The only thing I can't understand about Griggs is his liking for the man. It's incomprehensible to me."

"I don't think Mr. Griggs really likes him," said Katharine. "There's a mystery about it. But I'm almost sure he doesn't really like him. I believe he thinks he's responsible for Crowdie in some way. They knew each other long ago."

"Nobody knows much about Crowdie's antecedents, anyway. I never could understand the match."

"Oh — it's easily understood. They fell in love with each other. Of course he would have been delighted to marry her, if he hadn't cared a straw for her, for the sake of the social position and all that. Then he had a sister — at least, people said so, but nobody ever saw her that I know of

—somewhere in New Jersey. She didn't come to the wedding, I know, for I was Hester's bridesmaid. Charlotte and I were the only two."

"She didn't come to the wedding because she was dead," said Ralston. "That's an awfully good reason."

"I didn't know. I've often wondered about her, but I didn't like to ask questions. One doesn't you know, about people who don't turn up. They always are dead, or something—and then one feels so uncomfortable."

"Yes," answered Ralston, as though meditating on the fact. "At all events," he continued, "nobody ever knew much about Crowdie, nor where he came from. So I don't exactly see how Griggs could be responsible for him. But, as you say, there's a mystery about it all—so there is about Griggs, for that matter."

"Oh, no! Mr. Griggs is all right. There's nothing mysterious about him. He was born abroad, that's all, and I believe he was awfully poor as a boy—a sort of orphan lying about loose on the world, you know. But he's got a lot of tremendously proper relations in Rhode Island. He goes to see some of them now and then. He's told me."

"Well—it's very queer about Crowdie, anyhow," said Ralston, thoughtfully. "But there's something I wanted to talk to you about, dear," he continued after a little pause. "It's about our marriage certificate. You know we're living in danger of an explosion at any moment. That thing is tucked away somewhere amongst poor uncle Robert's papers. We've spoken of it once or twice, you know. They're going through everything, and sooner or later it's sure to turn up. It's just as well to be prepared beforehand. I don't know what will happen if we tell your father now, but he's got to be told, and it's my place to do it."

"No, Jack," answered Katharine. "It's my place. I made you do it — I've never made up my mind whether it was the wisest thing we could do, or whether it was a piece of egregious folly. Suppose that we had quarrelled after it was done. We should have been bound all our lives by a mere ceremony."

"But we knew we shouldn't," protested Ralston,

"Nobody knows anything," said Katharine, wisely. "We know now, because we know each other so much better. But I made you take a tremendous risk, and you didn't want to do it at all — "

"It wasn't on account of the risk — "

"No — of course it wasn't. But you're quite right now. That thing may turn up any day. I shall go to papa this very evening and tell him that we're married. It's the only sensible thing to do."

"Indeed, you shan't do that!" cried Ralston, anxiously. "You know him —"

"Shan't?" repeated Katharine, looking up into his face and smiling. "I will if I please," she said with a little laugh.

"Will you?" asked John, meeting her eyes with an expression of determination, but smiling, too, in spite of himself.

"Of course!" answered Katharine, promptly. "Especially as I think it's a matter of duty. Of course I'll do it —this very evening!"

"Don't!" said Ralston. "There'll be a row."

"Not half such a row as if you try to do it," observed Katharine. "You'll have each other by the throat in five minutes."

"Oh, no, we shan't. We're very good friends now. I don't see why there should be any trouble at all. He wants us to marry. He said so in his letter, and he's taken a sort of paternal air of late, when I come to the house. Besides, haven't you noticed the way in which he turns his back on us when we sit down to talk? If that doesn't mean consent — well, he won't have the trouble of a wedding, that's all, nor the expense, either. He ought to be glad, if he's logical."

"I don't think he'd mind the expense so much now," said Katharine, with perfect gravity. "I think he's getting used to the idea of spending a little more, now that we're to be so rich. He was talking about having a butler, last night. Fancy! But I do wish those administrators, or whatever you call them, would hurry up and give us something. We're awfully hard up, my mother and I. We've had to get such a lot of clothes, and I'm frightened to death about it. I'm sure the bills will come in before the estate's settled, and then papa will take the roof off, as you always say — he'll be so angry! But I don't think he'll make such a fuss about our marriage."

"No — that's just what I say. That's why I want to tell him myself."

"Jack!" cried Katharine, reproachfully. "You just said there'd be a row if I went to him about it."

"Well — I think I can manage him better," said Ralston. "You and he are used to fighting every day as a matter of habit, so that you're sure to go at each other on the smallest provocation. But with him and me, it's been a sort of rare amusement — the kind of thing one keeps for Sundays, and we don't like it so much. Besides, since you say that he won't be so angry after all, why shouldn't I?"

"Exactly. And I say, why shouldn't I? — for the same reason. I shall just say that we got married because we were afraid we should never get his consent, but that since he's given it frankly, — he did in that letter; — we've agreed to tell."

"That's just what I should say," answered
Ralston. "Those are the very words I had in my
mind."

"Of course they are. Don't we always think
alike? But I want to tell him. I'd much rather."

"So would I — much rather. It will end in our
going together. That's probably the most sensible
thing we can do. There'll be a certain grim surprise, and then the correct paternal blessing, and
the luncheon or dinner, according to the time of
day."

"It will be dinner, if we go home and do it
now," said Katharine, thoughtfully.

"Come on! Let's go!" answered Ralston.
"There's no time like the present for doing this
sort of thing. Where are we? Oh — South Fifth
Avenue's over there to the left. That's the
shortest way, round that corner and then straight
up."

They turned and walked in the direction he
indicated, both silent for a while as they thought
of what was before them, and the final telling of
the secret they had kept so long.

"You don't know how glad I shall be when
everybody knows," said Katharine after a time, as
they paused at a crossing to let a van pass by.

"Not half so glad as I shall be," answered Ralston. "But it couldn't be helped. I know it's
been hateful to have this secret — well, not exactly

hanging over us, but to have it a part of us all this time. Still — I don't see when we could have announced it. There's been one thing after another to make it impossible, and somehow we've got used to it. They say there's nothing like having a secret in common to make two people fall in love with each other. It seems to me it's true."

"We didn't need it, dear," said Katharine, softly, as they began to cross the street.

"No — not exactly." Ralston laughed. "But it hasn't made it any worse, at all events. But what moments we've had. Do you remember when they began to talk about secret marriages that night?"

"Don't I!" laughed Katharine. "I thought I should have gone through the floor! How well you behaved, Jack! I expected that you'd break out every minute and fall upon poor cousin Ham. But you didn't. As for me, I got scarlet, and I don't often blush, do I? Dark people don't. Well — it's all over now."

"Not till we've had our talk out with your father. We can't be quite sure of what will happen till then."

"No — but he can't unmarry us, can he? So what can he do? He can say that he'll disinherit me. That's the worst he could possibly do, and what difference would it make? You're going to be one of the rich, rich, rich men, Jack — with ever so many millions more than you can possibly spend on onions and honey — like the wayward old man of Kilkenny, you know. Besides, papa will not be angry at all. He'll simply dance with delight. I believe he's secretly afraid that we're cheating him, because we never speak of ever announcing our engagement. He thinks we're revenging ourselves now, and each means to marry somebody else, and he's in fits lest he should lose you for a son-in-law. Isn't it fun?"

"Yes — your beloved father in fits, as you call it — and dancing with delight — it doesn't lack the comic element. But it looks so simple now, just to go and tell him, and be done with it. Why haven't we done it before?"

"Oh — we couldn't. It wouldn't have been safe until the will was settled. He was really dreadfully nervous all that time. I never saw him in such a state before. It really wouldn't have been safe. No — this is our first chance. We might have spoken a day or two ago, of course, but not much sooner."

"No — we couldn't," said Ralston. "But I'm glad — oh, tremendously glad that it's coming at last."

"And then — Jack," said Katharine, with some hesitation, "after we've spoken, you know — what are we going to do?"

"You and I? Why, get married, of course —

I mean — as if we were getting married. There
won't be any people nor any cake, nor any gorgeous
dress for you — poor dear! But we shall have to
pretend, I suppose — go off with your mother and
my mother, and as many more mothers as we can
pick up, to make us perfectly respectable, and then
we shall come back married, and choose a house
to live in. That's the first thing, you know. My
mother will never hear of our living with her, now
that there's to be lots of money. She's much too
wise for that. Relations-in-law are just bones for
husband and wife to fight over. But of course my
mother will come very often."

"And my mother," said Katharine.

"Yes — your mother, too," assented Ralston.
"Naturally, they'll both come. So long as they
don't live with us, we shan't mind."

"But you're very fond of your mother, Jack,
aren't you?" asked Katharine.

"Of course I am. We're more like brother and
sister than anything else. You see, we've always
been together so much."

"And yet you'd rather not have her live with
us?"

"Certainly not. And she wouldn't wish to."

"It's strange," said Katharine, thoughtfully. "I
don't think I should mind having my mother with
us. She'd be such a comfort when you were down
town, you know."

"Yes," answered Ralston, in a doubtful tone.

"I couldn't take my mother down town to comfort me at Beman's, could I?"

"What an absurd idea! But, Jack, — shall you still go to Beman's? You can't, you know. Everybody would laugh at you. A man with forty millions or so, doing clerk's work in a bank! It's ridiculous!"

"No doubt! But what am I to do with myself? What do people like that do? I can't hang about the clubs all day."

"You can stay at home and talk to me," said Katharine. "We can tell each other how much nicer it is than when we had to meet in Washington Square in the early morning — when I had to put red ribbons in my window — do you remember? It's only three or four weeks ago, but it seems years."

"It does, indeed. What tight places we've been through together since your father refused to hear of me as a son-in-law! Holloa! There goes Ham Bright! What in the world can he be doing down here at this time of day?"

Bright was walking towards them, as quickly as it was natural for him to walk, with his long, heavy stride.

"It's of no use to run away — he's seen us," said Katharine.

"He looks in a better humour than I've seen him lately," answered John in a low voice, as they approached Bright.

They met and stood still a moment on the pavement. Even under his great disappointment Hamilton Bright had never shown the least ill-temper, though he had avoided the Lauderdales and the Ralstons as much as possible, and had managed so that he scarcely ever saw John at the bank except from a distance. But he had been very gloomy of late. Now, however, as Ralston had said, he looked more cheerful.

"Going down town again?" asked John. "Not that I come from Boston, you know, Ham — but when one meets a man going down South Fifth Avenue at half past five in the afternoon, one's naturally curious. What's up?"

"Oh — nothing. I was just going as far as Grand Street about a house I've bought there. Did you know they'd found the other will?"

"Found the other will?" repeated Ralston, in the utmost surprise. "Well — what sort of a will is it? Will it be good?"

"I'm so glad!" exclaimed Katharine, thoughtlessly.

Bright fixed his clear, blue eyes on her with considerable curiosity, and hesitated an instant before he spoke.

"Of course!" he exclaimed. "They always said you knew what was in it, cousin Katharine."

"Did they? I don't know how they knew that I did," she answered. "But I'm glad it's found, all the same."

"Are you? Well — I hope it's all right. Of course nobody knows what's in it. Allen wants to collect the family at your house to-morrow morning to hear it read. It seems to me it might have been managed to-night, but he said there wasn't time to send round. I think cousin Alexander objected, too. He wants all the family. Will you tell your mother, Jack? Eleven o'clock at Clinton Place. Write a note to Beman to say why you don't turn up at the bank."

"All right," answered John, gravely. "I hope it will be all right, Ham, old man," he added, putting out his hand as Bright showed signs of being in a hurry.

"Thank you, Jack," answered the latter, heartily. "Not that you and I shall ever quarrel about money. Good-bye, cousin Katharine."

And he went on and left them to pursue their way in the opposite direction. They walked slowly, and looked into one another's eyes.

" I thought he'd burned it," said Ralston at last, in a tone of wonder.

" So did I," answered Katharine. " Jack," she continued, after a slight pause, " it won't do to go and see papa now. Not till the will's been read to-morrow. You don't know what a state of mind he'll be in until he's heard it — and then — then I'm afraid it will be worse than ever."

" Yes — let me see — how was it ? You and

Charlotte and I are to have everything, and pay half the income to the parents. Isn't that it?"

"That's it. And there's a million set aside for the Brights. But Heaven only knows what that dreadful court will do this time!"

"I don't much care," answered Ralston. "But all the settling up will be suspended again for ever so long. You'll never get the money to pay for your new frock, dear, with all your millions!"

"Oh, Jack — really? I'm frightened to death about those bills!"

"I was only laughing at you," said John, laughing himself. "Besides, as I'm really your husband, I'm responsible for your dressmaker's bills in the eye of the law. But, I confess, I begin to wonder whether any of us will ever see any of that money."

CHAPTER XXXII.

LONG after midnight Hester Crowdie sat beside her sleeping husband, watching him with unwinking eyes. The soft, coloured light was shaded so that no ray could fall upon his face to disturb his rest, as he lay back upon the yielding pillow, sleeping very soundly. The house was still, but the servants were not all gone to bed, for Hester was anxious. At any moment she might need to send for a doctor. But she sat watching the unconscious man alone.

His eyes were closed, and his face was flushed. He breathed very heavily, though she did not quite realize it; for the sound of his breathing had increased very gradually during many hours, from having been at first quite inaudible until it filled her ears with a steady, rhythmic roar, loud and regular as the noise of a blacksmith's bellows. But she was scarcely conscious of it, because she had watched so long.

Hour after hour she had sat beside him, hardly changing her position, and never leaving the room. To her the house seemed still, and only now and then the echo of the steam horns reached her ears,

271

made musical by the distance, as it floated from the
far river across the dozing city.

On a fine spring night New York is rarely asleep
before two o'clock. It dozes, as it were, turning,
half awake, from time to time, and speaking
drowsily in its deep voice, like a strong man very
tired, but still conscious. It breathes, too, sometimes, as Crowdie was breathing, very heavily,
especially in the nights that come after days of
passion and struggling; and the breathing of a
great city at night is not like any other sound on
earth.

Hester was conscious that all was not well with
the man she loved, though he had slept so long.
She rose, and moved uneasily about the room.
She was very pale, and there were dark shadows in
her pallor, the shadows that fear's giant wraith
casts upon the human face when death is stalking
up and down, up and down, outside the door, waiting to see whether he may take the little life that
falls as a crumb from the table of the master, or
whether he must go away again to his own place,
out of sight.

But Hester did not know that he was there, as
she rose and crossed the room and came back to
stand at the foot of the bed, gazing at Crowdie's
face. She was anxious and uneasy, though she
had watched him once before in the same way.
But at that first time she had not done what she

had done now, with feverish haste, thinking only of helping him.

All at once she shivered, and she turned to see whether the window were not open. But it was closely shut. It was as though something very cold had been laid upon her. She stared about, nervously, and the pupils of her eyes grew very large, with a frightened look. She laid both hands upon the foot of the bedstead, and grasped it with all her strength, bending forwards and staring at Crowdie's face, and the chill thrilled very strangely across her shoulders and all through her, so that she felt it in her elbows and in her heels. She glanced over her shoulder into the softly shadowed corner farthest from the bed; for she was sure that something was there, in the room, a bodily presence, which she must presently see. The chill ran through her again and again, cold as ice, but with a painful pricking.

She looked at Crowdie again and saw that his eyes were no longer tightly closed. The lids were a little raised, and she could see the edge of the dark iris, and the white below it and on each side of it. He had moved a little just as she had turned to look into the corner. He ought not to have moved, she thought, without reason. It was as though a dead man had moved, she thought. And again the chill came. She was sure that the window must be open, but she could not look

round. Suddenly she remembered how when she
had been a little girl she had been taken to be
photographed, and the man had put a cold iron
thing behind her head that seemed to hold her
with two frozen fingers just behind her ears. She
felt the frozen fingers now, in the same places, and
they were pressing her head down. For a moment
everything swam with her, and then it all passed.
The iron hand was gone — the window was shut —
there was nothing in the corner.

But instantly the terrible, stertorous breathing
rent her ears. It had gone on for hours. The
servants could hear it downstairs. The bedstead
trembled with it under her hands. But she had
not been conscious of it. The unnatural thing
that had touched her — the thing that had come
in through the window and that had stood in the
corner — it had unsealed her hearing. She heard
now, and fearfully.

With one slender arm under the pillow she raised
him, for she thought that he might breathe more
easily if his head were higher. His laboured
breath deafened her, and she could feel it through
her sleeve upon her other arm. Desperately she
hastened to arrange the pillows. But the dreadful
sound roared at her like the flames of a great fire.
In sudden and overwhelming terror she left him as
he was, half uncovered, and ran to the door, calling
wildly for help, again and again, down into the

dimly-lighted staircase. Then she came back in a
new terror, lest her screams should have waked
him. But he slept on. In the movement of the
pillow as she had withdrawn her arm, his head had
fallen on one side. His eyes were half open, and
the breath was rough and choking.

She had never known how heavy a man's head
was. Her small, bloodless hands made an effort to
turn him — then some one was with her, helping
her, anxiously and clumsily.

"Not so! Not that way!" she whispered,
hoarsely, with drawn, dry lips, and her little
hands touched the servant's rough ones with
uncertain direction, in haste and fear.

Then he breathed more easily, and she herself
drew breath. But she had been terrified, and she
sent for old Doctor Routh, and sat down in her old
place to wait and watch until he should come. It
was better now. The coming of the servant had
broken the loneliness, and there was life in the air
again, instead of death. Her heart fluttered still,
like a wild bird tired out with beating its wings
against the bars. But there was no chill, and presently the heart rested. He was better. She was
quite sure that he was better. The rough breathing would cease presently, he would sleep till
morning, and then he would waken and be himself
again, just as though nothing had happened. Now
that the fear was gone, she rose and went to the

window and let the shade run up so that she could see the stars. They had a soft and sleepy look, like children's eyes at bed-time. The musical echo of the horns came to her from the river. In the old Colonnade House opposite and to the right, a single window was lighted high up. Perhaps some one was ill up there — all alone. Then the city moved in its dozing rest, with a subdued thumping, rumbling noise that lasted a few seconds. Perhaps there was a fire far away, and the engines and the hook-and-ladder carts were racing away from the lumbering water-tank down one of the quiet eastern avenues. The light in the window of the Colonnade House went out suddenly — no one was ill there — it had only been some one sitting up late. Hester missed the light, and the great long building looked black against the dim sky, and the stars blinked more sleepily. She drew the shade down again and turned back into the room.

She started. Crowdie had seemed better when she had left his side for a moment. It had eased him to move his head. But now he was worse again, and the room almost shook with the noise of his breathing. It was as though he were inhaling water that choked him and gurgled in his throat and nostrils. She was frightened again, and ran to his side. She took her little handkerchief which lay on the small table at her elbow, and passed it delicately over his mouth. Her hand trembled as soon as she had done it, and the handkerchief fell upon the woollen blanket, and gently unfolded itself a little after it had fallen. It caught the light and seemed to be alive, as though it had taken some of the sleeping man's life from him. She started again, and seized it to crumple it and thrust it away, with something between fear and impatience in her movement, and she bent over her husband's face once more, and realized where her real fear was, as she tenderly smoothed his fair hair and softly touched his temples.

There was nothing to be done but to wait, and she waited, not patiently. Sometimes the noise of his breathing hurt her, and she pressed her hand to her side, and hid her eyes for a moment. The dismal minutes that would not go by, nor make way for one another, dragged on through a long half-hour, and more. Then there was a rumbling of wheels on the cobble stones, and she was at the window in an instant, flattening her face against the glass as she tried to look northward, whence the sound should come. It was Routh's carriage. That was a certainty, even before she caught sight of the yellow glare of the lamps, moving fan-like along the broad way. It was not likely that any other carriage should stray into the loneliness of Lafayette Place at that time of night. The carriage stopped. Hester saw a man get out, and heard the clap of the door of the brougham as it was sharply closed behind him. Immediately she was at the door, her hand on the handle, but her eyes turned anxiously upon Crowdie's face. The steps came up the stairs, and she looked out. It was Doctor Routh himself, for she had sent a very urgent message.

Without going upon the landing, she stretched out her hand and almost dragged him into the room, for somehow her terror increased to a frenzy as she saw him, and she felt that her heart could not go on beating long enough for him to speak. Her face was very grave, but she was only conscious of his deep violet-blue eyes that glanced at her keenly as he passed her. He had half guessed what was the matter, for the terrible breathing could be heard on the stairs.

Without hesitation he took the shade from the light, and held the little lamp close to Crowdie's face. He raised first one eyelid and then the other. The pupils were enormously dilated. Then he felt the pulse, listened to the heart, and shook his head almost imperceptibly. A moment later he was scratching words hastily in his note-book.

"Why didn't you send word that it was morphia?" he asked, sharply, without looking up. "Send that by the carriage, and tell them to be quick!" He thrust the note into her hands and almost pushed her from the room. "Make haste! I must have the things at once!" he called after her as she flew downstairs.

Then he tried such means as he had at hand, though he knew how useless they must be, doing everything possible to rouse the man from the poisoned sleep. He smiled grimly at his own folly, and laid the head upon its pillow again. Hester was in the room in a moment.

"It's morphia," he said, "and he's had an over-dose. How did he come to get it? Who gave it to him?"

"I did," answered Hester, in a clear voice, and her lips were white. "Will he die?" she whispered, with sudden horror.

She almost sprang at Routh as she asked the question, grasping his arm in both her hands.

"I don't know," he answered, slowly. "I'll try to bring him round. Control yourself, Mrs. Crowdie. This isn't the time for crying. Tell me what happened."

She told him something, brokenly, her memory half gone from fear — how something had happened to distress him, and he had turned red and fallen, twisted and unconscious — she did not know what she told him.

"Has it ever happened before?" asked Routh, who was holding her hands to quiet her, while she moved her feet nervously.

It had happened once, she told him, on a winter's evening when they had been alone. She could say that much, and then her eyes were drawn to Crowdie's face, and to the horror of it, as a bent spring flies back to its own line when released. Routh pressed her hand.

" Look at me, please," he said, authoritatively. " We can't do anything for him till my things come.   Tell me why you gave him morphia."

She had thought it was the right thing.   Her husband had told her that he had formerly taken a great deal of it.   He had suffered great pain when he had been younger, from an accident, and had fallen into the habit that kills.   But before they had been married he had given it up — for her sake.

Her eyes turned to him again.   She snatched her hands from Routh's and pressed them desperately to her ears to keep out the sound of his breathing.   But Routh drew her away and made her look at him again.

And these attacks came from having given up morphia, she told him.   Crowdie had said so.   He had told her that, of course, a dose of the poison would stop one of them, but that he was determined not to begin taking it again.   It would ruin his life and hers if he did.   The attacks gave him no pain, he had said.   He did not remember afterwards what had happened to him.   But of course they were bad for him, and might come more frequently.   He had been terribly distressed.   It had seemed to be breaking his heart, because it must give her pain. He had made her promise never to give him morphia when he was unconscious. He was determined not to fall back into the habit of it.

"Then why did you do it?" asked Routh, scrutinizing her pale face and frightened eyes.

She had imagined that it would save him pain, though he had told her that he recollected nothing of his sensations after the attack was past.

"He was all stiff and twisted!" she cried, in broken tones. "His hands were all twisted — his eyes turned up."

"But where did you get the morphia?" asked the physician, holding her before him, kindly, but so that she had to face him.

"He had it," she said. "I made him show it to me once. He kept it in a drawer with the little instrument for it. He showed me how to pinch the skin and prick it — it was so easy! There was the mixture in a bottle — the cork wouldn't come out — I did it with a hairpin — "

"How much did you give him?" enquired the doctor, bringing her back to her story, as her mind groped, terror-struck amongst its details.

"Why — the little syringe full — wasn't that right?" She saw the despair of life in his eyes. "Oh, God! My God!" she shrieked, breaking from his hands. "I've killed him!"

"I'm afraid you have," said Routh, but under

his breath, and she could not have heard him speak.

She threw herself wildly upon her husband's breast, clutching him with her small white hands, lifting herself upon them, staring into his face, and then shrieking as she fell forwards again, her hands tearing at her own thick brown hair. Routh knew that Crowdie could not be disturbed. He stood back from the bedside and watched her with far-seeing, dreaming eyes, while the first fever of despair burned itself out in a raving delirium. He had seen such sights many times in his life, but he remembered nothing more terrible than the grief of this woman who had killed her husband by a hideous mistake, thinking to save him pain, thinking it well to break a promise he had taken of her for his safety, and which she had believed had been only for his self-respect.

Crowdie was past saving. Routh did all that his science could do, trying in turn every known means of breaking the death sleep, trying to hem in the life before it was quite gone out, that the very least breath of it might be imprisoned in the body. But it was of no use. The poison was in the veins, in the brain, the subtle spirit of the opium devil distilled to an invisible enemy. The little hand of Fate, that had been so small and noiseless a few hours earlier, spread, gigantic, and grasped Science by the throat and shook her off. There was not anything to be done. And Hester twisted her hands, and moaned and shrieked, and beat her breast, like a woman mad, as indeed she was.

Routh had understood. Crowdie was an epileptic. He had perhaps believed himself cured when he had married his wife, and had been horrified by the first attack. He loved her, and he would naturally wish to hide from her the secret of his life. The general feeling about epilepsy is not like what is felt for any other human weakness. An epileptic is hardly regarded as a natural being, and the belief that the disease is hereditary brands it with an especial horror. It had been ingenious on Crowdie's part to invent the story about the morphia, and to carry it out and impress it on her by showing her the instrument and the bottle of poison. It was possible that there might have been some foundation of truth in the tale. He might have had the implements from a physician. But Routh, who had known him long, was convinced, for many reasons, that he had never been a victim to the habit of using the drug regularly. It had been very ingenious of the poor man. Hester could hardly have known anything of the after effects of breaking off such a habit, still less was it probable that she should know much about epilepsy, and trusting him as she did, it was natural that she should never have reported what he had told her to any one who might have explained the truth.

The only mistake he had made had been in not throwing away the poison, and refilling the bottle with pure water. He had miscalculated the anxiety she would feel to relieve him, if he ever had an attack again. The mistake had cost him his life.

Towards morning the house in Lafayette Place was very still again, though there were lights in the windows, and the shadows of people moving about within passed and repassed upon the shades. Only the policeman on his beat, looking up eastward and seeing the dawn in the sky and glancing at the windows, knew that there had been trouble in the house during the night, and guessed that for a day or two the blinds would not be raised. But all the great city began to breathe again, turning in its sleep, and waking drowsily in the cool spring dawning to begin its daily life of work and play and passion, unconscious of such trifles as the loss of a man, or the madness of a frantic woman's grief.

CHAPTER XXXIII.

It would have needed more imagination than Katharine Lauderdale possessed to suppose that the scene in which she acted a part during the afternoon could possibly lead to serious consequences. Had she been told how jealous Hester really was of her, she could not have realized what such jealousy meant. She had gone away much more hurt by Hester's coolness, and by her refusal to return to the old terms of friendship, than disturbed by the thought of the domestic quarrel she had left behind her. If Hester was jealous, foolishly, and if Crowdie had displeased both her and Katharine, the young girl considered it only fair that they should talk the matter over, and if Hester were angry, it might teach her husband to be more careful in future.

What had really affected her was the disenchantment she had felt when she found that Hester had no intention of renewing the relations which had existed before the affair of the will had produced a temporary estrangement. It had been another blow to another ideal, and another possibility of life was wiped away from the future.

Little by little her whole existence was being narrowed to one thought, one happiness, one belief, all centred in John Ralston. Of all the many people who had come into her young life, he alone had not brought her any permanent pain, nor any pain at all, save once, when she had been terribly mistaken about something he had done during the previous winter. More than once, indeed, and even within the past few weeks, they had been near to what would have made a disagreement between most lovers. But only near — no more. Just at that point when others might have taken offence foolishly, or spoken the hasty word that sets the whole fabric of love vibrating, and sometimes makes it rock and topple over and fall — just at that point one or the other of them had always yielded, and the danger had been over in an instant and as soon forgotten. It seemed as though they could never quarrel; and when they were weary, as they often had been of late, it rested them to be together even for a few moments.

So it had happened on that day when Ralston had met Katharine as she was coming from the Crowdies', and they had walked together, and made a plan which would have been put into execution at once, but for the news Bright had given them, and which momentarily checked them when they were on the point of disclosing their long-kept secret. Then they had parted, judging it wiser that John should stay away from the house that evening, and avoid the danger of irritating Alexander Junior's temper, which had most probably been more or less roused by the finding of another will.

Katharine went into the library before going to her room, with a vague idea of ascertaining the state of the family humour, if any one happened to be there. She was not disappointed, for her father and mother were together, Alexander sitting upright in Katharine's favourite chair, and Mrs. Lauderdale lying upon the sofa and staring at the ceiling. Katharine saw her first, and understood her mother's warning glance. It was clear that there had been a pause in the conversation. Alexander's face was cold and expressionless as he looked at his wife.

"Well," he said, in a tone of repressed but righteous indignation, "have you heard the news, Katharine? They've found another will."

"Yes," she answered, kissing her mother by force of habit rather than from any other motive. "I just met Hamilton Bright in the street. He told me."

"Oh, yes; he knows all about it." Alexander spoke with profound resentment, as though Bright were personally responsible for the second will. "Katharine, my dear, I don't think you've kissed me to-day. I didn't see you this morning."

Katharine looked at him in some surprise, smiled
a little foolishly, as people do when they cannot
understand exactly what is wanted of them, and
then rose almost before she had sat down. She
went to him and laid her cheek against his with
precision, and both he and she kissed the air audibly and simultaneously. Alexander Junior had
always detested anything like demonstration, but
he insisted, on the other hand, upon the punctual
execution of certain affectionate practices, as a
matter of household discipline.   Early or late the
air must be kissed when the cheeks were in contact.

"I thought I'd seen you," said Katharine, as she
retired again to her seat.

"No," answered Alexander, meditatively. "No
— I think not. My child," he continued, in a tone
unusually gentle for him, "do you think that without feeling that you are betraying my poor uncle
Robert's confidence, you could tell me what that
will contains ? "

She fancied from the way in which he spoke
that he had framed the question at his leisure
before she had come home, so as neither to offend
her nor to refer to his previous attempts to gain
her confidence. She hesitated a moment before
answering him, but he did not appear to be impatient. In her quick weighing of the case, she
could see little or no reason for not satisfying his
curiosity.

"Recollect, my dear, that I only wish you to speak about it, if you feel that you can do so with a perfectly clear conscience," he said.

"Oh, yes; of course!" she answered, repressing a smile. "But I don't really see why you shouldn't know. I think, while he was alive — well, that was different. But now — I think it's quite fair. Of course, I don't know what will this is. He may have made several, for all we know. But the one he told me about was like this. His idea was to make three trusts, all equal. Oh! — in the first place there was to be one million for the Brights, amongst the three, aunt Maggie, Hamilton, and Hester. Then the three equal shares of the rest were to go in trust to Charlotte and Jack Ralston and me — what did you say, papa?"

Alexander Junior had uttered an indistinct exclamation.

"Nothing," he said. "Go on."

"Each of us three was to pay half the income of a share to one of you three, you and mother, and Mrs. Ralston. But before that — I forgot to say it — each of us was to contribute something to make up an income for grandpapa — about fifty thousand dollars altogether, I think. Then the fortune was all to be in trust for our possible children. That was all. I don't think there was anything else."

"Do you mean to say that there was nothing

left outright to any of us older ones ? " asked
Alexander, in a tone of stupefaction.

" Well — you three had half the income amongst
you," answered Katharine.

" What an absurd will ! " exclaimed her father.

Then he bit his lip and sat in silence, looking at
his clasped hands.

" But it may not be that will, after all," he said,
in a low voice, after a long pause. " A man who
will leave one old will behind him may leave twenty.
Lawyers always say that any one who changes his
will once is sure to do it again and again."

He drew little consolation from the thought,
however, and he was suffering all that his arid
nature was capable of feeling, in the anticipation
of losing the control of the fortune which had been
practically within his grasp. But he had grown
used to uncertainty and emotion within the last
two months, and his face was set and hard. Nevertheless, he felt that he could not long bear the
eyes of the two women upon him in his trouble,
unless he made an effort of some sort.

" Did the will say nothing about the trusteeship? Who were to be the trustees ? " He asked
the question with a revival of interest.

" I don't know," answered Katharine. " I never
saw the will, of course. He only told me what I
have told you."

Alexander said nothing, but he slowly rose to

his feet, with less of energy and directness than he usually showed in his movements.

"We'll talk about it this evening," he said, and left the room.

When he was gone Katharine rose and went over and sat upon the sofa at her mother's feet. Mrs. Lauderdale had said nothing during the brief interview, but had watched her husband's face anxiously when he spoke, as though she had anticipated some outbreak of temper, at least.

"I'm glad you told him at once, dear," she said. "I'm very much troubled about him. I was afraid he'd be angry."

"Isn't it dreadful that any one should care so much?" Katharine spoke thoughtfully, and looked at the floor.

"I'm very anxious," answered Mrs. Lauderdale, not noticing what her daughter had said. "He has talked in his sleep all night. He talks of nothing but the money. Of course, it's incoherent, and I can't make out half of what he says. It's all the worse. I'm afraid his brain will be seriously affected if this goes on much longer."

"Mother — hasn't every one got some great passion like that, locked up inside of them, and trying to get out?"

Katharine looked up as she asked the question. Neither she nor her mother thought of those months of insane envy, which had almost separated them in heart forever.

"I never did," said Mrs. Lauderdale, innocently. "I never cared for anything like that."

"I have," said Katharine. "I do. It's just like my caring for Jack. You might as well try to face an express train as to stand in the way of it. I know just how papa feels — now. Only with him it's money. He'll upset the whole world to have it, as I'd turn the universe inside out rather than lose Jack. I suppose that's the meaning of the word passion — I'm beginning to understand it."

"It sounds much more like the meaning of sin," observed Mrs. Lauderdale. "I don't mean in your case, dear. Love's quite another thing. Perhaps I shouldn't have said it at all."

CHAPTER XXXIV.

EVEN Alexander Junior, more than preoccupied by his hopes and fears in regard to the will, was profoundly shocked by the news of Walter Crowdie's sudden death. Doctor Routh, as a friend of the family, took it upon himself to notify all the relations of what had taken place in the night, for during the first hours Hester had been incapable of any thought. He had undertaken to inform Hester's mother, and he wrote to the Lauderdales and the Ralstons at once, in order that they might not learn the news from the papers and accidentally.

No one of the family had ever liked poor Crowdie, but all of them had been fond of Hester at one period or another of her life, though she had never seemed to possess the power of keeping upon terms of intimacy with more than one of them at a time, and never with any for very long. The fact that the loss was hers softened every judgment of the man who was gone, and in the first anxiety which every one felt to show a sympathy which was genuine, Alexander Junior was perhaps the only one who remembered that

293

Mr. Allen was coming at eleven o'clock to open the document which had been found, before the eyes of the whole family. With a delicacy which might be attributed to the implacability of circumstances, but for which he was afterwards willing to take more credit than he got, he sent a message down town, explaining what had happened, and putting off the meeting until the afternoon. Alexander spent his morning in making sure that every one could be present, except Mrs. Bright. Hamilton would represent his mother and sister.

It seemed heartless to Katharine that no one — not even Hamilton Bright himself — should have suggested putting off the reading of the paper at least until the next day, and once more the ruthlessness of humanity was thrust upon her so that she could not help seeing it. It was true, she admitted, that in reality Crowdie had been the husband of a very distant cousin, and in theory neither the Lauderdales nor the Ralstons would be expected to suspend a curiosity which concerned the fate of a colossal fortune, for the matter of a death which hardly touched them. Yet Katharine thought that in practice people might show some feeling in such a case. What she saw was that the first shock was real and startling, but that half an hour after hearing the news her father and mother were discussing Crowdie's character with about as much

consideration as though he had been a dead China-
man, or a foreign prime minister. She registered
another bit of strong evidence against the efficacy
of professed religion, and shut herself up in her
room for the morning, for the mere satisfaction of
being alone and of asking herself what she had
really thought of Crowdie.

She had detested him. She had no doubt of
that. When she recalled a certain smile of his,
and thought of the redness of his lips, she shivered
and was disgusted. She did not like to remember his undulating, womanish gait, nor the pallor
of his face. Everything about him had repelled
her intensely. And yet, when she thought of
him lying dead at that moment, she felt a sharp
pang, which was very like what she might have
felt if she had really missed him. She could
not understand that. Then she remembered his
voice, and the enchantment of his singing on that
night at the Brights' the song of Lohengrin —
the song of the swan, she thought, as it had turned
out to be in truth, so far as she was concerned.
She wondered whether it were his voice that she
was really thinking of with regret. For she certainly felt the little pang. It came again when she
remembered that he was dead. She tried it two or
three times. It came once more, then very faintly,
then not at all, try as she might to think of him as
he probably looked. She had never seen any one

dead except old Robert Lauderdale, but that was a
recent memory. All the details of death were fresh
in her mind, and she could picture to herself the
quiet household, the subdued voices, the darkened
rooms, the flowers. The faint smell of them came
back to her. She wondered whether the smell had
been so peculiar, and faint, and sickening, because
they had been almost all white. But there was
no pang of 'missing' when she thought of the
old man. Yet she had been fond of him, and she
had detested Crowdie. She did not understand,
as she sat all alone thinking about it. She came
to the conclusion that when people die they are
missed in proportion to their vitality by those who
have not really loved them. Perhaps she was
right. The nature and causes of those sudden
thrusts which ordinarily sensitive people feel have
been very little studied.

But Katharine was sincerely sorry for Hester.
She did not know whether to go to her at once, or
to wait until the next day. Her impulse was to
go immediately, though she asked herself whether
Hester could possibly wish to see her, and she
tried to put herself in Hester's place. But the
thought that John Ralston might die brought such
a burst of pain with it that she rose from her seat
and walked about the room, breathing a little faster.
Then, having risen, she went downstairs and consulted her mother.

"If I were you, I should go," said Mrs. Lauderdale. "I'll go with you, if you like. You've always been her best friend. I'm sure she's been much nearer to you than your sister ever was, hasn't she? Of course she has. It can't do any harm to go and ask for aunt Maggie, and if Hester wants to see you, you can go up and I'll come home alone, or stay downstairs with aunt Maggie until you're ready."

"That sounds very sensible," said Katharine. "I'll get ready."

At the house in Lafayette Place everything seemed familiar to the young girl. It was just as she had anticipated. The blinds were drawn down. Old Fletcher, the butler, shuffled and looked red and lachrymose, as he opened the door. There was a strong smell of white flowers.

Presently Mrs. Bright appeared, pale and very grave, in a black frock which was too tight for her and rather old-fashioned — the last one she had worn in her long mourning for her husband. They went into the little room which had been the scene of the trouble on the previous evening. The drawing of old Robert Lauderdale still lay upon the table, where Crowdie had placed it; only the little tea-table was gone. Again Katharine felt that thrust at her heart which she could not explain. It all seemed so near, and yet what was upstairs made such a great difference.

They talked together in subdued tones for a few minutes. Aunt Maggie said that Hester was behaving very strangely, and that she was anxious about her. Walter had always seemed to possess a strange influence over her. Mrs. Bright could not understand it. She herself had never quite approved of the match, and Walter had never endeared himself to her, in spite of his talent and apparent devotion to his wife. Hester was acting very strangely. She was not wild now. She did not scream nor throw herself about. On the contrary, she was so calm that her quiet was positively terrifying. The people — by which term aunt Maggie meant the undertakers — could do nothing without her. She would hardly let them touch poor Walter — she wanted to do everything herself. She must certainly break down, and perhaps lose her reason. People sometimes went mad in that way, but it would be a pity — especially for such a man as Crowdie. No. Walter had never endeared himself to Mrs. Bright.

Katharine looked at the kind-hearted, stout, elderly woman, with her refined face and her air of superiority over the common herd, and wondered whether she had any real feelings. She hardly made a pretence of regret for the young life that had been cut short, though she seemed really anxious for her daughter. She was like the rest of them, thought Katharine, and she really had no heart. That was clear. She asked whether Hester would be willing to see her.

"Really," answered Mrs. Bright, "she's behaving so strangely, poor child, that there's no knowing what she may do. She may be angry if I don't tell that you're here. She's insisted on having him carried into the studio. Poor darling! I let her do as she pleases. But I'll go and ask her if she'd like to see you. It can't do any harm, at all events."

Aunt Maggie left the room, walking on tiptoe and listening before she actually went out, after opening the door.

"Mother, is everybody as heartless as that?" asked Katharine when she was gone, in a tone which seemed to expect no answer.

"Heartless?" repeated Mrs. Lauderdale. "I don't think she's heartless. She's dreadfully anxious about Hester."

"Yes; but about poor Mr. Crowdie — she doesn't seem to care in the least."

"Oh, no — she never liked him. Why should she? Take care, though! somebody might hear us talking."

Katharine sighed and was silent. Her mother did not seem to understand what she meant any more than any one else. After the first shock they all appeared to be perfectly indifferent. Crowdie was dead. Bury him! Doubtless they were already wondering whether Hester would marry again, and if so, when. Yet Katharine knew that they would all be shocked if Hester wore mourning less than three years. It was her business to mourn; it was theirs, in the interest of society, to see that she mourned long and decently for a man whom they had all disliked.

Before long Mrs. Bright returned, softly as she had gone, shut the door noiselessly behind her, and looked round the room as though she thought that some fourth person might be present and listening. Then, with an air of secrecy, she spoke to Katharine.

"My dear, she'll see you if you'll come upstairs."

"Certainly," answered Katharine. "I'll go at once."

"But you mustn't be surprised by anything she does," said Mrs. Bright, anxiously. "She'll want you to see him, I think. She's looking very quiet, but she's very strange. Humour her, Katharine — humour her a little."

Katharine nodded, but said nothing.

"She's waiting for you on the landing outside the studio," added Mrs. Bright. "I needn't go up with you, need I? I've just been up all those stairs."

"Of course not," Katharine answered.

As she went something oddly like fear got hold of her, and her heart fluttered unexpectedly. She was conscious that she was pale as she ascended to the top of the house. Probably, she thought, it was the idea of seeing the dead man's face that affected her unpleasantly. She nerved herself to make an effort and went on, wondering that it should be so strangely hard to go.

As she began to go up the last flight of stairs she was conscious that Hester was standing at the top, waiting for her. She wished that she had not offered to come. Then she looked up and met the deep eyes, and saw the ghastly face turned towards her. Hester was excessively pale, and even her lips were colourless. Her slight figure looked taller than usual in the straight loose gown of black, and her hands, clasped together upon the banister, had the emaciated, nervous look of some hands in pictures by the early painters. Exhaustion, in some people, shows itself in the hands before it appears in the face.

Katharine reached the top of the flight and stood still, looking at her, wishing to speak but not finding words just then. They had parted almost, if not quite, as enemies, on the previous day. Katharine went a step nearer. Her face showed well enough the deep sympathy she felt, but Hester did not exactly look at her face, but only into her eyes, with a fixed stare that made the young girl feel uneasy. That stare alone would have justified Mrs. Bright in saying that her daughter was behaving strangely. The transparent hands unclasped one another, but they fell straight to her sides. As Katharine extended her own, Hester drew back, the stare became more fixed, the eyes opened more, till they were very wide, the finely pencilled brows were raised haughtily, and the shadowy figure seemed to grow taller. Then she spoke, slowly and distinctly, in a voice that did not tremble.

" I wanted to see you.   Come with me."

She turned and opened the door of the studio, leading the way. Katharine was startled by what she saw. The great room had been darkened as much as possible by drawing all the thick shades, which had been made to keep out the sun in summer, and a great number of candles were burning with a dim, yellow light. The air was thick with the smoke of burning perfumes, which rose in tall, straight, grey plumes, from two censers placed upon the hearth before the huge chimney-piece. In the absolutely still atmosphere the smoke rose to the height of a man before it broke and opened, hanging then like draped grey curtains in the heavy air. The strange, cool smell of burning myrrh predominated, but in spite of it the drowsy, overpowering odour of frankincense reached Katharine's nostrils. She stood still and stared through the smoke.

In the middle of the room Crowdie lay dead,

clothed in a long garment of stuff that was soft and dark. The couch was covered with a silken carpet which hung down to the floor. The pale light of death softened and beautified the repulsive features, in their solemn calm, to a degree which Katharine would not have believed possible, had she been capable of thought just then. But she was taken by surprise; she was a little frightened, and she was dazed by the glare of the many candles, and dizzy with the sudden breathing of the perfume-laden air. She stood still at a little distance from the couch and looked at the dead face, stretching her head forward with a sort of timid curiosity, holding her body back with the instinctive dread of death which the young feel in spite of themselves.

Hester did not stand beside her. With slow steps, as though she were moving with a solemn procession to the rhythm of a funeral march, sweeping her long black gown noiselessly behind her, she passed to the other side, and came up to the couch and stood over her husband's body, facing Katharine. In the shadowy smoke of the incense, with the flaring light of the wax candles upon her, she was like a supernatural being. She might have been the freed soul of the dead man, come back to look once more at Katharine's face.

"Come nearer to me," she said, in deadly calm, without a tremor.

An older woman might not have obeyed the summons, and might have realized that Hester Crowdie was to all intents and purposes mad, since it could not be supposed that she had planned a tragic scene, with a theatrical instinct nowhere at fault, even in a single detail. But there was something really terrible and grand in it, as it struck Katharine; and there was the grim reality of death lying there and vouching for the widowed woman's sincerity. To those not familiar with the dead, nothing can seem like comedy in their silent presence. To those for whom death has lost all horror, there is scarcely anything but comedy, anywhere.

Katharine obeyed and went nearer, but not as near as Hester herself. Instinctively she held back her skirts, as though fearing even the contact of the carpet on which Crowdie lay. Her right hand she still carried in a scarf.

Hester's fixed gaze met her again, and she was conscious that her own eyes were uncertain. There was an irresistible something which drew them to the dead man's face. But when Hester spoke again the young girl looked at her.

"Katharine Lauderdale, this is your doing, and this is what you have done to me."

The words came clearly, like those she had spoken before, monotonously and distinctly, as though she had learned them by rote. Katharine started at first, and opened her eyes wider, as though doubting whether she were in her senses. But she found no word to say, though her lips were parted.

"You have killed my husband. You have destroyed my life. I have brought you here to see what you have done."

Katharine did not start this time, but she drew back a little, with an indescribable horror that was not fear.

"You must be mad," she said, in a low voice, keeping her eyes on Hester's.

A strange, fantastic smile played upon the pale lips, and looked more than unnatural in the yellow glare of the candles.

"I wish I were mad," she said.

In the long silence which followed, Katharine glanced at the dead man's face. Its set, waxen smile was like Hester's, and the girl felt a creeping shudder in her shoulders. She bent her body a little.

"He cannot hurt you," said Hester, holding her with inexorable eyes. "He knows that you have killed him, but he cannot hurt you. If he could, he would — for my sake. Come close to him and look at him."

Katharine came forward again, more because she was brave and would not even seem afraid, than for any other reason.

"My dear Hester," she said, trying to speak

naturally, but in a low voice, "you're beside yourself with grief. You don't know what you're
saying."

"I know what I am saying," answered the
widowed woman, solemnly. "You shall listen to
all I have to say. Then you shall go, and I will
never see you again until you are dead. Then I
will come and look at you, for his sake. You tried
to steal him from me while he was living. He is
mine now, to keep forever. You cannot get him.
Look at him, for he is mine. The last words he
ever heard me speak were cruel, unkind words.
Then he fell. He did not speak afterwards. I
gave him the morphia. I told you my story once
— but it was not the true story. It killed him.
It was my hand that killed him, through your
soul, and your soul shall pay me. I am not mad.
You have done this to me. You know it now.
You made me speak those last words he heard."

Katharine listened in silence — chilled with a
sort of horror of which she had never dreamt.
There was an unnatural terror for her in the
woman's deadly calm. There was no passion in
the voice, no hatred, no jealousy. It was as
though she were possessed by an unseen power
that used her mouth to speak with, and controlled
her, and against which she could do nothing.

"Have you heard? Do you know now?" she
asked after a pause.

Still Katharine did not speak. A new sensation of fear crept upon her. She began to think that the dead man's lips moved and that the quiet lids trembled, and she could not take her eyes from the face.

"You have no heart," said the voice. "You are the worst woman alive to-day, anywhere in the whole world. You said you were my friend, and you have done this thing to me. You have done it. No one else has done it. It is all your fault. You pretended that you loved me like a sister, and you came often, and he saw you. You are more beautiful than I am, and he saw that you were. But he did not love you. Oh, no! He loved me. You pleased his eyes as everything beautiful pleased him. He did not know how bad you were. But I made him say that he hated you, — he said it twice before he died, — and you had only pleased his eyes. But now they are closed, and you cannot please him any more, because he cannot see you."

Katharine looked up slowly, realizing that the woman was insane. She had never seen an insane person, and it had been hard to understand at first. She did not know what to do. Her blood froze at her throat — she could feel the cold at her collar. Still the monotonous voice went on speaking, while the incense and the myrrh sent up their straight plumes of smoke into the cloudy air, and the heavy perfumes grew more and more oppressive and stupefying.

"You pleased him so much that he broke his promise to me, and it was almost the only promise I had ever asked of him. He sang to you, because you pleased him so much. I will not forgive you. I never will. But he is dead now. See! I kiss him. He does not open his eyes as he used to do when I kissed him softly."

The dark figure bent down and Hester kissed the dead face, and again her unnatural smile seemed to be reflected in it.

"He smiles," she said. "But he cannot kiss me. And he cannot sing to you any more. You made him do it once. He will not do it again. Once you made him break his promise. He will not break it again. He will keep it. The dead keep their promises, and he has promised to be mine always now. I am not so sorry that he is dead, because he will be always mine. He smiles, you see. He knows it. He does not want you, because you cannot please him now that his eyes are shut so fast. He does not want you now. Go away, Katharine Lauderdale. Walter does not want you."

There was no rising intonation in the voice that spoke, no emphasis, no authority. But the calm, unchanging tone was far more terrifying than any passionate outburst could have been. Katharine shrank back, and then stood still a moment.

"Why do you stay?" asked the voice. "We hate you. Go away. You see that we want to be alone together. We do not want you."

Katharine felt herself growing white with the horror of it all. She bowed her head in silence and went to the door, turning a moment to look back as her hand was on the spring. She felt as though she were in some mysterious tomb of ancient days, where the living and the dead were buried together — the rigid dead upon his couch, the living beside him, flexible, mad, dangerous with the overstrain of an incredible, inexpressible grief.

The dark figure stood erect with dropped and folded hands. The white face stood out luminously pale against the grey smoke-clouds of the incense and myrrh, the yellow flaming candles flickered still from the draught of Katharine's dress as she had passed and threw an uncertain, moving light upon the motionless mask of the dead man.

"Leave us alone together. We want to be alone together. Go away and never come back to us again."

Katharine was going, but her terror suddenly overcame her, and she opened the door, went out, and closed it behind her in a flash, gasping for a breath of unscented air. She reeled as she came out, under the clear daylight of the glass roof which covered the staircase, and she steadied herself against the door-post, stupidly staring at the tapestry on the opposite wall. She felt sick and faint, and for a moment she knew that she could not get downstairs without falling. She felt that she was full of the perfume-loaded air she had breathed, that it clung to her like a blanket, and hindered her from drawing a full breath. She raised her left arm to her face mechanically, and smelled it. The stuff was full of the incense, and she threw her head back with parted lips, to draw in freshness if she could.

She was so strong that she did not faint, but stood erect against the door-post until she could trust herself to walk. She listened at the door for a moment to hear whether the mad woman were still talking over her dead husband, or whether, perhaps, the madness had suddenly yielded to the merciful tide of tears. But there was no sound. They were alone together, as Hester had said that they wished to be.

Katharine pressed her hand to her eyes with all her might, as though to crush out the memory of what she had seen. Then she went forward at last, and began to go down the stairs.

She heard a man's footstep, swift, nervous and strong, coming up from below, and as she reached the first landing she came face to face with Paul Griggs. His weather-beaten face was so grey and drawn that she should hardly have known him in

a crowd, and the weary, dark eyes that met hers had
something in them which she could not understand.
He stood aside to let her pass, but would have said
nothing had she not spoken.

"She's alone with him, up there," she said in
a sort of scared whisper. "She's going mad—it's
dreadful."

Griggs looked as though he would have gone
on without answering, though he did not actually
make a step. His dark eyes were dull and glassy,
and his jaws were set, as though he were in great
pain.

"Can't you do something for her?" asked
Katharine, hesitating. "Shouldn't we send for
Doctor Routh? He might give her something."

She made the suggestion vaguely, as women do.
There is something pathetic about their blind faith
in medicine, though they may have seen it fail
a hundred times.

"If you like," answered Griggs, in a far-away
tone, as though he scarcely knew what she was
saying. "Send for him if you like. I don't
care."

Katharine stared at him in surprise. He was
sometimes a little absent-minded, but she could
not understand his being so at that moment. She
laid her left hand upon his arm with a gesture half
of appeal, half of authority.

"Something must be done," she said. "She's

really going mad. She mustn't be left alone with
it any longer."

"I don't think she'll go mad," Griggs answered.
"But I shall," he added, with an unnatural smile,
which recalled Hester's.

"You!" exclaimed Katharine, in a sudden astonishment which made her forget everything else
for an instant. "Why? I know you liked him—"

"Liked him!" repeated Paul Griggs, in a voice
that was almost loud, and the dull eyes flashed for
a moment, and then became glassy again. "I can't
talk now," he said, rapidly. "Forgive me—I
can't stop!"'

Without waiting for her to go down, he sprang
up the stairs. Katharine looked after him with
wonder. A moment later she heard the door of
the studio open and shut quickly, and she was sure
that she heard one word, a name—Walter—
spoken in the broken accent of a man's despair.

Again she paused before she went downstairs,
and hesitated, not as to what she should do, but as
to what she should think. At least, she felt that
her friend Griggs was not without heart, whatever
the true ground of his extraordinary emotion might
be. She had stumbled upon one of those mysteries
which lie so near the dull surface of society around
us, and had seen a human soul at that moment of
all others when it would not have been seen. As
she thought of it, she felt at the same moment the

instinct to tell no one, not even Ralston, of the few
words she had exchanged with Griggs on the stairs.
The resolution formed itself in her mind unintentionally, as a natural prompting of honour against
the betrayal of a secret accidentally learned. What
the secret could be she could not guess, and it was
long before she knew, but she did not break the
promise which had formulated and pledged itself.
Long afterwards, when she learned the strange
story of Griggs' life, which no one had ever suspected, she wondered that on that day he had not
killed her with his hands rather than be delayed
the smallest fraction of an instant on his way up
those stairs. In his place, woman as she was, she
would have been less merciful, and she would not
have been courteous at all.

But she knew nothing of the wanderer's existence, save that he had of late strayed into her own,
and that he had seemed oddly attached to a man
who was almost universally disliked without any
well-defined reason. Her intuition told her that he
had something to conceal, and her faith in him, such
as it was, led her to believe that it was something
not wrong, but sacred almost beyond anything
imaginable.

She went quietly downstairs, and many things
happened to her, good and bad, before she saw the
face of Paul Griggs again. She found her mother
and Mrs. Bright sitting side by side, and aunt

Maggie was holding Mrs. Lauderdale's hand, and admiring her bonnet. A death which does not come too near to them draws certain types of women together. As Katharine entered the room and saw the two together, she wondered whether the death of Walter Crowdie was to have the effect of reconciling the Lauderdales and the Brights.

"Well, child, have you seen her?" asked Katharine's mother, with a considerable show of interest.

CHAPTER XXXV.

"People don't often really go mad from grief," said Mrs. Lauderdale, as she and Katharine walked slowly homeward in the bright spring afternoon. "I shouldn't be surprised if Hester married again in a few years. Not very soon, of course — but in time. She's very young yet. She'll be very young still in five years — for a widow."

"I don't think she can ever get over it," answered Katharine, rather coldly, being displeased at her mother's careless way of speaking.

"It's a mistake to take things too hard," said the elder woman. "And it's a great mistake to underrate time. A great many curious things can happen to one in five years."

Katharine was not in search of unbelief, nor of encouragement in not believing that human nature could really feel. Her faith in it had been terribly undermined during the past winter, and she had just been with two persons, Hester Crowdie and Paul Griggs, whose behaviour had at least tended to restore it. She did not wish the recuperative effort of her charity towards mankind to be checked. So she did not argue the point, but walked on in silence.

She had not recovered, and could not recover for many days, from the impression produced upon her by the ghastly scene in the studio. Her young vitality abhorred death, and its contrary and hostile principle, and when she thought of what she had seen, she felt the same sickening, shrinking horror which had led her to hold back her skirt from any possible contact with the carpet on which Crowdie's body had been lying. She might have been willing to admit that her mother, who had seen nothing, but had sat downstairs talking with the comfortable, fat and refined aunt Maggie, was not called upon to feel what she herself felt after going through such a strange experience. But since her mother felt nothing, her mother could not understand; and if she could not understand it was better to walk on in silence and to make her hasten her indolent, graceful steps.

In reality, Mrs. Lauderdale was much more preoccupied about the possibilities of the second will turning out to be favourable to her husband or the contrary, and her preoccupation was not at all sordid, though it was by no means unselfish. She was anxious about him, in her unobtrusive, calm way. He talked of money in his sleep, as she had told Katharine, and he was growing nervous. She had even noticed once or twice of late that his hand shook a little as he held the morning paper after breakfast, during the ten minutes which he devoted to its perusal. That was a bad sign, she thought, for a man who had been famous for his good nerve, and who had been known all his life as an unerring shot. She did not like to think what consequences a great disappointment might have upon his temper, which had shown itself so frequently of late, after nearly a quarter of a century of comparative quiescence. Nor was it pleasant to contemplate the new means of economy which he would certainly introduce into his household if by any evil chance he got no share of the Lauderdale fortune. But that, she told herself, was impossible, as indeed it seemed to be.

It was of no use to be in a hurry, she told Katharine, as they had at least an hour to get rid of before the time at which Mr. Allen was to be expected. The Ralstons and Hamilton Bright would only come a few minutes earlier. Every one would understand how unpleasant it might be to be shut up together in such suspense for half an hour before the truth could be known—each hoping to get the other's money, as Mrs. Lauderdale observed with a little laugh that had hardly any cruelty in it. But, of course, nobody would be late on such an occasion. There was no fear of that. And she laughed again, and stepped gracefully aside on the pavement to let a boy with a big bundle go by.

She had not been deceived in her calculations, for there was still plenty of time to spare when they reached the house in Clinton Place. Katharine disappeared to her room, glad to be alone at last. There was a hushed expectation in the air of the house, which reminded her of the place she had just left, but she herself felt not the smallest interest in the will. So far as she was concerned, she was perfectly well satisfied with the course taken by the law, independently of any will at all.

The Ralstons and Hamilton Bright came almost at the same moment, though not together, and Katharine had no chance of exchanging a word with John out of hearing of the rest. They all met in the library. The old philanthropist was there, and every one was secretly surprised to discover what a very fine-looking old man he was in a perfectly new frock coat with a great deal of silk in front. But his heavy, shapeless shoes betrayed his lingering attachment to the little Italian shoemaker in South Fifth Avenue, whose conscientiously durable works promised to outlast old Alexander's need for them.

Alexander Junior stood before the empty fireplace, coldly nervous. He could not have sat still for five minutes just then. When he spoke of Crowdie's death to Hamilton Bright, and immediately afterwards of the weather, his steel-trap mouth opened and closed mechanically, emitting

metallic sounds — it could not be called speaking
— and his glittering grey eyes went restlessly
from the window to the door and back again, without even resting on Bright's face.

Bright himself was grave, manly, quiet, as he
generally was. He was eminently the man who
could be reckoned with and counted upon. He
would make no attempt to conceal his disappointment if he were disappointed, nor his satisfaction
if he were pleased, but the expression of either
would be simple, quiet and manly, with few words,
if any.

Mrs. Ralston watched the two as they stood side
by side. From her position on the sofa she could
see Alexander Junior's hands twitching nervously
behind him. But she was talking with Mrs. Lauderdale at the same time. She made no pretence
of being very sorry to hear of Crowdie's sudden
death. She rarely saw him and she had never
liked him. To her, he was merely the husband
of a very distant cousin — of a descendant of her
great-grandfather through a female branch. It
was too much to expect that she should be profoundly affected by what had happened. But her
dark, clearly cut features were grave, and there
was a certain expectancy in her look, which showed
that she was not really indifferent to the nature
of the events momentarily expected. She admitted
frankly to herself that it would make an enormous

difference in her future happiness to be very rich
instead of being almost poor, and she had told her
son so as they came to the house.

John was trying to talk to Katharine near the
window, but he found it impossible to shake off
Alexander Senior, whose fondness for his favourite
granddaughter was proverbial in the family. The
old gentleman stood by, approvingly, and insisted
upon leading the conversation which, with old-
fashioned grandfatherly wit — or what passed for
wit in the families of our grandfathers — he constantly directed upon the subject of matrimony,
with an elephantine sprightliness most irritating to
John Ralston, though Katharine bore it with indifferent serenity, and smiled when the old man
looked at her, her features growing grave again as
soon as he turned to John. She could not shake
off the terrible impression she had brought with
her, and yet she longed to explain to John why
she felt and looked so sad. She, also, glanced often
at the door. The arrival of the family lawyer
would put a stop to her grandfather's playful per-
secution of her, and give her a chance to say three
words to John without being overheard.

Ralston stood ready, knowing that she wished
to speak to him alone, and he paid little attention
to Alexander Senior's jokes. He glanced about
the room and said to himself that the members of
the Lauderdale tribe were a very good-looking set,

from first to last. He was proud of his family just then, for he had rarely seen so many of them assembled together without the presence of any stranger, and he was most proud of Katharine's beauty. Pallor was becoming to her, for hers was fresh and clear and youthful. It ruined her mother's looks to be pale, especially of late, since the imperceptible lines had been drawn into very fine but clearly discernible wrinkles. Mrs. Lauderdale had told herself with tears that they were really wrinkles, but she would have been sorry to know that John, or any one else, called them by that name.

At last the lawyer came, and there was a dead silence as he entered — a tall, lantern-jawed man, clean shaven, almost bald, with prominent yellow teeth, over which his mobile lips fitted as though they had been made of shrivelled pink indiarubber. He had very light blue eyes and bushy brows that stood out in contrast to his bald scalp and beardless face like a few shaggy firs that have survived the destruction of a forest.

He spoke in an impressive manner, for he was deaf, emphasizing almost every word in every sentence. He was a New Englander by birth, as keen and provincial in New York as ever was a Scotchman in London.

Having been duly welcomed, and provided with a seat in the midst of the assembled tribe, he leisurely produced a pair of gold-rimmed glasses and a handkerchief, and proceeded to the operation of polishing the one with the other. He was provokingly slow. His chair was placed so that he sat with his back to the window, facing Mrs. Lauderdale and Mrs. Ralston, who occupied the sofa on the right of the fireplace. The two Alexanders and Bright completed the circle, while Katharine and John placed themselves behind the lawyer. John could see over his shoulder.

Not a word was spoken while Mr. Allen made his careful preparations. It could hardly be supposed that he had any traditional remnant of the old-fashioned attorney's vanity, which made him anxious to produce an effect by taking as long as possible in settling himself to his work. He was simply a leisurely man, who had been born before the days of hurry, and was living to see hurry considered as an obsolete affectation, no longer necessary, and no longer the fashion. There is haste in some things, still, in New York, but not the haste that we of the generation in middle age remember when we were young men. Mr. Allen, however, had never been hasty; and he found himself fashionable in his old age, as he had been in his youth, long before the civil war.

When his glasses were fairly pinching the lower part of his thin grey nose, he thrust one bony hand into his breast-pocket, leaning forward as he did so, and quietly scanning the faces of his audience, one after the other. He was so very slow that John and Katharine looked at one another and smiled. From his pocket he brought out a great bundle of papers and letters, and calmly proceeded to look through them from the beginning, in search of what he wanted. Of course, the big blue envelope was the last of a number of big blue envelopes, and the last but one of all the papers.

"This is it, I think," said Mr. Allen, with dignity and caution.

The two elder women drew two short little breaths of expectation, sat forward a little, and then thoughtfully smoothed their frocks over their knees. Alexander Junior's knuckles cracked audibly, as he silently twined his fingers round one another, and pulled at them in his anxiety. Hamilton Bright uncrossed his legs, and recrossed them in the opposite way. Katharine sighed. She was tired of it all, before it had begun.

"Yes," said Mr. Allen, with even more dignity, but with less caution in making the assertion, "I believe this is it."

"Thank the Lord!" exclaimed John Ralston from behind the lawyer, who was deaf.

Mrs. Ralston smiled a little, and avoided her son's eyes. Hamilton Bright looked absolutely impassive.

"You all see what it is," said Mr. Allen. "It

is a large blue envelope, gummed without a seal,
marked 'Will,' in a handwriting which may be
that of the late Mr. Lauderdale, though I should
not be prepared to swear to it, and dated 'March'
of this year. It is reasonable to suppose that it
contains a will made in that month, and therefore
prior to the one of which we have knowledge.
Mr. Lauderdale " — he turned to Alexander Senior
— "and you, Mrs. Ralston — with your consent, I
will open this document in your presence."

" By all means — open it," said Alexander
Junior, with evident impatience.

" Certainly, certainly, Mr. Allen," said his father.
" That's what we expect."

Mrs. Ralston contented herself with nodding
her assent, when the lawyer looked at her. He
searched for a penknife in his pocket, found it,
opened it, and with infinite care slit the envelope
from end to end. After carefully shutting the
knife, and returning it to his pocket again, he
withdrew a thick, folded sheet of heavy foolscap.
As he did so, a smaller piece of paper, folded only
once, fluttered to the ground at his feet. It might
have been a note of old Robert Lauderdale's, expressing some particular last wish of such a nature
as not to have found its proper place in a document of such importance as the will itself. The
eyes of every one being intent upon the latter, as
Mr. Allen opened it, no one paid any attention
to the bit of paper.

Mr. Allen was old and formal, and he had no intention of bestowing a preliminary glance at the contents of the paper before reading it. He began at the beginning, for the first words proved it to be a will, and nothing else. It began, as many American wills do, with the words, "In the name of God. Amen." Then followed the clause revoking all previous wills, each and every one of them; and then the other, relating to the payment of just debts and funeral expenses. Then Mr. Allen paused, and drew breath.

The tension in the atmosphere of the room was high, at that moment of supreme anxiety.

"'It is my purpose,'" Mr. Allen read, "'to so distribute the wealth which has accumulated in my hands as to distribute it amongst those of my fellow creatures who stand most directly in need of such help —'"

There was a general movement in the circle. Everybody started. Alexander Junior's hands dropped by his sides, and his steel-trap mouth relaxed and opened.

"Go on!" he said, breathlessly.

Mr. Allen went on, shaking his head from time to time, as his only expression of overwhelming stupefaction. It was by far the most extraordinary will he had ever seen; but it was legally and properly worded, with endlessly long, unpunctuated sentences, all of which tended to elucidate the already sufficiently clear meaning. In half-a-dozen words, it is sufficient to say that the will constituted the whole fortune, without legacies, and without mention of heirs or relatives, into a gigantic trust, to be managed, for the final extinction of poverty in the city of New York, by a board of trustees, to exist in perpetuity. Many conditions were imposed, and many possible cases foreseen. There were elaborate rules for filling vacancies in the trusteeship, and many other clauses necessary for the administration of such a vast charitable foundation, all carefully thought out and clearly stated. The perspiration stood upon the old lawyer's astonished head, as he continued to read.

Alexander Junior seemed to be absolutely paralyzed, and stared like a man distracted, who sees nothing, with wide-open eyes. Even Mrs. Ralston bent her dark brows, and bit her even lips, in disappointment. Hamilton Bright bent down, leaning his elbows upon his knees, and looked at the fourth page of the vast sheet of closely written foolscap.

"We're a pack of fools!" he exclaimed, suddenly. "The will isn't signed."

Alexander Junior uttered a loud exclamation, sprang to his feet, and snatched the will from the lawyer's hand so roughly as to brush the gold-rimmed glasses from his thin nose, on which they had pinched their unsteady hold, and they fell to the ground.

"Eh? What?" he asked, very much disturbed by such rude interruption.

Alexander had turned to the end, and had seen that it was a blank, without signatures either of testator or witnesses.

"Thank God!" he exclaimed, fervently, as he dropped back into his chair. "That almost killed me," he added in a low voice, regardless of the others.

But no one paid much attention to him. Hamilton Bright remained impassive. Each of the others uttered an exclamation, or breathed a sigh of relief. For some minutes afterwards there was a dead silence.

Mr. Allen was fumbling on the floor for his gold-rimmed glasses, still very much confused. They had managed to get under the low chair in which he sat, and which had a long fringe on it, reaching almost to the ground, so that he took some time in finding them.

"Of course he would never have signed such a thing!" said Hamilton Bright, with emphasis. "He had too much sense."

"I should think so!" exclaimed Mrs. Lauderdale. "The only thing I can't understand is how it ever was kept and marked 'Will.'"

"Uncle Robert once told me that he had often made sketches of wills leaving all his money in trust to the poor," said Katharine. "He never

meant to sign one, though. This must be one of
them — of course — it can't be anything else!"

"His secretary probably put it away, supposing
he wanted to keep it," said Ralston, from behind
Mr. Allen. "Then he forgot all about it, and so it
turned up among the papers. It's simple enough."

"Oh, quite simple!" assented Alexander Junior,
with a half-hysterical laugh.

Mrs. Ralston was watching the lawyer as he felt
for his glasses on the carpet. He paused, wiped
his brow — for it was a warm afternoon, and he
had been nervously excited himself in reading the
document. Then he continued his search.

"There's a bit of paper there on the floor, beside
your hand," said Mrs. Ralston. "I saw it drop
when you opened the envelope. Perhaps it's something more important."

Mr. Allen recovered his glasses at that moment,
and with the other hand took up the little folded
sheet. With the utmost care and precision he
went through the same preparations for reading
which had been indispensable on the first occasion.

"Let us see, let us see," he said. "This is
something. 'I hereby certify,' — oh, an old marriage certificate of yours, Mrs. Ralston. John
Ralston and Katharine Lauderdale — married —
dear me! I don't understand! This year, too!
This is very strange."

Again every one present started, but with very

different expressions. Hamilton Bright grew slowly red. There was a short pause. Then John Ralston rose to his feet and bent over Mr. Allen's shoulder.

"It's our certificate," he said, quietly. "Katharine's and mine. We were married last winter."

And he took the paper from the hands of the wondering lawyer, and held it in his own.

"Katharine!" cried Mrs. Lauderdale, when she had realized the meaning of Ralston's words.

"Katharine!" cried Alexander Junior, almost at the same moment.

At any other time some one of all those present might have smiled at the difference in intonation between Mrs. Lauderdale's cry of unmixed astonishment, and her husband's deprecatory but forgiving utterance of his daughter's name. Both conveyed, in widely differing ways, as much as whole phrases could have told, namely, that Mrs. Lauderdale was sincerely pleased, in spite of all her former opposition to the marriage, and that her husband, while he would much rather have his daughter married to Ralston secretly than not at all, felt that his dignity and parental authority had been outraged, and that he would be glad to have an apology, if any were to be had, of which condition his voice also expressed a doubt.

"I'll tell you all about it, from the beginning," said John Ralston.

He told the story in as few words as he could, omitting, as he had done in telling his mother, to give Katharine her full share of responsibility. She bent far forward in her seat while he was speaking, and leaned upon the back of Mr. Allen's chair, never taking her eyes from her husband's face. More than once her eyes brightened with a sort of affectionate indignation, and her lips parted as though she would speak. But she did not interrupt him. When he had finished he stood still in his place, looking at his father-in-law, and still holding the certificate of his marriage in his hand.

Alexander Junior would have found it hard to be angry just at that moment. He had his desire. In the course of five minutes he had been cast down from a position of enormous wealth and power, since there could be no question but that the half of the great estate would really be in his control if there were no will; he had been plunged into such a depth of despair as only the real miser can understand when his hundreds or his millions, as the case may be, are swept out of sight and out of reach by a breath; and he had been restored to the pinnacle of happiness again, almost before there had been time to make his suffering seem more than the passing vision of a hideous dream. Moreover, the marriage being already accomplished and a matter of fact, made it a positive certainty that all that part of the fortune which belonged to the Ralstons would return to his own grandchildren. His outraged sense of parental importance was virtuously, but silently, indignant, and he admitted that, on the whole, the causes of satisfaction outnumbered any reasons there might be for displeasure. Something, however, must be done to propitiate the prejudices of the world, which had much force with him.

"I think we'd better all go into the country as soon as possible," he observed, thinking aloud.

But no one heard him, for Katharine had risen and come forward and stood beside her husband, slipping her arm through his, and invisibly pressing him to her — unconsciously, too, perhaps — whenever she wished to emphasize a word in what she said.

"I want to say something," she began, raising her voice. "It's all my fault, you know. I did it. I persuaded Jack one evening, here in this very room — and it was awfully hard to persuade him, I assure you! He didn't like it in the least. He said it wasn't a perfectly fair and honest thing to do. But I made him see it differently. I'm not sure that I was right. You see, we should have been married, anyway, as it's turned out, because papa's been so nice about it in the end. That's all I wanted to say."

There was probably no malice in her diplomatic

allusion to her father. The only person who smiled at it was Mrs. Ralston.

"Except," added Katharine, by an afterthought, "that the reason why we did it was because we wanted to be sure of getting each other in the end."

"Well," said Hamilton Bright, who was very red, "I suppose the next thing to do is to congratulate you, isn't it? Here goes. Jack, I'm sorry I slated secret marriages the other day. You see, one doesn't always know."

"No," observed Mrs. Lauderdale, who had her arms around her daughter's neck. "One doesn't — as Ham says."

"That's all right, Ham," said John Ralston. "I didn't mind a bit."

But Hamilton Bright minded very much, in his quiet way, for he had played a losing game of late, and the same hour had deprived him of all hope of marrying Katharine, faint as it had been since she had so definitely refused him, and of all prospect of ever getting a share of the Lauderdale fortune. But he was a very brave man, and better able than most of those present to bear such misfortunes as fell to his lot. As for marrying, he put it out of his thoughts; and so far as fortune was concerned, he was prosperous and successful in all that he undertook to do himself, unaided, which is, after all, the most satisfactory success a man can have in the long run. The right to say 'I did

it alone' compensates for many fancied and real
wrongs. And that was something which Hamilton
Bright had very often been able to say with truth.
But his love for Katharine Lauderdale had been
honest, enduring and generally silent. Never had
he spoken to her of love until he had fancied that
his friend John Ralston had no intention, nor she,
either, of anything serious.

It was with the consent and approval of all her
family that Katharine entered upon her married
life at last, after having been secretly and in name
the wedded wife of John Ralston for more than five
months. The world thought it not extraordinary
that there should be no public ceremony, considering the recent decease of Robert Lauderdale and
the shockingly sudden death of Walter Crowdie.
The Lauderdales, said the world, had shown good
taste, for many reasons, in having a private wedding. Having always lived quietly, it would have
been unbecoming in them to invite society to a
marriage of royal splendour, when he who had left
them their wealth had not been dead two months.
On the other hand, the union of forty millions
with twenty could hardly have been decently accomplished by means of two carriages from the
livery stable and a man from the greengrocer's.
The world, therefore, said that the Lauderdales
and the Ralstons had done perfectly right, a fact
which pleased some members of the tribe and was

indifferent to others. The only connections who were heard to complain at all were the three Miss Miners, whose old-maidenly souls delighted in weddings and found refreshment in funerals.

And the only person whom Katharine missed, and cared to miss, amongst all those who congratulated her was Paul Griggs. She did not see him, after they had met on the stairs of the house in Lafayette Place, for a long time. During the summer which followed the announcement of her marriage, she heard that he was in the East again — a vague term applied to Cairo, Constantinople and Calcutta. At all events, he was not in New York, but had taken his weary eyes and weather-beaten face to some remote region of the earth, and gave no further sign of life for some time, though a book which he had written before Crowdie's death appeared soon after his departure. Katharine received one letter from him during the summer — a rather formal letter of congratulation upon her marriage, and bearing a postmark in Cyrillic characters, though the stamp was not Russian, but one she had never seen.

Here ends an act of Katharine's life-comedy, and the chronicler leaves her with her beauty, her virtues and her imperfections to the judgment of that one reader, if perchance there be even one, who has had the patience to follow her so far, with little entertainment and no advantage to himself. And to that one reader — an ideal creation of the chronicler's mind, having no foundation in his experience of humanity — the said chronicler makes apology for all that has been amiss in the telling of the events recorded, conscious that a better man could have done it better, and that better men are plentiful, but stout in asserting that the events were not, in themselves and in reality, without interest, however poorly they have been narrated.

Moral, there is none, nor purpose, save to please; and if any one be pleased, the writer has his reward. But besides moral and purpose in things done with ink and paper, there is consequence to be considered, or at least to be taken into account. In real life we take more thought of that than of anything else; for, consciously or unconsciously, man hardly performs any action, however insignificant, without intention — and intention is the hope of consequence.

All that happened to Katharine Lauderdale, and all that she caused to happen by her own will, had an effect upon her existence afterwards. She was entering upon married life with a much more varied experience than most young women of her age. She had been brought into direct and close relation with people influenced by some of the strongest passions that can rouse the heart. She had been hated by those who had loved her, and for little or no fault of hers. She had seen envy standing in the high place of a mother's love, and she had seen the friendship of her girlhood destroyed by unreasoning jealousy. Above all, she had known the base hardness and the revolting cruelty which the love of money could implant in an otherwise upright nature. The persons with whom she had to do were not of the kind to commit crimes, but in her view there was something worse, if possible, than crime in some of the things they had done.

So much for the evil by which she had passed. For the good, she had love, good love, pure love, honest love — the sort of love that may last a lifetime. And if love can weather life it need not fear the whirlpool of death, nor the quicksands of the uncertain shore beyond. It is life that kills love — not death.

Therefore, as the chronicler closes his book and offers it to his single long-suffering reader, he says that more remains to be told of Katharine and of the men and women among whom she lived; namely, the consequences of her girlhood in her married life.

THE END.